Praise for Tess Stimson's books

'Dark. Twisty. Addictive. I couldn't put it down'

Lisa Jewell

'More chilling than *Gone Girl* and twistier than *The Girl on the Train*, this emotional, raw, dark family drama keeps you guessing until the end'

Jane Green

'Truly gripping: the opening is heart-breaking and it never lets up, all the way to a genuinely shocking denouement'

Alex Lake

'Well-drawn characters, believably complex relationships and relentlessly twisting plot keep the reader guessing. Plus, Tess Stimson writes beautifully'

Debbie Howells

'*Tense*, twisty, and that ending – wow!'

Jackie Kabler

'Such a gripping, fast-paced book. I just couldn't put it down and read it within a day!'

Short Book and Scribes

STOLEN

Tess Stimson is the author of thirteen novels, including top ten bestseller *The Adultery Club*, and two non-fiction books, which between them have been translated into dozens of languages.

A former journalist and reporter, Stimson was appointed Professor of Creative Writing at the University of South Florida in 2002 and moved to the US. She now lives and works in Vermont with her husband Erik, their three children, and (at the last count) two cats, three fish, one gerbil and a large number of bats in the attic.

By the same author:

The Mother (originally published as *Picture of Innocence*)
One in Three

STOLEN

TESS STIMSON

avon.

Published by AVON
A division of HarperCollins*Publishers* Ltd
1 London Bridge Street
London SE1 9GF

www.harpercollins.co.uk

HarperCollins*Publishers*
1st Floor, Watermarque Building, Ringsend Road
Dublin 4, Ireland

A Paperback Original 2021

First published in Great Britain by HarperCollins*Publishers* 2021

Copyright © Tess Stimson 2021

Tess Stimson asserts the moral right to be identified as the author of this work.

A catalogue copy of this book is available from the British Library.

ISBN: 978-0-00-838605-4

Typeset in Meridien by Palimpsest Book Production Limited,
Falkirk, Stirlingshire
Printed and Bound in the UK using 100% Renewable Electricity at CPI Group (UK) Ltd

MIX
Paper from
responsible sources
FSC® C007454

This book is produced from independently certified FSC™ paper
to ensure responsible forest management.

For more information visit: www.harpercollins.co.uk/green

For my sister, Philippa.
Memory-keeper and best friend.

the present

The hot sand at the side of the road burns her bare feet. Her lungs are on fire and there's a really bad pain in her side. Her legs feel like jelly. It's sheer panic that propels her forward now.

She saw what they did to Mummy; she knows what they'll do if they catch her.

They didn't find her because she was hiding behind the bougainvillea planter in the courtyard when they came, like she used to do when she was little. *We're going to play a game. I want you to be as quiet as a mouse.* She didn't make a squeak.

The road ahead of her shimmers and she doesn't know if it's because it's so hot or because she's exhausted. Sweat trickles into her eyes and she wipes it away. She has no idea where she is. Nothing looks familiar. There are no houses or people anywhere. All she can see is sand and scrubby grassland, stretching for miles in every direction. Nothing she can hide behind if they come after her. No one she can ask for help.

Terror wells up in her. She knows Mummy is dead. She's nearly six years old, now. She understands what dead means.

Mummy told her to *run! don't look back!* and even though she didn't want to leave her, she did as she was told. But she's *so* tired now. Her feet are raw and blistered, and her legs are so wobbly she's weaving drunkenly back and forth at the side of the road. She doesn't know why they want her, only that she mustn't let them find her.

Run!

Don't look back!

She runs.

1

two years earlier:
forty-eight hours before the wedding

chapter 01

alex

If I'd terminated my pregnancy, I'd be turning left now as I board the plane.

I'd have room on the small desk at the side of my privacy booth for both my case files and the pad of foolscap paper on which I take notes by hand, the old-fashioned way, because five years of legal practice have taught me it's the best method to find the loophole everyone else has overlooked. I'd decline a glass of chilled champagne so that I could keep a clear head, and kick off my shoes – cream and camel Grenson brogues, shoes that are businesslike and understated and make clear that I am a woman to be taken seriously.

But I didn't.

So I'm herded right, not left.

My brogues are from New Look, although you'd really have to know your footwear to detect the difference. I can't afford highlights *and* nursery fees, so my medium-length hair is more its natural ginger than the classy auburn I used to favour. At twenty-nine, I'm still on the fast track to partner at human rights law firm Muysken Ritter, but when I get up at 4.30 a.m. these days, it's not to fit in an hour with my personal trainer before getting to the office by six. I used to love weekends, because it meant I could work straight through without the interruption of meetings and client conferences.

Not any more.

The woman in the row ahead of me twists around as the trolley passes, peering between the seats. She's smiling, but the expression in her eyes is strained. I don't blame her: we're less than half an hour into a nine-hour flight.

'Could you ask your little girl to stop kicking?' she says nicely.

'Lottie, stop kicking the lady's chair,' I say, in a tone that gives no hint I might as well be commanding the sun to set in the east.

Lottie stops instantly, her fat little legs suspended mid-swing. The woman smiles again, more honestly this time, and turns away.

She's fooled by the curls.

My three-year-old daughter is blessed with white-blonde ringlets that reach her waist, the kind of fantasy hair Disney princesses used to have before they got feisty. It misdirects attention from the pugnacious jut of her jaw, the stubborn, bull-headed set of her shoulders. She isn't conventionally pretty – her features are too quirky for that, and then there's her weight, of course. But you can tell she's going to be striking when she's older: what my grandmother's generation would call 'handsome'. She just has to grow into her face, that's all.

The curls are nature's sly sleight of hand. They make people think of angels and Christmas, when they would be better off sharpening stakes and searching for silver bullets.

Lottie waits just long enough for the woman to relax.

'Please, dear, could you *stop* that?' the woman says. There's no smile this time, pained or otherwise.

Kick. Kick.

The woman looks at me, but I'm studiously flicking through the inflight magazine. You have to choose your battles. We still have eight and a half hours to get through.

Kick.

Trying another tack, the woman pushes a bag of Haribo sweets through the gap in the seats. 'Would you like some gummy bears?'

'You're a stranger,' Lottie says. Kick.

'Yes, very good, that's right.' Another unrequited glance in my direction. 'Don't take sweeties from strangers. But we won't be strangers if we introduce ourselves, will we? I'm Mrs Steadman. What's your name?'

'Charlotte Perpetua Martini.'

'Perpetua? That's . . . unusual.'

'Daddy said I had to have a Catholic name because he's Italian, so Mummy googled saints and picked the worst one she could find.'

My daughter and I have no secrets.

'And where is Daddy, Charlotte? Isn't he going on holiday with you?'

Kick.

'Daddy's dead,' Lottie says, matter-of-factly.

The nuclear option. Golden princess curls *and* a dead daddy? There's no coming back from that.

'Oh, dear. Oh. I'm so sorry, Charlotte.'

'It's OK. Mummy says he was a bastard.'

'Lottie,' I reprove, but my heart's not in it. He *was*.

The woman subsides into her seat, radiating the peculiar combination of tongue-tied embarrassment and ghoulish curiosity with which I've become so familiar in the fourteen months since Luca was killed when a bridge collapsed in Genoa. He was visiting his elderly parents, who split their time between their apartment there and his mother's ancestral family home in Sicily. It's just luck it was my weekend to have Lottie, and not his, or she'd have been with him.

Taking pity on the woman, I give Lottie my mobile phone. It's quite safe: at thirty thousand feet she can't repeat the in-app purchase debacle of last month.

With my daughter distracted, I flip open my case file, trying to keep my paperwork in order in the cramped space.

This trip couldn't have come at a worse time. The asylum hearing for one of my clients, a Yazidi woman who survived multiple rapes during her captivity by IS, was unexpectedly brought forward last week, meaning I've had to hand it over to one of my colleagues, James, the only lawyer at our firm with a free docket. He's extremely competent, but my client is terrified of men, which will make it difficult for James to confer with her at her hearing.

The case should be open-and-shut, but I worry something will go wrong. If we weren't going to the wedding of my best friend, Marc, I'd have cancelled the trip.

I'm midway through composing a detailed follow-up email to James when Lottie suddenly spills a full cup of Coke across my table.

'Goddamn it, Lottie!'

I shake my papers furiously, watching rivulets of Coke streaming from the pages.

Lottie doesn't apologise. Instead, she crosses her arms and glares at me.

'Get up,' I say sharply. 'Come on,' I add, as she mulishly remains in her seat. 'You've got Coke all over yourself. It'll be sticky when it dries.'

'I want another one,' Lottie says.

'You're not having another anything! Move it, Lottie. I'm not kidding around.'

She refuses to budge. I unbuckle her seatbelt and haul her

out of her seat. She yowls as if I've really hurt her, attracting attention.

I know exactly what my fellow passengers are thinking. Before Lottie, I used to think it myself every time I saw a child have a meltdown in a supermarket aisle.

I hustle Lottie down the narrow aisle towards the bathroom. She responds by slapping the headrest of every seat as she passes. 'Fuck you,' she says cheerfully, with each slap. 'Fuck you. Fuck you. Fuck you.'

I stopped being embarrassed by my daughter's bad behaviour long ago, but this is extreme, even for her. I grab her shoulders. 'Stop that right now,' I hiss in her ear. 'I'm warning you.'

Lottie screams as if mortally wounded, and then collapses bonelessly in the aisle.

'Oh my God,' a woman sitting near us exclaims. 'Is she all right?'

'She's fine.' I bend down and shake my daughter. 'Lottie, get up. You're making a scene.'

'She's not moving,' someone else cries. 'I think she's really hurt.'

The buzz of concern around us intensifies, and a few people half-stand in their seats. A steward hurries down the aisle towards us.

'This woman hit her kid,' a man accuses.

'I did *not* hit her. She's just having a tantrum.'

The steward looks from the man to me, and then at Lottie, who still hasn't moved. 'Does she need a doctor?'

'There's nothing wrong with her,' I say. 'Lottie, get up.'

An older woman a few seats away pats the steward's arm. 'It's the terrible twos. They all go through it.'

'Lottie,' I say calmly. 'If you don't get up right now, there will be no Disney World, no ice-cream, and no television for a week.'

In a battle of wills, my three-year-old daughter is easily my equal. But she's not just stubborn: she's smart. She can make a cost/benefit analysis in an instant.

She sits up, and the concerned whispers around me change to exasperated mutters of disapproval.

'I hate you!' Lottie says. 'I wish I'd never been born!'

I pull her to her feet. 'That makes two of us,' I say.

chapter 02

alex

A blast of moist, soupy tropical air envelops us when we leave the aircraft, as if someone has opened the door of a tumble dryer mid-cycle. My sunglasses instantly fog and Lottie's hair fluffs in a platinum nimbus around her shoulders. I can only imagine the effect the humidity is having on mine.

We join the crumpled, weary queue snaking towards passport control. When the US border guard asks me whether my visit is for business or pleasure, I'm tempted to tell her neither.

If you like eating dinner at 5.30 p.m. and wear sandals that fasten with Velcro, Florida is for you. But for those not aged under seven or over seventy, it's less enchanting.

We're here because Marc's bride is the kind of woman who wants Insta-ready wedding photos of cerulean oceans and sugary beaches, regardless of the inconvenience to everyone else.

I can't be the only person who finds the current craze for destination weddings the apogee of entitled narcissism. If it's romance you're after, elope. Otherwise, is it fair to expect a brother with three young children, student loans and a mort-gage to fork out for five plane tickets or risk becoming a family pariah? And what about elderly relatives whose own life events – marriage, children – are now behind them, and for whom a grandchild's wedding is one of the few genuine pleasures left?

For me, flying four thousand miles to enable my daughter to be a bridesmaid at my best friend's wedding is an expensive nuisance. For the lonely and infirm, unable to travel, such distant celebrations are an exercise in heartbreak.

It's the reason Luca and I married twice, once in his mother's ancestral church in Sicily to please his extensive family, and once in West Sussex for my considerably smaller one. Perhaps a third wedding would have actually made it stick.

I reclaim our suitcase from the carousel, and Lottie and I join yet another queue, this time for a taxi. We're both hot, tired and disagreeable by the time we get in the cab, but fortunately my daughter soon falls asleep, her head pillowed in my lap.

I stroke her hair back from her sweaty face, smiling as she wrinkles her nose and bats my hand away without waking.

Mothering Lottie is the hardest thing I have ever done. It's the only task, in my accomplished life, at which I've struggled to succeed.

There's no Hallmark coda to that statement, no *but nothing has been more fulfilling*. I don't find motherhood satisfying or rewarding. It's tedious, repetitive, solitary, exhausting. Luca was a much more natural parent. But my love for my daughter is visceral and unquestioning. I'd take a bullet for her.

I check my emails as we sit in bumper-to-bumper traffic on the causeway across Tampa Bay, careful not to disturb Lottie.

It's as I feared: while I've been in the air, my Yazidi client has had her request for asylum denied, principally because she was unwilling to confer with her male legal counsel and participate fully and properly in the interview.

I fire off several quick emails in response, setting in motion the steps necessary to lodge an appeal. I'm not being precious or egotistical when I say my absence from London has real-world consequences, and every minute I'm away from the office counts.

But Marc put his entire life on hold for me when Luca was killed. He knows I don't particularly like Sian, his bride; failure to attend their wedding, no matter how I might spin it, would test our friendship. And I'll only be away six days. James can hold down the fort at work till I return. I'll just have to pull a few all-nighters once I'm home to get things back on track.

I put my phone away and gently reposition my daughter's head in my lap as we take the exit towards the neon-lit drag of St Pete Beach, with its jostle of hotels, bars, chain restaurants and tourist shops.

We turn off the main strip away from the crowds and into a more residential neighbourhood. A few minutes later, the taxi stops at a gate at the foot of a short bridge, which leads to a tiny barrier island a few hundred feet off the coast. The skyline is dominated by the Sandy Beach Hotel, a primrose-yellow, six-storey crenellated building that rises against the sky like a wedding cake.

Our driver lowers his window to talk to the security guard and, after a moment, the white barrier is lifted and we cross over onto a tiny spit of land jutting out into the Gulf of Mexico.

I shake Lottie awake as the taxi pulls into the courtyard in front of the hotel. A porter whisks away our luggage, and I pick up my drowsy daughter and carry her into the lobby.

A huge wall of glass opens directly onto the white sugary beaches and Lottie instantly buries her face in my shoulder. She's always been terrified of the sea; I have no idea why.

A number of beachfront rooms have been reserved for the wedding party. I change ours to one overlooking the pool, so Lottie doesn't have to wake up to a view of the ocean. A vivid orange and red sunset is spreading across the sky, and I'm just about to take my weary child upstairs when Marc and Sian come in from the beach.

Marc pretends to ignore me completely and extends his hand to Lottie. 'Miss Martini,' he says gravely. 'A pleasure to see you again.'

'It's *Mizz*,' she corrects.

'Mizz. My mistake.'

Sian slips her hand through Marc's arm. The gesture is possessive rather than affectionate. 'We should be getting back to the others,' she says.

'Want to join us?' Marc asks. 'Paul was just getting in another round.'

'I would, but Lottie needs to get to bed. She's shattered.'

'Why don't you get her settled, then come back down and find us? We're at the Parrot Beach Bar, just the other side of the pool. Zealy and Catherine are with us, too.'

Thus speaks the man who has yet to have a child and learn what it is like to spend the rest of your life with your heart walking around outside your body.

'She's *three*, Marc,' Sian says. 'Alexa can't just leave her on her own in a strange hotel.'

Marc takes the handle of my carry-on bag with proprietary authority. 'At least let me help you upstairs with this.'

'Everyone's waiting for us,' Sian says.

'You go back out. We'll be down again in a minute.'

His bride-to-be smiles, but it doesn't reach her pretty eyes.

There's never been the slightest chance of a romantic liaison between Marc and me. We met when he started coaching the women's football team at University College, London, where I studied law; for the first three years we knew each other, he only saw me sweaty and mud-spattered, in unflattering Lycra shorts and sporting a mouthguard.

I've liked some of his girlfriends. But he's let several good ones get away by missing the proposal window: by the time he's realised they're perfect for him, they've grown tired of waiting and moved on.

Marc's thirty-six now; a wealthy marketing director with every trapping of success bar a wife and family, and he's been itching to get married for several years. Sian just happened to be the one holding the parcel when the music stopped.

My phone rings just as I slide the keycard into the hotel room door.

'I'm sorry,' I say. 'I wouldn't take it, but it's James—'

'Go, go,' Marc says. 'I'll get Lottie sorted out. Sian won't mind if I stay a bit longer.'

I seriously doubt that, but I need to talk to James and find out what's happening with my client, so I take Marc up on his offer to look after Lottie, and go back along the corridor to take the call somewhere quiet.

By the time I return to our room fifteen minutes later, Lottie is dressed in her pyjamas and tucked into one of the two queen-sized beds. Marc is perched next to her, reading her a story.

'Ready to go down?' he asks me, putting the book aside.

I hesitate. I'm wired from my conversation with James and wide awake; a glass of bourbon would put that right. But even though I'm fully aware I'm not a natural mother, I do my best to be a good one.

'I can't leave her,' I say.

Lottie folds her fat arms crossly across her chest. 'You didn't read my story properly,' she tells Marc. 'You *missed* a page.'

'It's OK,' I say. 'I've got this, Marc. You go. I'll see you tomorrow.'

I settle down on the bed, leaning against the padded head-board and pulling Lottie into the crook of my arm. She hands me the book, *Owl Babies*, turning the well-thumbed cardboard pages for me as I read aloud the story of three baby owls, perched on a branch in the wood, waiting for their owl mummy to return.

And she does, swooping silently through the trees: *You knew I'd come back.*

Then I add the line that's not in the book, the line Lottie's been waiting for, the line that Luca, making up for my shortcomings, always used to add, with more faith than my history warranted: 'Mummies always come back.'

thirty-six hours before the wedding

chapter 03

alex

Lottie wakes hours before dawn, still on London time. I toss her my phone, buying myself another valuable half-hour, and burrow back under the covers. Of all the many trials of motherhood, sleep deprivation is one of the worst.

I never wanted a child. This doesn't mean I don't love the very bones of her now she's here; Lottie is my oxygen, the reason I breathe. But I can't be the only woman who didn't see herself as a mother until it happened, and, if I'm ruthlessly honest, for quite a long time after she arrived.

In fairness, I didn't much see myself as a wife, either.

Luca and I met nearly five years ago, in March 2015, a few months after he'd moved to the UK from his hometown of Genoa, in northern Italy, to head up the London office of his family's coffee import business. In those days, I rented a ground-floor flat one street away from Parsons Green Tube station in Fulham with a couple of friends, and we were sick and tired of having our drive blocked by commuters dumping their cars in nearby roads before getting the train into central London.

One evening, unable to drive to my father's sixtieth birthday party in Sussex until the owner of the car obstructing mine returned, I lay in wait, seething, and then exploded in the driver's face.

Italian to his marrow, Luca gave as good as he got. As I recall, our first conversation consisted almost entirely of imaginative swearwords in two languages.

Sometime around the point I stormed back into the flat, grabbed a tub of Ben & Jerry's ice-cream, and smeared it all over his windscreen, I noticed how good-looking he was. Our encounter descended into clichéd rom-com meet-cute: he asked me out to dinner, I accepted, and we ended up in bed.

At the time, I was twenty-four and had just started full-time work at Muysken Ritter. I was putting in eighteen-hour days, six and often seven days a week. I didn't have time for a relationship.

But Luca was charming, well-travelled, and fun. I enjoyed spending time with him. The sex was excellent, and I found myself refreshed and more productive after a night together. It was easy to fancy myself a little bit in love with him.

Or perhaps I really was; from this distance, it's hard to be sure.

Some four months after that first, cystitis-inducing night, I discovered that, thanks to a bout of food-poisoning and consequent antibiotics, I was six weeks pregnant. If I didn't have time for a relationship, I certainly couldn't cope with a baby. I booked a termination, and told Luca, because I felt it would've been dishonest not to, not because I expected him to have a say in the matter.

To my astonishment, he fell on bended knee and asked me to marry him. I rather wounded his pride by laughing.

He was Italian, of course, and Catholic: for him, the idea of abortion was anathema. He begged me to keep the baby, promising he'd do all the childcare, I'd 'barely know the baby was there'.

He was passionate, and persuasive.

And I was young enough, and arrogant enough, to believe I really could have – and do – it all.

20

And then there was my sister, Harriet. At the age of nineteen, she'd been diagnosed with cervical cancer, and although the aggressive chemotherapy treatment saved her life, it'd rendered her infertile. It was impossible not to have her tragedy at the forefront of my mind when I made my decision.

The next time Luca proposed, I said yes. Reader, I married him – twice. We moved into a two-bedroom terrace in Balham, turning one of them into a nursery, and set about building our little family. And when it all fell apart, as it inevitably did before we'd even reached Lottie's second birthday, I took it on the chin and put marriage and children on the list of experiments worth trying once, but never repeating, along with parachute jumpsuits and floral tea dresses.

I'm woken a second time when Lottie flings the phone at my head. It makes brutal contact and I sit bolt upright, rubbing the side of my skull. 'Fuck!' I exclaim. 'What did you do that for!'

'You're not listening to me,' Lottie says.

'Damn it, Lottie. That really hurt.'

'I don't want to be a bridesmaid.'

I fling back the bedcovers. 'I don't give a damn what you want. You said you'd do this, and you're going to.'

'My blue mummy says I don't have to.'

I have no idea what she's talking about. 'Well, *this* mummy says you do.'

I need to pee, but when I try to open the bathroom door, it's jammed shut. I kneel down and prise out the dozens of bits of paper Lottie has shoved beneath it, an irritating habit she started in the traumatic aftermath of her father's death. She does it with any door that doesn't fit tightly to the floor, convinced monsters are going to slide between the gaps. She refuses even to go into my parents' kitchen, because the door down to the cellar has a half-inch gap she can't block.

21

'For heaven's sake, Lottie. I thought we'd talked about this.'

She hunches her shoulders, juts out her chin and glares at me mulishly.

I use the bathroom and then come back and sit on the edge of her bed. 'What's going on, Lottie?' I say, my tone brisk. 'You've been looking forward to this wedding for months.'

'I don't like Marc any more.'

'Since when?'

Her scowl intensifies. 'He touched me.'

Nothing, but *nothing*, in more than ten years of friendship, has ever given me cause to doubt Marc. Not by a glance, insinuation or chance remark has he suggested his tastes run towards children. But when your daughter tells you a man has *touched* her, you take it seriously.

'What do you mean?' I ask sharply. 'When?'

'Last night. I didn't like it.'

My mouth dries. I can't believe Marc would *ever*, but then it's always the ones you least suspect.

Lottie has many faults but I've never known her to lie. Her default position is to tell the truth and shame the devil. The thought that anyone may have touched her, *hurt* her, is enough to ignite a murderous rage in me. I would go to the ends of the earth to protect my daughter.

'Where did he touch you?' I ask, as calmly as I'm able.

'I'm not telling.'

I want to grip her by the shoulders and shake the details out of her, but she'll simply refuse to talk to me if I pressure her. Her longest retributory silence to date lasted three full days, when she punished me for trying to establish what she wanted for her third birthday. She wasn't the one who caved to end the standoff.

'OK,' I say, getting up again.

'He was very *rude*,' she says.

22

'What sort of rude?'

'He squeezed me!'

'Squeezed? You mean, like a hug?'

'No!' She gathers a fistful of her ample belly in each hand. 'Here! Like this! He said I was *getting chunky*!'

I'll deal with the fat-shaming aspect of this clusterfuck later. Right now, I'm just relieved I don't have to accuse my best friend of molesting my daughter on his wedding day.

'He's only saying that because he's marrying an ironing board,' I say.

'She *does* look like an ironing board,' Lottie agrees delightedly.

'You should feel sorry for him, really.'

'All right. I'll be his flower girl.'

'Good,' I say mildly.

The wedding rehearsal starts at six tonight, an hour before sunset, the same as the actual ceremony tomorrow. It's still not yet seven in the morning, which gives me eleven hours to fill without allowing Lottie to eat herself sick, drown, get sunstroke or cut off the hair of any of the other four brides-maids (quite within the realms of possibility; there was a rather disastrous incident with the paper scissors her first term at nursery school).

I'm not optimistic.

chapter 04

alex

I've never really understood Lottie's fear of the ocean. There was no childhood trauma in the sea that might have triggered it, no near-drowning incident, and water itself isn't the problem; she loves the pool and has been able to swim without armbands, even well out of her depth, for almost a year.

But this is a beach wedding and Lottie has to get used to the nearness of the sea, so, after lunch, I fortify myself with a stiff gin-and-tonic (full disclosure: not my first of the day) and take her down to the beach.

Fortunately, although her chin goes down and her shoulders hunch forward so that she resembles a bonsai charging bull, she doesn't detonate as I'd feared. We walk slowly towards a raked section of powdery white sand, where the hotel staff is setting out rows of beribboned gilt chairs in front of a wedding arbour entwined with plastic starfish and shells. I lead Lottie down the sandy aisle she will tread at the wedding rehearsal in a couple of hours, and show her where she'll sit in the front row tomorrow.

'There's no tide here,' I explain, crouching down beside her as she stares towards the ocean, her features grimly set. 'Well, not much of one. The sea isn't going to come any closer, I promise.'

Lottie takes a firm step towards the shoreline, which is about six metres from where we're standing. Trust my girl to face her fears, challenge them head on.

I hear Sian's voice behind me. 'Are you going for a swim, Lottie?'

Sian and her best friend and maid of honour Catherine are picking their way across the hot sand in matching pink flip-flops, their wet hair slicked back from their faces after their dip in the ocean.

'We're just on our way back to the hotel to get ready,' I say.

'But the sea's so warm,' Sian says. 'And she's got plenty of time before the rehearsal.'

'It's an *ocean*, not a sea,' Lottie says.

Sian crouches next to her. 'I hope you're not worried about people seeing you in a swimming costume, Lottie. No one minds what you look like.'

I want to smack Sian across her pretty face. But I need not worry; Lottie has the situation handled.

'Why would I be worried?' she asks bluntly.

'Never mind,' Sian says quickly. 'Are you afraid of sharks, then?'

'Of course not!' she retorts. 'I *like* sharks.'

'She's got no reason to be scared,' Catherine says. 'They'd take one bite of her and spit her out.'

Lottie appears to view this as a compliment.

My phone vibrates in my pocket as Sian and Catherine return to the hotel. I'm surprised to see my sister Harriet's name on the screen. 'Lottie, sit here and don't move while I talk to Aunt Harriet,' I say, pointing to a nearby sunlounger. 'I'll only be five minutes.'

I take a couple of paces towards the shoreline, tempted by the sea. The warm water ripples over my bare feet and I find myself wishing Lottie could get past her fear; the water really *is* perfect.

25

'I wasn't expecting to hear from you,' I tell my sister. 'Is everything all right? Are Mum and Dad OK?'

'As far as I know. Why?'

'Because you *called* me!'

'Shit, sorry. Must have been a butt dial.' Harriet sighs. 'I thought something must be wrong when I saw the missed call.'

I take the implicit rebuke in my stride.

Harriet and I haven't been close since we were children; we love each other, of course, but we're chalk and cheese. We often go months without speaking, unless there's a family crisis. Mum's only fifty-seven, but she's been in hospital twice in the last three years to have malignant polyps removed from her colon.

On each occasion, I've been the one who's had to break it to Harriet, who lives up in the Shetland Isles with her husband Mungo, an oil-rig engineer. Despite the wonders of modern technology, I know she often feels very cut off from the family, especially with Mungo frequently away on the rigs. She's an artist, working from home, so she has plenty of time to feel lonely.

'Sorry,' I say. 'I didn't mean to worry you.'

'It's all right. False alarm.'

There's a slightly awkward pause.

'Lottie must be excited,' Harriet says, finally.

My daughter is the one place where Harriet and I meet. She adores Lottie and, even though she and I don't talk often, Lottie often hijacks my iPad so they can FaceTime.

I glance at Lottie, who isn't sitting on the sunlounger as instructed, but weaving in and out of the neat rows of gilt chairs, arms spread as if she's pretending to be a plane, and getting under the feet of the hotel staff.

'It's Lottie,' I say. 'It's hard to tell.'

I'm surprised to hear the sound of a flight announcement

26

in the background of the call. 'Are you at the airport?' I ask. 'Where are you going?'

'It's just the TV,' Harriet says. 'Look, I've got to go. I just wanted to be sure everything was OK. Take lots of photos of Lottie for me, won't you?'

'Of course,' I say.

I slip my phone back into my shorts and turn back along the beach, and see my daughter talking to a man I've never met.

His hand is on her shoulder and something about the way he's leaning over her sets every maternal alarm bell ringing. I call Lottie's name loudly and the man glances in my direction and then briskly walks away. By the time I reach Lottie, he's already disappearing around the side of the hotel.

'Who was that?' I demand of my daughter.

'I don't know.'

'What have I told you about talking to strangers?'

'I wasn't talking to him. *He* was talking to *me*.'

'What did he want?'

She glares at me, clearly irked. 'He said he couldn't find his little girl, and asked if I'd seen her.'

A shiver runs down my spine. Lottie is smart and intelligent, and I've drummed into her the dangers posed by strange men, but she's still not yet four. I was less than fifteen metres away from her; I only took my eyes off her for a few moments.

I frogmarch her back to the hotel, ignoring her furious yanks on my arm. I should have kept a closer eye on her: Florida has one of the highest numbers of sex offenders of all fifty American states. Its population, which comprises a significant number of tourists and retirees from other states, is transient and in a constant state of flux. There's little sense of community and it's an easy place to get lost in the crowd.

I'm a lawyer. I looked it up.

27

As we reach the hotel lobby, Lottie finally breaks free from me and races over to join the cluster of little girls who'll be bridesmaids with her. I'm about to go after her when Marc's sister, Zealy, steps out of the hotel lift.

'Alex! I thought it was you! You've had your hair cut.'

Reflexively, I touch the back of my head. I had a good eight inches lopped off my long hair last month, so that it now sits just below my collarbone; I just didn't have the time to style it properly before. 'It was driving me mad. Do you like it?'

'I love it. It really suits you.'

Zealy and I have been friends for years, although we don't see each other as often as I'd like; my fault, of course. Those friendships that weren't crushed by my workload fell by the wayside once I had Lottie. Zealy is actually Marc's half-sister, from his mother's first marriage to a black South African. The first time Sian met her, she asked if she could touch Zealy's hair and remarked how wild it was she 'sounded so white'.

Zealy loops her arm through mine. 'Come have a drink with me in the bar,' she says. 'Help me drown my sorrows.'

I don't let her lure me into the bar, but I do yield to a cocktail by the pool, keeping a close eye on Lottie's bright platinum head as she and the other little girls dart back and forth around us like dragonflies.

I'm in two minds about whether to report Lottie's encounter with the man on the beach to the police, or at least to hotel management. The more I think about it, the odder it seems.

But I've nothing concrete to offer them. If every mother who ever had a 'bad feeling' filed a police report, they'd be drowning in paperwork.

I accept a second martini when Zealy presses me, and put the incident to the back of my mind.

twenty-four hours before the wedding

chapter 05

alex

Lottie upends my expectations and performs perfectly at the wedding rehearsal, which makes me fear for tomorrow. Her genius is in the art of bait-and-switch.

Marc and Sian run through their vows three times before the blushing bride is satisfied. The young bridesmaids fidget on their gilt chairs, clearly bored, nudging each other in the ribs and pulling faces. Only Lottie behaves, hands folded primly in her lap. It's a bad sign.

Finally Sian is happy, and she and Marc process back down the sandy aisle.

Zealy and Catherine corral the bridesmaids and they all fall into step behind Marc and Sian, with Lottie bringing up the rear.

As soon as the bridal party reaches the gate from the beach to the private courtyard by the hotel pool, where the reception will take place, the five little girls break ranks and hurtle towards their parents.

Lottie crashes into my legs, glowing with pride.

'Did I do good, Mummy?'

'You were perfect,' I say, ruffling her curls and trying not to sound too surprised. 'I hope you'll be just like that tomorrow. I won't be with you, so I'm trusting you, Lottie. Best behaviour.'

'Where will you be?'

'Just behind you, over there.' I point to my reserved seat a couple of rows behind the bridesmaids' chairs, along with the other parents. 'I'll see you as soon as we get back to the party at the hotel.'

'Just follow me, Lottie, and stay with the other girls,' Zealy says, as she joins us. 'Mummy will be right behind you, with everyone else.'

'Whatever,' Lottie says.

'*Lottie*,' I say.

'I don't envy you the teenage years,' Zealy says.

Lottie tugs on my arm. 'Can I have some ice-cream now?'

'*May* I. After dinner.'

Her eyes narrow. 'You said I could have *as much ice-cream as I wanted* if I behaved.'

She has me over a barrel, and she knows it.

'Fine,' I say. 'But you'd better eat all your dinner, Lottie.'

We leave the courtyard and pass through the Palm Court dining room, where a long table has been set up for the rehearsal dinner, then into the main hotel lobby. There's a small shop near the entrance selling the usual tourist tat: postcards, T-shirts, shot glasses bearing the name of the hotel. It has an ice-cream freezer Lottie scoped out as soon as we came downstairs this morning.

I lift her up to the freezer so she can pick out what she wants. She selects an ice-cream cookie the size of a wheel and Zealy and I sit on a bench in the lobby while she eats it.

By the time she's finished, and I've cleaned her face and sticky fingers, the rest of the wedding party has assembled in the Palm Court for dinner.

We take the last three free seats at the crowded table next to Marc. Lottie immediately grabs both her bread roll and mine, devouring them in a couple of greedy bites.

'Where does she *put* it all?' Zealy asks, as Lottie reaches down the table to help herself to Zealy's roll.

'She'll eat herself sick just to spite me,' I say.

Marc's college roommate and best man, Paul Harding, leans across the table and gives Lottie his own roll.

'I like a girl with an appetite,' he says, giving her a wink. 'I'm always hungry at weddings, too. They never feed you properly.'

Zealy and Paul have hooked up a couple of times over the years but, although I know Zealy would like to make the arrangement more formal, I don't think Paul's the kind to settle down. An international art consultant, he's dark-haired and at least six foot five, his large nose leavening otherwise glossy good looks. They'd make an attractive couple.

Flic Everett, the mother of one of the other bridesmaids, Olivia, signals to a waiter for another cocktail. 'Are you sure you don't want Lottie to eat with Olivia and the other girls upstairs?' she asks me. 'I'm sure it'd be more fun for her.'

'I'm not letting her out of my sight,' I say.

'My eldest, Betty, is babysitting. Lottie would be fine, I promise—'

'That's not what I meant.'

Flic gives me an odd look, and then turns to Marc's father, Eric, who's seated on her other side.

Lottie takes yet another roll. I realise she's not actually eating them, but slipping them into the pockets of her cardigan. 'What are you doing?' I say.

'They're for my blue mummy,' she says.

That's the second time she's mentioned her 'blue mummy'. Before I can ask her what she means, there's a disruption at the other end of the table.

A good-looking man I don't recognise has entered the restaurant, and Sian rises to her feet to greet him. He's clearly part of the wedding group; he must be one of the ushers. But there isn't a free place for him at the table, and I realise my daughter has probably taken his seat.

'Lottie shouldn't be here,' Sian says to me. 'It's just adults. We've only paid for twelve people.'

'I'm happy to—'

'She's only a kid,' Marc says. 'It's not like she's going to eat much.'

I don't hold Sian's sceptical expression against her.

David Williams, Sian's father, touches his daughter's bare arm. 'It's all right, love. I'll sort it out with the hotel afterwards.'

'There isn't *room*,' Sian says.

Catherine pushes her chair back slightly from the table and pats her lap. 'She can sit on my knee, if she wants?'

'Why don't we all just move our chairs down a bit?' Sian's mother, Penny, says. 'We can squeeze together, and make space for Ian.'

Sian looks like she wants to object, but she reads the table and subsides. Marc beckons to a waiter and another chair is produced, and everyone shuffles along to make room.

'Who's he?' I ask Zealy.

'Ian Dutton,' she says. 'He's one of Marc's friends. He was a professional tennis player for a bit, though I think he's retired now. He used to coach Marc, that's how they met.'

He certainly looks the part, his linen shirt failing to hide a rippling six-pack.

'Sorry I missed the wedding rehearsal,' Ian says, sitting down. 'My flight was delayed and I only just got in. Anything special I need to know?'

'Not really. Paul can fill you in,' Marc says.

'It's more for the little ones,' Penny adds. 'And Lottie did a lovely job, didn't she, Sian?'

'Yes,' Sian says, grudgingly.

Two waiters serve our appetisers; Lottie has picked mussels in white wine. Not the choice of most three-year-olds, but then my daughter isn't most children.

'Good for her,' Paul says, admiringly.

'I don't know how she can eat those things,' Sian says, with a shudder. She toys with her rocket salad, no dressing, no almonds, hold the shaved parmesan.

One of the mussels suddenly shoots out of Lottie's hand, spraying white wine everywhere, and skids along the table, landing neatly in front of Sian's plate.

An accident, obviously.

Lottie giggles and then claps two starfish hands over her mouth.

Ian roars with laughter. 'Slippery little buggers,' he says. 'Here. Let me winkle a few out for you, kid.'

Lottie, normally reluctant to part with her food, hands him her bowl of mussels without complaint. Ian swiftly finesses half-a-dozen and returns it. 'There you go. Don't bother with a fork for the rest; just use your fingers.'

Catherine leans forward. 'I've just realised,' she says, in a breathy whisper. 'Now Ian's here, there's thirteen of us. Isn't that unlucky?'

'I don't believe in luck,' I say.

chapter 06

From my hidden vantage point, I watch the little girl run down the beach, her white-blonde hair streaming like a bleached flag behind her. She's pretending to be a plane, or a bird perhaps: her arms are stretched wide as she swoops and dives across the sand.

No one is with her. No one is watching her.

Except me.

The little girl stops suddenly, plopping down on her fat bottom in the sand. She tugs off her sandals and flings them into the sea, laughing with delight as the tide quickly whips them away. It's hard not to smile, watching her. She is still young enough to be unfettered by should *and* ought. *She's impulsive, living in the moment. She skips joyfully along the beach in her bare feet, her skirts flapping wetly around her calves, and I wonder briefly at what age we stop skipping and surrender to the pedestrian discipline of walking and running.*

I'm glad she's having fun now, because I know she'll be frightened when I take her. I can't help that, but I'll make sure it's all over as quickly as I can.

The child veers closer to the shoreline, oblivious to my presence as I emerge from the rocks behind her, and I quell my instinct to pull her back from the water's edge and tell her to be careful, that the tide is stronger than it looks. Life is dangerous. If she doesn't know that by now, she soon will.

And the biggest threat to her doesn't come from the sea.

It comes from me.

the wedding day

chapter 07

alex

As predicted, Lottie literally eats herself sick at the wedding rehearsal dinner. I'm up three times in the night with her and, as a consequence, we both sleep in until after nine.

She seems fine when she wakes up, but I'm not taking any chances. We spend a quiet morning in our room, skipping the bridal party lunch, though I let Lottie order chicken soup from room service when she complains she's hungry. She's uncharacteristically cooperative and watches cartoons on my iPad while I get some work done. By the time the hairdresser needs her mid-afternoon, her colour has returned and she's back to her old self.

As soon as the stylist has finished plaiting her hair in a striking fishtail braid, I take her down to Zealy's room, where the little bridesmaids are getting ready.

Even though her last dress fitting was just three weeks ago, it takes some serious tugs on the zip to get her pouffy pink dress done up. But there's a lump in my throat when she finally does a twirl. She may not be the world's idea of a beauty, but she's never looked lovelier to me.

I warn Zealy to keep a plastic bag handy, just in case Lottie's sick again, and go down to the beach to take my seat with the rest of the wedding guests.

Ten minutes later, Zealy texts me a photo of my daughter, arms folded, scowling at the camera. I laugh out loud. It's so very much the essence of Lottie I immediately make it my screensaver.

Sian follows the American custom of having the bridesmaids precede her down the sandy aisle. I'm so proud of Lottie as she leads the way, scattering fistfuls of pink rose petals with a wild, joyous abandon that draws smiles from more than a few wedding guests and elicits a snort from Marc.

I watch my daughter take her place at the end of the front row of gilt chairs beside the other bridesmaids, facing down the ocean with determination. I wish I was close enough to tell her how beautiful she is.

The ceremony is brief and picturesque. Marc is visibly moved as Sian comes down the petal-strewn aisle in her ivory Vera Wang dress, her cold beauty warmed by the genuine glow in her eyes. The sun sinks photogenically into the sea as they complete their vows and a scattering of tourists, hovering at a polite distance along the water's edge to watch, claps sentimentally.

The release of two white doves as Sian and Marc walk back up the aisle together isn't to my taste, but it brings us closer to my first glass of champagne, which most assuredly is.

I join the stream of wedding guests following the bridal party back to the hotel for the reception. We're all given pink wristbands before being permitted through a small gate into the private courtyard adjacent to the pool, where waiters are circulating.

Taking a glass from one, I locate Zealy and Paul.

'Didn't Lottie do well?' Zealy says. 'Although I thought she was going to take someone's eye out with her flower basket.'

'Talking of,' I say, glancing around.

'She's over by the ice-cream station with the other brides-maids,' Paul says, pointing to a knot of pink taffeta skirts just visible through the throng. 'I saw her a few minutes ago tucking into the chocolate fudge brownie.'

'In that case, let's hope Sian's not planning to recycle the dresses.'

'Jesus, aren't they hideous?' Zealy exclaims, plucking at her own. '*Pink*, for God's sake. I look like an uncooked sausage.'

The good-looking tennis player comes over to join us, his rippling muscles somehow enhanced by his formal attire. I didn't get a chance to talk to Ian Dutton last night, since he was seated at the far end of the table, but that's something I intend to rectify now.

I collect a second glass of champagne from a passing waiter. I don't have time for relationships, but sex is a different matter.

In most failing marriages, sex is the first thing to go. With Luca and me, it was the last.

No matter how bad things got between us, how vicious the knock-down, drag-out arguments, somehow we always ended up in bed together, our fury and hate acting as an aphrodisiac in a way that mirrored our very first encounter. At the time, I consoled myself with the thought that our marriage couldn't really be on the rocks, because no couple could be this good in bed if it were.

What I didn't realise, until the day I threw him out for yet again breaking his fingers-crossed promise of fidelity, was that we communicated through sex because we had nothing else.

In the eight months between our separation and Luca's sudden death, I was celibate, unable to envision ever being with another man. But death has a strange way of recalibrating your perspective. It makes you grasp life, and sex is the ultimate expression of that instinct. I couldn't live with Luca, but I never expected to have to inhabit a world without him, either.

I don't broadcast my after-hours activities, but I refuse to

41

apologise for being a single twenty-nine-year-old with a healthy sexual appetite, either.

Ian is witty and charming, and I find him attractive. Judging by the level of flirtation between us as the evening deepens, my feelings are reciprocated. His lines aren't particularly original, and the flattery a little too thick, but I'm not in this for the long term.

We've drifted to the edge of the throng of wedding guests by the time Sian's father clinks his fork against a champagne glass to signify the start of the speeches. Over Ian's shoulder, I can see the occasional flash of Lottie's pink dress as she goes back to the buffet table for second helpings, and then thirds.

Zealy and Paul are sitting at a table near the gate to the beach, her feet in his lap, an empty bottle of champagne amid the dirty plates in front of them.

'Could you keep an eye on Lottie for a bit?' I ask.

'No problem,' she says, casting Ian a knowing glance. 'Have fun.'

The drifts of powdery sand are oddly cool beneath my bare feet, and it's surprisingly dark once we get beyond the immediate penumbra of light from the hotel. The susurration of the waves on the shore is erotic and, when Ian pulls me towards one of the serried ranks of double "honeymoon' sunloungers, I don't hesitate.

'Know anything about stars?' Ian asks, gazing up at the night sky.

'Ursa Minor,' I say, pointing. 'That W? That's Cassiopeia. And Andromeda, over there, look. The bright star.'

'How d'you know all that?'

I shrug. 'It interests me.'

'What's your star sign, then?'

'Not astrology,' I say. 'Astronomy. There's a difference.'

The moon has risen higher in the sky while we've been on

42

the beach, bathing us in its cool, eerie light. I realise we've been gone longer than I'd thought.

'I should be getting back to the hotel,' I say. 'I need to get my daughter to bed.'

'I won't be seeing you again, will I?'

'No,' I say. It would be an insult to pretend otherwise.

I've become expert at compartmentalising my life, separating out the strand that is a parent from the workaholic lawyer. It's a safety mechanism. I don't know if it's healthy, but I don't know any other way to be.

But Ian's comment stings a little. I'm not the hardened man-eater he seems to think. I can't afford to get involved; even if I had the time, there's Lottie to consider. Any man I date is a potential stepfather. The responsibility of choosing the right man for my child is overwhelming, and one I'm not ready to face.

I show my pink security bracelet to the waiter on attendance at the gate and rejoin the thinning number of wedding guests.

The speeches have finished; I must have been gone longer than I thought. Zealy and Paul are dancing cheek to cheek by the pool with a few other couples, and I scan the courtyard for my daughter.

When I fail to find her, I go and tap Zealy on the shoulder.

'Hey,' I say, not yet frightened. 'Have you seen Lottie?'

chapter 08

alex

'She was just here,' Zealy says, pulling away from Paul and glancing around the courtyard. 'We saw her a few minutes ago.'

'Did you see where she went?'

'Sorry. But it can't have been very far,' she adds.

Paul slings his arm around Zealy's shoulders. 'She was headed back towards the ice-cream station with some of the other kids,' he says. 'It was literally only about three or four minutes ago.'

I thank them and head over to the buffet tables. As Zealy said, Lottie can't have got very far in a couple of minutes. I'd have seen her as I came in if she was anywhere near the ocean side of the courtyard.

I must have just missed her at the ice-cream station. The waiter manning it shrugs when I ask after Lottie, and a quick recce along the buffet tables tells me she's not helping herself to wedding profiteroles or softening tortilla chips either.

I turn back to the courtyard, wondering where she can have got to, and catch a glimpse of pink skirts disappearing around the corner. There's a small section in the rear of the courtyard devoted to kids' games: air hockey, a pool table, a pinball machine and whack-a-mole. Lottie spent an hour here yesterday, before I ran out of American quarter coins and had to drag her away. No doubt she's begged or borrowed some more money from Marc or another guest, which is slightly embarrassing. Clearly, I need to set firmer boundaries.

But when I round the corner, there's no sign of Lottie. One of the pre-teen bridesmaids is setting up a rack of balls on the pool table; it must have been her skirts I saw.

'Have you seen Lottie?' I ask.

She looks at me blankly.

'The little flower girl. The one with the blonde hair.'

'Oh, the fat one?'

The smart one, you buck-toothed human haemorrhoid. 'Yes,' I say.

'Nah. Not for ages.'

A faint wisp of anxiety curdles my stomach. We're probably just missing each other in the crowd, that's all. But it's a lot less busy than it was; quite a few people have already left the reception, and waiters are beginning to clear plates away.

I scan the courtyard for a glimpse of blonde hair. Lottie must be here somewhere. She can't have got out to the beach; there's a waiter on duty at the exit gate checking security bracelets, and anyway, I'd have seen her as I came in that way myself.

I skirt the pool, refusing to acknowledge the depth of my relief when I verify its turquoise waters are undisturbed, and then go inside the hotel. There are three receptionists behind the desk and a doorman at the front entrance; one of them would have noticed if a three-year-old wandered out of the hotel on her own.

But when I ask if anyone's seen her, they all shake their heads. One of the receptionists offers to look for her with me, but I decline. Escalating the search would be admitting something is wrong. And everything's fine.

I just can't find my daughter, that's all.

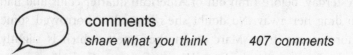

comments
share what you think   407 comments

ButterFly57, Florida, USA
I can't imagine what that poor woman is going through.
God bless that beautiful little girl. Hope and pray she
comes home safely.

Fizz_for_fuzz, Devon, UK
Why would anyone leave their kid alone just coz they're on
holiday? Why??

Happysmile, Edinburgh, UK
If this was my child I would be searching with my bare
hands until they were down to the bone . . . .

Fair-minded, Brittany, France
This poor woman, she must be out of her mind with worry.
She was at a wedding, her child should of been safe.

sharpcat21, London, UK
Good parenting is not leaving a 3 yr old unsupervised at
night.

> **WideAwake @sharpcat21**
> She wasn't unsupervised, she was at a wedding with
> friends. Where's your compassion?

Nothing_To_See_Here, Greater Manchester, UK
Why does this snoozepaper feel the need to tell us how
much her flat is worth? Her child is missing for God's sake.

chocciegirl, Florida, USA
I sure hope this little girl is found safe and well. How can a child disappear in the middle of a wedding???

BriarRose @chocciegirl
It's like nowhere's safe anymore.

chapter 09

alex

The panic doesn't strike immediately. I make another circuit of the courtyard, checking every inch. Once I'm certain Lottie isn't there, I go back into the hotel and search all the public areas leading from the lobby, including the dining room – always Lottie's first port of call – and toilets. I go upstairs and check she hasn't returned to our room, although she doesn't have a keycard, so she wouldn't be able to get in. She is nowhere to be seen.

I'm suddenly very sober.

'Think,' I tell myself out loud. 'Don't panic.'

Lottie is not in the courtyard. She's not sitting outside our room, or in any of the public areas of the hotel. She'd never have gone to the beach without me, and even if she had, the hotel staff manning the gate are under specific instructions not to allow children to leave on their own. That leaves only one logical option: she must have gone off to play with one of the other bridesmaids in their room.

Actually, it leaves two options, but I refuse to put the second on the table.

I return to the reception desk and ask the helpful girl behind it for the room numbers of the four other bridesmaids.

'I can't give you those,' she says, 'but I can call them, if you'd like?'

Lottie is not in any of the other families' rooms.

It's twenty minutes now since I came back from the beach; twenty-three or twenty-four minutes since Zealy and Paul saw Lottie. I imagine that pinprick of certainty – *she was headed back towards the ice-cream station with some of the other kids* – as the glowing blue dot in the centre of a circle. With every second that passes, the radius of possibility widens.

How far can a three-year-old go in five minutes? In ten? In twenty?

What if she's not alone?

I can't ignore the second option any longer. I run back to the courtyard, consumed by fear. She's hiding, I tell myself. She must be hiding.

I know she's not here, but I check again: under the tables and behind large concrete bougainvillea planters, not caring that I'm starting to attract attention. I feel dizzy, as if I have vertigo. My eyes ache and my throat is dry. I know, already, that my search has somehow shifted.

This will be the moment I come back to, again and again. The decisions I make now, whether I go down to the beach, even though I'm sure she's not there, or out into the car park in front of the hotel in case she slipped past the doorman; whether I draft other guests to help in the search, risking chaos or confusion, or keep looking by myself. What I do next will be something I live with forever.

'You still haven't found her?' Zealy asks, as I make my third circuit of the buffet tables.

'She can't have got far,' I repeat.

Except that's not true any more. In half an hour, Lottie can walk a mile. And that's assuming she's moving under her own steam. I picture a hand clamping over her mouth, a strong arm scooping her up, and struggle not to vomit.

Zealy hitches up her ridiculous pink skirts and strides over to the DJ managing the music. A moment later, Elton John falls quiet, and people turn in surprise.

'Listen up, everybody,' Zealy says, clapping her hands for attention. 'We seem to have lost one of our little bridesmaids. There's no need to worry, but if everyone could help us track her down, we'd all be grateful.'

She strikes just the right note of contained concern. As wedding guests start to look about them, Zealy marshals a couple of hotel staff and sends them down onto the beach, just in case.

Part of me is sure that in a few minutes, when Lottie has been discovered hiding behind a rack of postcards or fast asleep in the lobby, I'm going to wish Zealy hadn't raised the alarm prematurely. Lottie's just gone upstairs looking for our room and got lost. She's probably stuck in the lift, or sitting on the stairs, waiting for someone to find her.

'She'd never go near the sea,' I tell Zealy. 'I don't want to waste time looking for her there.'

'She might if she thought that's where you were.'

If she saw me leave with Ian.

The beach is the only place I haven't looked. Zealy and I run down there now, and I'm not even pretending to be calm any longer.

I yell Lottie's name, shouting myself hoarse, as we turn and run in opposite directions. The sand, which seemed so beautiful just hours ago, is now a treacherous bog serving only to slow me down. It's like one of those hideous nightmares in which you try to run but find yourself trapped in quicksand, your limbs moving in slow motion as a faceless pursuer hunts you down.

The sound of the sea is louder in the darkness. I shine the torch from my phone between the sunloungers, in case Lottie is hiding there, too afraid to move. She must be so scared. For all her bravura, she is still a three-year-old child alone in the dark.

I don't know how far down the beach I should go. Panic clutches my heart. Suppose this is the wrong direction? Suppose I am moving further away from Lottie, instead of closer?

Ahead of me, a beached catamaran looms out of the darkness. I run towards it. In my mind's eye, I picture Lottie crouched down behind it, lost and frightened, her knees pulled into her chest, her blonde hair tangled by the wind. The vision is so real that when I draw level with the fibreglass pontoons, I am fully expecting Lottie to be there.

The shout that I have *found her!* dies on my lips. My disappointment is so visceral I lean on the catamaran and vomit onto the sand.

I wipe the back of my hand across my mouth and circle around the catamaran. There are so many places she could be, so many directions she could have gone. To my right is the inky sea; to my left, the bright lights of the St Pete Beach strip. Ahead of and behind me are miles of shadowed, dimpled sand. I spin in circles, panic choking me. She could be anywhere.

With anyone.

A voice calls my name. Marc is jogging down the beach towards me.

'Have you found her?' he calls.

'Where is she, Marc?'

He draws level with me and squeezes my shoulders. 'We'll find her. She can't have got far.'

'There was a man,' I say, suddenly remembering.

'What man?'

I can't believe this slipped my mind. 'Yesterday afternoon, when we were down on the beach. I saw him talking to Lottie. He had his hand on her shoulder.' I frown, trying to remember the details. 'Mid-forties, receding hair. Thin.

Smartly dressed – too smart for the beach. There was something off about him.'

'We need to call the police,' Marc says.

Calling the police will mean this is real. My daughter isn't just lost or hiding from me. She's *missing*.

'Better safe than sorry,' he adds. 'By the time they get here, I'm sure we'll have found her.'

There are people scattered all over the beach now, calling Lottie's name. The atmosphere at the hotel has changed when Marc and I return, desperate for news. Floodlights have been turned on in the courtyard, tables pushed back. The hotel manager is addressing staff clustered in a small knot beside the desk in reception. They're instructed to check inside anywhere a child could crawl or hide and possibly be asleep or unable to get out: cupboards, piles of laundry, large appliances, outbuildings and crawl spaces.

A child is missing. Everything is to be put on hold until she's located.

Marc talks to the hotel manager. It's been an hour already. If she was in the hotel, she would have been found. The police are being called. Already my world is splintering into *before* and *after*.

I know – we all know – that in the case of a missing person, the first seventy-two hours are crucial. Of those precious hours, the first is the most vital of all. We've already wasted that. Every moment that passes takes my daughter further from me. The chances of her safe return will shrink hour by hour, minute by minute, until I'm left hoping for a miracle.

Luca and I used to joke about Lottie being abducted. If anyone takes her, we used to say, they'd soon bring her back.

Zealy reaches for my hand and doesn't let go. We sit on the sofa in the hotel lobby, waiting for the police to arrive. This is

America, I tell myself. The police know what they're doing here. They have the FBI and the most sophisticated technology in the world. If someone has taken my daughter, they'll track them down.

There's a sudden shout from the corridor. 'I've found her!' Paul cries.

We leap up. Everyone is running towards him.

He's holding a bundle of pink taffeta in his arms. A little girl's blonde head lolls against his shoulder.

It's impossible to tell if she's alive.

chapter 10

alex

The child Paul has found is not Lottie.

It turns out he has confused my daughter with one of the other bridesmaids, five-year-old Olivia Everett, who'd fallen asleep in the hotel recreation room. It takes a moment for the significance of his mistake to register and, when it does, I feel as if an abyss has opened at my feet.

'Was it you or Paul who saw Lottie at the ice-cream station, just before I came back from the beach?' I ask Zealy urgently.

She looks at him and then back at me as she, too, realises the seriousness of the error. 'It was Paul.'

Paul, who has mistaken Olivia for Lottie. He's been muddling them all night. They don't look alike: Olivia's hair is much darker, a dirty blonde close to mouse, and she's far skinnier than Lottie. But to a childless man in his thirties, one fair-haired little girl in a pink dress is much like another.

Which means it wasn't my daughter he saw *headed back towards the ice-cream station with some of the other kids* an hour and ten minutes ago.

It was Olivia.

The timeline from which we have been working, the blue dot at the centre of the circle of possibilities, is not where, or when, we thought it was. Everything must be recalibrated. We must retrace our steps from the very beginning.

Fear shears the thin thread of hope to which I've been clinging. I know, *I know*, Lottie has been abducted. The guilt is a physical sensation, a constant, nauseating drumbeat of pain in my ears: I left my child, and now she is missing. I have failed her in the most basic and fundamental of ways: I couldn't keep her safe. And my failure is amplified by the appalling revelation that I don't even know when she was taken. I've fallen into the same trap as Paul, blinded by the pink skirts.

When did I last see Lottie for *sure*? Not just a glimpse of pink taffeta, flitting between the buffet tables or disappearing around corners, but Lottie herself?

I realise, with a chill, that I haven't seen her with absolute certainty since the wedding ceremony on the beach, when she was sitting on her gilt chair a few rows away from me.

Not an hour and fifteen minutes ago.

Four hours ago.

My child may have been missing for four hours and *I didn't even notice*.

Even as I suppress my panic, I fix that snapshot in my mind, knowing it may be the last time I ever saw my daughter alive: Lottie glaring ferociously at the sea, clutching her empty flower basket on her lap, her platinum hair whipped free from its fishtail braid by the breeze.

It'll be the first question the police ask when they arrive: when did you last see your daughter? And when I tell them this new truth, it will affect every aspect of their investigation.

In any case like this, a disappearance or a murder, the first person under suspicion is always the victim's nearest and dearest. But when the police learn I lost sight of my child four hours ago, their consideration of me will transition from routine to serious. They'll waste time delving into my history, my record as a mother, when they should be out there, looking for her.

I've failed my daughter twice over.

'For God's sake, where are the damn police?' Zealy exclaims, just as two uniformed officers enter hotel reception.

The adversarial nature of the legal system means that, as a lawyer advocating for some of the most disadvantaged people in the world, I'm used to viewing the police as the enemy. I've seen the aftermath of dawn raids: children wrenched from their parents, decent people treated like criminals, property destroyed. But I've never been so glad to see a police uniform as I am now.

One of the officers hangs back, talking into the radio at her chest. The other introduces himself. 'Officer Spencer Graves, ma'am. I understand your daughter is missing?'

'Someone's stolen her,' I say.

'Did you witness the abduction, ma'am?'

'No, but we've looked everywhere. I know she's been taken!'

'How old is your daughter, ma'am?'

'Three. She'll be four next February.'

'We're wasting time,' Zealy interjects. 'You need to send out an alert and set up roadblocks before it's too late!'

'Ma'am, we just got to establish some facts,' Graves says. 'Is it possible she's wandered off on her own?'

'We'd have found her by now,' I say. 'Half the hotel staff is out looking for her. We've got a hundred wedding guests searching the beach. She's only three, she couldn't get very far on her own.'

'Could she be with another family member?'

My frustration intensifies. Time is not my friend. With every second that passes, whoever has taken my daughter is moving further away, and the area that must be searched, the diameter of possibility, exponentially expands.

'There's no other family here. I'm telling you, someone has *stolen* her!'

'What about the father, ma'am? Is it possible she's with him?'

'He's dead,' I say shortly.

'He was killed in the Genoa bridge collapse last August,' Zealy says.

'Sorry to hear that, ma'am.'

One of those random, when-your-number's-up, pointless deaths. Luca was visiting his parents in Genoa, following his mother's recent diagnosis with dementia. He just happened to be driving across the Ponte Morandi, the main bridge across the city, when the cables in its southern stays broke. He was one of forty-three people killed that day. His body was crushed beyond recovery, but his beautiful face was unmarked, except for a small, deep cut above his right eye.

When I saw him lying in his coffin before the altar in the same church where we'd married, near his mother's home village in Sicily, I remember thinking he looked like he was sleeping. Any moment now, he'd open his beautiful eyes and smile at all the fuss he'd caused.

I couldn't tear my eyes from his broken parents, hollowed out with grief. To lose a child. It is beyond imagining.

'Please,' I beg. 'Lottie hasn't wandered off or got lost. Someone's *taken* her.'

Graves gives me a searching stare and then rejoins the female officer. I watch them confer for a few minutes, my agitation escalating. It's clear they think I'm overreacting. Another hysterical mother convinced her daughter has been kidnapped, when the child has just fallen asleep in a corner somewhere. The rational part of my brain doesn't blame them: ninety-nine times out of a hundred they'd be right.

The female officer's radio crackles and she goes back outside.

57

'I'm sure there's nothing to worry about,' Graves says, returning to me. 'These cases, most every kid turns up safe and sound. But your daughter's pretty young. It's kinda late for her to be out on her own, so we're gonna call in back-up from the CAC.'

She's three, I want to scream. *She's too young to be on her own whether it's late or not!*

I suppress the urge to tear the hotel apart with my bare hands, to run back out to the beach and turn over every grain of sand. I have to wait, *wait*, for the slow wheels of procedure to turn.

Zealy refuses to leave me, but I insist Paul goes back out and keeps searching with the others. Every pair of eyes matters. I can't shake the fear we're doing everything wrong. This is the time I will look back on, the crucial minutes when I had the chance to save my daughter but instead let her slip through my fingers.

It's close to midnight when two new detectives arrive. They throw acronyms at me and then, when Zealy demands clarity, explain longhand that they're from the Crimes Against Children division of the Investigative Operations Bureau at the Pinellas County Sheriff's Office. Once again, they're a male/female pairing, but this time, a fortysomething woman is the ranking officer, a Lieutenant Bamby Bates. It's a ridiculous name, a stripper's name, but she looks shrewd and efficient, with sharp black eyes that miss nothing, and I feel someone is finally taking me seriously.

'We're issuing an Amber alert,' she tells me. 'We've notified the FDLE – the Florida Department of Law Enforcement,' she adds. 'It should go out within minutes.'

'What's an Amber alert?' I ask.

'It means Lottie's details will go out to the media,' she says. 'They'll be broadcast on radio and TV, and via text message alert. They'll also be up on the interstate electronic gantry system. This isn't Portugal,' she adds. 'Lottie isn't going to disappear through the cracks here.'

She knows my child's name. She knows what happened to Madeleine McCann, and where. She's telling me she's experienced and well-informed; she knows what she's doing. Her department won't trample vital clues into the ground or let the trail go cold.

'Do you got a recent photo of Lottie on your cell?' the lieutenant asks. 'We can embed it in the Amber alert.'

I pull up the picture Zealy texted me this afternoon, the one I made my screensaver, and forward it to Bates. Lottie is wearing the pink dress she was last seen in and glaring at the camera with her customary ferocity, her unruly blonde hair already escaping from its French plait. It's not a flattering photo, but it's Lottie, the very essence of her.

'What about the media?' I ask. 'Should I do an appeal?'

'We're not there yet,' Bates says. 'I know this is real hard, Alexa, but you gotta trust me. I'm going to find your daughter.'

Nothing is comforting. Nothing makes me feel any less frantic. But I recognise that this woman is Lottie's lifeline, and she knows what she's doing.

'You're not going to be able to sleep,' Bates says, her voice softening. 'And I know you want to be out there, looking. But you have to let us do our job.'

There is a sudden commotion from the courtyard. Marc's elderly father, Eric, is rushing towards us as fast as he can manage. He's holding something, but I can't see what it is until he's almost upon us.

A small, pink shoe.

chapter 11

quinn

It takes Quinn a few moments to realise she hasn't been buried alive. Her nose is pressed up against a splintery wooden board, but so too is her left cheek, and, as far as she's aware, convention dictates some kind of pillow when you're laid to your eternal rest.

She rolls onto her back and stares up at the underside of a porch roof. Losing her right eye last year has thrown off her spatial awareness, but even she can see the roof is canted away from the building at a precarious angle. She meant to tell Marnie to get it fixed the last time she woke up on her ex-girlfriend's front stoop.

It's not yet dawn; early morning October mist drifts across the grey fields of stubble surrounding the farmhouse. Quinn runs a tongue around her remaining teeth. Her mouth feels like the bottom of a bat cave. She hates falling asleep without flossing, even though at this point it's akin to repainting the railings on the *Titanic*.

Her phone vibrates in her back pocket, but she ignores it. It'll be the News Desk, and she has no intention of interrupting her hangover to schlep back to Washington. They can get one of the junior correspondents to follow whatever chum the president has just thrown in the water.

The screen door opens. 'Jeez,' Marnie says. 'Again?'

Quinn struggles to sit up, pushing against her functioning arm. 'You need to get your porch roof fixed.'

'What the fuck you doing here, Quinn?'

'Selling Girl Scout cookies?'

Marnie pulls Quinn to her feet. 'I'm not kidding around. This has got to stop.' She doesn't invite Quinn in, but she doesn't shut the door in her face, either. Quinn follows her into the warm kitchen, feeling like a stray cat let into the house after a night on the tiles.

'You can't keep getting wasted and driving out here,' Marnie says, pushing a cup of coffee across the counter towards her. 'You're gonna end up in a ditch. And I gotta tell you, you look like crap.'

Quinn would smile if she could, but she's lost most of the muscles on the right side of her face. 'That ship has sailed,' she says, without a trace of self-pity.

She demanded one of the nurses bring her a mirror just three days after the IED exploded beneath her Jeep in Syria. She couldn't actually tell the woman what she wanted, of course: her jaw was still wired shut. She'd had to write it with her left hand on the pad they'd given her. One silver lining to all this: it's her right arm that's paralysed, and she's a leftie.

Her desire to see what she looked like wasn't provoked by vanity: she's a *television* reporter. Viewers may not expect their war correspondents to be pretty blonde auto-cuties, but they don't want to be put off their dinner, either.

Senior management at INN said all the right things when they medevacked her home, promising to keep her job open and to pay for private medical care and one-on-one rehabilitation, but Quinn knew as soon as she looked in the mirror her career was fucked.

And she was the lucky one: her cameraman, fixer and

translator had all been killed in the roadside bomb, along with the two US troops accompanying them. Quinn 'just' lost an eye, her right lower jaw, and ninety percent of the use of her right arm. The plastic surgeons patched her up pretty well, but there was no way INN would ever let her on prime time TV again.

Instead, they had the company shrink sign her off the reporters' roster with PTSD, and offered her a job they didn't expect her to take, as Washington Bureau Chief. In theory, it was a promotion.

She's aware she's become a cliché: the embittered journalist looking for redemption and a way back into the premier league, but she's not going to be the one to blink first. Their standoff has lasted fifteen months so far. INN sends her on bottom-feeding stories that never make it out of the graveyard bulletins. Quinn returns just enough of their calls to stop them being able to fire her.

Marnie folds her arms and watches Quinn sip her coffee. 'You coulda caught your death. It was down in the thirties last night.'

'Alcohol doesn't freeze. Slit my wrists and I'll bleed pure bourbon.'

'Not funny, Quinn.'

Even with sleep in her eyes and pillow-creased cheeks, Marnie is still the most beautiful woman Quinn has ever seen, with a torch of red hair and delicate Celtic bone structure. They met nine months ago at a petrol station in rural Maryland; Quinn had been struggling one-armed to change a flat tyre when Marnie had stopped to help.

Conversation had led to dinner; dinner to bed.

The other woman hadn't been put off by Quinn's disfiguring injuries. What put an end to their relationship, after just over six months together, was Quinn's inability to stay sober for longer than eight hours at a stretch.

62

Quinn reaches for the pitcher of coffee on the hotplate, wrapping her bad hand around her mug as she refills it. She's learned the hard way that adding the non-visual signal, from the sense of touch, helps her brain judge distance and location more accurately.

'How long this time?' Marnie asks.

'What day is it now?'

'Sunday.'

Quinn has many faults, but telling the truth and shaming the devil is hardwired into her DNA. 'Three days,' she says.

'Goddamn it, Quinn. You wanna screw up your life, be my guest. But I don't want a ringside seat.'

Quinn was a screw-up long before the IED. She suffered a one-two knockout punch when she was seven and her parents divorced, and then fought *not* to have custody. Forced to spend her childhood shuttling between homes in London and Scotland, in neither of which she was welcome, she didn't grieve much when they died from cancer while she was at college, within six months of each other. She specialises in rooting out all that's dark and ugly in human nature, because it's what she knows.

Her phone buzzes again.

'Take it,' Marnie says.

Quinn suppresses her craving for a slug of Eagle Rare from the hip flask inside her jacket and swipes right on the call from the News Desk.

twelve hours missing

chapter 12

alex

I keep trying to explain my daughter's fear of the sea to Lieutenant Bates, but no one will listen to me.

'She'd never go near the ocean,' I say, again and again.

Marc's father shows us the section of shoreline where he discovered Lottie's shoe floating at the water's edge. It's clear the police want this to be a drowning rather than an abduction. Florida is a tourist hotspot, after all: its economy depends on its reputation for fun-filled, family-friendly vacations. It took years for Praia da Luz to recover from the damage to its image caused by the McCann case. A drowning would be a tragedy, yes, but only for me.

There are searchlights all along the beach now, rendering it as bright as day. Forensic integrity matters less than locating Lottie but, apart from that single pink shoe, nothing else is found.

I know Bates wants me to keep out of their way and stay at the hotel, but I can't sit still. As dawn breaks, Zealy, Marc and I resume our search together, covering every inch of the tiny barrier island.

In addition to the main hotel, the complex also comprises a dozen separate holiday villas and staff accommodation, and a nine-hole golf course. We jump over low walls and rake through scrubby undergrowth, looking in drains and ditches, and beneath the bridge that connects the island to St Pete Beach. It's eerily quiet: most of the other wedding guests have gone to bed, and the police searchers have moved to the mainland. We're completely alone. It feels as if no one is looking for Lottie. Just me, and my two dearest friends.

Someone suddenly calls my name from the bridge. I glance up and find myself staring at a man holding a long-lensed camera.

'Fuck off!' Zealy yells.

I put a restraining hand on her arm. 'Don't. We may need the press.'

Lieutenant Bates is waiting for me when we return to the hotel. 'We want you to speak to the media,' she says, with perfect timing.

We are here already: the point she told me just a few hours ago she didn't want to reach. Any last crumb of hope that this is a false alarm, a near miss, vanishes.

Bates correctly interprets my silence as acquiescence. I would stand on my head and spit pound coins if I thought it would bring Lottie home.

'We've spoken to the local networks,' Bates says. 'We'll do the appeal at six tonight, to catch their evening shows. Don't worry about what you're gonna say. We'll help you with that.'

'She's in no state to face the media,' Marc says.

'I know it's tough, but the sooner we get this story out there, the better.'

'You don't need Alex for that.'

'An appeal from the mother always gets traction,' Bates says.

We both know what she really means. The media don't just want a photograph, or a stiff-necked detective appealing for information. That's not going to get them the clicks and likes and shares and tweets they're after. They want tears and pain. They want *me*.

'What are you going to do in the meantime?' Zealy demands.

'I promise you, we're throwing everything at this,' Bates says. 'We've got a lot of people out there looking for her. We're pulling CCTV from tolls and gas stations. And I've got a team putting a timeline of the reception together: where everyone was during the evening, and when. It'll help us figure who could have seen something. Folks oftentimes don't realise the significance till later.'

'Everyone was taking photos,' Zealy says. 'She's bound to be in quite a few of them, at least in the background. They'll be time-stamped—'

'We've already asked everyone to give us what they got,' Bates says. 'Trust me, Zealy, we're on it.'

Her phone buzzes and she mouths an apology, then steps away out of earshot.

I dig the heels of my palms into my eyes, exhausted and frightened beyond reckoning. Lottie's been missing all night. I'm so tired I can barely stand, and yet I'm consumed with a restlessness I can't seem to control. I feel very cold, and my hands keep twitching, a physical manifestation of my urge to search.

I realise I can't put off calling my parents any longer. This will shatter their world. They adore Lottie; she's their only grandchild and the light of their lives. Ever since Luca died, I've taken her home to them most weekends. I dread to think what this news will do to them. But I have to tell them before they find out from someone else.

Just saying the words out loud to Mum and Dad makes the nightmare real.

When Mum starts to sob, I break down completely, and have to hand the phone to Zealy.

She asks Dad to tell my sister and Luca's parents, Elena and Roberto. I've never been close to my in-laws; they made it clear from the start they wanted their only son to marry a nice Italian girl who'd stay at home and have babies, not an ambitious career woman. They tolerated me while Luca and I were together, but after our divorce I became persona non grata. They haven't spoken to me, or seen Lottie, since his funeral. But they're both old and frail: Roberto has serious heart problems and Elena is in the early stages of Alzheimer's, one of the reasons Luca travelled back to see them so often. They deserve to hear this news from family, not to wake up and read it in the papers.

'Your dad says he and your mum will be on the next flight out,' Zealy says.

'What about Harriet?'

'He's going to call her now.'

'They shouldn't come out,' I say. 'Mum hasn't been well. And by the time they get here, we'll have found Lottie, anyway.'

'Of course we will,' Zealy says, stoutly.

We go back downstairs to find Marc, but Bates intercepts us in the lobby. 'I'd like you to look at something,' she says, handing me her phone.

'What is it? Is it Lottie?'

'Please.'

The screen is paused on a grainy black and white CCTV image at a petrol station. It's from last night: the timestamp on the bottom of the screen says 23:42. Bates plays it for me. An overweight, middle-aged man in cargo shorts, flip-flops and a sleeveless T-shirt comes out of the petrol station and heads towards a four-door pickup truck. He leans in through the window of the front passenger seat, as if talking to someone, and then thumps his meaty fist on the vehicle's roof.

I glance up at Bates. 'What is this?'

'Please, just keep watching.'

The man walks around the truck and gets into the driver's

side. Suddenly, one of the rear doors opens. A child starts to get out; a little girl in a full-skirted dress rendered grey by the security camera. Her feet are bare.

Then the child is yanked back inside the vehicle, and the person in the passenger seat – it's impossible to tell if they are a man or a woman – reaches across the car for the rear door handle and pulls it shut from inside. The car drives off.

The whole scene has taken no more than a few seconds.

chapter 13

When I beckon, she comes to me, her eyes bright with curiosity. She should know better, but she's evidently one of those children who likes breaking the rules.

I spin her my story and then turn as if to leave, knowing curiosity will be her undoing. I'm right. She catches up to me and slips her hand in mine, because she trusts me. We walk together in plain sight along the beach, past dozens of people. No one even tries to stop us.

I can't believe it's this simple. This is the moment of greatest risk, the only period of time when, for all my careful planning, events are largely beyond my control. If someone sees her with me and challenges us, I have my excuse ready. But no one even notices. We are made invisible by our very ordinariness, the child and me.

I walk a little faster. The clock is already ticking. The child may be missed at any moment. Time is of the essence.

I turn onto a stony path leading away from the shore. She's barefoot, though she doesn't complain. But she is slowing us both down as she hops gingerly from foot to foot, so I pick her up and she doesn't protest.

We reach my rental car, which I've parked in a church car park chosen because it has no security cameras. The ID I gave the car hire company is obviously false; you'd be shocked how quickly you can obtain a fake driving licence online. The 'dark web' is not some distant, sinister land in Middle Earth; it's right there, Mordor at your fingertips, just a click away.

I used the same ID to rent a cheap hotel room. I didn't even have to deal with a human being; a security key code was sent to my burner phone.

The child frowns for the first time when I open the door to the back seat of the car. 'Where's my car seat?' she says.

'Aren't you too old for that?' I ask, although of course she isn't.

'Yes,' she says, pleased.

She doesn't ask questions as we drive to the hotel. I've been careful to pick a route with few traffic cameras and no road tolls. We've been driving for more than forty minutes when she requests the bathroom, but I tell her we're nearly there. I have no intention of making any unscheduled stops anywhere I haven't had a chance to reconnoitre first.

I park behind the hotel. I will abandon this car soon, but there's something I have to do first.

Opening the car boot, I take out a generic navy holdall.

Inside it is a roll of black plastic rubbish bags, some wire ties and a large pair of scissors.

chapter 14

alex

Another false alarm. The child in the back of the pickup truck at the petrol station isn't Lottie. It looks like her. The little girl is the same age, the same build. She has long fair hair like my daughter, though I can tell, even from the grainy, grey CCTV footage, that it isn't the same Nordic shade of platinum as Lottie's.

It *could* be my daughter. But it isn't.

Lieutenant Bates presses me to be sure. The little girl in the CCTV film appears to be under some sort of duress. She's wearing a stiff, formal skirt that strongly resembles Lottie's bridesmaid dress, unusual clothing for a trip to the beach. Am I absolutely *sure*—

I am.

The sudden hope, and then the vicious disappointment, devastates me. My fear and powerlessness reach breaking point; I feel like a caged, demented animal. This is, without doubt, torture of the cruellest kind. I don't know I'm screaming and smashing my fists against the marble-topped reception desk until Marc wraps his arms around me, physically restraining me so I don't hurt myself. I collapse against him, keening my agony in harsh, raw sobs. It's as if my heart has been ripped from me. I didn't realise, until this moment, that the child I never wanted to have has become my reason for living.

Zealy and Marc beg me to go upstairs to get some rest, but I know sleep is impossible. It's only when Bates points out that I must be coherent for the press appeal this afternoon that I agree at least to try.

Zealy helps me change out of the pale blue cocktail dress I've been wearing since yesterday afternoon. It's unrecognisable now: ripped and stained by hours of searching through brush and scrubland.

I dump it straight in the bin and Zealy selects a clean white T-shirt and pair of taupe linen drawstring pants from my wardrobe. She tries to persuade me to shower before putting them on, but I refuse. I don't have the patience.

I lie down in the darkened bedroom while Zealy dozes in an armchair, refusing to leave me alone, but I can't sleep. I can't imagine sleeping again until my daughter is found. I have to keep vigil with my daughter.

I drift in and out of an exhausted, fitful twilight, haunted by nightmarish images of my daughter's mottled body lying cold and still on a marble slab, her face bloodied and bruised. I wake, my heart pounding, clothes soaked in sweat. Even when I get up and change my T-shirt, I can't rid myself of the images dancing behind my mind's eye. I don't know if I'll ever be able to close them again.

Bates and her colleague, Sergeant Lorenz, want to talk to me before the press conference. In the last few hours, the police have taken over the business centre overlooking the pool. Two small suites are being used as interview rooms, while in the main conference room the photo of Lottie I gave them has been blown up and taped to a glass display wall.

Smaller headshots of the principal players in this drama – me, Marc, Sian, the bridesmaids and ushers, even an old picture of Luca, presumably downloaded from social media – are tacked in a semicircle around Lottie. Colour-coded arrows connect us in ways I cannot decipher.

They're putting together a detailed timeline now. Filling in the gaps, piecing together Lottie's last known movements from eyewitness reports and photographs from people's phones.

As I follow Bates through the conference room to one of the interview suites, she tells me that they think the last person to speak to Lottie was Sian's mother, Penny; several guests saw Lottie chatting to her just as everyone trooped up from the beach to the hotel. But Penny has nothing useful to add. She doesn't even remember the encounter.

After that, the trail goes cold.

The police can't find a single person who recalls talking to Lottie after the wedding ceremony ended. There isn't one photo of her at the reception, despite the fact so many of us saw her – or *thought* we saw her – flitting back and forth between the buffet and the ice-cream station.

My head swims with nausea. I have been clinging like a drowning man to the hope she *was* at the reception, even if I didn't see her; that she wasn't missing for hours before I raised the alarm.

It's possible, of course, that she just doesn't happen to be in any of the photos. But given the volume the police have obtained from the phones of dozens and dozens of guests, not to mention the official photographer, the chances are vanishingly small that she wouldn't be in the background of at least some of them. Far more probable is the terrifying truth that all those apparent sightings of a blonde girl in a pink dress weren't Lottie after all.

We all made the same mistake Paul did: one little girl in a frothy pink frock looks much like another.

Even, unforgivably, to her mother.

While I've been upstairs, trying to sleep, the police have sequenced the photos. The last one they have of her was taken at 18.33, by Flic Everett, who was taking a picture of Olivia.

Bates shows it to me, pushing it across the Formica table between us. Lottie is sitting on her gilt chair at the end of the front row on the beach, her head turned away from the camera as if something – or someone – has caught her attention just out of shot. If we knew what, or who, that was, perhaps it would tell us where she is now. They're cross-referencing all the photographs they have, Bates says, trying to find the object of Lottie's attention, but it's a slow, laborious process, and in the meantime, my daughter is still missing.

18.33.

Nearly four full hours before I reported her missing.

Before I even noticed she was gone.

I realise now why the tenor of the questions from Bates and Lorenz has subtly changed, and why I'm in an interview room, rather than sitting on the sofa in reception.

I understand the logic: statistically, I'm the person most likely to have harmed my child. But while they're probing for cracks in my story, quizzing me about what Lottie was like as a baby or whether I find it difficult to cope as a single mother, they're not out there, looking for her.

'You let a three-year-old kid make her way back to the hotel on her own?' Lorenz says. This is the third time he's asked the same question, albeit in different ways. 'You were fine with that?'

'She wasn't on her own! All the bridesmaids followed Sian and Marc down the aisle together, and then all the guests went back in a big group. It was a *wedding*!'

'But you didn't go find her once you got to the reception?'

'She's a really smart little girl,' I say, and even to my own ears I sound defensive. 'She doesn't need me checking in on her every five minutes.'

And then Bates asks me what I was doing in the crucial window between 18.33, when Flic Everett took that last photo of Lottie, and 22.28, when the police logged the first phone call reporting her missing.

I tell her the truth: I was having sex on the beach with a stranger.

It didn't take long: we took advantage of the privacy afforded by the hooded sunloungers, and Ian was an athletic lover. I orgasmed twice, in hard, sharp succession, before Ian came with a grunt of his own. Twenty minutes, start to finish.

We spent another twenty minutes, half-an-hour at most, gazing up at the stars and talking. I was away from the party less than an hour.

I'm not ashamed of the sex: I'm single, with as much right as any man to enjoy a fling with no strings attached.

But I'm also a mother, and it's clear to everyone in the room I prioritised myself over my daughter. I didn't go and find her once the wedding was over because I was too busy drinking champagne and flirting with a stranger.

Even if I had nothing to do with her disappearance, I'm culpable.

'What do you know about Ian Dutton?' Lorenz asks.

'He's a friend of Marc's. I'd never talked to him before last night.'

'Was it his idea to go to the beach?'

'No, mine.'

I stare at the photograph of Lottie lying between us on the table. 'Ian couldn't have had anything to do with this,' I say. 'He was with me when she disappeared.'

'You're assuming only one individual is responsible,' Bates says.

Her words conjure images I don't want in my head. Sex trafficking rings, paedophile circles, men working in concert to spirit children away to dark basements and stained mattresses.

'I understand why you have to ask these questions,' I say, trying to hold my voice steady. 'But I didn't hurt Lottie, and nor did any of our friends. I told you about that man I saw talking to her on the beach. Have you checked into him?'

Lorenz leans back in his chair. 'We're looking at every possibility.'

'You say Lottie is a smart kid,' Bates says.

'She *is*. She didn't wander off or get lost. She'd never have gone near the water. And she's not the kind of kid to be fooled by stories about lost puppies. Someone *took* her.'

'A stranger?'

'Obviously!'

'See, this is what confuses me,' Bates says. 'Lottie disappeared into thin air in the middle of a wedding, and yet *no one* seems to have noticed. No one saw anything, no one heard anything.'

Blood roars in my ears. Suddenly I understand what she's saying, the realisation slamming into my stomach with the speed and force of a train.

If a stranger had snatched Lottie by force in broad daylight it would have attracted huge attention. My daughter may be only three, but just getting her into her car seat is like wrestling with an alligator. She'd have screamed, lashed out, created such a scene no one could have ignored it.

Abducting her from the reception under cover of darkness and loud music might have been easier. But access would have been far more difficult. The beach is public, but the reception area by the pool was restricted to wedding guests, enforced by hotel security. And the lack of any photographs or genuine sightings of my daughter at the reception lends weight to the theory that she never came back to the hotel.

'It's possible she left the beach under her own steam, of course,' Bates muses. 'But if not, it seems more plausible to me that she was with someone she knew and trusted.'

I don't know if that makes it worse.

'We *will* find her,' Bates says.

But we both know time is running out. No one has seen Lottie for nearly twenty-four hours. I don't have to be told that if she isn't found in the next forty-eight, she may never be found at all.

Lottie, three, snatched as her mother attends wedding

FLOWER GIRL STOLEN

THE distraught mother of missing three-year-old Charlotte Martini was clinging to hope she was still alive last night.

As the desperate hunt continued in Florida, her mother relived the terrifying moment she discovered her daughter had vanished from a wedding reception at the upmarket Sandy Beach Hotel on a private barrier island off the coast of St Pete Beach, while she was chatting with guests just yards away.

Alexa Martini, 29, a human rights lawyer, has told family and friends she believes her daughter was snatched just moments after performing her duties as a flower girl at the wedding of family friend Marc Chapman.

Desperate

The child's grandmother, Mary Johnson, 59, who flew out with her husband, Anthony, 65, to be with Mrs Martini yesterday, described the frantic phone call she received after her daughter discovered her child was missing around eleven o'clock on Saturday night. 'It's the call no mother ever wants to make or hear. She said: "Lottie's been taken, Lottie's been taken." She was hysterical. 'She only took her eyes off her for a split second. It was broad daylight, they were at a wedding. Lottie is the apple of her mother's eye.'

Florida police yesterday sealed off the beach and patio area by the pool where the wedding reception was held, and forensic specialists combed through the area, looking for clues. An Amber alert – a nationwide appeal to find the missing child – was issued, and all airports and ports have been notified.

But despite a massive search throughout the night involving police, divers and volunteers, there has been no sign of Lottie, who was wearing a pink bridesmaid's dress and ballet-style shoes when she disappeared.

Thin man

Police have appealed for a 'thin man' who was spotted carrying a child near the hotel at the time of Lottie's disappearance to come forward. Lieutenant Bamby Bates, of the Pinellas County Sheriff's Office, said they 'urgently' needed to speak to the man to rule him out of the inquiry.

Last night, as police helicopters scoured the sea, beach and surrounding area, Lottie's mother issued a statement. 'This is a very difficult time for all the family and we are all devastated. At the moment, all we can think about is Lottie's safe return, and we ask anyone who may know anything to contact the police.'

It's the second tragedy to strike the family in just over a year. Last August, Mrs Martini's Italian husband, Luca Martini, 38, was killed in the Genoa bridge collapse while visiting the city, where his wealthy family own an import export coffee business. The sister of the groom, Zealy Cardinal, 32, said: 'Alex had only just started to recover from losing Luca. She's a strong woman, but this would knock anybody for six. We're just praying Lottie comes home soon.'

She said the tot was 'smart and intelligent, very strong-willed and determined. She'll be four soon and will start school in the New Year.'

Driven

Alexa Martini, who is considered a rising star at her London-based law firm, Muysken Ritter, had recently moved into a £650,000 townhouse in Balham, south London.

A friend of the family, who asked not to be named, said: 'There has been some negative spin put on this, with people criticising Alex for leaving Lottie to make her way back from the beach on her own. Alex is very driven. She's a career woman, and she works hard, so it's only reasonable she lets down her hair a bit now and again. But it's ridiculous, she was close by, and there were dozens of people about. Everyone was keeping an eye out for each other. No one was drunk.'

twenty-four hours missing

twenty-four hours fasting

chapter 15

alex

The police haven't decided yet if they believe I'm guilty. But they're certainly keeping the possibility on the table.

'If something happened to Lottie,' Bates says. 'If there was an accident, Alex, and you panicked. Now would be the time to tell us.'

'When?'

'When?'

'*When* was this accident?' I ask incredulously. 'Twenty witnesses will tell you I went straight from the wedding to the reception by the pool. According to your own evidence, Lottie was alive and well at that point. Another dozen people can confirm I wasn't on my own for a second at the reception. *When* could I have hurt her?'

'Alex, no one is accusing you of anything,' Bates says. 'As I told you, we simply have to consider all the possibilities.'

'There's a significant period of time when you're not in any of the photos,' Lorenz says. 'Over an hour, in fact.'

'And I've told you what I was doing then, and with whom!'

'Mrs Martini—'

I push back my chair. 'I don't think I should continue this conversation without a lawyer.'

I'm not foolish enough to think the innocent have no need

of lawyers; that those with nothing to hide have nothing to fear.

Bates and Lorenz follow me back to the main conference room where Zealy is waiting for me. A group of college students is playing volleyball on the powdery white sand outside. A catamaran slices through the turquoise ocean in the distance. Already life is returning to normal. *Stop all the clocks*, I think. How can people sail and play ball while my daughter is missing?

I imagine plunging into the ocean, swimming as hard and fast as I can until I am so far out and so exhausted I can allow the water to just pull me under, and bring an end to all of this.

A young Black female officer approaches Bates, too focused on the urgency of what she has to say to pay attention to me. 'Lieutenant, we got a witness thinks she saw something,' she says. 'A man carrying a kid around the time the girl disappeared. Says she thinks he looked off.'

'What does that mean?'

'I'm just telling you what she said.'

'Who's the witness?'

The officer belatedly notices me and hesitates. Bates gestures for her to continue.

'One of the wedding party,' the officer says. 'The maid of honour, Catherine Lord.'

'Why has she only just come forward with this?' Bates asks.

'Says she didn't realise what she'd seen till now.'

'Fuck's sake. Where is she?'

'Interview two.'

Bates turns to me, but I forestall her. 'She told me she hadn't seen Lottie all night,' I say. 'I want to hear this.'

'If it's important, you'll be the first to know.'

'Let her do her job,' Zealy says. 'You need to eat something. At least come and have a coffee. You're not going to do Lottie any good if you don't look after yourself.'

Bates and Lorenz are already heading towards the interview suite. I allow Zealy to lead me to a couple of bilious-green armchairs printed with pink flamingos in the hotel lobby. She orders us a couple of toasted club sandwiches, but after the first couple of bites I can't eat any more and put the plate down. There's a hard lump in my throat, making it difficult to swallow. Even with the benefit of two cups of coffee in my bloodstream, I feel light-headed and oddly detached from my surroundings.

I'm haunted by the truth of the lieutenant's observation: Lottie knew her abductor. Someone she *trusted* took her. Someone here, at this wedding.

Someone who, even now, is pretending to be my friend.

chapter 16

alex

Bates returns within the hour to brief us.

'The description Catherine Lord gave is of a white male, mid-forties, thin, average height, with dark receding hair,' she says. 'Sound like anyone you know?'

It sounds exactly like the man I saw talking to Lottie on the beach, and I say as much. Lorenz can't quite look me in the eye, and suddenly they're treating me with kid gloves again. But any vindication I might feel is swept away by a tsunami of guilt. I should have reported the incident when it happened. I should have kept Lottie close to me, knowing she might be at risk.

Should have. Could have.

If only.

Louder than the drumbeat of blame is the thud of terror in my heart. Before, the monster of my nightmares was blessedly vague: a dark, hazy shadow. Now, he has a face. As agonising as it is not knowing what's happened to Lottie, the idea of her in this man's hands is worse. A man who may be doing indescribable, unthinkable things to her as we stand here.

'What else did Catherine say?' I ask.

'Alex, we don't know for sure this is—'

'Just tell me!'

The lieutenant looks me in the eye. 'Ms Lord saw a man carrying a child between the side of the hotel and the staff apartments about twenty minutes after the wedding ceremony finished. She'd gone to the restroom to freshen up, and saw them through the window.'

'Why didn't she say anything before?' Zealy demands.

'The kid was wrapped in a beach towel,' Bates says. 'She didn't connect it with Lottie because she didn't see a pink dress. And the kid she saw had bare feet. Catherine remembers that, because the kid's feet were dirty, like it'd been walking barefoot on the sidewalk. Lottie was wearing ballet slippers when she disappeared.'

'She hates shoes,' I say. 'She's always taking them off.'

Bates glances at Lorenz, who nods as if scribing a mental note.

Much as I want to know what's happened to my little girl, I can't bear for it to be this. 'There must have been a lot of fathers carrying their kids back from the beach yesterday,' I say desperately. 'Why does she think this was Lottie?'

'She says he didn't look like a tourist,' Bates says. 'She thinks the kid was asleep – she can't be sure if it was a boy or a girl. But she says he didn't look comfortable carrying the child, like he wasn't used to it. He had her scooped flat in his arms, instead of up against his shoulder, you know, like you do with older kids. Catherine said they just looked off.'

'Jesus,' Zealy says. 'And she didn't think it might've been useful to know this earlier?'

I don't have the energy to spare for anger. 'You really think this was Lottie?'

'It's too early to say. Either way, we need him to come forward.'

'We have a sketch artist in with Ms Lord now,' Lorenz adds.

'A sketch artist? What about security cameras?'

'They don't got any alongside the hotel. The liquor store across the way has a couple cameras, but this guy, whoever he is, he's been smart about dodging them.' Lorenz shrugs. 'Nothing from the parking lot, either. But we're eliminating the vehicles there, matching them to hotel guests. No one saw the guy carrying a kid across the bridge, so he must have had a car parked somewhere. We'll find him.'

Every time someone says that, it rings less true.

'I understand how hard this is, Alex,' Bates says. 'But we got a great team working on this. We've had a lot of calls from the Amber alert. It's just a question of time—'

Behind me, someone calls my name.

Even though I'm supposed to be the strong one, the moment I see Mum standing in the hotel lobby I run towards her and fling myself into her arms like a child.

Dad encircles us both and we cling together, drawing strength from our shared grief.

We've always been like this, a trio so close it can be hard to see the seams.

When Dad finally releases us, Marc and Sian are standing awkwardly a few feet away, clearly not wanting to interrupt.

Mum hugs them both in turn. 'I'm so sorry this happened to you,' she says.

Sian looks surprised and gratified. It hasn't even occurred to me to spare a thought for a bride whose wedding day was hijacked in the most terrible way. Grief makes you selfish. But Sian and Marc will never be able to celebrate their anniversary without remembering this. Only Mum would think to acknowledge their loss in the midst of our own.

'We wanted to be with you for the press conference,' Marc says to me. 'Some of the others are coming downstairs for it, too. Moral support.'

'We should be getting you a lawyer,' Dad says. 'No matter

what the police say now, they'll start to look at you, if they haven't already. And you'll need someone to handle the media, too. After this appeal goes out, the story will get a life of its own. We need someone to keep the press off your back so you can focus on doing what you need to do.'

'I'll do it,' Marc says. 'I've got a few media contacts here and at home.'

'Fine,' I say.

Mum is watching Lorenz and Bates as they confer with their colleagues by the door to the conference room. Beneath the sheen of maternal competence I've known all my life, she looks scared and suddenly old. She's not yet sixty, but she's had two brushes with cancer, and her beloved grandchild is missing. Her skin is yellow and waxy, and there are grey pouches beneath her eyes. I'll be glad when my sister arrives to take care of the person I need to take care of me.

'What time does Harriet's flight get in?' I ask Dad.

'The Shetlands are a long way away, love,' he says. 'Lottie will be home long before Harriet could get here.'

It takes a moment to register that my sister isn't coming.

Our relationship has always been complex. We're sisters, after all. Friends and rivals in equal measure. I always envied Harriet's ability to take advantage of the battles I fought as the firstborn with our parents over curfews and boys and school; she was resentful she never got to do anything first. As a child, it never occurred to me she might feel excluded from the self-nourishing triumvirate my parents and I had established before she was born two years later. Only recently have I wondered if her retreat to the Shetlands was a tactical withdrawal, precipitated by an instinct for self-preservation.

I'm aware, too, of the cruelty of fortune: that the sister who prioritised work over family was given a child she hadn't asked for, whereas Harriet, who only ever wanted a baby, will never have one of her own. But we love each other dearly. I've never questioned that.

And she worships the ground Lottie walks on; I've never doubted that, either. Harriet was the first to visit me in hospital after Lottie was born and, unlike me, she was a natural with the baby. Lottie suffered from colic and, within days of taking her home, Luca and I were on our knees with exhaustion. Nothing we did settled her: we rubbed her back, put a warm hot water bottle on her tummy, gave her gripe water; I even changed my diet and cut out anything spicy, in case something in my milk was upsetting her. But no matter what we tried, she screamed unrelentingly, for hours at a time. Sometimes I didn't know if it was Lottie crying or me.

When she was about a week old, I called Harriet, who was staying with Mum and Dad, and begged her to come and take Lottie out for an hour, just so we could get some sleep.

The second Lottie was in my sister's arms, she stopped crying.

The baby-whisperer, we called her. Lottie only had to hear Harriet's voice and she became calmer. To her shattered parents, it was like dark magic. Harriet saw us through the first six weeks, and I'm sure I wasn't the only one who thought Lottie had been born to the wrong sister.

After Luca died, Harriet came down again to rescue us. For all our differences, I don't think I'd have coped without her. Neither Lottie nor I were ready for me to be a full-time single parent, and Harriet saved us both.

Which is why I can't believe she's let me down now.

As Mum and Dad go upstairs to change after their long flight, the wedding party gathers in the hotel lobby in an unconscious parody of yesterday's formal photographs: Marc and Sian in the centre, with Sian's parents behind her, and Marc's dad, Eric, at his son's shoulder. Flanking them are Catherine and Zealy on one side, and Paul and Ian on the other. It's the first time I've seen Ian since our encounter on the beach and, when he catches my eye, he flushes and looks away.

Only the little bridesmaids are missing from the tableau, a truth that lands like a blow to my solar plexus.

The lieutenant touches my arm. 'Before you talk to the media,' she says, 'there's something you need to know.'

She hands me a small, clear plastic evidence bag. It takes me a few moments to understand what I'm holding.

My daughter's hair.

chapter 17

quinn

The mother doesn't come across well. She delivers her prepared statement as if reading from a shopping list, and she looks almost bored to be here.

The police may have told her not to show any emotion, of course. They'll have explained that in cases like this, the perps often watch media coverage and get off on the family's pain.

But the public expects a desperate mother to react in a certain way. Quid pro quo: give me your tears, your grief, your trauma, and we'll give you our sympathy and understanding. Until something else catches our attention, anyway.

Show us *some*thing, Quinn thinks. Throw us a bone.

Sure, everyone reacts to trauma in different ways. She's seen one woman bury five children killed by the same bomb in Syria without shedding a tear, and another sob her heart out over a torn dress. But as Quinn glances around the press pack, she notices it's not playing as sympathetically as it should. The story is still largely local; most of the journos present are touchy-feely Americans. Alexa's cool British reserve isn't doing her any favours.

Quinn signals for her cameraman, Phil, to take some wide-angled shots that include the grandparents of the missing girl who're sitting quietly at the side of the room. Both of *them* are in tears, she notes, the grandmother clinging to her husband's arm. So this stiff-upper-lip thing isn't a family trait, then.

She hates human interest stories like this; they're voyeuristic and intrusive, turning personal tragedy into a saleable commodity. She became a journalist to cover events that change the course of the world, and the disappearance of one kid, however tragic for the family, doesn't matter in the wider scheme of things.

But she can sense something dark at work here that piques her interest. Something sinister and ugly; something that's brought this family's world crashing down upon them.

She jams a plastic Evian bottle in the crook of her withered right arm and untwists the cap with her left hand. It contains neat vodka; not her beverage of choice, but she can hardly rock up to a press conference swigging bourbon from her hip flask.

This might not be Quinn's kind of story, but it's the perfect springboard back to prime time. She's aware she only got it because the rest of INN's Washington team was scattered across the country following Democratic presidential candidates, leaving Quinn the assignment editor's bottom-of-the-barrel option at seven on a Sunday morning. But this is going to be big. INN is a UK-based news network and Florida a popular destination for British families.

If Lottie Martini isn't found safe and well soon, this'll get a lot of play back home. Front-page stuff. A little English girl from a nice, middle-class family, disappearing from a wedding, and not in some dodgy third-world country like Thailand or Mexico but in *America*, just a hop and a skip from Disney World. The tabloids are going to eat it up.

She watches Alexa Martini as the vodka warms its way down her gullet. *Is* this a nice, middle-class family? The missing girl's father is dead, killed in the Genoa bridge collapse last year, so that should elicit some sympathy. Everyone loves a pretty young widow. It's a shame the kid isn't more photogenic, though. No one's going to want to plaster *that* face on a 'Have you seen this child?' T-shirt.

Her phone pings with a news-feed alert and she leans in to talk to Phil, whose eye is glued to his camera viewfinder. 'Can you stay with this till they're done?' she says. 'I need to call the Desk.'

'Want me to toss the mother any questions?'

'She isn't taking any. I won't be long, anyway.'

Quinn hits speed dial before she's even out of the conference room. 'Sandy, did you just see what dropped on the wires about Raqqa?'

'Don't worry, Quinn. Terry's on it.'

'Fuck Terry. I should be there.'

'No one's going there while the Russians are bombing the shit out of the place,' the assignment editor says. 'Least of all you.'

'Come on, Sandy,' she presses. 'Terry doesn't have the contacts on the ground like I do. He'll never get inside the city. You know I'm the right person for this.'

'Have they found the missing kid yet?'

She sighs impatiently. 'I can hand this story over to Daryl or Anya. They don't need to sit on Biden and Warren every minute of the day. Or you can fly someone out from London.' She hates having to beg, but she's literally given her right arm for this story. 'Please, Sandy. I can go directly to Raqqa from right here, I've got all my personal shit with me. I'll swing through the Beirut Bureau and pick up—'

'Forget it, Quinn. Christie would have my balls.'

Christie Bradley, the first female editor in INN's history, and possibly the only person, other than Marnie, who Quinn respects. She's been Quinn's inspiration since she first joined

INN as an entry-level desk assistant fourteen years ago, one of an elite band of fearless reporters like Christiane Amanpour and Christina Lamb who blazed a trail for women like Quinn to follow.

'You want me to sign a waiver?' Quinn tells Sandy. 'No one's going to sue you if I get killed. Come on, Christie will be fine with it—'

'You're on speakerphone,' a voice says. 'And I bloody well am not fine with it, Quinn, so quit pushing.'

Christie sat by Quinn's bed in the ICU all night after she was medevacked out of Syria, waiting for her to regain consciousness, and the first thing she said when Quinn came round was, 'Your story led the bulletins.' Quinn thought *Christie* would get it.

'You know I'm right,' Quinn says. 'No one knows that story like I do.'

'And when I think you're ready for it, it'll be all yours.'

Quinn takes another slug from her bottle. The vodka isn't sitting well with her.

Maybe skipping lunch was a bad idea.

'You're not being sidelined, Quinn. This missing kid is a lead story. I want it done properly, no shortcuts. Once it wraps up, *then* we'll talk about Raqqa.'

Quinn seethes as she slips her phone back into her jeans. Lead story or not, Daryl or Anya could easily handle it. It's a waste of firepower to keep her here when she could be in Syria.

The press conference has finished by the time she returns to the business centre and everyone bar the TV crews has left. The room dims abruptly as the powerful lights are turned off and Quinn picks her way around producers coiling cables and packing equipment away.

'Can you go out and get me some shots of the beach?' Quinn

asks her cameraman. 'They're not going to let us get too close, but you should be able to get some long shots from the shore. And the gate from the beach to the hotel. Give me something moody. Maybe a tracking shot along the alley round the side of the hotel, too, if you can get it.'

She ducks out onto the terrace behind the conference room and lights a cigarette. The area in front of the pool where the reception took place is sealed off with police tape, but she can still get a sense of the key locations in this story, and how they relate geographically to one another.

She inhales a deep hit of nicotine as she walks from the hotel to the beach. Lottie Martini disappeared in more or less broad daylight, under the noses of a hundred wedding guests. Surely the kid would have screamed and yelled if some weirdo she didn't know had grabbed her off the beach? Even in the chaos of a crowd, you'd think someone would've noticed.

Of course, it's conceivable he – or she – lured the kid away with some plausible story, but odds are she went with someone she knew.

Quinn unscrews the cap of her Evian bottle again. This whole thing is such a fucking waste of time. It'll turn out to be the mother, or a boyfriend. It always is. She could be on her way to the Middle East right now, and instead she's stuck babysitting a seedy domestic drama.

As she tilts back her head to drain the bottle, Alexa Martini comes out onto the balcony a floor above her. The woman stands for a long moment with her hands on the railing, staring out to sea like a ship's figurehead. Quinn can't see her face, but her posture is ramrod straight. It's like she's carved out of ice.

Someone comes out onto the balcony to join her. A man; too young to be her dad. Quinn edges forward to get a better view. It's the bridegroom. Marc something-or-other. Good-looking guy.

He puts his arm around the small of Alexa's waist, and she leans back against him. She's not made of ice *now*. They look like newlyweds – except this isn't the woman he just married.

Interesting.

Quinn screws the top back on the empty plastic bottle and dumps it in the nearest recycling bin. Her spidey senses are tingling again.

Every good story begins with a loose thread.

five days missing

five days missing

chapter 18

alex

At sunrise on the fifth full day since Lottie's disappearance, I go down to the beach where I last saw my daughter. The police tape has finally been removed, the wedding arch dismantled and the gilt chairs stacked and put away. It's as though the last traces of my daughter are being deliberately erased.

Despite all the police activity, the helicopters and divers and searchers on the ground, despite the Amber alert and the press appeal, it feels as if I'm the only one still looking for Lottie. The rest of the world already wants to move on.

I walk along the shoreline, scanning the sand in front of me, as if looking for clues. I'm not sure what I expect to find: the missing pink ballet shoe, a ribbon from her hair, some message scrawled in the sand that only I can decipher?

There isn't a minute in the day when I don't go back to the moment I last saw my girl, cradling the image like fine china in my mind's eye. Lottie sits on her chair, her head turned away from me. Her hair escapes from her plait, an unearthly, silvery nimbus around her head. Her plump arms are crossed over her chest.

With each return to the memory, there is a sharper clarity, a new detail summoned from my subconscious: a lengthening shadow falling across the sand behind my daughter, a black skimmer flying over the shallows, looking for fish. Lottie swings her legs and I think – no, I'm sure – that she's already kicked off her pink shoes. She's perched on the edge of the gilt chair, which is too high for her, so she can dig her bare toes into the sand. Another minute, and she'll slide off her seat.

Except I *know* I couldn't see her feet from where I was sitting, four rows behind her. The angle of sight from my chair afforded me a partial glimpse of my daughter from the shoulders up, nothing more. Sifting through my memories may prove as futile as my search along the sand.

Bates now seems convinced we're dealing with a stranger abduction, but I *know* my daughter would never have gone with someone she didn't trust. If the 'thin man' Catherine saw is connected to Lottie's disappearance, he wasn't working alone. Someone Lottie knew persuaded her to leave the beach and led her to him. Someone with whom she felt safe.

It was Lieutenant Bates who first pointed this out, but she's now pivoted away from her own theory.

Because of the hair.

They couldn't be sure it was Lottie's, Bates said, when she handed it to me. They hadn't had time to run the DNA tests. But the tangled hanks of hair in the bag were the same white-blonde as my daughter's, the same length and texture. The ends were blunt where they'd been hacked from her head.

I only just made it to the bathroom in time. I vomited into the lavatory until there was nothing left but bile, consumed by the thought of the terror my daughter must have felt. Be feeling.

If the lieutenant's intention was to make me emotional and sympathetic for the TV appeal, it backfired. The difference between the British and American response to crisis, I suppose. I've seen footage of myself at the press conference, which took place just ten minutes later. It is clear to me I was in shock, barely able to function. I read Bates' prepared script like an automaton. But to anyone watching, I must've looked like I didn't care.

This isn't a popularity contest: my child is missing and it shouldn't matter whether I'm *liked*. But if people are suspicious of me, if they think I had something to do with my daughter's disappearance, they won't be out there, looking for her.

It's as if Lottie has vanished into thin air. Despite dozens of reported sightings all over Florida, not one has turned into a definitive lead. Forensic teams have combed every inch of the motel room where her hair was found, but they're looking for a needle in a haystack. There are hundreds of fingerprints from previous guests they have to rule out, even supposing the kidnapper was careless enough to leave his own. Unless he's been caught before, they won't be on the police database anyway.

Five days since my baby was stolen from me, and the police are no closer to finding her than when they started.

I reach the end of the beach, where it gives way to a wide drainage culvert, and turn back. The crenellated, primrose-yellow hotel rises like a tiered cake against another azure Florida sky. It's a little cooler today, less humid, and a soft breeze lifts the hair on the nape of my neck. A perfect, bucket-and-spade beach day.

Lottie's photo has been on the front page of newspapers across Florida and at home in the UK, and the local TV stations have been running her disappearance as their top story for days. But the media is already starting to lose interest. We've had virtually no uptake from national networks, which means if Lottie's been taken out of Florida, no one's looking for her. I know Bates and Lorenz think she's dead. Even my parents are trying to prepare me for the worst.

But Lottie is alive. My daughter is *alive*. She's tenacious, determined, ferocious. She couldn't be extinguished without creating a disturbance, a rent in the fabric of the world that I would feel. We're not looking in the right places, that's all.

Somewhere, buried in the back alleys and dark hallways of my memories, is the key to all of this.

I just have to find it.

six days missing

chapter 19

alex

I'm on the beach again, following what has now become a familiar route, when my sister calls me. I'm aware I've become a local curiosity, like a Victorian fisherman's widow haunting the wharf; I feel the eyes follow me as I walk along the sand. There are pictures of me in the local papers: *grieving mother's lonely vigil*. But I can't stay away. I feel close to Lottie here.

I watch the flaming sun sink into the glittering silver sea. Sunset: the golden hour, beloved by photographers for its warm, flattering light.

The hour my daughter disappeared.

'What time is it where you are?' I ask Harriet.

'I don't know. Late. Or early, I suppose. I couldn't sleep. How are you doing?'

'Not good.'

'I wish I could be there,' Harriet says. 'I just don't want to get in the way. I thought I could do more good here, trying to keep the press interested.'

'It's fine,' I say, and almost mean it.

'Is there anything I can do?' she says. 'What about money? Do you—'

'I'm good. The hotel says I can stay here as long as I need. Mum and Dad, too.'

Lottie and I should have been checking out today. Our flight home is scheduled this afternoon. One of the senior partners at Muysken Ritter called me the day after the press conference to tell me that the resources of the firm are at my disposal; I only have to ask. I'm not to worry about work. They've redistributed my cases to my colleagues and put me on paid leave. I feel as if I'm letting my clients down.

'I've told Mum and Dad to stay as long as you need them,' Harriet says. 'I'll cover their expenses every month till this is over. Mungo can afford it. We *want* to do it.'

I can't imagine another week of not knowing where Lottie is, never mind another month.

As I say goodbye to my sister and pocket my phone, I see Marc coming down the beach towards me. My brain reflexively processes this as I do everything now, through the prism of Lottie's disappearance: *he isn't running, so she hasn't been found.* My parents have done their best to look after me, but supporting them through their own grief depletes what little reserves I have. Marc is the one who's held me together.

He hasn't left my side since Lottie went missing.

He's a small man, Marc, short and wiry, like a jockey. His features are irregular, unremarkable. But he's constantly in motion, filled with barely suppressed energy. He's set up a website and GoFundMe account for Lottie, and become our de facto media liaison officer. He can't stay here forever, but I have no idea how I'll manage without him.

I know what Sian thinks. She's always felt there's more to our relationship than either of us will admit. Perhaps she's right.

He's holding his phone out to me now, turned sideways so I can see the video paused on the screen. I can't tell from his expression if it is good news or bad.

'You're not going to believe this,' he says.

For a moment, I wonder why he's showing me footage of the president of the United States fielding questions about China from the steps of his Florida estate at Mar-a-Lago. I wait impatiently for the next story, the one about Lottie.

And then suddenly the president interrupts his own press conference.

'This kidnap, this Lottie Martini, did you hear about that?' he says. 'Here, in Florida, in this great state. Did you hear about it? It's a horrible thing, a horrible thing. A girl, a little girl, I mean, British. She's British. I love England. We have a great relationship, they love me over there. I have a mother born in Scotland. And as you know, Stornoway is serious Scotland. You don't get any more serious than that. It's so beautiful. My mother loved Scotland. My mother also loved the Queen.'

'Jesus,' I breathe.

'This is going to change everything,' Marc says.

'That's good, isn't it? Everyone's going to be looking for her after this!'

'Yes, but it also means the police are going to be swamped with calls and sightings from Alaska to Honolulu,' Marc says, as we turn and walk briskly back towards the hotel. 'They're going to have to check out every single one of them. It'll be like looking for a needle in a haystack. They don't have the manpower for this. We need to help triage the calls, so they can focus their attention on the ones that could be genuine.'

'Us? How are we supposed to do that?'

'It's easy enough to weed out the time-wasters with a few simple questions. Bates says at least half the tips coming in are sightings of kids who aren't even close to the right age. Teenagers, some of them. But the calls clog up the lines. That's something we can help with.'

He stops by the gate from the beach to the hotel. A make-shift shrine has developed there over the past few days: flowers

111

wilting in the Florida heat, cheap teddy-bears made in China, bobbing *Frozen* helium balloons. Those who leave them mean well, but I can't bear it; it's like Lottie is already dead.

'This is going to explode now,' Marc says, turning back to me. 'We're going to have the world's press on our doorstep. Alex, they're going to find out about Kirkwood Place.'

THERE BUT FOR THE GRACE OF GOD

COMMENTARY by Lisa Jenkins

TIME and again over the last few days we've heard it: 'I would never have left my child alone like that.' We shake our heads, our faces grave, and reassure one another such a tragedy could never happen to *us*, because we would never take such a terrible risk.

But as we cling to the hands of our own sons and daughters just that little bit tighter this week, an uneasy voice inside us calls us out for the hypocrites we are.

It's so much more comfortable to think that someone's at fault, and point the finger at Alexa Martini.

The truth is, there but for the grace of God go all of us. Lottie's mother only did what all of us have done in some form or another.

Alexa Martini is now living an unspeakable nightmare, blaming herself for allowing her daughter to walk a hundred yards from a beach to a wedding reception with four other young bridesmaids, instead of taking her child's hand herself.

Random

Sometimes dreadful things happen completely at random. The mother we saw this week pleading to whoever had taken her daughter could just as easily be you or me. And that's what terrifies us, and, in our fear, we look for someone to blame. When is a child old enough to use a public bathroom alone? To get the bus to school? What age should you let them stay in the house without a babysitter when you have an evening out? Ten? Twelve?

We've all left a child in the car while we nipped into the post office, or allowed them to walk down to the corner shop for some sweets, telling ourselves we can't wrap them in cotton wool forever.

We know the risk of anything happening to them is statistically small, and yet we can't help breathing a sigh of relief when they come back safe and sound.

It's tempting to blame Lottie's mother because we want to believe we can stop awful things happening to our children. We have a desperate need to feel we can control our lives.

Lottie wasn't snatched from a rough council estate, while her drug-addled single mother entertained her boyfriend. This happened in a luxury resort to a professional, educated woman. And that's why we've been so busy protecting ourselves by saying: 'I'd never have done that.' Alexa Martini wasn't neglectful or thoughtless. She made the kind of decision every parent does on a daily basis. She shouldn't be condemned for that.

Let's not turn this tragedy into a referendum on another woman's mothering. Instead, we must all hope and pray for Lottie's safe return.

seven days missing

seven days missing

chapter 20

alex

Marc has set up our campaign headquarters in an empty office space on the neon strip of St Pete Beach, about ten minutes' drive from the hotel. An anonymous well-wisher came forward after yesterday's appeal by the president, offering to make it available to us for as long as we need it.

Getting out of my car, I stare at the windows papered with flyers appealing for my daughter's safe return. Beneath her photograph is an 800 contact number and the words: *Have you seen Lottie?*

It's the same picture I gave the police for the Amber alert. I can't imagine she's still wearing her pink bridesmaid's dress. Her hair will be different, too. The fact that the kidnapper went to such trouble to change her appearance is a good sign, Bates tells me. If he'd killed her, he wouldn't have bothered.

I try not to think of my daughter's curls, sealed and tagged in an evidence bag.

Inside the office space, folding tables have been set up, equipped with phones and laptops. Marc has organised the hundreds of volunteers who have come forward into a rota to man the new Find Lottie tip line.

Others have been tasked with posting up flyers. Marc has given each of them a map of the St Pete Beach area, with their targeted section highlighted in yellow marker. Grocery stores, pharmacies, nail bars, hair salons. Anywhere there may be eyes. 'We want her face to be at the forefront of everyone's mind,' he says.

I can't believe how much he's accomplished in just twenty-four hours. Every lamppost or telegraph pole I passed on my way here had a flyer tacked to it. Our biggest problem has been handling the sheer number of people who want to help.

The press interest has become the firestorm Marc predicted. The hotel has moved my parents and me to their penthouse suite on the top floor, which is accessible only by a private lift, but every time we leave the building we have to run the gauntlet of a growing scrum of journalists shouting questions and shoving cameras in our faces. The manager has been very kind, and the staff are doing their best, but it's only a matter of time before the situation becomes untenable. Dozens of hotel guests have cancelled their bookings because of the media attention, and I don't blame them. This can't go on much longer.

Marc detaches himself from the cluster of people around him when he sees me.

'What do you think?' he says, indicating the phone banks lining the sides of the room. 'Most of the volunteers are local residents, but we've got quite a few tourists from back home, too.'

'It's incredible,' I say.

'A lot of the local churches are doing special services for Lottie tomorrow,' he says. 'We thought it'd be good if you attended Sunday Mass at the Catholic cathedral downtown, maybe said a few words afterwards—'

'Marc, I don't know. Church isn't really my thing.'

'Church matters here, Alex. We need to keep people on your side.'

I'm suddenly assailed by the memory of the last time I was

in a church. It was hot then, too. The black dress I'd bought in London was too warm for Sicily, even in October, and I was so hot I thought I'd pass out. Luca's parents had surrounded his coffin with so many flowers I couldn't even get close to him, and their cloying scent mingled with the sour smell of sweat from the press of bodies in the tiny family chapel. The dark wooden pews were packed with weeping, black-clothed mourners, dark as crows. Choking clouds of incense swirled around the nave as the priest raised his thurible, the metal censer clinking against its chain. I had to suppress a sudden, violent urge to drag my smart, cosmopolitan husband's corpse out of his open coffin and away from the medieval superstition and mummery. He didn't believe in it any more than I did.

Luca was a lousy husband, but an excellent father. Our daughter would never have disappeared on his watch. If he exists in some parallel dimension or afterlife, I hope he is watching over Lottie now.

'No church,' I tell Marc. 'I'll give a press statement if you think it's worthwhile, but I can't do church.'

A volunteer in her mid-fifties interrupts us, grabbing my hand and pressing it between her own. My daughter's face stares up at me from the cotton T-shirt stretched across her large breasts. 'Alexa, I just wanted to say how sorry I am,' she says, as if she knows me. 'We're just praying the Lord brings Lottie home safe.'

'Thank you,' I say.

Everyone is watching me, even as they pretend to busy themselves with their phones and stacks of flyers. I'm Ground Zero for this whole carnival, *the mother*, here, in person. I'm sure many of the volunteers are sincere in their desire to help find my daughter, but there's a rubbernecking, morbid element, too – a frisson of excitement at being part of a major news story. They'll go home and tell their friends they met me today.

119

'I have to go,' I tell Marc abruptly.

He offers to come with me, but I'm suddenly desperate to be alone.

Yet once I'm outside, I get in my car with no idea where to go next. I left the hotel because I felt trapped there, too. There are too many people who need my attention; our extended entourage is ballooning, and I'm overwhelmed.

Most of the wedding guests have returned home, but now there are other friends and relatives who have flown over to join the search: my mother's sister, Aunt Julie; a childhood friend I haven't seen in fifteen years. I know they only want to help, but the presence of so many people struggling to contain their own distress and grief is exhausting. Harriet was right not to come.

My phone rings. I've personalised Lieutenant Bates' ringtone; hers are the only calls I care about now. I scrabble for it in my bag, and then recklessly empty its contents onto the passenger seat, heedless of the coins and tampons spilling in every direction.

'We haven't found her,' Bates says, putting me out of my misery.

The wild hope dies. Disappointment fills my lungs and makes it hard to breathe. Lottie isn't dead, I tell myself. They haven't found a body, either. I have to hang onto that.

'Alex, I need you to come down to the precinct,' Bates says.

Something in her tone alerts me. 'Why?'

'I'll explain when you get here—'

'No. Tell me now.'

'OK,' Bates says. 'Alex, something has come up, and we'd like to ask you a few more questions.'

'What about?' I ask, although I already know.

'Kirkwood Place,' she says.

120

chapter 21

quinn

Quinn isn't happy with the president. His intervention in the Martini case has put the kibosh on any chance she might have had of persuading INN's editor to let her off the hook on this story. Public interest is off the charts now. Even Quinn has to concede it makes sense to have a senior correspondent covering the story.

The assignment editor has sent one of the new batch of graduate trainees out to Florida to act as her fixer. His job is to do all the scut work, like attending press briefings or chasing down the correct spelling of interviewee names, so Quinn's free to work the story the way she wants to.

But the kid's sticking to her like bloody Velcro. She can't take a shit without him following her to the bathroom. And he nearly took a swig from the contents of her Evian bottle yesterday. She doesn't mind going toe-to-toe with the News Desk over editorial decisions, but her reputation as a journalist is paramount. Which means there really *is* water in the damn bottle today.

Timothy – 'please don't call me Tim' – is harmless, Quinn supposes. Despite the ginger hair. And at least he's figured out where the nearest Starbucks is, which will keep her cameraman, Phil, happy.

The kid returns to their motel room now with a cardboard tray of pumpkin spice lattes and puts it down on the large table where Phil has set up their editing equipment. INN has gone cheap, as usual, booking them into the one-star Starlight Inn on the St Pete Beach strip, even though the negative publicity means the Sandy Beach Hotel now has plenty of free rooms.

Quinn shoves her chair back from the editing table. Enforced sobriety is doing nothing to improve her mood. 'This piece is shit, Phil,' she snaps. 'We can't keep showing GVs of the hotel and the same fucking photo of Lottie.'

'We don't have anything new,' Phil says, cracking the lid of his latte to let the steam escape. 'All we've got today is Alexa arriving at the campaign HQ. We can drop in yesterday's talking heads from the presser, but otherwise GVs are all we got.'

He doesn't point out they can't pad the story with a piece-to-camera, as most correspondents would. She might get away with her jaunty eye-patch reporting from Raqqa, but not on something sensitive like this. Given how huge the story is becoming, she's surprised INN haven't big-footed her by sending out a more camera-friendly reporter from London. The bulletin editors are already bitching because they can't use her for live two-ways.

'We need footage of the kid at the bloody wedding,' Quinn says. 'Christ! This is the twenty-first fucking century. Every bastard with a phone thinks he's Stephen Spielberg. How can we *still* not have pictures of her?'

Phil knows better than to respond. She's made the same complaint every day since they got here.

Timothy doesn't.

'Wouldn't it be bad taste to use them, anyway?' he says. 'I mean, they might be the last pictures of her alive. It seems a bit . . . tabloid.'

'No, we wouldn't want to lodge those images in anyone's

122

mind,' Quinn says sarcastically. 'Just in case they remembered something.'

'Don't be a bitch,' Phil says.

Quinn drops back into her chair. 'Jesus! Fine. Fine! Give me fifteen seconds of Alexa Martini arriving at the campaign offices,' she says. 'Then go to yesterday's presser with the hair in the evidence bag. Tim, how far into the conference is that?'

He leafs through his notebook. 'Five minutes twenty-one.'

She feels like Rumpelstiltskin, weaving gold from straw. Somehow she pulls together a two-minute piece for the lunchtime bulletin, stitching together soundbites from the lieutenant and Marc Chapman, who seems to be Alexa Martini's de facto spokesman, along with reheated general footage from the preceding few days. This story is next to impossible to illustrate with pictures. The police investigation is all happening behind closed doors. Until the kid is found, alive or dead, all Quinn's got are talking heads and filler.

She watches as Phil lays down the soundbite from Marc. The most frustrating part of all this is that's she's got one hell of a story in her back pocket, and she can't use it. Sian Chapman's revelations are dynamite, but Quinn simply doesn't have enough to go public with it yet.

Quinn hasn't liked Alexa Martini from the start. She has no problem with ambitious, successful women; she respects anyone who's carved out her place in the world. What she has no time for are women who want to have it all, and then expect allowances to be made.

She's lost count of the times she's had to cover for mothers taking time off for their kids' braces to be fitted or to attend school sports days. And why is it the single women who always have to work Christmas Eve? If a woman wants the baby *and* the job, fine. But she should compete on a level playing field. Raising the next generation of taxpayers doesn't confer special status, as one of her former colleagues once insisted. Quinn isn't going to be around long enough to collect her pension anyway.

Marnie says Quinn sees all mothers as the enemy: baby-making factories who've let the side of feminism down. Maybe there's a grain of truth in that. But it's not fair on the kids, either. Women have no business having children if they're just going to dump them in a boarding school before they turn eight. The nursery and the boardroom don't mix. Some women shouldn't have children, it's as simple as that.

This isn't about you, Marnie said yesterday. *And just because Alexa Martini doesn't wear her heart on her sleeve, it doesn't mean she doesn't feel things deeply. The woman's daughter is missing!*

Except that's just it: Quinn isn't convinced Lottie Martini is missing at all.

Eleven years ago, she covered the disappearance of a nine-year-old girl in West Yorkshire. Twenty-four days later, the mother, Karen Matthews, was arrested for conspiring with a family friend to kidnap her own daughter. For more than three weeks, Matthews had played the tearful victim, pleading for the release of her 'beautiful princess daughter', who, it turned out, had been drugged and hidden in the base of a divan bed at her friend's flat the whole time.

So no, Quinn doesn't feel bad for being cynical and suspicious. It's what she's paid for.

She grabs the bag slung over the back of her chair. 'Enough of this crap,' she says. 'We need to start holding some feet to the fire. Tim, I want you to drive over to the sheriff's office and make some new friends. I don't care what you have to do. Sleep with the chief if necessary. But I want to know every single thing that's happening over there, down to what Bates has in her sandwiches.'

'Actually, it's Timothy—'

Quinn is already halfway towards the door. 'Find out if they're looking at anyone other than this "thin man". My money says they're pinning it on him because they haven't got any other suspects. Have they even managed to connect him to the motel where they found the girl's hair? And I don't want the usual bullshit about promising leads, blah blah. Are they looking for a body? Is Alexa Martini involved, or not?'

'What do you want me to do?' Phil asks.

'Do you know how many kids are currently missing in Florida?' Quinn says abruptly.

He doesn't seem surprised by the non-sequitur. He's worked with her long enough to know how her mind works. He notices Timothy googling the question, and gently takes the phone out of the kid's hands.

'Three hundred and forty-five,' Quinn says. 'Three hundred and forty-five missing kids in Florida alone. We're not talking runaways or family abductions—'

'What's your point, Quinn?'

'If you were the mother of one of those Florida kids, how would you be feeling right now?'

This is why Quinn is so damn good at what she does. She's never afraid to punch the bruise.

'I don't get it,' Timothy says.

'Your president takes the time to appeal for the return of a white British child visiting the US on a luxury foreign holiday, but *your* kid, your Hispanic or Black kid, doesn't get a mention,' Quinn says. 'America can afford to let a few hundred low-income kids slip through the cracks. Who's going to notice? But don't mess with our tourist industry. Don't lose any *white* kids.'

'But this has nothing to do with race,' Timothy says.

'It's America,' says Quinn. '*Every*thing here has to do with race.'

125

chapter 22

alex

Kirkwood Place. I knew it'd catch up to me, sooner or later.

If we could just go back to a time when we were spiteful and judgemental, but only behind one another's backs. If we could stop scolding each other in public, accept that for some women it's possible to love your spouse more than your child, acknowledge there are those of us whose lives are not completed by a baby, but ruined by it.

If there was space for women like me, would that have made a difference?

Before our divorce, Luca was the one who took Lottie to daycare. I had to be at work by seven-thirty and the Montessori nursery Luca had insisted on was twenty minutes in the opposite direction. Luca set his own hours and often worked from home, so it made sense for him to be the one to drop her off. And he *liked* taking her. If he wanted to sit in traffic singing 'Baby Shark' every morning, he was welcome to it.

I was singularly unsuited to be anyone's mother, let alone the mother of a child like Lottie. She erupted from my womb angry and indignant, as if she'd absorbed my ambiguity towards parenthood like nutrients through her umbilical cord. For Luca, it was love at first sight the moment he saw her, but for me it was always more complicated. There was the urge to protect her, of course; the biological pull to nurture, a hormonal surge that tugged my nipples with silver fishhooks every time she cried. But side by side with that was a lingering sense that with every feed I was diminishing, dissolving, like a bar of soap.

I never minded that Luca was the person Lottie turned to when she needed her nose wiped, or to whom she raised her outstretched arms to be carried when she was tired. She was growing up in a household where a woman held down a complex, difficult, important job, and a man cooked homemade ravioli and took her for swimming lessons. I couldn't think of a better example to set her.

Two or three times a year, Luca had to visit the family's coffee plantation in Brazil, since his mother's dementia and father's failing health made it impossible for them to travel. Normally, when he was away, an experienced childminder called Rachel helped out with Lottie.

But when Lottie was about sixteen months old, Luca had to make an unscheduled trip to Rio at the last minute, because of some production problems at the plantation. Rachel was away on a cruise around the Norwegian fjords with her sister, and Mum was still recovering from surgery after her second brush with cancer.

So I was left, quite literally, holding the baby.

At the time, I had a number of complex cases on my desk. But with no one else able to look after Lottie, I had no choice but to make the best of it.

I juggled my schedule so that I could drop her off at nursery on the dot of seven, and arranged to leave the office early for three days until Rachel got back, so that I'd be there in time to collect her at six.

The night Luca flew out, I couldn't sleep. Our marriage was in deep trouble and I knew we couldn't go on the way we were. Luca wasn't in Rio alone. He'd had flings before, but none of the others had lasted more than a few weeks. Juiliana was different. He hadn't troubled to hide this indiscretion, for a start.

I've never been a jealous person, appreciating the distinction between sex and love, but the disrespect hurt. It was becoming painfully obvious to me I couldn't keep looking the other way over Luca's infidelities; I had to make a decision, and soon. Lottie adored her father and I hated the thought of subjecting her to the back-and-forth of divorce and two homes. But what kind of feminist role model was I if I tolerated a man who treated his wife like this? Mum's argument that he was 'just being Italian' had long since worn thin.

My response to stress, as always, was to throw myself into work. The next morning I was at my desk at Muysken Ritter, head down, trying to make sense of a risible response by the Crown to our objections over deportation when my secretary knocked on my door around lunchtime. It was closed; Jade knew that meant I was only to be disturbed if the building was on fire.

'Excuse me,' Jade said. 'But there are two policemen to see you.'

Looking back, it was like a macabre rehearsal for what was to come. A year later, almost to the day, two different police officers arrived at my office to break the news that Luca had died in the Genoa bridge collapse.

Oddly enough, on neither occasion did the sudden appearance of the police at my place of work cause me to panic. I hadn't yet learned to fear the ambulance that passed me on the way home or the unexpected knock at the door.

I can't remember what I thought when I looked up and saw them standing behind Jade, their faces grave. I probably just assumed it was something to do with one of my clients.

It never occurred to me they'd come to arrest me.

eight days missing

chapter 23

alex

The room is small and grey and bland. Two hard plastic chairs have been placed either side of a large square table, on which sits an oddly old-fashioned machine with dials and graph paper and a long stylus. The polygrapher stands in front of the table, his arms by his sides. His posture is a study in neutrality, neither alert nor relaxed.

'Ashton Hyatt,' the polygrapher says, extending his hand to me. 'I'm sorry to be meeting you in such circumstances.'

'I'll leave you to it,' Lieutenant Bates says.

Hyatt shuts the door behind her and motions for me to take one of the two chairs. He's a thin man, mid-forties, beige in every way: the kind of person you'd struggle to remember five minutes after meeting him, if not for the striking blaze of white hair in the centre of his cropped brown curls.

He tells me to place my feet flat on the floor, with my hands on my knees. I do so, my stomach fizzing with nerves. He loops cables around my chest and I stiffen self-consciously as he attaches sticky pads to my pulse points. The room is stuffy and airless, despite the noisy conditioning unit in a solitary window high up one wall.

Just routine, Bates said yesterday, when she called me into the precinct and asked me to take a lie-detector test. As if she was simply dotting 'i's and crossing 't's, when we both know her discovery of what happened in Kirkwood Place has changed everything.

I've liaised with American lawyers on a number of client cases over the years, and I'm aware polygraphs are much more common in the US, particularly in situations like this. But it's never *routine* when it happens to you.

'I won't ask you to relax,' Hyatt says now. 'If you *didn't* find this stressful, then we'd worry. Your heart rate's likely up a notch. That's normal.'

He takes a seat opposite me and pulls a legal pad towards him, making a couple of notations before switching the machine on. Immediately, the needle begins to scratch four blue lines across the graph paper.

'Some of these questions will seem obvious,' Hyatt says. 'And I'll likely repeat some. I'm not looking to trip you up, OK?'

I swallow. I should have nothing to fear, but my palms are sweaty and my heart feels like it's going to burst out of my chest.

'OK, then. Here we go. Is your name Alexa Martini?' Hyatt asks.

I nod.

'I need you to give me a verbal answer.'

'Sorry. Yes.'

He glances at the scratch marks on the graph paper and makes a note. 'Is your birth date January first, 1990?'

'Yes.'

The mundane questions continue. *Were you born in the United States?*

Is London, England, your place of residence?

Are you age twenty-nine?

Do you work as an attorney?

'No,' I say.

The needles instantly leap across the page, a massif of blue spikes. Hyatt peers at them and writes something on his legal pad. 'Is the legal firm of Muysken Ritter in London your place of employment?'

'Yes.'

'I'll ask the question again. Are you an attorney?'

'I'm a lawyer,' I say.

His expression clears. 'Ah. Yes. Of course. Two countries divided by a common language.'

The tone of his questions starts to change as he asks me about Lottie and I dig my fingernails into my palms. I can't take my eyes from the stylus moving across the graph paper.

Is Lottie your only child?

Have you ever regretted having children?

Have you ever physically punished Lottie?

Have you ever harmed her?

The needles spike across the graph paper again. Hyatt studies the page, writes in his notes. 'No,' I repeat.

By the time we are finished, I am drenched in sweat. Hyatt removes the sticky pads and cables and I bury my face in my hands, struggling to control my breathing. He has reduced the infinitely complex grey shades of motherhood to binary black and white, leaving me disorientated and confused.

Bates told me to just tell the truth, but I'm not sure what that is any more.

Doesn't every mother wish at some point, if just for a fleeting, guilty moment, that she was child- and responsibility-free? Does that mean we regret having them? I love the very marrow of my daughter's bones, but there've been times I've found the burden of raising a child crushing.

And how do you define harm? Lottie's hair colour was determined by genetics, but how she turns out – the emotional

133

baggage she carries with her into adulthood – is on me. I don't even have Luca to share the load.

The responsibility is overwhelming.

My parents are waiting for me in the precinct reception area when I emerge. I've splashed water on my face in the bathroom, but I can see from their expressions that my distress is obvious.

'This is *harassment*,' my mother says, loudly. 'That Lieutenant Bates is just looking for an easy target because she's run out of ideas!'

'Mary,' Dad says.

'Please, Mum,' I say. 'I just want to get out of here.'

We took precautions to avoid the press but, the second we go outside, a feral pack of at least a dozen journalists surges towards us, shouting questions and shoving their cameras and microphones into my face. Not one single police officer comes out to help us deal with the attention. I realise I've been thrown to the wolves.

Dad forges a path through the scrum to our hire car, roughly pushing away a TV camera as I duck inside the vehicle. The paparazzi surround us, pressing their cameras to the windows, still yelling their questions. As we drive away, they run back to their own cars so they can follow us.

In the days since Lottie vanished, I've become almost numb to the relentless media scrutiny, the constant presence of cameras every time I step foot outside. Before the hotel manager moved us to the penthouse suite, one enterprising muck-raker even disguised herself as a chambermaid and ambushed me as I came out of the shower. But the attention has never been hostile or aggressive like this before. *What can you tell us about Kirkwood Place?*

'Ignore them,' Mum says. 'They're vultures. They don't care about Lottie. They just want a good story.'

It was naive to hope no one would find out. I'm only surprised it didn't come to light sooner. After a lengthy investigation, the police in London dropped all charges against me, but that doesn't mean the slate was wiped clean. These days, it's almost impossible to fully expunge your history from the internet.

And even I can see that, in this instance, my record is particularly pertinent.

chapter 24

alex

Lottie had been unusually accommodating that morning. It was as if, in her father's absence, she'd taken pity on me.

She ate her yoghurt and Cheerios without protest and for once she didn't stiffen like a board when I tried to get her arms into the sleeves of her T-shirt. She even threw me a tolerant smile when I put her flashing blue trainers on the wrong feet, and had to take them off and start again. Perhaps the novelty of spending more time with each other had worked its charm on her, as it had on me.

Nonetheless, it'd already been seven-twenty by the time I got her buckled into her car seat, and I had an eight o'clock meeting on the other side of London I was never going to make.

I texted Jade frantically every time we hit a red light, and managed to get the meeting delayed till eight-thirty, but then I had to circle the block twice before I finally found a place to park four streets from the Tube station, and I sat in a tunnel for twenty minutes just outside London Bridge, unable to call or email anyone.

My stress levels were sky-high by the time I got to work. I shut myself in my office and told Jade I wasn't to be disturbed unless it was life or death. She'd worked with me long enough to know I wasn't kidding.

But I hadn't meant it literally.

Wilful exposure of a child to risk of significant harm. That's what the police officer said when they arrested me. As if I'd deliberately set out to hurt my daughter.

I've never pretended to be a perfect mother, but until that day I'd always prided myself I was at least a competent one. I frequently checked the straps of Lottie's car seat, adjusting them if they'd stretched a little loose, just like you're supposed to. I put her to sleep on her back when she was a baby and installed plastic protectors on all the wall outlets, even though it meant breaking my fingernails to get them off again whenever I wanted to plug something in. I looped blind cords out of reach and put up stair gates, ensured she was vaccinated on schedule, never covered her food with BPA-laden plastic wrap, cut her hotdogs into lengths (on the rare occasions I allowed her to have them) so that she wouldn't choke and covered her in Factor 50 even on cloudy days. Every time I drove on the motorway, I'd lock the car doors in case one of them malfunctioned and sucked Lottie out of the car, like a movie in which a plane door is opened mid-flight.

When Luca, carefree and eternally optimistic, asked, 'What's the worst that could happen?' I always had an answer.

It never occurred to me that *I* was Lottie's greatest danger.

I have no excuse for what happened. I was tired and overworked and stressed, but so are tens of thousands of other mothers. I doubt I was the only one preoccupied with the fact her husband was having an affair, either.

It was the reliably appalling British summer that saved Lottie's life. The temperature that day was only 18°C, cool for August; but even so, Lottie was sweating and dehydrated by the time a passerby spotted her, forgotten where I'd left her in the back seat of my car.

The name of the street where I'd parked was Kirkwood Place.

137

twelve days missing

twelve days missing

chapter 25

alex

'You don't have to do this,' Mum says. 'It's not too late to change your mind.'

'I'll be fine,' I say.

Mum presses her lips together, holding back the words with a visible effort as she tucks a stray strand of hair behind my ear. 'You look lovely, darling. Good luck.'

I look far from lovely: my face is shadowed and drawn, and this olive linen shirt drains my skin of colour. But that's the point. *Let your pain show*, Marc said. *You have to look the part.*

People aren't interested in how I really feel. My grief is so intense it's settled in my heart like permafrost and I realise that makes me come across as unfeeling. But I can't help it. It's so intolerable to be me, even for a moment, that I've walled myself off from my own feelings, because it's the only way I can survive. Half the time, it feels like I'm outside my own body, watching myself from a distance. And yet, even second-hand, the pain still takes my breath away.

I have grave reservations about giving this interview but, as Marc pointed out yesterday, I don't have much choice now.

'We've got to change the narrative,' he said. 'This is the only way. And it has to be television. It's much harder to misrepresent you on TV than if you did a newspaper interview. This way, no one will be able to misquote you. You've got to connect with people, get them on your side again.'

Dad and Zealy both agree with him. Mum's the only holdout. I don't need to explain myself, she says. Every mother out there understands what it's like to make a mistake, to drop the ball: *there but for the grace of God*. She says it's only chance this terrible thing happened to me and not them. Any one of us could have fallen asleep in bed during a night feed and smothered our baby, or left a second-floor window fatally unlocked, or forgotten our daughter was sleeping in the back of the car.

I don't care if people think I'm a bad mother. I only need them to believe I had nothing to do with Lottie's kidnap. I have to get everyone looking for her again.

The backlash over Kirkwood Place has dominated the news cycle for four days now. Every aspect of my parenting is being viewed through its lens: the day I forgot to pack Lottie lunch for nursery; the time I left her in the supermarket trolley while I nipped into an adjacent aisle and returned to find her in the arms of a concerned shopper. People are crawling out of the woodwork with their stories, hungry for vicarious celebrity.

A woman who was on the plane when Lottie and I flew out two weeks ago has come forward, claiming I hit my daughter when she spilled her drink. She even has phone footage of me shaking Lottie's shoulder as she lies crumpled in the aisle.

It plays on every channel. Again and again, I watch myself yank my daughter to her feet, and I don't see a fraught, exhausted mother struggling to match wills with her stubborn child, and be a good parent. I see what everyone else sees: an angry, violent woman who looks as if she can't wait to be rid of her child – a child who is now missing.

Did I mean to leave her in the hot car that day on Kirkwood

Place? I honestly don't know any more. Maybe I abandoned Lottie in that car because I *wanted* her to be taken from me.

Maybe all those people who think I'm wicked are right.

It feels as if no one is searching for my daughter any more, including the police.

The case is still officially open, of course, but there's no more talk about the thin man. No one stops to ask why on earth I'd cut off my daughter's hair. I'm now the prime suspect. The Florida tourist board must be thrilled.

This TV interview is the very last thing I want to do, but Marc is right: I have to change the narrative.

'Turn that up,' Dad says suddenly, pointing at the muted television screen in my hotel room.

Zealy reaches for the remote. A sweating, overweight man in a white suit is standing at the top of a flight of steps in front of a municipal-looking building, facing a bank of microphones. A ticker-tape runs along the bottom of the screen: *Mayor accuses mom in Lottie Martini case.*

'Mayor Eagleton, is Mrs Martini gonna be arrested?' a reporter calls, off-camera.

'That's a matter for the police,' says the mayor.

'But do *you* believe she's guilty?'

'This is a beautiful city,' the mayor says, spreading his arms. 'It's a real safe place. A real safe place. We have thousands of families visit our city every year and enjoy our beautiful beaches, and I'm tellin' you, it's a safe place.'

Another voice calls out: 'So do you think Mrs Martini killed her daughter?'

'Listen. All I'm saying is, we have a little girl disappeared in the middle of a weddin', and none of the folks there saw or heard a thing, which seems mighty strange to me.' He shakes his head. 'Mighty strange. My little girl, she'd holler like all get-out if somebody she don't know tried to take her some place she don't want to go.' He jabs a pudgy finger in the air. 'And we have a lady left her baby in a hot car, a *workin'* woman off takin' her *important* London meetings and who knows what all, while her baby *baked in the sun*. Y'all seen the film of her assaultin' that innocent child on the airplane. We're gonna find the truth and we're gonna find that poor baby. Now if y'all will excuse me . . .'

Zealy turns off the television with an exclamation of disgust. 'Jesus Christ. What is this?'

'*This* is small-town America,' Marc says. 'Which is why you've got to do this interview, Alex.'

He accompanies me downstairs to the second floor where the INN television crew have set up in one of the hotel suites.

It seemed smarter to go with a British network; as Marc said, they have less skin in the game politically than the American stations, who make no pretence of impartiality.

Quinn Wilde is the reporter doing the interview. I know her by reputation through my work in human rights law: she's covered numerous conflicts in places like Syria, whose refugees my firm has represented. I've seen her at press conferences over the last two weeks – she's hard to miss, with that piratical eye patch – but I'm a bit surprised she's covering this story. I thought she was a war correspondent; when I hear her name, I picture her standing in front of bombed-out buildings pock-marked with bullet holes. Maybe she lost her nerve after she got blown up by that IED a year or two ago.

Whatever the reason, Marc thinks it's a good thing she's doing the interview; he says she'll give it credibility and gravitas. I hope he's right.

A skinny kid with a quiff of ginger hair ushers me across the INN suite to two armchairs in the centre of a web of cables and lights. Three cameras have been set up on tripods, one

144

pointing towards each chair and a third with a wide-angle view of the entire set.

A cameraman is checking each viewfinder in turn and making adjustments to the height of the tripods. On a table behind the chairs are two small monitors, currently showing a rainbow of vertical bars. Two labels identify them as 'preview' and 'live'.

The skinny kid points to the nearest armchair. 'We're a bit tight for time, so if you could sit here, Phil can get you miked up and check for levels,' he says. 'Um, Marc, is it? You can wait in the edit suite next door, if you like. There's a monitor, so you can watch the interview live with me when we go on-air.'

A jolt of panic hits me. 'Live?'

'This was supposed to be pre-recorded,' Marc says. 'There was never any discussion about a live interview.'

'The editor's given you the *PrimeTime* slot,' the skinny kid says. 'We're on-air in five minutes. There's no time for a pre-record. Don't worry, Mrs Martini, you'll be fine. You won't know the difference once the cameras start rolling. Quinn'll help you through this. And you'll reach so many more viewers on *PrimeTime*. Everyone will be watching, which is what we want, isn't it?'

Marc frowns. 'This isn't what we agreed—'

'It's OK,' I say.

The cameraman hands me a small microphone attached to a slender cable. 'If you could thread this up the front of your blouse,' he says. 'Just clip it on your lapel. Yep, that's perfect.'

He reaches behind me and fastens something to the waistband of my khaki jeans. I've lost so much weight in the last two weeks they hang off me, so he has to prop the device against the cushions.

Suddenly the room is filled with a purposeful urgency that

reminds me of the operating theatre when I had my appendix out at sixteen: the same brisk efficiency of people who know what they're doing and have done it a thousand times before. The cameraman asks me what I had for breakfast so he can check his sound levels, while the skinny kid coordinates with someone on the phone.

Quinn is the last to enter the room. She whispers something in the cameraman's ear and then settles in the seat opposite me, attaching her own mike with her left hand. Her right arm is stiff and immobile.

'Two minutes to on-air,' the kid announces.

The cameraman adjusts the camera pointed towards Quinn, angling it so that it captures a three-quarter profile of her good side on the preview monitor behind her. It's hard to see beyond the defiant eye patch, but she must have been beautiful before the accident. Her remaining eye is an intense, Elizabeth-Taylor violet-blue, and her choppy, jaw-length black hair dips to a dramatic widow's peak before falling in a thick wedge across her damaged face.

'One minute!'

Quinn pins me like a butterfly beneath her singular gaze. She hasn't lost her nerve, I realise suddenly. She's spoiling for a fight.

The kid holds up his right hand. 'Coming to you in five . . . four . . .'

chapter 26

alex

Quinn doesn't even glance at me as the skinny kid silently closes his fist to signal we're on-air. Instead, she studies the sheaf of papers on her lap as, over her shoulder, the live-feed monitor shows Andrew Tait, the presenter of *PrimeTime* back in London, introduce INN's evening bulletin.

'A beautiful three-year-old little girl, baby Lottie, snatched from a glamorous destination wedding,' the newscaster says. 'Her mother drinks and parties at the reception a hundred metres away, leaving little Lottie on the beach alone. Tonight, the mystery continues.'

I tense. This is the interview that's supposed to rehabilitate me and refocus attention back where it belongs, on Lottie. Tait just made it sound like my daughter belongs in care.

The newscaster introduces a pre-recorded piece from Quinn and his face is replaced by footage of a white sandy beach.

'This is the last place Lottie Martini was seen alive, the Sandy Beach resort in St Pete Beach, Florida,' Quinn's recorded voice says, as the camera zooms in to the gate between the hotel reception area and the beach, left moodily ajar. 'Lottie was a flower girl at the wedding of a family friend. Lottie's mum, Alexa, says her little girl had been looking forward to being a bridesmaid.'

Quinn efficiently recaps the facts of the case. There's nothing antagonistic in her reporting and I wonder if I'm imagining her hostility. Surreptitiously, I wipe the palms of my hands against my jeans.

'According to police, the wedding ceremony ended just before sunset, which that night was at six fifty-eight p.m.,' Quinn's voice continues. 'Several witnesses saw Lottie talking to various wedding guests on the beach, including the bride's mother, Penny, but after that, the trail goes cold. Alexa Martini has admitted leaving her three-year-old daughter to walk back to the hotel alone. And in this tropical climate, it gets dark quickly once the sun goes down.'

The camera wobbles and jerks as it follows the fateful path from the beach up to the hotel gate. The footage has been shot three feet from the ground: a child's view of the world. It's sickeningly effective.

Quinn lets the journey play out in real time without comment. I had no idea a hundred metres could be so far. The room starts to close in on me, and black spots dance before my eyes. What was I *thinking*, letting my baby find her way back to the hotel alone?

Suddenly I hear my own voice being played back to me, a clip from the press conference the day after she disappeared. 'Lottie's a smart kid,' I say. 'It's not like she was on her own. Lots of people were around.'

Even to my own ear, I sound careless and indifferent. I was in shock when I said that, but no one will think about that now. They'll only see a woman who comes across as defiant and defensive; a neglectful, deadbeat mother.

I glance at Quinn, feeling ill. She's a respected, serious journalist. She's simply reporting the facts. So is this truly how I appear to the outside world?

Is this who I *am*?

'A waiter at the hotel that night told INN Alexa Martini had drunk several cocktails with friends before the wedding ceremony even began,' her voiceover continues. 'She was then seen drinking a number of glasses of champagne at the reception itself. At about seven-twenty p.m., the maid of honour, Catherine Lord, saw a thin man walking away from the resort carrying a small child wrapped in a blanket. Alexa Martini insists it was the kidnapper, but in the light of the revelations from London, police here are questioning her account.'

On the preview monitor next to the one carrying the live-feed, I see my own face, white and hunted, as I leave the police station after the polygraph.

Mum was right: I should never have agreed to do this interview. Simply by being here I'm opening the door to debate, invading my own privacy and putting my fitness as a mother at the heart of the story, when all that should matter is finding my daughter.

'Despite extensive police investigations, there hasn't been a single confirmed sighting since this photograph was taken –' the camera cuts to the wedding photo of Lottie, sitting on the end of the row of gilt chairs '– at six thirty-three p.m. But Alexa Martini didn't raise the alarm for nearly another four hours.' She pauses to let that sink in. 'Police didn't receive the first call, which came from the hotel staff, not the little girl's mother, until ten twenty-eight p.m.'

I'm shocked to see Mum's face suddenly appear on screen. 'Lottie's not the type of little girl to wander off,' Mum says. 'She knows about stranger danger, we've drilled that into her. She'd never go off with someone she didn't know.'

I close my eyes. I didn't know Mum had spoken to the press. I know what she meant, but that's not how it sounds. The insinuation is clear: *It had to be someone she knew*. And I can't argue with that, because I don't *know* how my daughter vanished in front of dozens of people without anyone seeing or hearing a thing. I'm starting to doubt my own version of events myself. I feel like I'm going mad.

'Nearly two weeks later, Lottie is still missing,' Quinn's voice says. 'No one knows if she's alive or dead. Her story has captured the world's attention, the ear of the US president, even a papal blessing.' The tone of her voice suddenly changes. 'The level of interest in the case has not been without controversy, not least because some community leaders have suggested a child from a poor, non-white family wouldn't have received so much attention.'

The camera cuts to a wall filled with photographs of smiling Black children and then to a man seated at a desk laden with thick, overflowing files.

I glance at Quinn, who's studiously sifting through her notes while the pre-recorded piece airs. Where's she going with this?

The on-screen tag identifies the man as Terrence Muse, of the Black and Missing Children Foundation. 'There are so many families of colour who are desperately searching for their missing loved one. They are just asking for a couple of seconds of media coverage and it can change the narrative for them,' he says. 'But the decision-makers don't look like us. These large-scale searches, they're always for *white* children.'

Quinn's voiceover resumes as a young Black woman appears on screen. She's holding a large portrait of a bright-eyed, smiling young boy.

'Shemika Jackson's son, Jovon, disappeared in December 2016,' Quinn says. 'He was just nine years old.'

I recognise the unquantifiable grief in the woman's eyes.

'It makes me angry to see y'all reporting on somebody else's child,' Shemika says. 'I had to fight to get Jovon on local news and this white baby's on national news with the FBI overnight. I'm tired and I'm frustrated and I'm mad.'

The camera follows Shemika into her son's bedroom, clearly untouched since his disappearance. She sits on the edge of his bed and bows her head in grief. For the first time since Lottie vanished, I'm yanked out of my own suffering. This woman has endured the same hell as me for almost three years, and she doesn't even have the fragile comfort of knowing that the world is out there looking for her son.

I've spent my working life giving voice to those who would otherwise be unheard and yet I never gave a thought to mothers like Shemika Jackson, who don't have my contacts and resources, who can't afford to take indefinite time off work. I feel ashamed.

I've lost track of what Quinn is saying and I jump when I hear my name again. 'Alexa Martini escaped tragedy once before, when she left her baby daughter in a hot car,' Quinn says in her voiceover. 'She insists she's being framed, the victim of a bungled investigation. Rumours are rampant, facts scarce. Those hours of the evening of October the nineteenth remain a mystery, except to the person or persons who harmed Lottie Martini.'

The live-feed monitor abruptly switches to me, trapped like a rabbit caught in the headlights in my plush hotel armchair. I have no idea if I'm about to be eviscerated or finally given my chance to set the story straight.

Quinn leans forward, her blue gaze alight with malice. She's out for blood. She's cloaked it in journalistic impartiality, but this whole thing has been a set-up from the start. The interview with Shemika Jackson was deliberately included to make me look even less sympathetic, if that were possible. A privileged white woman in her five-star luxury suite, who at best is guilty of reckless neglect, at worst something far more sinister.

'INN has received leaked details of the results of the recent polygraph you took, Alexa,' she says. 'Would you like to know what they say?'

chapter 27

quinn

The tide has turned. Public opinion can change on a dime, and Quinn has a spooky ability to sense the tipping point and stay one step ahead of the curve.

Like everything else these days, public sympathy is a popularity contest, and Alexa Martini is too self-contained and guarded to win any prizes. She could be falling apart on the inside, of course, but people don't give a shit about that. The generation raised on *I'm a Celebrity* . . . and *Love Island* is used to a diet of high-octane drama and vicarious emotion. They want Alexa's grief obvious and in-your-face so they can get a kick out of her suffering. It was only a matter of time before they turned on her for not giving them what they wanted.

Quinn wonders what the woman is thinking as she watches the footage of her daughter's last known journey play out on screen.

Phil did a masterful job with the camerawork: retracing the little girl's steps from a kid's-eye view was inspired, and he shot it just after sunset, the time Lottie disappeared, with shadows already lengthening eerily across the dimpled sand. Alexa's face is grey, her skin suddenly taut across her cheekbones and jaw, as if she's been shrink-wrapped.

This isn't personal. Quinn is simply going after the story.

She introduced the Shemika Jackson angle because the idea of this woke, do-gooding human rights lawyer coming face-to-face with her own white privilege appealed to her sense of irony.

There's a hierarchy even for the parents of a kidnapped child. At the top of the pile: articulate, well-connected, white middle-class parents like Kate and Gerry McCann and Alexa Martini. And at the bottom, people like Shemika Jackson.

Shit, who's she kidding? Of course it's personal. There's something about Alexa Martini that's really got under her skin.

As the pre-recorded piece comes to an end, Quinn leans forward. This is the moment she lives for, the high that almost makes her forget how much she wants a drink: when her quarry is cornered and she moves in for the kill.

'INN has received leaked details of the results of the polygraph you took four days ago, Alexa,' she says. 'Would you like to know what they say?'

Alexa blanches. 'How did you get them?'

'We've verified them as genuine,' Quinn says, ignoring the question. 'Were you aware, Alexa, that you *failed* that lie-detector test?'

She lets the silence bleed. Alexa grips the arms of her chair with whitened knuckles, glancing around the makeshift studio as if tempted to flee.

'Your polygraph shows a "probable lie" to one or more answers,' Quinn presses. 'Can you explain that for us?'

'I don't know—'

'*Did* you lie?'

She waits for the protestations of innocence, the accusations of fake news and media bias.

'Maybe,' Alexa says.

Quinn isn't often surprised, but she is now. 'I think you need to explain that,' she says.

Alexa slumps in her seat, a marionette whose strings have been cut. 'The questions on the polygraph were so confusing,' she says. 'They asked if I hurt Lottie, and I didn't, not on purpose, but I let it happen, didn't I? So does that make a liar out of me?'

'You tell me, Alexa.'

'Which questions did I fail?'

'Our source didn't go into details.'

There's a flash of defiance in the other woman's eyes. 'So, for all you know, I could've just been fibbing about my age,' she says.

'What were you doing when your daughter disappeared, Alexa?'

The woman looks down at her hands.

Quinn waits her out. After twenty seconds of dead air, the intern moves into her (single) eye-line, signalling for her to move things along. She turns her head so he's presented with her eye patch.

'I was having sex,' Alexa says, finally.

Quinn already knows *exactly* what Alexa Martini was doing when her child was abducted; the Pinellas County Sheriff's Office leaks like a sieve. 'You were having sex?' she repeats, prolonging the moment. 'So, who was looking after Lottie?'

'I was at a *wedding*! I thought she was safe!'

'So you didn't make arrangements for someone to watch her?'

'I know I'm not a perfect mother,' Alexa pleads. 'But I love my daughter. I do the best I can. I support both of us, I look after her and make sure—'

'You left her in your car,' Quinn says.

'I made a mistake!'

'And then you abandoned her to have sex with a stranger. You can see why some people might question your ability as a parent.'

154

'Would they question it if I was a man?' Alexa asks. 'I *didn't* abandon her. I was at a wedding with my friends. I told you, I thought she was safe! Wouldn't you? Wouldn't anyone?'

'That isn't the—'

'If I was her father, not her mother, would my sex life be an issue?' Alexa demands. Suddenly, she's sitting up straighter. 'Why am *I* held to a higher standard? If her dad had got drunk and had a one-night stand, everyone would accept it was a mistake, not a moral failing, wouldn't they? They'd say losing his daughter was its own punishment. But because I'm her mother, because I'm a woman, I'm expected to be *perfect*. I'm held to a different standard. How is that fair?'

Quinn realises this interview is running away from her, and she can't quite understand why. 'It's not about your sex life,' she says, in an attempt to wrench it back on course. 'You left a three-year-old wandering around in the dark, and it's clear you prioritise your work over your daughter. What kind of mother *are* you?'

Too late, she realises she's gone too far.

Alexa Martini may be the poster child for bad parenting but, unless she's actively involved in her daughter's disappearance, she's still a bereaved mother who's lost her child.

Quinn could kick herself. She let her personal bias take over, and she's just given Alexa what she needed: the sympathy of her audience.

'Do you think I somehow *deserved* this?' Alexa asks.

'This isn't personal, Ms Martini.'

'Of course it is! Do you think I shouldn't care about my work because I have a child?'

'Not if it's at your child's expense.'

'I have a career,' Alexa says. 'In the minds of a lot of people, that's enough right there to make me a bad mother. It's hard enough when stay-at-home mothers accuse me of putting

155

myself first because I love my job. Trust me, many of them have been kind enough to share their views with me on social media over the past two weeks. But you know what's worse, Ms Wilde?' Her sarcasm is thick, and bitter. 'When other women, career women like me, do it, too.'

The barb hits home. Quinn doesn't know why she went after Alexa like that, and she doesn't want to dig too deeply. *This* is why she prefers covering wars. Being shot at is so much less complicated.

She's not surprised when her mobile vibrates with an incoming call from INN's editor less than five minutes after they come off-air.

'What the actual fuck?' Christie Bradley says.

'Look, I know, but—'

'You just created one hell of a shitstorm,' Christie says. 'Hashtag QuinnWildeApologiseNow is already trending on Twitter. I've had INN's board chair on to me! Since when do we go after the victim, Quinn? Not to mention attacking women for trying to juggle kids and a career. Jesus.'

'She opened that door—'

'Then shame on you as a journalist for letting her set the agenda.'

The editor's judgement burns, not least because Quinn knows she's right.

'Well, you've got what you wanted,' Christie says, her tone heavy with disappointment. 'You're off the story. I don't want you anywhere near Alexa Martini. I've told the International Desk to book you a flight to Syria first thing.'

Except Quinn has never let a story go in her entire journalistic career.

chapter 28

The child chafes against my rules, even though I explain they're for her own good. I've cut that distinctive bright blonde hair, but I still don't risk taking her out in public, except when I'm forced to get food. She's more of a handful than I expected, and I lose my patience with her quite quickly.

'Where's my mummy?' she demands, with increasing frequency.

'I'm your mummy,' I tell her.

She flies into a rage, kicking and biting. My legs are soon covered with bruises, and, in the end, I'm forced to do things I'd rather not. She's quieter after that.

None of this is going the way I thought it would. I expected her to be upset at first, but surely she realises by now I'm doing this for her? It hurts she can't see how much I love her. Her precious 'mummy' wasn't any kind of real mother to her. What was she doing, letting a child this age wander the beach on her own? I doubt the woman even misses her now she's gone.

Whereas I've proven my devotion. I've risked everything for her.

But she doesn't make herself easy to like. She's sulky and rude, and throws a tantrum whenever she doesn't get her own way.

I try to make allowances. We're both suffering from cabin fever, trapped within the same four walls day after day. I didn't expect to be here this long. I'd planned to lie low for a few days, while the fuss died down, and then we'd start our new life together.

But the fuss doesn't die down. Her name is on everyone's lips. Her photograph is everywhere.

I follow every development in the story obsessively, waiting till she's asleep before going online and trawling through news sites and social

157

media. They parade the mother on television – as if that'll do any good – and she doesn't come across well. It doesn't take long for the press to turn on her. The police need someone to blame for their lack of progress, too, and she's a handy scapegoat. No one questions their failure to turn up a single lead when everyone is busy blaming the woman who should have kept the child safe in the first place.

But I worry we'll start to attract attention if we stay in this roadside hotel. It's the kind of place people pass through for a night, maybe two. No one stays longer than they have to.

It's a risk to move, but it's more of a risk to stay.

My options are limited. I can't chance anywhere decent, so I pay cash in hand for a small room at a cheap B&B in a transient part of town. It smells damp and musty, and the child complains the sheets feel slimy. She's fractious and complaining, and constantly, constantly hungry. There are no cooking facilities here so she has to make do with crisps and sandwiches, and she doesn't do so gratefully. This isn't the start to our new life I'd envisaged.

I'm beginning to realise I've made a mistake.

I'd hoped it wouldn't come to this.

chapter 29

alex

Stay alive. That's all you have to do, Lottie. Nothing else matters.

Just stay alive.

Wherever you are right now, just concentrate on that. Oh, God, you must be so frightened. I'm coming for you, Lottie, I promise, and I'm going to find you. I'll never stop looking, no matter how long it takes. You just have to be brave and hold on for me. I know you can do that. You're the toughest, bravest, most stubborn person I've ever met.

– oh my baby, my baby –

No more crying. I won't if you don't.

Did I ever tell you about the day you were born? You were nearly two weeks late and, even then, they had to induce you, as if you didn't want to be born at all. So angry, so *outraged*, at the indignity of it all. Daddy fell in love with you the moment he saw you, red-faced and furious, but all I could see was a stranger I didn't know and was expected to love, and it terrified me. Your hair was dark, then. It only went blonde when you were two or three months old. We used to joke we'd brought the wrong baby home from the hospital, but the truth is, you're just like me. Neither of us have found it straightforward to get along with the world, have we? You were a difficult baby. You didn't make yourself easy to like. But as Daddy said, why should you? You didn't ask to be born.

You had two baby teeth at birth, did I ever tell you that? Natal teeth, the paediatrician called them. So typical of you. You made my life hell breastfeeding.

I'm so sorry I didn't protect you. I promise, when you come back, I'm going to do a better job of that; of everything. I'll even quit work, if that's what you want. Daddy was always so much better at all of this, wasn't he? I'm so sorry I'm the one you were left with.

Baby girl, please don't be scared. You just have to find a way to keep going, to stay alive. That's all you have to do. *Stay alive*. Nothing else matters, do you hear me?

They can't hurt who you are. I'm going to find you. Just hold on, baby.

I'm coming.

fifty-two days missing

fifty-two days missing

THE MORNING EXPRESS
Monday 9 December, 2019. Transcript/p.4
<u>Panel:</u>
Carole Bucks
Pete Lee
Nasreen Qaisrani
Jess Symonds

JESS: Sorry, I'm just not buying that. Even Alexa Martini's sister—

CAROLE: Oh, here we go.

JESS: No, Carole, no, sorry, I'm not having that. You've had your say, let someone else get a word in. Even Lottie's aunt says it's time to wind down the search and for Alexa to come home.

CAROLE: If it was my child, I'd not stop looking, no matter how long it took.

PETE: We have to be realistic. I think it's very sad but, in the cold light of day, it does seem like this has gone on, more and more money is being put into the search, in America and here at home, and it doesn't seem to be getting any nearer, tragic as this is, to getting solved.

CAROLE: Can I, can I—

NASREEN: Before you go on, and this is an incredibly difficult conversation, I'm the parent of a two-year-old, but there are issues of race that come into this—

PETE: I wondered how long it'd take before—

163

[overlapping speech]

NASREEN: I think – and I have to say, my heart goes out to Lottie's family, and it's really sad, and I feel for them, I have to start by saying that – but at the same time, it's been seven weeks now since she disappeared.

PETE: Fifty-two days.

NASREEN: And there *are* issues of race, and as a brown person, as the only brown person here—

CAROLE: I think that's incredibly racist, you're implying that as a white person, I can't speak to—

[overlapping speech]

NASREEN: All I'm saying is, there's the case of Shemika Jackson, and she's very vocal about the fact that because she's Black, she isn't getting the attention. Alexa Martini's lucky, in a way—

CAROLE: *Lucky?*

NASREEN: In a perverse way, she is, because at least her missing child, she knows that every day, somebody is out there looking for her. All these parents of other children, their kids, they've been forgotten.

JESS: Nasreen's right, but I think there's something else going on here as well. I think there's definitely a race issue, if Lottie had been brown or Black, this wouldn't be one of the most expensive and publicised inquiries since Maddie McCann, but I think something else is going on, which is the Martini story is box office.

PETE: She sells newspapers.

JESS: Sexy Lexi, all that.

NASREEN: Oh, can we not.

CAROLE: If the media's been a part of it, I feel a huge—

PETE: Of course the media's been a part of it.

NASREEN: Yeah, but you can't get away from the race issue – wait,
            I'll shut up in a minute – if this was a Pakistani mother
            from Bradford who'd left her kid on her own, there
            wouldn't be all this attention, the president of the United
            States, for God's sake.

CAROLE: So should we police according to race, is that what
            you're saying?

NASREEN: Well, in this instance, yeah, what I'm saying is, and I'll
            repeat it again, if this was a single mother from Bradford,
            we wouldn't be here.

JESS: I don't want to cast blame, but some of the stories that've
            come out, putting aside the fact she's admitted she was
            having sex on the beach when her daughter disap-
            peared—

CAROLE: For God's sake. It's not 1950. She's entitled to a sex
            life.

PETE: Hashtag TeamAlexa.

CAROLE: We wouldn't be having this conversation if she was a
            man.

NASREEN: The truth is, no one wants to admit it, but it's simple
            biology – I'm sorry, Carole, it's true – kids need their
            mums. Something has to give, and it's the kids who
            suffer.

CAROLE: When did this stop being about finding a missing child, and turn into a referendum on whether Alexa Martini is a good mother?

NASREEN: She opened the door with that interview.

JESS: It's not about taking sides, but this isn't the first time she left her kid on her own. And just looking at the pictures of Lottie, I'm not fat-shaming here, but looking at the photos of her—

[overlapping voices]

JESS: It's not the child's fault, the parent's the one responsible for cooking and feeding them, you don't get to that size, we're not talking about a cheeky McDonald's now and again, this is child abuse.

PETE: Oooh, you've done it now.

CAROLE: She's three! You're fat-shaming a baby!

PETE: What did I tell you?

NASREEN: I think we're getting away from the—

PETE: So you think Sexy Lexi is innocent, do you, Carole?

CAROLE: I do, yes.

JESS: I'm not saying she isn't, though if I were the FBI, I'd be looking at the groom, Marc, he's way too invested, he's on TV every five minutes. But the question is, all the resources being put into finding this one girl, here in England and in America, sad as it is, when a child goes missing in the UK every three minutes. What about all the other kids who never come home again?

166

CAROLE: It shouldn't be about money. If there is even the slim-
            mest chance of finding Lottie, we have to keep looking.

PETE: The problem is, and I don't want to sound cold-hearted
            here, but the problem is there have been cases solved,
            and it just gives false hope. There was that case in South
            Africa, where there was a little baby, it was taken out
            of its mum's arms—

NASREEN: Zephany.

PETE: She turned up seventeen years later, but not because of
            expensive police searches. You can't keep throwing good
            money—

JESS: There was one in Austria, wasn't there, kept in a cellar
            eight years. Natascha Kampusch. She escaped, didn't
            she?

NASREEN: And Jaycee Dugard, she was missing for eighteen years
            before she turned up alive.

PETE: Thank you, you've all just made my point. They make
            the news because it hardly ever happens. Even though
            we know the chances are almost nil, people say, oh,
            Jaycee Dugard or whatever, they found her, you can't
            give up hope.

CAROLE: Are you saying we should give up?

PETE: No one wants to be the person to pull the plug, but we
            have to be realistic here. The trouble is, and I appreciate
            the irony here, we're just keeping the story alive every
            time we do a show like this and talk about her, and it's
            not doing the family any favours in the long run. They
            need to be able to move on.

167

CAROLE: How can Lottie's mother possibly move on when her
            child is still out there?

PETE: No one wants to say it, but the chances she's still alive
            are—

[overlapping voices]

PETE: I'm just being realistic.

JESS: We all know, if a child isn't found in the first seventy-
            two hours, it's basically over.

CAROLE: Can I just say, the Lottie Fund, they've raised nearly a
            million pounds online already. And Jack Murtaugh, the
            Tory candidate for Balham Central—

PETE: Bandwagon alert.

CAROLE: Can we just put the party politics aside for five minutes?

PETE: Don't be naive.

CAROLE: He's promised if he's elected on Thursday, he's going
            to raise the issue of Lottie Martini with the Foreign
            Office.

NASREEN: This is where it comes back to race and class again
            – no, I'm sorry, but it does. You have a white, middle-
            class lawyer who's getting all this support from MPs
            and politicians. I mean, if she was poor, she wouldn't
            be able to afford to stay in Florida for months on
            end.

JESS: It's a horrific, horrific, tragic situation, but the fact is,
            all she's doing now, staying out there, is sucking atten-
            tion from people like Shemika Jackson, who really
            need it.

168

CAROLE: It's not about race or money—

PETE: Of course it is.

CAROLE: We're the ones who're privileged. We go home to our kids at night. What does Alexa Martini have to go home to?

chapter 30

alex

I pull into my reserved spot in front of our campaign office and steel myself to run the gauntlet of protesters camped on the pavement outside: #TeamAlexa on one side, #JusticeForLottie on the other.

They've been here for six weeks now, ever since the INN interview aired. Their numbers vary, depending on whether it's a slow news day, but the core supporters of each group show up every morning, waving their placards and shouting slogans whenever someone enters or exits the building. I've long since stopped wondering if they have jobs and homes to go to.

Ignoring the catcalls, I hitch my bag on my shoulder and keep my head down till I'm safely inside. At least the abuse is only verbal, now. In the immediate aftermath of the interview, I had death threats and, on one occasion, someone threw eggs.

When Quinn Wilde cornered me on live television, I defended myself as best I could, wanting only to change the narrative and refocus the spotlight on the search for Lottie, but all I did was open up a whole new front in the media war. Of course I care about the struggles of women in the workplace, and the hypocrisy around male and female parenting, but the noise I've created has almost drowned out the mission to find

171

my daughter. I'm starting to wonder if I'm doing more harm than good by staying in Florida.

Jon Vermeulen, the Find Lottie campaign's new manager, is waiting for me inside. When Marc returned to the UK three weeks ago, he hired Jon to take over. An ex-CNN producer, he's a tough, shrewd South African in his mid-fifties who bears more than a passing resemblance to a Sherman tank.

'Your fan club is back in force today,' he says, handing me a cup of Colombian dark roast.

'Channel 5 devoted the whole of their *Morning Express* segment to Sexy Lexi yesterday,' I say.

'Still with that dikshit?' Jon says. 'Fokkers.'

The red-top *Daily Post* in London was the first to come up with the humiliating nickname, the day after the Wilde broadcast aired. The tabloid made much of my 'beach romp' with a 'hot tennis hunk', and while the other newspapers weren't quite as salacious, they all picked up the ridiculous tag.

No one cares that I've never been called Lexi in my life or that using the word 'sexy' in the context of a child's abduction is sickening. I'm thankful that at least the media haven't managed to track Ian Dutton down. He left Florida the morning after the first press conference, along with most of the other wedding guests, and seems to have gone to ground since then. Despite the insinuations of the *Post*, he's the one person I know couldn't have taken Lottie: he was with me when she disappeared.

Jon hands me a stack of opened mail. 'I've logged the donations and binned the crazies. These are the ones I thought you'd want to see.'

'Thanks. I appreciate that.'

'Aweh,' Jon says: a catch-all Afrikaans term of acknowledgement that can mean anything and everything.

On more than one occasion in the past few weeks, I've had

172

reason to feel grateful for Jon's protectiveness. Ten years ago, his wife and five-year-old son were murdered during a botched home invasion in Cape Town, when Jon was away covering the war in Iraq for CNN. He's never forgiven himself, and helping people like me is his way of being able to sleep at night. Now that everyone else has returned home to their own lives, he's the closest I have to a friend here.

It took some persuading to get Mum and Dad to leave. But Mum's misplaced optimism was too much for me to bear. She insisted Lottie would never have gone with a strange man, so it must be a woman who'd taken her; a bereaved mother, perhaps, someone who'd lost her own baby and so took mine. But the grieving mothers of her imagination snatch infants, not small children. Mum repeated the idea that Lottie was being spoiled and showered with love, over and over, until I couldn't stand it any longer and begged Dad to take her home.

Jon folds his meaty arms together as I sift through the mail, radiating disapproval.

'Is there something else?' I ask.

'Simon Green called.'

Simon's one of Marc's hires, too, an ex-MI6 agent whose private investigative firm, Berkeley International, specialises in finding missing children. He has a number of former special forces investigators and surveillance experts on his payroll, and connections to the intelligence services on both sides of the Atlantic.

Jon is sceptical of bringing in paid outsiders, wary of scammers exploiting my desperation, and Simon's firm doesn't come cheap.

But in the three weeks since he was hired, he's already identified several potential leads the police have missed, including a second witness who believes she saw the 'thin man', and provided an e-fit we handed over to Lieutenant

Bates. We've had thousands of tips from the new Lottie Hotline that Simon set up, including several from convicted paedophiles saying they know where she is. While the thought makes me sick to my stomach, those tips are the first concrete leads we've had. Simon says it's not *if* we find Lottie, but *when*.

'What did he want?' I ask now.

Jon grunts. 'Money, I'm guessing.'

I call Simon back, but it goes straight to voicemail. I leave a message, crushing the tiny flicker of excitement that flares despite my best efforts to remain calm. Jon's right. It's probably just an admin question. Two months of dead ends and red herrings have taught me that hope is the enemy.

To distract myself, I read some of the post Jon has filtered for me. Letters of support from across the world: a child's drawing inscribed 'to lottys mommy', prayers, poems, a card signed by the pupils of an entire primary school.

'Mrs Martini?'

I glance up. A Black man in his mid-forties, conservatively dressed, stands near the main door, his path blocked by Jon's protective bulk. He's accompanied by a Latinx woman a few years younger. Not police, but not civilians either.

'It's OK,' I tell Jon.

'My name is Darius James,' the man says, as Jon steps aside. 'This is my colleague, Gina Torres. We're with the National Center for Missing and Exploited Children in Lake Park, Florida. We've received a message from the British embassy in Washington—'

I'm already on my feet. 'Have you found her?'

'The ambassador has asked us to take you to the embassy,' James says.

'Is she there?'

'I'm so sorry, Mrs Martini. It's not quite that simple.'

chapter 31

alex

A wave of nausea hits me and I shout to the embassy driver to pull over. He picks up the urgency in my voice and immediately swerves to the side of the Washington motorway, ignoring the furious sound of horns from the vehicles around us as he cuts across three lanes of busy rush-hour traffic.

I leap out of the car and rush to the verge, my hands on my knees as I bend over and retch into the blackened, polluted grass.

Gina Torres touches my shoulder. 'It might be good news,' she says. 'We don't know yet.'

I jerk away. 'So you've said.'

'Alexa, I realise how hard this—'

'Don't tell me that,' I say fiercely. 'You turn up and tell me I have to get on a plane to Washington *right now*, but you can't tell me why! You've got no idea what's waiting for me when I get to the embassy. A video of my daughter in a basement? Pictures of her rotting corpse in the woods? How can you tell me you *don't know*? What am I supposed to do with that?'

'I understand how you feel,' Torres says.

'You can't possibly—'

'My son disappeared four years ago.'

I wipe my mouth with the back of my hand. My throat is

raw with stomach acid. I feel nauseous still, but there is nothing left in me but bile.

'He was competing in a swim meet in Jacksonville,' Torres says, her voice steady. 'He's a really good swimmer, he's been on the school swim team since third grade. Fourteen kids got on the school bus, but only thirteen kids came home. The coach didn't do a head count before they left, so nobody realised he was missing. He was at his dad's that week, and my ex assumed there'd been a screw-up and I'd collected Nicolás from the meet myself. No one raised the alarm till next morning.'

Four years. I can't even imagine.

In four years, Lottie will be nearly eight. Old enough to read and write, go to Brownies, ride a bike. I can't get my head around *four years*. The only way I manage to keep going is to focus on getting through the next hour without her. And then the hour after that. I can't think about tomorrow, or next week. I don't know how Torres is still standing.

'How old was he?' I ask.

'Twelve. He's sixteen now.'

I don't say *I'm sorry* or tell her *how awful* this is. I give her the only thing I can: the present tense. 'What is he like?' I ask.

She smiles. 'He has so much energy. I mean, he's never still, not for a second. When he was little, we used to make him stand in the corner when he was naughty, and man, it used to chap his ass. He can be real hard on himself, too. He struggles with math and when he does his homework, he'll snap pencils, the dining room ends up covered in broken pencils. He'll say, what's the point, Mom? Why do I got to learn about fractions? Whoever ate five-eighths of an orange?'

We're members of a club no one ever wants to join. Everything looks different where we are: there's a shadow

176

that covers the world. Losing a child – in the most literal, unbearable sense – changes you in ways you'd never have believed possible.

We are living every parent's worst fear. Their nightmare is our story.

The driver sits on his horn and leans out of the window. 'Hey! You coming?'

A lorry whooshes past, rocking our vehicle as we get back in. We cross the Potomac river and turn onto Massachusetts Avenue, where half-a-dozen national embassies are located. The car pulls up opposite an attractive red-brick building behind high railings.

Darius James gets out of the car and speaks to the security guard on the gate, and after a few minutes' wait, we are all ushered inside.

I'm shaking so hard Torres has to sign my name for me in the visitors' log. Lottie isn't here; if there was a live child waiting for me, the faces around me wouldn't look like this.

A secretary shows us into a small sitting room on the third floor and offers us coffee, which I decline. I feel like I'm going to be sick again. Gina Torres takes my hand as we sit together on the yellow sofa and this time I don't pull away.

The door opens again. The man who enters looks even younger than me. 'David Pitt,' he says, shaking my hand. 'I'm with the National Crime Agency in the UK. I'm so sorry to put you through this.'

'Have you found her?'

'The Italian police have received a call,' Pitt says, mercifully dispensing with any more preamble. 'From a Serbian mobile phone. A man identifying himself only as Radomir says he has information on Lottie, but he insists he'll only speak to you. I have to warn you, it could well be a hoax. But we've conferred with the Italian and Serbian police and, for reasons I'm not going to go into now, both forces have concluded this could be genuine.'

The room swims. They must be fairly confident or they wouldn't have brought me all the way to Washington. This could be . . . oh, God, this could be the break we've been waiting for.

Even the police have admitted the only way Lottie will be found now is through a tip-off from someone either involved in her abduction or close to those who are. She's too young to be able to escape on her own, unlike some kidnap victims who've hit the headlines. Natascha Kampusch, the Austrian girl who was snatched when she was ten, had to wait eight years before she got the chance to flee. In eight years, if Lottie is still alive, she won't even remember me.

'Did you trace the call?' I ask. 'Do you know where this Radomir is?'

'It was a burner phone,' Pitt says. 'But he's now called twice. The Italian police have given him the number of a mobile we're going to give you. Radomir said he'd call at seven p.m., our time, so that's' – he checks his own phone – 'three hours and ten minutes from now.'

Don't hope. This is just another crank call. Even if it turns out to be genuine, there's no guarantee it'll lead to Lottie.

I lick dry lips. 'What do you want me to do?'

'We're going to be right here with you,' Pitt says, and suddenly he doesn't seem like a college kid any more. 'We're working with the Italian and Serbian police, which is why we brought you here, to the embassy. We're going to be right beside you, Alex. This Radomir could be a whistle-blower or he could have a ransom demand. Or it could be nothing. All you need to do at this stage is establish contact. We'll take it from there.'

Pitt talks me through what will happen next, but there's a buzzing in my ears, and I'm finding it hard to concentrate. If

178

I get this wrong, Radomir could disappear and with him any chance of finding my daughter.

I can't stop shaking. Gina tries to get me to eat the sandwiches the embassy staff have provided, but my stomach turns at the thought of food. I can barely keep down water. This is probably a false alarm. Another attention-seeking troll, getting kicks from my misery.

And yet.

Thirty minutes before Radomir is due to call, we're joined by two Italian specialist kidnap officers, who confer with Pitt, Torres and James. The whole team radiates professionalism and experience, which sustains me as the final minutes slowly tick past. I can't imagine how hard this must be for Gina, holding out this hope to me, however slim, while she waits, waits for her own miracle.

6.58 p.m.

6.59 p.m.

My hands are too clammy to hold the phone they've given me, so I set it on the coffee table in front of me, and wipe my palms on my skirt.

7.00 p.m.

7.01 p.m.

'Are you sure you didn't get the time wrong?' I ask. 'He said seven, you're sure?'

'Give him time,' Gina says.

Five minutes turn into ten. Ten into fifteen. The phone screen stays resolutely dark.

Pitt murmurs something to one of the Italian officers, who nods and leaves the room. I suddenly wish Luca was here. We may have been lousy at marriage, but the one thing that united us was our love for Lottie. No matter how supportive my parents and Marc have been, there's no one to share my agony in the bleakest hours when I awake in the middle of the night, flayed by guilt. I'm unmoored, clinging to near strangers for comfort.

'You allowed for the time difference?' I say. 'Radomir didn't mean—'

'Vincenzo is checking that now,' Pitt says.

The Italian returns a few minutes later. 'Seven US Eastern time,' he confirms, in accented English. 'There is no doubt.'

Another ten minutes pass. I realise now how bright the hope inside me had burned, despite my best efforts. The heavy, dragging feeling in my chest intensifies. No one is going to call. There is no miracle. The descent back into hell is even worse this time.

And then, at 7.52, the phone buzzes.

chapter 32

alex

The phone buzzes again.

A text. The identity of the sender is withheld.

'It's a video,' I say, showing Pitt. 'There's no message. Should I open it?'

He takes the phone from me. 'We'll be back in a few minutes.'

I get up and pace the sitting room, too agitated to sit down. I understand why they've taken the phone but, whatever the video shows, it can't possibly be worse than what I'm imagining.

'There are some things no mother should see,' Gina says, quietly. 'I know you think you've prepared yourself, Alex, but you can't. No one can. If they think you need to see whatever Radomir has sent you, they'll show it to you.'

It seems to take a lifetime, but Pitt returns in less than ten minutes. 'We've hooked up the phone to a larger screen,' he says. 'We'd like you to come and view the video.'

'What is it? Is it Lottie?'

'We're not sure,' he says. 'But it's not bad news. Whoever it is, they're alive.'

Please, God, let it be Lottie. Please, God, let us find her.

We go downstairs to a room that seems to be used for

security monitoring, judging by the array of screens along one wall. A video is paused on one of them. It's hard to make out what it shows: it's been shot at night, and the picture is grainy and grey.

'It doesn't last long,' Pitt says. 'Maybe twenty seconds. We'll play it in real time, and then we can slow it down and take it frame by frame.'

Pitt's colleague plays the clip. A man carries a young child from a terraced house to a nearby parked car, the pair partially illuminated by a streetlamp a couple of metres away. A second figure, a woman, is a few paces ahead of them. The footage has been shot covertly: the angle is odd, framed by the edge of a brick wall, and the video ends abruptly, with the camera swinging wildly towards the ground.

'Play it again,' I say.

I step closer to the screen, focusing intently on the child. She – or he – is wearing a woolly cap, so it's impossible to see the colour of the hair, and their face is buried in the man's shoulder. The child looks to be about three or four, but the footage is such poor quality I can't be sure.

'Again.'

Pitt's colleague taps a few keys. I strain my eyes trying to see something that isn't there, but I still can't tell if it's my daughter. I don't recognise the man or woman, either. Both are wearing baseball caps and androgynous jeans and trainers, and they have their backs to the camera. They could be anyone. There are no street or traffic signs visible; the number plate of the vehicle is obscured by the angle from which the video's been shot. We can't tell what country this is or if the car is left- or right-hand drive. This could have been taken anywhere.

'Wait,' Pitt says, as the camera swings towards the ground for the third time. 'There. Go back.'

This time, I see it, too. As the footage tilts wildly, for a brief moment a bus shelter is visible in the far left of the frame.

Pitt reaches past his colleague and pauses the footage on the image of the bus shelter. The advert on the end of it is clear, even in the darkness.

'Marmite,' I say.

'It's in the UK,' Pitt says. 'Nowhere else would have an advert for Marmite.'

'How could Lottie be in *England*?'

'We still don't know it's Lottie,' Gina reminds me.

Pitt leans forward on the desk, staring intently at the screen. 'Let's take another look at the child, frame by frame,' he says. 'See if there's *any*thing you recognise.'

How can I not know my own daughter? But there's nothing to distinguish this toddler from any other. Maybe if the child was walking by itself, there might be something familiar that chimed with me: a way of moving, perhaps, or a certain gesture. But held in the man's arms like this, the face turned away, there's nothing for me to go on.

'Our analysts will go over this,' Pitt says, finally. 'They'll look for reflections, fragments, things we might have missed. If there's anything there, we'll find it.'

His tone is upbeat, but I feel as if I've failed yet again.

'What's that?' Gina says abruptly, pointing to the screen, which is frozen once again at the beginning of the clip. 'Is that a tattoo? There, on the inside of his wrist?'

'Zoom in,' Pitt says.

His colleague tightens the shot, focusing on the man's wrist. An inch or so of skin is visible below the edge of his jacket, revealing part of a tattoo. Enlarged, the image is even more blurry. Pitt leans over and taps a few keys. The picture goes in and out of focus, and then suddenly it clarifies and is recognisable as a compass rose.

A compass rose. Why is that so familiar?

Pitt's expression sharpens. 'Alex? You've seen this before?'

My mouth is dry. I feel as if I'm falling.

A compass rose. I remember where I saw it.

'I know who that is,' I say.

two years missing

chapter 33

alex

The meeting is held in a classroom at a small primary school in Tooting Bec, two minutes' walk from the Tube station. I'm half an hour early, so I stop for a coffee to kill time. Edie, the woman who runs the café, brings me my usual: American, black, no sugar. She sets it down in front of me without a word. She knows what day it is.

A little before seven p.m., I leave the café and head to the school. I never got the chance to be a school mum myself, but it smells exactly as I remember from my own school days: boiled carrots, floor polish, erasers and marker pens. No one seems to have considered the irony of holding the meetings here, in a primary school.

The caretaker lets me in and I make my way upstairs to the Year 2 classroom. The corridor is painted a bright, cheery yellow and an illustrated alphabet is tacked to the walls at the height of a five-year-old: *Harry Hat Man. Munching Mike. Quarrelsome Queen.* On either side of the classroom door are a row of coat pegs and I scan the names taped beneath them, looking for Lottie's. George, Taylor, Ava, Muhammad, Oscar. Lottie's should be third from the end, but I don't see it. And then I remember it's October, and a new school year has started since I was last here, with a new intake of Year 2 pupils. Lottie has moved up to Year 3 and a little boy called Noah now has her peg.

It's stupid, of course. It's not *my* Lottie. But there was something oddly comforting about seeing her name there, as if, in some parallel world just out of reach, my daughter was going to school, hanging up her coat on a peg with her name on it, making snowmen out of cotton wool, learning to read.

Inside the classroom, the tables have been pushed to the side to create space for a circle of chairs in the centre. The first time I came here, not long after I returned to England, the group was using the classroom chairs, designed for six-year-olds. It took a minor mutiny to obtain the full-size chairs that are now brought in from the school auditorium when the group meets each month.

It's been a while since I came to a meeting, but I recognise all but one of the faces. Our group leader, Ray, is setting out thick china cups and saucers on a table beneath the window. I know from experience the tea will be weak, the coffee undrinkable. But Ray was a pastry chef in a former life and his chocolate eclairs and puff pastry elephant ears melt in your mouth.

I help myself to a couple of palmiers, and take my seat in the centre of three vacant chairs, so that there's no one immediately on either side of me. I never used to be claustrophobic; until Lottie was stolen, I wasn't afraid of anything. Now, the list runs off the page. Crowds, open spaces, flying, the dark. It makes no sense: the worst has already happened, so I should have nothing left to fear. It's down to grief, Mum says. It attacks you in the most unpredictable ways.

The newbie to my left is clutching her cup and saucer as if they're the only thing tethering her here.

I smile. 'You really should try one of these,' I say, taking a bite of my palmier.

'I'm not really hungry.'

188

Before Lottie, empathy wasn't my strong suit. Now, I make the effort. 'My name's Alex,' I say.

'Molly.'

'How long has it been?' I ask.

'Thirteen days. You?'

'Two years.'

She blanches. Ray's seven-year-old son, Evan, had been missing six years when I first came to group. I remember wondering how he could have survived that long: six Christmases without his son, six birthdays, six anniversaries of the last night he tucked his son into bed. But I know now you learn to exist in the spaces around your grief. You keep on living, whether you want to or not.

'Is it your son or daughter?' I ask Molly.

'My daughter,' she says. 'She's sixteen. They say she's a runaway, but you *know*, don't you?'

'What's her name?'

'Mallory,' she says. 'What about you?'

'A little girl. Lottie. She'll be six in February.'

I see the sudden recognition in her eyes as she kicks herself for not having realised who I was before. She drops her gaze to the cup and saucer in her lap, and I know she wishes now she hadn't come. I'm an A-lister in this bleak new world of missing children and grieving parents: *Lottie Martini's mother*. If she's part of a group that includes me, it means her nightmare is real.

When I finally returned to England twenty-one months ago, I thought being home would make me feel less alone. But I quickly realised the opposite was true. I was living in a foreign country where no one spoke my language. The same mothers who'd once invited me on playdates and made me their pet pity project in the wake of Luca's death – the poor widow, in need of friends – now crossed the road to avoid me. I was a living reminder of their worst fear.

Even my bond with Zealy has become strained. She's on the board of the Foundation, of course, and her fundraising efforts have been heroic, but at the end of the day she still has a life, whereas I'm suspended in limbo. Finding Lottie is the only thing that matters to me, other than work, and even though Zealy has never said anything, she must miss the friend I used to be: the woman who'd take her out to lunch to commiserate after a bad date and text instantly if Sweaty Betty had a sale. These days, we hardly see each other any more and, when we do, we have pitifully little in common.

I joined a support group for the parents of missing children because I was desperate to be around people who knew what it was like, but it took me a full year to accept I was one of them. *First you have to admit you have a problem.*

Ray waits a few minutes for any last stragglers and then shuts the classroom door. We introduce ourselves, giving our names and that of our missing child. Some people add a few details – Andrew would be thirteen now, April used to love *Frozen* – while others barely look up. Ray doesn't really belong here any more: his son's body was found a few months after I started coming to meetings, at the bottom of a well half a mile from his mother's house. But the little boy's killer has never been found and Ray doesn't need to explain why he still comes to group.

'Do you want to start today, Alex?' he says.

I glance around the classroom at the dozen or so people here. So much misery; so many lives put on hold.

'It's the anniversary today,' I say. 'Two years since Lottie was taken. Last year, for the first anniversary, I went back to Florida to launch a new appeal. The police there did a reconstruction, which got a lot of coverage. Quite a few of you probably saw it on TV.'

Nods and murmurs of affirmation around the room.

'We had a lot of calls to the hotline. There was a strong lead in South Africa, but it was another dead end.' My voice is flat. 'They're always dead ends.'

South Africa. Morocco. New Zealand, Belgium, Mexico, Honduras. Every lead, no matter how slim, has to be followed up. For the first year after Lottie went missing, I travelled the globe meeting prime ministers and foreign secretaries, powerful figures who, with the eyes of the world upon them, promised to leave no stone unturned in the effort to bring my daughter home. And I'm no closer to finding Lottie now than I was the day she disappeared.

On my good days, I imagine she's dead. Everyone has their own mechanisms for self-protection and, for me, this is better than the alternative. The awful images that scroll through my mind in my bleakest hours, of Lottie held in some dark place, passed around some unspeakable child sex ring, no sane human being would want in their head. *Better dead than that.*

For me, hope is now the enemy. People mean well when they tell me stories about children found alive after years, even decades, in captivity, and insist I mustn't lose faith. But all I can think about is what those children suffered before they were found. The rapes. The beatings.

How can I hope for that? It's selfish of me to want Lottie to survive at any cost. I'll never stop looking for her, but when I pray now, it's a plea to a God I no longer believe in that she didn't suffer, and that her death was quick. That her body will be found, so that she – so that *we* – can rest in peace.

I no longer rush thousands of miles across continents at every report of a blonde child in a gas station on the outskirts of Cairo. I've learned the hard way to let Simon Green and the rest of his investigative team do their job. I can't help Lottie, but there are other children whose lives my skill and talent *can* save.

So, ten months ago, I returned to work. This year, I've treated the second anniversary as just another day. I've put my phone on silent and ignored the missed calls from Mum. I appeared in court this morning and fought for my client, a fourteen-year-old Syrian boy who the Home Office insisted was eighteen and therefore subject to deportation to a country that will probably kill him, and I won. For me, this is a day like every other: filled with guilt and grief and the endless agony of not knowing.

And, like every other day, I will survive it.

At the end of the meeting, we stack the chairs and Molly helps me carry them back to the auditorium. 'Do you come to a meeting every month?' she asks.

'Not always. But usually.'

'Does it help?'

'Not exactly. But at least here, no one expects you to move on.' I look her in the eye. 'You need to know this, Molly. I wish someone had told me. What we're living with isn't like bereavement. There's no closure, so we're stuck in our grief mid-cycle. Time doesn't heal for people like us. Our pain compounds, like interest.'

'Do you ever want to . . . give up?'

'Every day.'

Molly twists and tugs a hank of her hair. This isn't the first time: her scalp is scabbed where she's ripped her hair out at the roots. People don't realise how physical grief can be.

'Can I ask you a personal question?' she says.

I nod. I know what it will be.

'Do *you* think he did it?' she asks. 'Your friend? The one with the tattoo?'

chapter 34

quinn

Quinn loiters in the corridor outside the classroom, waiting for the meeting to start before going in. She doesn't want to attract attention, although it's difficult to fly under the radar when you sport a black – and diamanté, thank you, Marnie – eye patch. She waits until a woman telling her story in the centre of the circle breaks down into noisy sobs and, under cover of the distraction, slips into a chair at the back of the room.

She checks her phone surreptitiously as she sits down. Nothing yet.

The sobbing woman subsides into gentle weeping and the man sitting next to her puts his arm around her and helplessly pats her back. Another woman in the circle, younger, thinner, takes over, her voice so quiet it's hard to hear.

Quinn wonders impatiently how long this is going to go on. She's on a deadline here. As far as she's concerned, group therapy is right up there with all the other woo-woo bullshit like crystal healing and sound baths. If you're starving and you go and sit in a room with other people who're also starving and talk about how hungry you all are, it doesn't make you want to chew your own shoe leather any less.

She shifts uncomfortably. It's like these chairs are made for six-year-olds. She's had trouble with her spine ever since the

IED, and without the cushion of at least half a bottle of Jack Daniel's, she's in a fair degree of pain.

Her phone vibrates, and her pulse quickens, but it's just a routine news alert from the Associated Press: *Family marks second anniversary of Lottie Martini's disappearance.*

Quinn doesn't get the big obsession with anniversaries and milestones, particularly negative ones like this. She's never even bothered to celebrate her birthday, taking her lead from her parents, who managed to forget both her seventh *and* eighth, at which point she stopped trying to remember it, too.

She scrolls through the AP story. They're playing it safe, keeping their coverage neutral. *Friends and neighbors say prayers as the Lottie Foundation refreshes the public's memory with new appeals and a documentary, blah, blah.*

Probably smart, all things considered. The public mood towards Alexa Martini rapidly swung back in her favour after the Florida police officially named the tattooed man from the video as their main suspect. Alexa still has her haters, but most people are cautiously sympathetic these days, viewing her as an inadequate, rather than wicked, parent. With the main suspect on the run, and the child still missing, the story has largely fallen off the front pages.

Quinn knows she should just let it go, too. INN's editor made it crystal clear she's not to go anywhere near Alexa Martini. But she can't leave it alone. She's like one of those grizzled cops, obsessing over the one case they never managed to solve.

She might not have wanted the story when she was first saddled with it, but being pulled off it has driven her crazy. She was stuck in Syria when news of the video broke and had to watch one of the kids from the Washington Bureau churn out uncritical regurgitations of police press releases, instead of investigating the real story.

Even if the man with the compass tattoo is guilty – a big *if,* since no one can prove if the child in the video is Lottie – it still doesn't make Alexa Martini innocent. The man was her *friend*. They could be working together. Why has no one ever dug into that?

Because everyone wanted to close the case, that's why. Far easier for all concerned to pin the blame on a man whose guilt is unlikely to be tested in court. The police were happy, because they could check the box marked *solved*, even if they hadn't actually caught their man. The mayor of St Pete was *very* happy, because the kidnapper was British, not local. And the social media mob was happy, because their poster girl for working mothers was exonerated. Everyone wins. Except Lottie, of course, but no one seriously thought the poor kid was still alive, anyway.

Yet Quinn just can't stop picking the scab.

You're letting your ego get in the way, Marnie said, after months of listening to her conspiracy theories. *This isn't about finding out what happened to Lottie; it's about you being taken off the story. If you're so keen to know where she is, why don't you quit bitching and do something about it?*

So she got herself transferred back to London, where she had access to the right sources, and pursued the Martini story in her own time.

She's cashed in every favour she's ever had with her contacts, legit and otherwise. Her diplomatic sources have a pretty good idea the man's in Dubai, though they haven't been able to find him. Even if she tracks him down, there's no extradition treaty with the UAE. But she has to talk to him. She has to *know*.

She's rewatched her interview with Alexa Martini so many times now, she's memorised it: each frame of footage, every micro-expression that flits across the woman's face. And she's *still* not sure if she's lying.

Quinn is so engrossed in her phone, she's startled when

she's addressed by name. She glances up to find everyone in the room looking at her.

'Quinn? Would you like to share?' asks Leo, who's leading group this week.

Crap.

'I'm not really feeling it today,' Quinn says.

'Six months,' her sponsor says. 'It's an achievement, Quinn. Take a moment to feel proud of yourself.'

Six months of sobriety. There's only one way she wants to celebrate, but that would defeat the object of being here.

She goes up to collect her chip, feeling like a fraud as she returns to her seat. Unlike everyone else here, she has no intention of staying sober. She misses her old friend Jack too much. But she's going to stay clean long enough to solve the mystery of what happened to Lottie Martini, or fucking die in the attempt.

As Leo brings the AA meeting to a close, Quinn's phone finally beeps with the message she's been waiting for. She skips the Serenity Prayer, ignoring Leo's look of disapproval, and heads straight from the school to the café on the corner, where Danny is waiting.

'How was it?' he asks, as she pulls out a chair.

She brandishes her chip. 'Six months sober.'

'Cool.'

Danny's still in his twenties, but he's the best investigator she's ever worked with. He runs rings round Simon Green and his goons at Berkeley International, the team of private investigators hired by the Lottie Foundation. Last she heard, Green had taken the Foundation for nearly a half a million quid, without a single firm lead to show for it. But maybe Alexa Martini wants it that way.

'What've you got for me, Danny?'

Danny slides his phone across the table. She swipes through the pictures, her good eye narrowing. 'What am I looking at?'

'Immigration CCTV from Abu Dhabi. Your sources were right. He's in Dubai. Been there pretty much since the shit hit the fan with that video. It makes sense – neither the UK nor the US have an extradition treaty with the UAE.'

Quinn sighs impatiently. 'We knew that. Dubai's a big fucking city, Danny. Did you find him?'

'Better,' Danny says. 'We found them both.'

two years and two days missing

chapter 35

alex

'Jesus Christ,' Jack Murtaugh says. 'Half a *million*? You've got to be kidding me!'

He glances around the table. You could cut the tension in the room with a spoon. Jack's been an outspoken supporter of ours since he was re-elected as the local MP for Balham Central back in December 2019, two months after Lottie disappeared. But this is the first time he's become directly involved with the Foundation, and the reason he's doing so now, at my request, is because we need to bring an outsider's clear-eyed scrutiny to what we do next.

The original campaign to find my daughter morphed into the Lottie Foundation after I returned to England. Our mission is not just to search for my daughter, but to raise the profile of missing children who would otherwise slip through the cracks: children like Jovon Jackson, whose parents don't have the same resources and contacts I have. Legal restrictions meant the Foundation couldn't be formed as a charity. Instead, we set it up as a not-for-profit company run by a board made up of friends and relatives, including Dad and me, Paul and Zealy.

And Marc, of course.

Without him, we no longer have anyone with marketing expertise on the board. One of our greatest strengths – our close-knit loyalty – has become our biggest weakness. With the exception of Jon Vermeulen, who continues to manage things on the ground in Florida, the rest of us are well-meaning amateurs, not fundraising professionals. The Foundation has been run too much from the heart, not the head, which is why we're almost bankrupt.

Paul Harding, our treasurer and the man who once mistook one little girl in a pink dress for another, has the grace to look embarrassed. 'That money was spent over a two-year period,' he says.

Everyone shifts uncomfortably. We're all aware how expensive the search for my daughter has been in the abstract, but seeing the numbers in black and white makes disturbing reading.

'This man, Simon Green. He's bleeding you dry,' Jack says. 'Who hired him?'

'Marc Chapman,' Paul says. There's an awkward silence.

Jack sighs and tosses the ledger of accounts across the table. 'Well, this can't go on,' he says. 'The Foundation's barely solvent. If nothing else, Green is going to have a comfortable retirement.'

'The man's a crook,' Jon says, his South African accent more pronounced than ever. He's flown over especially for this board meeting, and he and Jack are clearly on the same page. 'Half a million quid, and all we have to show for it are shots from Google Earth and some photos of a travelling salesman.'

'The salesman was a legitimate line of inquiry at the time,' Paul protests. 'Berkeley International were only able to eliminate him after three months of surveillance—'

Jon snorts. 'Three months of fat fees.'

I don't believe Simon Green is a crook, but we can't keep spending money the way we have been. All the surveillance, the voice analyses, the profiling, the deep background checks – we just don't have the money for it. People have lost interest

202

in Lottie. It's been too long since she vanished and, without a single hard lead to show for the millions spent on the search for her, people have stopped giving. We need to pivot to the Foundation's core mission and focus on other missing children if we want to attract new donors.

'Re-litigating the past isn't going to help,' I say, before the meeting descends into recrimination. 'We're here to talk about how we fund the Foundation going forward, not just the search for Lottie. That's why Jack's here.'

Jack rakes a hand through his thick, black hair. A shambling bear of a man in his mid-thirties, he's not particularly good-looking, but there's something oddly compelling about him. He commands the room without saying a word. He has a sartorial style that could best be described as unmade-bed: his jackets are usually rumpled and flapping open, his shirts spilling out, his collars awry, his ties rarely on an even keel. But he deploys his dishevelment in strategic ways, seemingly too passionate about the subject at hand to iron. In an increasingly airbrushed and filtered world, his style telegraphs unvarnished truth-telling and reality. It holds the allure of the anti-spin. I'm not surprised he's tipped for the front bench in the next reshuffle.

'As Alex says, it's not just about Lottie any more,' Jack says. 'You can't justify spending this kind of money on one kid – sorry, Alex – when there are so many other children out there who need help.'

'But once the Yard inquiry gets more funding—' Paul begins.

'I wouldn't count on that,' Jack interrupts. 'You're not getting any support from Number 10. You've been treading on too many toes.'

Paul bristles. Out of all of us, he's given the most time to the nuts-and-bolts running of the Foundation. 'I don't see what Downing Street has to do with it,' he says.

'Yeah, that's obvious.' Jack tips back his chair, his hands

tucked behind his head. 'Look, mate, every time you remind the Americans they lost a British citizen on their watch, the "special relationship" takes another hit. Post-Brexit, we need them more than they need us.'

'We have precedent on our side. The McCann inquiry—'

'She disappeared from Portugal. The US is a different kettle of marine life. You're comparing apples and oranges.'

'Jack and I have a meeting with the Foreign Office this afternoon,' I say, bringing the meeting to a close. 'We'll know a lot more after that.'

As we leave the boardroom, Jack falls into step beside me. 'I don't think I'm going to win any popularity contests with your friends,' he says.

'They'll get over it,' I say. 'You're not telling us anything we don't all know. Donations from the public aren't going to cut it. We need that government funding.'

'Like I said, don't get your hopes up.'

We reach the street. 'Do you want to get a cab?' I ask.

'I'm fine with the Tube.'

We're only two minutes' walk from the Stockwell station, so I have no plausible reason to object. As Jack swipes his Oyster card, I discreetly swallow a Valium pill. The Tube makes me claustrophobic: I've had several terrifying panic attacks while trapped below ground. The first time it happened, I had no idea what it was. It felt like I was being held underwater with no way of coming up for air. I was convinced I was dying. I was embarrassed and ashamed when the doctor told me it was 'just' a panic attack.

I'm thankful for the warm bubble created by the Valium as Jack and I find ourselves crammed halfway down the carriage, hemmed in by tourists and teenagers. He has to duck his head to avoid grazing it on the curve of the train roof.

We change to the Circle Line at Victoria and the train is less busy. I pick up a discarded *Metro* newspaper to make space to sit down and glance idly through the window as a train going in the other direction pulls into the platform opposite. My eye is caught by a young girl with bright blonde hair, sitting with her back to me in the other train. She's holding the hand of a woman standing next to her and, even through my Valium fog, my heart twists. In another life, I think, that could be Lottie and me.

I can't see the woman's face, but I notice the logo on her fleece: South Weald House. Small world. Mum and Dad used to take Harriet and me there on holiday every year when we were kids.

The doors close. Slowly, the two trains start to move in opposite directions. As we pull away, I see the child's face for the first time.

For a brief moment, all that separates me from my daughter are two panes of glass.

chapter 36

It's easier to avoid CCTV cameras than you think.

You don't have to go down the rabbit hole of conspiracy-theorist hacks you'll find online: laser pointers, frequency jamming, baseball hats that block electromagnetic fields using Faraday cages.

You just have to know where to look.

There are CCTV maps of most big cities on the internet these days. They'll tell you which street corners to avoid, what cameras are dummies, how to move unobtrusively from one blind spot to another.

But you can't dodge them all. And I've found the best way to avoid being noticed in the first place is to surround yourself with people who look like you.

When I first took the child, I made the mistake of hiding out in a sketchy part of town, where I thought no one would ask questions. But I quickly realised we stuck out like sore thumbs amid the cockle-pickers and asylum seekers, with our clean hair and white faces. As soon as we opened our mouths, we betrayed our middle-class, Boden origins.

We need to lose ourselves among our own kind if we want to blend in.

The girl is thrilled to leave the confines of the damp B&B. We drive north and I check into a hotel in a well-heeled part of the city, where we look like everyone else.

I can't keep her cooped up inside all the time, not if I want things to work between us. It's a risk to take her out in public, but I count on the fact we look like we belong together. She holds my hand and bounces excitedly in her seat on the train, eager for our next adventure.

We could be any mother and daughter. I even spot another woman wearing the same fleece as me, down to the contrast stitching on the cuffs. It's that sort of area.

Middle-class, respectable.

The sort of place where bad things only happen behind closed doors.

chapter 37

alex

The sudden deceleration when I pull the emergency lever flings people against each other. Shouts and cries of alarm echo up and down the carriage.

'What the fuck?' Jack exclaims.

The train screeches to a halt, half in and half out of the tunnel, leaving our carriage outside, still alongside the platform. I hammer on the train doors as people on the platform outside rush towards the exits, no doubt fearing a terrorist attack.

'Open the doors!' I shout. 'Open the doors!'

'Alex, what the hell?'

'I just saw Lottie on the other train!'

'Are you sure?'

'It was her, Jack!'

He doesn't waste time questioning me any further. He already has his phone out to call for help, and then curses as he realises he has no signal.

A female Tube employee stares at us from the platform, frozen in apparent indecision. Jack raps sharply on the glass, and flashes his House of Commons ID.

'Open the doors!' he demands.

The woman backs away. An alarm is sounding, an air-raid-style blaring. It contributes to the rising sense of panic around us. A group of young men barge their way through from the next carriage, which is in the tunnel, and barrel down the compartment towards us, shoving people out of the way. Voices are raised in protest, and a baby starts to cry.

'There must be an emergency release for the doors,' I cry, hitting every button I can see. 'What if there was a fire?'

One of the young men grabs my arm. 'What the fuck did you pull that alarm for, you stupid bitch?'

'Give it a rest, mate,' Jack says. His tone is light, but his voice carries an unmistakable air of menace.

'Yeah, well,' the yob mutters, releasing me. 'Some of us got places to be.'

I don't care that people are shouting at me, or that I'm being filmed on several mobile phones. My daughter is slipping through my fingers.

In three minutes, Lottie will be at the next Tube station. In six, she could be on a bus or in a taxi; in ten, who knows where. The ripple of possibilities is widening with every second that passes.

Panic chokes me: *not again*. I'm back on that beach in Florida and no matter how hard I try to run after my daughter, I'm caught in quicksand, my legs moving in slow motion.

My baby was here and now I'm losing her again.

A public announcement cuts through the hubbub. 'Ladies and gentlemen, it looks like there may be a short delay,' the announcer says. 'We're doing our best to get you on your way as soon as possible. Please move down through the carriages and exit the train via the platform. If the person who pulled the emergency alarm could make themselves known to a member of staff, we'll do our best to assist you.'

The female Tube employee is talking to two armed British Transport Police officers. There's a sudden hiss and the doors to the carriages still outside the tunnel open.

People spill out of the train, surging towards the exits. Frustration wraps itself around my lungs, my panic mounting. Lottie was almost close enough for me to touch.

I have to catch her, before it's too late—

Jack puts a gently detaining hand on my elbow. 'No point trying to chase her ourselves, Alex,' he says. 'We need to let the police handle this.'

I can't bear it, the idea of waiting, yet again, for someone else to find my child. The urge to run after Lottie is almost overwhelming. But he's right. We need the other train stopped and searched, the stations along the District and Circle Line locked down. It may already be too late. They may have changed lines, or exited the Tube system altogether.

Jack flashes his ID again and the police listen to him when he explains who I am and what we need.

We're escorted to a control room somewhere in the bowels of Victoria station, and I'm asked the same questions again by a more senior officer:

Are you sure it was your daughter?
Did you recognise the woman with her?
Did either of them see you?
It's been two years – are you sure?

'Two years is a long time in a young child's life,' the officer reminds me. 'They change so quickly at that age. By your own admission, you only saw her face for a few seconds and at an angle—'

'It was Lottie,' I insist.

Her face was thinner, and older, of course. But I know my own daughter. I recognised her in the truculent tilt of her head, the combative set of her jaw. Whatever has happened to her in the two years she's been missing, she is still Lottie.

210

'Is there *anything* else you can remember, Alex?' Jack asks. 'Anything you can tell us about the woman, beyond what she was wearing?'

'I told you. I didn't see her face.'

'You said she was holding Lottie's hand. Can you remember if she was wearing any jewellery? Was she white or Black?'

I close my eyes, summoning the brief snapshot of the woman to my mind's eye. I see again Lottie's hand clasped in hers, the slender silver ring on the woman's index finger.

'White. And young,' I add. 'Her skin was smooth. I'd say she was under thirty.'

'Anything else?'

'I couldn't even tell you what colour her hair was,' I say, frustration shading my tone. 'She was standing up; I could only see her from the chest down—'

I break off as it comes back to me.

The fleece.

South Weald House.

The officer relays the information to someone on the other end of a phone line.

'I can't just sit here,' I say. 'I can't just *wait*.'

'We've got people on all the exits between here and Earl's Court,' the officer says. 'We've had Lottie's picture circulated to all transport staff. We're pulling CCTV from the entire network system and putting it through facial recognition. If she's out there, we'll find her.'

She was out there before, I think. She's been out there for seven hundred and thirty-three days, and none of you has found her yet.

I stand up. 'We need to get to our meeting at the Foreign Office,' I tell Jack.

'What, *now*?'

'I can't do anything here,' I say. 'You're the one who said

211

there's no point trying to chase Lottie ourselves. The police can do that. We need to make sure Downing Street doesn't throw up any roadblocks when the Met applies for more funding. I'm not failing my daughter again, Jack.'

'Alex—'

'Lottie's *alive*,' I say. 'She's not buried in a shallow grave or locked in a basement somewhere. I'm not giving up on her again!'

'I'm not asking you to give up on her,' Jack says.

Something in his tone makes me pause. He ushers me into the hallway, out of earshot of the police.

'There are . . . things I can do,' he says. 'People I can talk to. But first, Alex, I need to know exactly how far you're willing to let me go.'

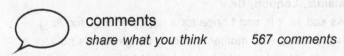

comments
share what you think   567 comments

ben_n_jerry, Vermont, USA
Two years nothing and then 1 wk before they pull the plug on the inquiry the child 'magically' appears in London. Coincidence? I don't think so.

Fastlane, Cardiff, UK
Where on earth did they get 2 million pounds from? it's a public fund it should be accounted for to the public. Clearly the mother has mental health issues and that MP is just using her to boost his career.

Fruit_Gum, Leicestershire, UK
What about the tattoo guy what happened to him ??

Tootsweet, London, UK
Why not just call it what it is: another sunny holiday fund for the bobbies.

ErikTheViking, Luton, UK
I agree with the pp what happened to the tattoo man? how can she of seen Lotty in London I thought he fled the country? it doesn't make sense.

ThisMinute, Rhode Island, US
It was never proved it was him, innocent till proved guilty.

ErikTheViking, Luton, UK
Innocent ppl don't run away.

213

Mandz, London, UK

As sad as it is and I hope for a happy ending, too long has passed. The mother is seeing things there's no way it was her daughter. I feel sorry for her but why would her daughter be in London when she disappeared 4000 miles away?

Woody_802, Dorset, UK

I reckon it's the sister.

two years and nine days missing

chapter 38

alex

South Weald House closed thirteen years ago, long before Lottie disappeared.

The woman who was with her couldn't be a current member of staff there. And when the police finally track down a retired employee, they discover there was never a uniform of any kind. Whatever I thought I saw embroidered on the woman's sweatshirt, it couldn't have been their logo.

Another dead end.

I want to cry with frustration. How can we have come so close to finding Lottie, closer than at any point since she disappeared, and be back where we started?

For two years, there have been mythical sightings of my daughter that we can never pin down. We don't have a single verifiable piece of evidence to prove she didn't vanish from that beach in a puff of smoke. And now we finally have a solid fact, one thing we know for sure: Lottie was *here*, in London, just seven days ago. We should be drowning in new leads, overwhelmed with information to follow up. And we have *nothing*.

The UK is one of the most surveilled nations on the planet, with more CCTV cameras per head of population in London than anywhere in the world, except China.

And the woman who has stolen my daughter managed to avoid *all* of them.

In the last week, the police have trawled through hundreds of hours of footage from the Tube and haven't found a single frame of a young blonde girl matching my description boarding a train.

Not at Victoria; not anywhere on the underground system.

No witnesses who saw either her or the woman in the fleece, despite extensive appeals. We have no proof either of them were ever on that train, let alone that the child I saw was Lottie.

It's clear the police think I imagined the whole thing, and I'm starting to wonder if they're right. Maybe the Valium messed with my head, taking fragments of memory and longing and jumbling them together. *Wishful thinking. When you think of the strain she's been under* . . .

Jack Murtaugh is the only person who doesn't question my account or my sanity. 'Don't start second-guessing yourself now,' he says when we meet at his office. 'Trust your gut. The woman you saw must have known where the cameras were and avoided them, which is why she didn't show up in the footage. No one gets that lucky otherwise.'

'Why was she in London with Lottie?' I ask. 'How did they get here?'

'We may know the answer to that soon,' Jack says.

As improbable as it seems to look at him now, shambling and rumpled as he is, Jack was in the SBS before he became an MP. His special ops unit was responsible for intelligence gathering and maritime counter-terrorism operations, and he still has friends in dark places.

He fiddles briefly with his phone and then turns the screen towards me. It's paused on the opening frames of a grainy black and white video. I've seen it a thousand times since it was first shown to me in Washington, but I *still* don't know if it's my daughter in the man's tattooed arms.

'This man was your friend,' Jack says. 'I need you to be sure you want me to do this, Alex.'

'He was never my friend,' I say coolly.

When the video came to light, my *friend* fled the jurisdiction of both British and American law enforcement without even attempting to clear his name. In my eyes, that makes him guilty until proven innocent.

I don't care about the niceties of the law any more. How he's connected to the woman in London, to Lottie, I have no idea, but if he knows something about my daughter, where she is, I want that information.

And I don't give a damn how we get it.

chapter 39

alex

Jack may believe in me, but I don't. For my own peace of mind, I need to prove to myself that I wasn't hallucinating; that I really saw Lottie on that train.

At the weekend, I go down to my parents'. The logo I thought I saw on the woman's fleece came to me from *somewhere*. I just have to find it.

'Why don't you let the police handle it, love?' Mum says, as I kneel beside the bookcase in my parents' living room. 'They know what they're doing.'

I pull another photo album off the bottom shelf. 'Mum, I told you, they don't even believe she was on the train.'

'Alex, love. It's no reflection on you. But—'

'It was Lottie,' I say.

'You're certain, are you?' Dad says. 'Certain enough to shut down the rest of the investigation and throw everything you have at this?'

I pause at that. Memory plays strange tricks on us; I know that better than anyone. In the last two years I've lost count of the number of times I've seen Lottie's reflection in a shop window or glimpsed her blonde head ahead of me in a crowd. *You see what you want to see.*

'There is no "investigation" any more,' I say. 'Unless we get more government funding, it's over anyway.'

Mum watches me sadly as I flip through the pages of the album. She thinks I'm on the edge of a nervous breakdown. She says she believes *I believe* I saw Lottie, which means she doesn't think I saw her at all.

'Darling, you're not making any sense,' she says.

'None of this makes any sense,' I say.

She and Dad spend the weekend tiptoeing around the subject, treading on eggshells, clearly afraid of setting me off. I put aside my agnostic convictions and go to church with Mum on Sunday morning because she asks me to, but it doesn't bring me any peace. Sitting in the pew, I feel raw and exposed, as if I have a target on my back. Afterwards, fellow parishioners come up and tell me how sorry they are about the 'false alarm' in London.

When we get home, Dad hands me a shoebox filled with loose photographs that didn't make it into the albums. 'Might as well be sure,' he says.

My throat tightens. 'Thanks, Dad.'

I sit down at the dining table and sift through the pictures. We returned to Devon year after year throughout my child-hood and there are photographs of me and Harriet at every age from toddlers to teens. During those holidays at South Weald House, when we only had each other for company, we shared a sisterly rapport that never quite translated back to normal life. The two of us used to watch TV together in the hotel bedroom when Mum and Dad had gone to the pub nearby and we were supposed to be asleep. We'd take it in turns to be lookout at the window and as soon as we saw them walking back up the hill to the B&B, we'd turn off the TV and jump back into bed. In those moments of complicity, we were as close as we ever came to being friends.

I scoop the photos into a neat heap and put them back in the box. Most of them are rejects, either out of focus or marred by a finger across the lens. God knows why Mum even kept them—

And then there it is.

At my shout, Mum hurries in from the kitchen, her hands dripping water and soapsuds. She leans over my shoulder and peers at the photo in my hand.

Harriet and I are sitting cross-legged with another little girl on a lawn somewhere, ice-cream cones melting in our hands. We look to be about seven and nine years old. Behind us, a woman in her late forties is laughing, her hand raised to shade her eyes against the sun. She looks familiar, but I can't place her.

'See her T-shirt? *That's* the logo I saw on the train,' I say.

'Mrs Garton,' Mum says, remembering. 'She was the housekeeper at South Weald House. Lovely woman. Harriet was friends with her daughter; that's her, sitting next to you.' She turns to Dad as he puts down his paper and gets up from his chair. 'What was the girl's name, Tony?'

'Buggered if I know.'

'Katie . . . no, Cathy, that's it. But it can't have been Mrs Garton you saw, love. She died years ago.'

'It wasn't her,' I say impatiently. 'But it was the same logo. The woman I saw was wearing a fleece, not a T-shirt, but it was definitely the same design.'

I didn't imagine it. I'm not going crazy.

A South Weald House logo *did* exist. There *was* a staff uniform, of sorts.

Whoever the police spoke to, that retired member of staff they traced, was wrong.

Or lying.

The photograph itself doesn't prove anything. I could be

222

mixing up childhood memories with something I wanted to see, something that was never really there. But this will give detectives something tangible to work with. The fact I can prove the logo *was* real gives my story credibility on some level, at least.

'The police should be able to trace the manufacturer of those T-shirts,' Dad says. 'Find out who bought them. Oh, love.'

I wasn't imagining it. It *was* Lottie I saw. And for the first time in two years, I have actually done something to help her.

The doorbell rings and I get up from the table. 'I'll go,' I say.

'It's probably just Wendy from next door,' Mum says, already heading into the kitchen. 'She said she'd drop by to borrow some cinnamon. Tell her I'll be right there.'

I tuck the photograph into my bag on the console in the hall so that it doesn't get lost, and open the front door.

'Hello, Alex,' Marc says.

chapter 40

quinn

Danny parks the car nose-in to the kerb beneath a palm tree and turns off the ignition.

'It's the second block from the left,' the investigator tells Quinn, pointing towards the row of high-rise apartments across the street. 'Al Dhafrah 1. His place is on the fourth floor, apartment E.'

'What time does he usually get home?'

'It varies. But he should be there by now.'

'You stay here,' Quinn says to Danny. 'I don't want to go in mob-handed. There may be more than one exit, so text me if you see him come out. Phil, just bring the handheld camera for now. If he agrees to a sit-down, we can come back for lights.'

Phil hitches his camera bag onto his shoulder. 'How does a bloody tennis instructor afford to live in a place like this?' he asks as they cross the road and skirt neatly manicured box hedges. The building isn't flashy, but it's a nice neighbourhood, and the cars parked along the street are Mercedes and BMWs.

'It's Dubai,' Quinn says. 'No income tax, remember. And he's probably making a fortune off bored expat housewives at the country club. He's a good-looking guy.'

'I'm in the wrong business.'

'You and me both.'

She leads the way up a shallow flight of steps into the air-conditioned marble lobby. There's no doorman or security. Quinn presses the button for the lift and the door immediately opens, but then closes again. She hits it a second time and the same thing happens. There's something jammed in the narrow gap between the elevator and the lift shaft.

'Fuck,' Quinn says. 'We'll have to take the stairs. I'll see you up there.'

The damage to her spine makes stairs particularly challenging. Phil is waiting for her when she finally reaches the fourth floor, his camera already out and on his shoulder.

She's surprised to see the door to apartment E ajar. 'Did you knock?' she asks.

'It was open when I got here.'

She pushes it wider. 'Hello?' she calls.

There's no response. She throws Phil a warning glance. A lothario tennis instructor may not seem like much of a threat, but he's been on the run from the FBI for almost two years. Who knows what he's capable of if he's backed into a corner.

As they step into the hall, Phil points to a pink doll's pushchair on its side in the hall. Her heartbeat quickens. Officially, this man doesn't have kids, but Danny's intel is right: there *is* a little girl living here.

Quinn buzzes with adrenaline. If they find Lottie Martini it'll be the biggest scoop of her career. She's already had Danny set things in motion so they can spirit the kid out of the country on a false passport, via Bahrain and Cyprus. She has no intention of playing by the rules and taking Lottie to the British embassy, only to have some government jobsworth slap her with a court injunction before she has the chance to tell the story. Once Lottie's on British soil, no one's going to give a shit how she got there.

225

They edge warily down the hall towards the open-plan living room, but it's deserted. Quinn glances out onto the balcony and checks a couple of doors leading off the kitchen, but there's no one in the bathroom or walk-in pantry, either.

She touches a half-drunk mug of coffee on the kitchen counter: still warm. Someone clearly left in a hurry, and not long ago.

'Do you think he was tipped off?' Phil asks.

She shrugs. 'It's possible—'

There's a muffled thud from the back of the apartment.

Phil is nearer. He flings open the door to a bedroom just off the hall. The blackout blinds are down and it takes a moment for their eyes to adjust to the gloom.

A figure looms out of the darkness. Phil ducks, cursing, and throws himself at the man's legs, dropping his camera as he brings him down. There's a brief tussle, but Phil grew up in the roughest part of Manchester's Moss Side. By the time Quinn finds the light switch, he has the other man pinned in an armlock beneath him on the floor.

The man struggles, but the fight has gone out of him.

'Jesus,' Phil pants. 'Keep the fuck still and I'll get off you.'

The other man stops squirming. Phil lets him go and the man wriggles awkwardly into a sitting position against the bed, breathing heavily.

'What the fuck did you do to him?' Quinn demands.

Phil snorts. 'Give over. That wasn't me.'

He's right: there's no way the brief altercation she just witnessed caused these injuries. Clearly someone got to the man before they did. His face is pulped to a bloody mess. One eye is already swollen shut and his nose is mashed almost sideways against his cheek. He's not going to be breaking many hearts at the tennis club anytime soon.

He coughs painfully, and spits out blood and bits of teeth.

226

'Christ almighty,' Phil says. 'What happened to you?'

The man swivels his good eye towards the door.

'There's no one else here,' Quinn says. 'You're OK, for now.'

Phil picks up his camera and shakes it. It rattles ominously. 'Fuck.' He throws the man a dirty look. 'Asshole. You sure this is the right guy, Quinn?'

She crouches down beside the man and grabs his right hand, turning it over so they can both see the inside of his wrist. A tattoo of a compass rose, identical to the one in the infamous video.

'Are you Ian Dutton?' Quinn asks.

The man sucks in a breath and then nods.

'What happened? Do you know who did this?'

The man glances towards the door again. He's not worried about someone lurking in the hall, she realises suddenly: he's looking towards the wardrobe.

Phil sees it, too. At Quinn's nod, he flings opens the closet door.

Cowering on the floor of the walk-in wardrobe, tangled amongst the trainers and tennis rackets, is a little girl.

chapter 41

alex

Much as I might want to, I can't leave Marc standing on the doorstep. I've been caught out too many times by paps with long lenses and, with the Foundation's funding on the line, I don't need any more scandal.

'I'll be right there, Wendy!' Mum calls from the kitchen. 'I wasn't sure if you wanted the ground cinnamon or the—'

She stops dead as she sees Marc standing in the hallway.

'Actually, I think I'll just take this over to Wendy now,' she says stiffly. 'Save her a trip. Nice to see you again, Marc.'

'You too, Mrs Johnson.'

She doesn't tell him to call her Mary, as she has done every time they've met since I left college. She can't even meet his eye, in fact, as she hangs her apron on the newel post and goes next door.

'Come into the study,' I tell Marc. I don't want Dad to know he's here. He's not as forgiving as Mum.

Marc hovers awkwardly by the door. I gesture impatiently towards the sofa. 'You're here now. Sit down.'

'I know you don't want to see me,' he says. 'But I had to come when I heard the news. I was in South Africa last week or I'd have come sooner.'

'You shouldn't have bothered.'

'Do you really think you saw Lottie?'

'Yes.'

'Alex, that's incredible,' Marc says. 'It's only a matter of time, now. The police will be able to track—'

'We both know you don't believe it was her. Let's drop the act. Why are you really here?'

He stares down at his hands, which are loosely clasped between his knees. No wedding ring, of course. His hair is thinning on top, I notice, and he's lost weight since I last saw him, almost a year ago. I know it's not fair to blame him for everything that happened, but I've long since lost the capacity to shoulder anyone's pain but my own.

'You know why I'm here,' he says.

'Nothing's changed,' I say.

He looks up, his expression hunted. There are bags beneath his eyes and his skin has a grey pallor. 'Alex, it was just a *kiss*.'

'We both know that's not true,' I say.

I'm not such a delicate flower that I can't cope with a man who crosses the line and presses his suit where it's not wanted. I swim with lawyers. I'm used to sharks.

And it was 'only' a kiss. I was never in any physical danger; Marc backed off the second I slapped him down. If it'd been anyone else, it would barely have registered.

But it wasn't anyone else. It was Marc.

We'd both been working late on a new marketing campaign at the Foundation. The rest of the team had left the office and, when we'd finally finished work, drained and exhausted, Marc had offered to give me a lift home as he had so many times before. Why wouldn't I accept? We'd been friends for more than a decade. There had never been a question of anything more between us. Marc was *married*.

And then, as he parked outside my house, he'd leaned across and kissed me.

229

Even as I shoved him away, he confessed he was in love with me and had been for years. As if that made it *better*.

An impulsive kiss, a clumsy pass: that I could have forgiven. But Lottie was abducted from his *wedding*. And now he was telling me it was all a mistake, because he'd been in love with me the whole time.

He should never have married Sian.

Lottie should never have been in Florida.

A photo of Marc's unwelcome kiss, taken by a nosy neighbour, had ended up in the papers that weekend. Sian threw Marc out and I had the epithet *home-wrecker* to add to *unfit mother* and *whore*. Donations to the Foundation dropped off sharply and, even though Marc left the board, they've never really recovered.

Marc couldn't have known the butterfly effect of his choices. But, God help me, I still can't forgive him. I've tried to get past it, but I can't. Every time I look at him, I see a wedding that shouldn't have happened, a lie that cost me my daughter.

I don't have a single relationship that hasn't been blighted by losing Lottie. Everyone who was at the wedding has the stain of suspicion on them, especially the so-called 'twelve apostles': the dozen guests who were at Lottie's 'last supper' the night before the wedding. Even those who weren't there aren't safe; online trolls have accused Harriet of snatching my child because she couldn't have her own.

The closeness I once shared with my parents has become claustrophobic. They worry about keeping me safe, when the sky has already fallen. And I've lost so many friends because they don't know what to say to me, how to be mothers around a woman who's lost her child. It's not sex that's the last taboo in society: it's bereavement.

'It's been a year, Alex,' Marc pleads. 'I've stayed away from you, like you asked. I don't know what more I can do to show you I'm sorry.'

'I know you are,' I say. 'But it's too late.'

'Please, Alex. Whatever mistakes I've made, it's only because I love—'

'Don't.'

'Lottie's gone,' he says, standing up. 'It breaks my heart, but she's gone, Alex. You still have the rest of your life. She wouldn't want you to waste it. She'd want you to be happy again.'

'You should leave,' I say, opening the door.

'After all I've done for you,' Marc says.

An odd chill ripples down my spine. There's a shadow in Marc's eyes, a darkness. *After all I've done for you.*

What does he mean?

My phone buzzes and Jack's number comes up on my screen.

Suddenly, my throat is dry. Jack said he'd call me the moment he had news about Ian Dutton. 'I have to answer this, Marc,' I say. 'You need to go now. Please, don't come back.'

I shut the front door behind him and take a steadying breath. In the next few seconds, I will know if—

'We haven't found her,' Jack says, ripping off the plaster. 'But there's something you need to see.'

chapter 42

alex

'Ian Dutton was set up,' Jack says.

We're sitting in his constituency office, less than two hours after he called me. Whatever plans he may have had for his evening, he cancelled so he could meet me straight away. He understands that even though my daughter's been missing for more than two years, every night of *not knowing* is as brutal and tormented as the first.

'What do you mean, Ian was set up?' I ask.

Jack hands me his phone. I stare at the photo of an attractive brunette in her late twenties. She looks Middle Eastern: Syrian, maybe, or Lebanese.

'Her name is Sanaa,' Jack says. 'She's Ian Dutton's girlfriend. She's the woman who was with him in the video. And *that*,' he adds, taking the phone and swiping to another picture, before handing it back to me, 'is the girl Ian was carrying in his arms. Sanaa's six-year-old daughter, Hala.'

I study the screen. The little girl's long hair is bright blonde, just like Lottie's. She's about the same age as my daughter would be, too, but the resemblance stops there. I pinch the screen and zoom in on her face. Close up, it's obvious she's a different child – wrong eye colour, wrong nose – but, of course, in the video all that was visible was the back of her head.

'Why didn't he come forward and explain who the girl was?' I say, handing back the phone. 'His name and photograph were all over the news! He could've ruled himself out as a suspect with a single phone call!'

'Because he and Sanaa were eloping,' Jack says.

'So?'

'Sanaa is Lebanese and so is her husband. Issues of child custody and divorce in Lebanon are generally decided in religious courts. If a father establishes that the mother is unfit or lacking good moral character, she loses any right to the child.' He gets up from the leather sofa and pours us both a measure of single malt from the bottle on the bookshelf. 'Running off with another man, especially a Westerner like Ian, pretty much makes a prima facie case on that score.'

'So he put himself at the centre of a *kidnap* investigation instead?'

'It wasn't just that Sanaa wouldn't get a fair hearing in court,' Jack says. 'The man's last wife died in mysterious circumstances. Sanaa was terrified of him. She knew if she left him, she'd have to disappear completely, and so would Ian.'

It certainly explains why Ian has been hiding out in Dubai under a false name, willing to sacrifice his reputation and go on the run to protect the woman he loves.

But he also sacrificed whatever hope I had of finding my daughter.

After the police identified him as their prime suspect, they all but gave up the search for anyone else.

'How reliable is this information?' I ask.

'Oh, it's reliable.' Jack knocks back his drink. 'My guys don't mess around. Ian didn't give it up straight away, but, like I said, they can be very persuasive.'

I don't feel sorry for Ian Dutton. His silence has wasted our time for almost two years. I feel ill when I think of the money and manpower that's been directed towards tracking down the wrong man. Every fact we've used to inform our search since the footage first surfaced has been predicated on a red herring. If Ian couldn't call the police, he could have phoned me, or sent a message. Told *some*one.

'Wait. If it was Sanaa's daughter Ian was carrying, why would anyone film it?' I ask. 'Why would they think it was Lottie?'

'They didn't. Alex, this wasn't a well-meaning tip-off. That video derailed the entire investigation. The whole thing with the Serbian burner phone, calling the Italian police – someone went to a lot of trouble to set Ian up and get the police chasing their tails. They *wanted* to waste time and resources, and they succeeded.'

I'm filled with sudden rage at the sadistic cruelty of it.

'Whoever took it, they were hiding in a doorway down the street, phone in hand, waiting to film Ian's midnight flit,' I say savagely. 'You can tell by the way the video starts before either of them even come out the door. The bastard must've known about it in advance.'

'Yep.'

'That has to be a pretty short list of people, Jack.'

'Ian says he didn't even tell his family. Still hasn't, in fact. They've got no idea he's in Dubai. Sanaa didn't tell anyone either – her parents would've supported her husband over their daughter. Ian insists the only people who knew were the two of them.'

'*Some*one knew!'

Jack rubs his thumb thoughtfully across his lip. 'Whoever sent that video was close enough to Ian to know what he was planning. That gives us some parameters.'

'Who could've known he was going to disappear in the middle of the night, if even his family didn't?' I say, frustration sharpening my tone.

'It might not seem like we're any further on, Alex, but trust me, we're making progress,' Jack says. 'When you identified Ian from the video, the police just concentrated on finding him, for obvious reasons. They weren't looking at the circle of people around him, which means there are leads that probably haven't been followed up.'

I want to believe he's right. Having a new focus of investigation *is* a major step forward. We've been treading water for so long, and this could be the break we need.

Or yet another dead end.

'We should find out if Ian has a connection to anyone at South Weald House,' I say. 'Maybe he knew someone who worked there.'

'It's certainly something to consider,' he says.

I know a brush-off when I hear one.

'You don't sound convinced,' I say.

Jack pulls sideways at his tie to loosen it. I'm struck again by the repressed energy he exudes. It's impossible not to be caught in its undertow and, despite my wrenching misery, knowing Jack believes we're getting somewhere makes me feel a little better.

'Look, we've established Lottie must've known her abductor, right?' he says. 'Or at least felt comfortable with them, or she'd have cried out when they approached her. Created some kind of disturbance, whatever. That's one of the reasons the police liked Ian for this in the first place.'

'Yes.'

'And now we know that whoever took her knew *Ian* pretty well, too,' he adds, balling up his tie and flinging it into a desk drawer. 'Well enough to have discovered his plans to vanish with Sanaa and be there on the right day, at the right time, to film it. So we're looking for someone who met Lottie *and* knew Ian.'

'The twelve apostles,' I say.

He pulls a pad of paper towards him. 'Yes. It's got to be someone who was at the rehearsal dinner. It's the only chance they'd have had to meet both Ian and Lottie. Ian was only in Florida one night and he told my guys he didn't speak to anyone else at the wedding. Give me the names of everyone who was at that "last supper" other than you and Ian.'

'Paul Harding,' I say. 'Zealy. Marc and Sian themselves, of course, and Sian's parents, Penny and David. Marc's dad, Eric. Catherine Lord, the maid of honour – she married Paul a few months after the wedding, so she's Catherine Harding now. And Flic and Johnny Everett, the parents of one of the bridesmaids, Olivia.'

'Anyone else?'

'That's it,' I say. 'But the police have checked them all out, multiple times—'

'The police spent the first half of the investigation thinking it was you and the second insisting it was Ian,' Jack says. 'I'm not taking anything they say on trust.'

I notice he's divided the ten names into two separate columns.

'Men and women,' Jack says. 'You saw a woman on the train with Lottie. So that's where we start.'

two years and fourteen days missing

...two years and fourteen days missing

chapter 43

alex

I'm woken by a noise downstairs. I sit up in bed, my heart pounding. The red numerals of the clock on my dresser read 4:33 a.m.

There's another soft thud and the unmistakable sound of someone moving about in the kitchen below me.

I flip back the covers and slide quietly out of bed. I'm not so much scared as furious: sleep is my most bitter enemy and only comes to me after hours of tossing and turning every night. I already know I'll never find the blessed relief of oblivion again tonight.

Another thump and then an odd, dull scrape of metal on metal.

I've been burgled three times since Lottie was taken; my unremarkable terraced house in Balham has graced newspapers often enough to make me a target for both cranks and thieves who seem to think I have bank notes from the Lottie Foundation stashed beneath my mattress. After the first robbery, I had a state-of-the-art security system installed, but technology is only as good as its human operator. I've got careless about setting it when I go to bed at night, especially as it has a tendency to go off if so much as a feather drifts across one of its sensors.

Grabbing my phone from my bedside table, I punch in three 9s and keep my finger over the green call button as I edge downstairs. A streetlamp outside my front door casts a rectangle of light through the stained-glass fanlight, splashing turquoise and purple abstract art across the black and white hall tiles.

The sound of footsteps in the kitchen brings me up short. I don't have a weapon and even if I did, I've no idea how to use it. When I was at college, I did a six-week course in self-defence, but the last time I actually went head-to-head with anyone my opponent was my seven-year-old sister.

Fuck it.

With a yell, I fling open the kitchen door so hard it bounces off the wall and slams back against me. A shadow bolts past me into the hall.

A small, four-legged shadow.

The fox stops as it reaches the front door, cornered. I take a step towards it and it bares its teeth with a ferocious growl.

I stop, holding up the palms of my hands as if in a hostage negotiation. 'Hey, take it easy,' I say. 'You scared me as much as I scared you.'

The fox growls again. I can't get to the front door to let him out, so I go back into the kitchen and unlock the back door. The fox zips past me and into the darkness, and I shut the door behind him.

The sash window over the sink is raised; that must be how he got in. I don't remember opening it, but my memory isn't exactly reliable these days.

I close the window. The fox has knocked over a packet of coffee beans I'd left out on the counter and worried at some porridge oats in their cardboard cereal box, ripping the packet open.

I tidy up the mess and am just sweeping it into the bin

240

when my heart starts banging in my chest so loudly I can hear the blood passing through my ears. My hands tremble on the dustpan and brush, and my vision is suddenly blurry. A wave of prickly heat sweeps through my body. I strip off the T-shirt I wear to bed and splash cold water on my face. My heart pounds even faster, even harder. I take a deep breath to calm myself, but my breaths are sharp and shallow. My chest tightens until it feels like I'm choking and my vision gets darker and narrower and then becomes kaleidoscopic, like when you close your eyes and press down on your eyelids to see stars. I have to grip the counter with tingling hands just to stay upright.

I yank open the drawer nearest to me, scrabbling through pizza delivery brochures and appliance instructions and spare coffee filters for the vial of Valium I keep there. I manage to coordinate my shaking fingers long enough to prise off the child-proof lid and swallow two of them dry.

It takes twenty minutes for the medication to kick in. I sink to the floor and curl up on the cool tiles, and tell myself I can get through this. *This is not too much for me. I have been through this before and it's not too much for me.*

Eventually, the panic attack abates. My anxiety starts to wind down, sweat cooling on my skin as my breathing slowly returns to normal.

I push myself into a sitting position and lean back against the nearest kitchen cupboard. I feel utterly exhausted, as if I've run a marathon. And in terms of my body's panicked response, I have.

I get to my feet and finish sweeping up the rest of the spilled coffee and porridge oats, moving like an old woman. We've had urban foxes around here before, although this is the first time one's been bold enough to come into the house. But it's my own fault for leaving my windows open.

241

I lean over the sink, double-checking I've fastened the catch at the top of the casement. And then I see the lock is broken. There are clear grooves in the frame around it. Someone has jemmied the catch open, and very recently. The exposed wood is pale and new. Someone was here, in my house, while I slept.

chapter 44

alex

My expensive laptop is exactly where it should be, on my desk in my study.

So, too, are the small diamond studs I stupidly left on the windowsill the other day, because I'd spent so long on the phone talking to a client they were irritating my earlobes. My office window is securely locked. My old case files are stacked neatly on the bookshelf beneath it, their corners perfectly lined up, undisturbed.

But the stand containing my pens is on the left of my keyboard, not the right. I always line up my mouse with the edge of its mouse mat; that, too, is in the wrong place.

No self-respecting thief leaves behind diamonds and electronics. Whoever broke into my house was clearly looking for something else.

Information?

I've caught journalists going through my bins and intercepting my post more than once, though none of them have yet broken into my home. But this could also be connected to one of the legal cases I'm working on, which worries me more. I represent several women who have a great deal to fear. One sought asylum here in the UK after her wealthy Pakistani husband and son murdered her daughter in an honour killing for refusing to marry the man picked out for her. Another Yemeni girl lives in constant fear for her life because she's gay. Both are sequestered in safe houses here in London. I'm their lawyer of record: someone may have come here, looking for their addresses.

But all the case files I'm currently working on are still in place on my desk and show no sign of being disturbed.

When I check my laptop, I find its sophisticated security system – installed by my law firm – hasn't been breached either. Perhaps whoever searched my office didn't have time to find what they were looking for before the fox roused me out of bed.

Knowing someone was in my home, going through my things, should freak me out more than it does. Now would be the logical time for a panic attack, but I'm immune to the normal sense of violation most people feel after a burglary: for more than two years now, I've been public property. There isn't a corner of my life that hasn't been exposed and laid bare to judgement.

I have no privacy left to invade.

The absence of fear leaves room for straightforward curiosity. Who broke in and what were they hoping to find?

There's no point calling the police. A break-in during which nothing was taken probably doesn't even warrant a case number, never mind an investigation. Nor do I want the publicity that would attend the inevitable leak to the press. I'll figure this one out myself. I have a hunch that if I discover what was taken, it'll lead me to the *who*.

I sit down at my desk and carefully go through each of my files and folders. I find nothing missing, not a page out of place, in any of them.

Except one.

I probably wouldn't even have noticed the discrepancy had I not been on high alert, looking out for it. But as soon as I open the folder I spot the paperclips collating my notes are on the left-hand corner of the collected pages, where most people would put it, rather than the right, as is my habit.

This break-in was never about work or getting a story. It's about Lottie. It's always about Lottie.

Quickly, I flip through the pages of notes to the back of the folder where I tucked the photograph of my sister and me eating ice-creams on the lawn with the housekeeper from South Weald House.

It's missing.

My pulse quickens. I check the folder again, and then around my desk, in case I've dropped it, but it's definitely gone. I've rattled enough cages and turned over enough stones for someone to have broken cover.

Jack may not believe there's a connection between Lottie and South Weald House, but I'm certain of it.

And there's only one person who can help me find it.

I'm not surprised when Harriet's mobile goes straight to voicemail. My sister has always been an early riser, especially since she moved to the Shetlands, but our communications over the past two years have been sporadic at best. When we do talk, we don't seem to know what to say to each other.

If we ever did.

'It's me,' I say, as soon as her recorded greeting ends. 'Look, I thought I might come up and stay with you for a few days. It'll be nice to spend time together.'

I pause. Is that enough?

'I'll be there tomorrow afternoon,' I add. 'I'll text you when I'm in Orkney.'

Slipping my phone into the pocket of my sweatpants, I go into the kitchen and insert a K-cup into the coffee machine. *One*, I think.

A stream of rich Colombian dark roast hisses into my mug. *Two*. I settle myself on a kitchen stool.

Three . . .

chapter 45

alex

My phone vibrates. 'Hey, there,' I say.

Harriet sounds a little out of breath. I imagine her listening to my message and panicking at the thought of having me turn up on her doorstep. I doubt I'm on speed dial. She'll have had to look up my number and type it in old-school. No wonder she's breathless.

'This really isn't a good time to come up here,' my sister says. 'The weather's been abysmal and Mungo only just got back from the rigs two days ago. You know what he's like when he's decompressing. I'd love to see you but—'

'Relax,' I say. 'I'm not coming up to bloody Shetland. I just said that so you'd ring me back.'

'Oh.'

'Although a more sensitive person might be a little offended by your eagerness to talk me out of it.'

I mean it as a joke, but it comes out as an accusation.

I know my sister loves me, just as I love her, but when I think of the closeness Zealy shares with Marc or the friendship many of my friends have with their siblings, I feel a sense of loss. Harriet and I have a strange disconnect, which I've never really understood. She isolated herself from me emotionally long before she put such literal distance between us.

'Mum OK?' my sister says, finally.

'She seemed fine at the weekend,' I say. 'A bit tired, maybe.'

Actually, now that I think about it, Mum wasn't quite herself. Dad said she hadn't been sleeping well, but I should check back in with her, make sure she's OK.

'I heard about what happened,' Harriet says, abruptly. 'In London, I mean.'

It's as if she's embarrassed to mention Lottie's name. *I heard about what happened. You know. When you saw your missing daughter on a train four thousand miles from where she disappeared.*

I get it a lot: the embarrassment. No one knows how to deal with grief any more. There's no template for anyone to follow and so, when catastrophe strikes, we hold candlelight vigils and put up roadside shrines and launch GoFundMe campaigns and then quickly move on, before we have to deal with any of the messiness of actual emotions.

The Victorians knew what they were doing with their widows' weeds and black armbands. Their etiquette for grieving a loved one was strict, and it may seem laughable now that the width of a black hatband was dictated by your relationship to the deceased, but everyone knew where they were. They knew what was expected of them. And when a widow cast off her mourning, her black bombazine and crepe, it was a signal to the world she was ready to engage with it again.

People cross the street to avoid me because they don't know what to say. It's extraordinary how many of them don't even mention Lottie 'because I didn't want to bring it up again', as if the loss of my baby is something I might *forget*.

I'll miss my daughter with every breath I take for the rest of my life, but I'm still human. Sometimes I crave normality so much it hurts: for someone to make a joke and not glance apologetically at me, as if they've just farted in church.

I know Harriet cares about Lottie almost as much as I do

247

and she's suffering too. But if I can endure my loss and still get up in the morning, she owes it to me to acknowledge my grief and use my daughter's name.

'Harry, I need to ask you something,' I say, abruptly. 'Do you remember that place in Devon we used to stay when we were kids? South Weald House?'

'Of course,' she says, sounding surprised. 'Why?'

'You used to be good friends with the housekeeper's daughter, didn't you?'

'Cathy?'

'Yes.'

'Years ago,' Harriet says. 'I haven't seen her since I left London. She was at UCL, you know, same as you.'

'I saw an old photo of her the other day when I was going through the albums with Mum,' I say. 'Eating ice-cream with us on the lawn. I really need to speak to her. Are you two still in touch?'

'Why don't you ask Marc for her number?' Harriet says.

'Why would *Marc* have it?'

The dead air between us is suddenly freighted with tension. In the silence, I can hear the wind whipping around her tiny croft hundreds of miles away.

'You really don't know?' Harriet says, at last.

The hairs on the back of my neck prickle. I'm not superstitious. I don't believe in women's intuition and sixth senses.

I grip the phone a little more tightly. 'What are you talking about, Harriet?'

'Marc Chapman coached Cathy, when she was on the UCL football team, that's how she and Sian became friends. Alex, I thought you knew.'

'Knew *what*?'

'Catherine Lord,' she says. '*Cathy*. She was Sian's maid of honour.'

248

chapter 46

No one gives us a second glance when we venture out now, though I still keep our outings to a minimum. We blend into a crowd of millions here in the city, but it only takes one person to recognise her.

Except the girl doesn't do well cooped up inside hotel rooms all the time. It's been too long since she had playmates. She's restless, bored, full of pent-up energy that manifests itself in tantrums and bouts of fury. She requires constant attention, constant entertainment.

I worry she's mentally unstable, that she's been irrevocably damaged by everything that's happened to her.

Or perhaps it's just me. I've never been a hands-on mother before.

Either way, I can't keep her indoors all the time. It's not healthy for her to spend hours staring at a screen and she's starting to look peaky.

We need to leave the city and go somewhere she can get outside and run around. Somewhere rural, where people keep themselves to themselves, but not too far off the beaten track that strangers attract notice. A place used to tourists and new faces in the village shop.

I rent a cottage on the coast and pay cash, three months upfront, but I don't plan for us to be here anywhere near that long. The skinny kid at the lettings agent doesn't ask for ID, though I have my fake passport ready. He's too busy counting bank notes.

The girl's photo is no longer on the front pages and, in this remote backwater, her name isn't on people's lips. I don't think anyone will be looking for her here, after all this time, but I can't be sure.

I'm careful when we go out, because people might be looking for me, too.

Every day, when I check online, I wonder if today's the day I'll see my own face staring back at me.

I can't believe no one's made the connection. For all my caution and planning, I couldn't tie up every loose thread. One tug in the right place and my carefully constructed world will unravel.

But with every day that goes by, I feel a little less anxious about being discovered, a little more confident no one's coming for the child.

She's stopped asking where her 'mummy' is, now. She doesn't demand to go home any more.

She knows how upset it makes me.

chapter 47

quinn

Quinn admires Zealy's tight arse as she follows her into a bright, open-plan sitting room with a spectacular million-dollar view across the Thames. There must be family money here somewhere or maybe a sugar-daddy; Zealy Cardinal is a dance teacher with a struggling studio in Islington and there's no way she could afford the Chihuly glass sculpture on the bookshelf or those Mies van der Rohe Barcelona chairs if she wasn't being bankrolled by someone.

Zealy folds herself gracefully into one of the chrome and leather chairs, tucking her bare feet beneath her. Quinn's eyes are drawn to her nipples, clearly visible beneath her white cashmere tunic.

'You've got fifteen minutes,' Zealy says.

Quinn puts her phone on the glass coffee table between them. 'Mind if I record this?' She indicates her withered arm. 'I find it difficult to take notes.'

'Fine.'

'What can you tell me about Catherine Lord?'

Zealy looks disconcerted. 'Catherine? You said on the phone you had information about my brother.'

'Bear with me. I'll get to that.'

Zealy plays with the slender silver bangle on her wrist. Her fingers are long and elegant, like the rest of her. 'I can't tell you anything,' she says finally. 'I don't really know her.'

'But your brother is close to her?'

'Not really. Marc coached her at college. She's Sian's friend, not his. He introduced them, that's all.'

'Have you seen Catherine since the wedding?' Quinn asks. 'No.'

'What about your brother? Has he seen her?'

'I don't know. I doubt it. I told you, she was Sian's friend, not his. I shouldn't think he's seen her since the divorce.' She sweeps her hair back from her face, looping the braids in a careless knot at the nape of her neck. 'Look, I don't see what any of this has to do with Marc.'

She's a heartbeat from telling Quinn to leave.

'You don't like Catherine much, do you?' Quinn says mildly.

Abruptly, Zealy leaps up from her two-thousand-dollar chair, clasping her slender arms around herself as if an Arctic blast has swept through the room.

Bingo.

'There's something *off* about her,' Zealy says. 'The whole time we were in Florida, she was just always . . . *there*. Every time you turned around. Listening in corners, watching you. It was weird. And she sucked up to Sian all the time, but I think she actually kind of *hated* her. One of those women who just doesn't like other women, you know?'

Quinn suspects Zealy has met a lot of women like that.

'What about Alexa Martini?' Quinn asks. 'How did Catherine get on with her?'

She shrugs. 'They only spoke a couple of times.'

'Did you ever suspect she might've had something to do with Lottie's disappearance?'

Zealy rubs her upper arms nervously. 'No. Maybe. I don't know.'

252

Quinn turns off the recording on her phone. 'Look, this is off the record,' she says. 'Just between you and me. Whatever you say won't go any further than this room.'

Zealy chews her lip. 'I don't have any proof.'

'I'm not asking for proof. What did your gut tell you, Zealy?'

The other woman's ambivalence plays across her face. She returns to her chair, perching nervously on the arm like a bird ready to take flight.

'I thought at first Catherine was just trying to fit in, you know, like people do when they're kind of on the fringes of things,' she says. 'She hardly knew anyone at the wedding. Sian said she only picked her as a bridesmaid because she needed an ugly one. I know she meant it as a joke, but she was never super nice to Catherine to be honest.' Zealy looks away, an ugly flush stealing across her caramel skin. 'I don't suppose I was, either.'

The ugly one. Quinn feels the familiar tingle along her nerve endings.

That's how Ian Dutton described Catherine, too.

Back in Dubai, Quinn and her cameraman, Phil, had patched Dutton up as best they could.

He'd refused to let them take him to hospital, so they'd poured a quarter-bottle of Scotch into him and settled him on the sofa with an ice pack.

Whoever had beaten him up had been very professional about it. They'd been looking for information, same as Quinn. They'd particularly wanted to know who he'd told about his plans to elope with Sanaa.

Dutton was adamant he hadn't breathed a word to anyone. They'd broken his nose and several ribs before they'd believed him.

'You're sure Sanaa didn't tell anyone either?' Quinn had pressed. 'Not even her parents?'

'They'd have gone straight to Sanaa's husband,' Ian said.

'Maybe someone followed you? Or overheard something?'

'We were careful. No one knew where Sanaa was. There's no way—'

He broke off suddenly.

'What?'

'One of the bridesmaids in Florida. She was like a peeping bloody Tom.' His words were distorted by his broken nose: *peepung bloodeh Tom.* 'I'd forgotten till now. I saw her lurking around one day when I was talking to Sanaa on the phone. I suppose it's possible she overheard me.'

'*Which* bridesmaid?'

He frowned, then winced with pain. 'The ugly one. I forget her name.'

Quinn had her suspicions then, but she's certain of it now: Catherine Lord is the woman who took that video of Ian and Sanaa eloping and sent it to the police.

Either she hated Dutton enough to land him in a world of hurt just for the fun of it, which, given she didn't even know him before the wedding, seems unlikely.

Or she was protecting someone else.

The so-called 'thin man'.

Who did Catherine *really* see carrying a child along the alley by the hotel that night?

two years and seventeen days missing

chapter 48

alex

Jack leans across the table to refill my wine glass and then tops up his own. I have to be up early tomorrow for a Zoom call with a client in Istanbul and this will be my third glass of a very heady Italian red, but I don't stop him.

'To answer your question, Alex, no, I don't think you're being paranoid,' he says. 'But I do think you're tired and under an incredible amount of stress.'

'Subtext: I'm being paranoid.'

'Maybe. But in your place, who wouldn't be?'

His fingers brush mine on the tablecloth. Jack wants to get into my knickers a little bit. I'm not foolish enough to take it personally. He's one of those men who simply loves women; wanting to get in their knickers is his default setting.

I move my hand. 'To paraphrase Oscar Wilde, to have one friend with a dark secret may be regarded as a misfortune,' I say. 'To have three looks like I need new friends.'

'Hardly dark secrets,' Jack says, taking his cue from me and leaning back in his chair, putting a little distance between us. 'Pale grey, at most. Newsflash: your platonic male friend is carrying a very unchaste torch for you. Who'd have thought? And Catherine Lord turned out to have gone to the same college as you, and met the same football coach. As conspiracy theories go, it's not exactly up there with the grassy knoll.'

'Ah, but you're forgetting about Ian Dutton.'

'Yeah, OK. I'll give you Dutton. That was pretty weird.'

'I'm planning a TED talk later in the week: *Poor Judgement or Why We Pick Men Who Elope With Other Women*. It'll be followed by a Q&A on *Sociopaths: the Science of Not Sleeping With*.'

He grins wolfishly. 'You just haven't slept with the right ones.'

If Jack didn't combine his supreme sexual confidence with a nice line in self-deprecation, he'd be insufferable. As it is, he's hard to resist.

I've occasionally taken a man into my bed over the last two years, when the loneliness has been unbearable. The encounters have been physically satisfying, but emotionally uninvolved: it's safer that way.

Jack, on the other hand, is far too risky a proposition. He's attractive on multiple levels and I have no time for a relationship, even if it was on offer. My focus has to be on finding Lottie and I can't afford distractions, however urbane and charming.

'Everyone has secrets, Alex,' Jack says, suddenly serious. 'Dutton's was more operatic than most, but we all have baggage. You could do a deep dive into the background of everyone at that wedding and you'd find something fishy on all of them: affairs, embezzlement, tax fraud—'

'Christ,' I say. 'What sort of friends do you have?'

'Politicians,' Jack says dryly.

'What about you?' I ask. The wine has gone to my head: my tone is more arch than I intend. 'What dark secrets do you have, Jack?'

'I'm married,' Jack says.

I laugh. Jack Murtaugh is famously single, a permanent star in the most-eligible-bachelor firmament of the gossip pages.

Jack doesn't laugh with me.

'Her name's Amira,' he says. 'We met in Libya about nine years ago. She needed to get out of the country in a hurry, so I brought her to the UK. Totally fake marriage. I haven't seen her in at least six years.'

A shadow passes across his face.

'You're not kidding,' I say. 'How d'you keep that quiet?'

'I told you, I have friends in low places.' He swirls the wine in his glass, but doesn't raise it to his lips. 'She lost her entire family in the aftermath of the Arab Spring. I couldn't just leave her there.'

The marriage may be fraudulent, but Jack clearly feels something for his fake wife or he wouldn't have risked his career to help her. I'm curious how they met, but I suspect, even if I asked, he wouldn't tell me.

The waiter clears our plates away. 'I don't know how you've kept this out of the papers,' I say. 'Does the party know?'

'Not even the chief whip. Apart from Amira, you're the only one.' He flashes me a broad smile, the clouds lifting as abruptly as they came. 'With great power comes great responsibility. Use it wisely, Alexa-san.'

Our server returns with two coffees and a small saucer of amaretti biscotti. I take one, unwrapping it and smoothing out the tissue-thin wrapper on the table.

'Lottie used to love these,' I say. 'Luca would do that trick for her, you know, setting it on fire. He'd tell her to make a wish.' My voice is suddenly thick. 'She always wished for a puppy. I said it wasn't fair, a puppy would be lonely stuck at home all day while she was at school—'

Suddenly, there isn't enough air in the room.

Jack takes the wrapper from me and rolls it into a cylinder, and then touches one end of it to the guttering candle on the table between us. My vision is blurred as it catches fire and floats up to the ceiling. Why didn't I just let her get the damned dog?

'Bloody widows,' Jack says. 'Always trying to pull at your heartstrings with their kidnapped baby stories. There was no need to add the puppy.'

I let out a sound that's half-laugh, half-sob.

His hand covers mine, and this time the gesture is honest and straightforward, the consolation of a friend. 'Hang on in there, Alex,' he says. 'If we weren't getting close, someone wouldn't have broken into your study. I don't know how the fuck our information leaked, but I'll find out. Something's going to break soon, I can feel it.'

Me.

I'm suddenly swamped by a tidal wave of pain so intense, it takes my breath away. Time does not heal. Nor does it stop: life goes on, however much of an insult that seems. Grief simply comes along for the ride. The wound is as raw now as the day Lottie was taken, a constant throb of heartache and misery.

Lottie was – is – my greatest achievement. I've never done anything else that matters, nothing of real worth, not in comparison to being her mother. My tragedy is that I didn't realise it until it was too late. I handed off my mothering to Luca, to her grandparents, to strangers at nursery, never knowing what I was giving up.

I'm so angry, so jealous of every mother who still has her child safely beside her. I'm sad *all the time*. People think I'm OK, that I'm getting better, moving forward, and sometimes there are moments when I almost believe it myself.

But these sobbing, agonised convulsions are not the lapses. They're my new normal; this is me all the time now.

The Alexa who copes, who works and smiles and talks and eats, is the front. I remember what normal used to feel like, so I do an impression of that and people buy into it. But I'm not OK.

I'm never going to be OK.

'Let's get out of here,' Jack says, flinging down a sheaf of twenties.

Outside, he hails a black cab and gives the driver my address, climbing into the back seat after me. He says nothing as I howl like a child, snot-nosed and hiccoughing and ugly. He doesn't try to soothe me or touch me. He simply sits vigil with me in my darkness.

Finally, I stop crying, as much from exhaustion as anything else. I close my eyes and rest the side of my head against the cool glass, my body aching all over, as if I've run a marathon.

'I had a son,' Jack says. 'He died.'

I'm too drained to feel anything, even surprise. Instead, there's simply a quiet sense of pieces slotting into place. Six words can tell the story of a man's entire life. *I had a son. He died.* I don't ask any questions because, in the end, what else do I need to know?

'I'm not the person I was before Ramzi,' Jack says. 'I have to remind myself who I used to be, and act like that. And what I've learned, Alex?' His voice is weary. 'What I've learned is that it doesn't matter. We're all acting, all the time.'

We travel in silence as the cab negotiates the short journey to my house, jolting over speed bumps in darkened residential streets. The cabbie double-parks outside and Jack gets out, then extends a hand to help me out. For a moment, I wonder if he's expecting me to invite him in, but then he climbs back into the cab.

'You still have hope, Alex,' he says, reaching for the door strap. 'Hold onto it. Trust me, it isn't always better to know.'

The cab idles in the road until I've safely reached my front door, its distinctive rumble echoing in the street. I watch Jack's tail-lights disappear and almost trip on an Amazon delivery box as I open my door.

I bend to pick it up. It's the only reason I see the sudden movement from the shadows behind me.

I swing around, my arm raised in self-defence. My forearm makes contact with flesh and bone, and there's a sickening crunch.

The motion sensor on the house next door suddenly trips, illuminating my scrubby patch of front garden.

'Christ almighty,' I say, as I see the face of my assailant for the first time.

chapter 49

alex

'Jesus H. Christ!' Quinn Wilde cries, staggering backwards. 'What the fuck! You've broken my nose!'

I have no sympathy. The woman jumped out at me from the shadows in the middle of south London at close to midnight. What did she think would happen?

Coolly, I pick up the Amazon box from the steps. 'Fuck off, Quinn,' I say, pushing open my front door.

'You're just going to leave me here?'

'Looks that way.'

The woman tries to stem the bleeding with her good hand, but she's struggling to keep her balance. 'Would you just help me the fuck inside?' she says.

Even under the best of circumstances, I'm not kindly disposed towards journalists, especially the bitch who eviscerated me on live television. But blood is pouring from her nose and I can't leave her exsanguinating on the street.

I indicate curtly for her to come in. 'Five minutes, then you're gone.'

She shoves past me. I fasten the security bolt, take off my coat and join her in the kitchen where she's sitting at my tiny breakfast table like she owns the place, her head tilted back. 'I need ice! Come on!'

'For God's sake,' I mutter, but I get her an ice pack from the freezer.

'What the fuck is wrong with you?' she says, her single eye fixing me with a malign glare as she holds the ice to her face. 'Do you try out your fucking ninja moves every time someone comes to the door?'

'Give me a break. You shouldn't have crept up on me.'

I take a bottle of single malt from the kitchen cabinet and pour myself a thick finger without asking if she'd like one. I knock a third of it back in a single gulp. 'Why are you here?'

'First off, I don't want to hear any shit from you,' she says. 'I'm not your favourite person, I get that. And trust me, I don't like you either.'

'Good to know.'

She shifts in the kitchen chair, clearly in pain. I could ask her if she'd like to move to the sitting room, to more comfortable chairs, but I don't.

'I've been covering this story since the beginning,' she says. 'I don't use official channels. There's a kid who works for me, Danny. He's a private investigator and brilliant at what he does. A lot better than the guy who's been fleecing your Foundation for the past two years.'

'Low bar,' I say.

'No shit, Alex.'

I shrug, but take another slug of my drink and let her finish.

'Danny tracked Ian Dutton down to Dubai, where he's been living since he skipped town.' Her blue gaze suddenly sharpens. 'But you knew that, didn't you? Someone got to him before we did and I'll bet you know something about that, too.'

'Where's this going, Quinn?'

'Catherine Lord. Well, Catherine Harding, these days, of course.'

Now she has my attention.

In and of itself, the fact that Harriet's childhood friend went to the same college as me and met the same football coach isn't that remarkable. Six degrees of separation connect us all. It could just be coincidence that Cathy became friends with my best friend's fiancée and ended up a bridesmaid at Marc's wedding.

But two weeks ago, I saw Lottie on a train with a woman who was wearing the logo of the holiday home where Cathy grew up. That feels like one coincidence too many to me.

I take a second tumbler from the cupboard and pour Quinn a whisky. 'OK. I'm listening,' I say, holding it out to her.

She hesitates for a moment, and then takes it. 'Ever wondered why Paul Harding married Catherine?' she asks.

We all have. On paper, Paul and Zealy were a much better match. But Paul was a player, with a girl in every port; even Zealy, gorgeous, sexy, eligible Zealy, couldn't seal the deal. And then, just three months after Marc and Sian's wedding, he suddenly married *Catherine*, a girl he'd never even looked at twice.

'Just spit it out, Quinn,' I say.

She cradles her glass against her chest, but doesn't drink it. 'I don't think the thin man ever existed,' she says. 'I think Catherine made him up, to protect Paul, and he married her to keep her quiet.'

'Wait. *What*?'

'I think Catherine knows what kind of man Paul is,' Quinn says. 'I think she's always known, but she doesn't care. She listened at doors and peeped through keyholes at that wedding, waiting for her chance. And when Lottie disappeared, she invented the whole spiel about the thin man to throw everyone off the scent.'

'What kind of man Paul is?' I repeat.

'Do you really need me to spell it out?'

My first instinct is to defend him. Paul Harding has been one of the Foundation's most loyal supporters from the beginning. There's never been any suggestion he likes little girls. He likes *women*. If Quinn had told me he was screwing around on Catherine, I'd believe it. But children? He's just not that kind of man.

If the last two years have taught me anything, it's that there's no such thing as *not that kind of man*.

Paul and Catherine.

Lottie would have trusted them both.

chapter 50

alex

'You're basing all of this on what, Quinn?' I demand. 'A hunch, or do you have hard evidence?'

'My investigator, Danny, he's pretty good at the tech stuff,' Quinn says. 'He knows his way around the dark web. He used to work for the National Crime Agency's online task force, infiltrating paedophile and human trafficking rings. He's got the kind of contacts money can't buy.'

I've become all too familiar with the sort of websites she means. I wish I didn't know there are dark places where you can browse a catalogue for obscene images of children, as if shopping for shoes. You can even filter by age or hair colour. Only two percent of dark websites are paedophile sites, but they account for more than eighty percent of dark web traffic.

How many men are out there, online right now, right this second, searching for a little girl with red plaits, or a four-year-old boy with blue eyes? How can we live in a world where we let this happen?

If four-fifths of dark web traffic was terrorists, not paedophiles, we'd be throwing billions of pounds at the problem. We'd be collaborating globally in the way we do when national security is at stake. Instead, all we have are a few tech geeks trying to reel them in, one at a time, from their back bedrooms.

'This IT guy you use,' I say. 'Danny. He's in contact with these people?'

'Yes. He's been doing this for years.' She grimaces. 'I don't know how he has the stomach for it. He has to build a relationship with them and gain their trust. It's the only way to get access to their websites.'

'How?'

She rolls the whisky around her glass. 'He has to provide images of children nobody's ever seen before.'

My stomach churns. 'Where does he get them?'

'He keeps back some of the material he finds in other investigations, to use as currency in new ones,' Quinn says. 'Fuck. The stuff he's seen, I don't know how he sleeps at night.'

My mouth is dry. I'm terrified of the answer, but I have to ask the question.

'Has he . . . has he seen—?'

'For the last nine months, he's been asking about Lottie,' Quinn says. 'Have they got pictures, have they heard of any videos. So far, the answer has always been no.'

'No?'

'I don't think she's out there,' Quinn says. 'Not in that world.'

The band around my chest eases, just a little. Ever since I saw Lottie on the Tube, and realised she was still alive, I've been tormented by the idea she's being passed around one of these horrific sex rings, trafficked between monsters like so much human cargo.

'If she was with these people, Danny would have heard something by now,' Quinn says, with surprising kindness. 'Lottie is a high-profile prize. I don't know what's happened to your daughter, Alex. I'm not saying she's alive. But I don't think she's being trafficked.'

'So you think Paul has her?'

'I don't know if he took Lottie. But he *is* part of a paedophile

268

ring Danny infiltrated.' She puts her glass down, untouched. 'Harding's good at covering his digital tracks, but not good enough. Danny's given the police enough evidence on him, and twenty-two more of these bastards, for them to make arrests. They may even be able to find some of these kids and rescue them.'

'What about Lottie?'

'I'm sorry, Alex. I don't know. I wish I could tell you. The Hardings are the only ones who might know that.'

The whisky curdles in my gut. I trusted that man. I welcomed him into my house. I shared meals with him, I let him hug me and literally cried on his shoulder. How could I not have *known*?

And what about Catherine? If she knew – if she even *suspected* – he'd taken Lottie, how could she say nothing? How could she *protect* him?

If she'd spoken up, maybe we'd have found my little girl in time. Maybe the nightmare would've ended before it'd even begun.

I make it upstairs to the bathroom just in time. When I have vomited until I'm bringing up nothing but bile, I rock back on my heels and wipe the snot and tears from my face.

Until now, I haven't wasted time hating the monster who took my child, not wanting to give him space in my head. I had to concentrate on finding Lottie. Revenge could come later, once my girl was safe in my arms.

But the bastard didn't have a face before.

two years and eighteen days missing

chapter 51

alex

I sleep better than I have in weeks. I've made my decision and even though I know there'll be no going back, it's oddly liberating to realise you've got nothing to lose.

At 6.30 a.m, I wake just as dawn is breaking. Flinging back the covers with new energy, I strip off yesterday's crumpled clothes and step into the shower, turning the setting all the way to cold. The freezing water takes my breath away, but I need to be sharp and focused.

I'm not waiting for the wheels of justice to grind slowly, if they grind at all. The police have had two years to find my daughter. I'm not going to risk letting them fuck this up, charging in in their size elevens. It's up to me now.

Pulling on a pair of jeans and a sweatshirt, I sit down on the bed to lace my trainers and braid my wet hair into a French plait to get it out of my face. I send a quick text to cancel the Zoom call I had scheduled with my client, and another to my colleague, James, asking him to take over the case for me.

When I go downstairs, I'm taken aback to find Quinn Wilde sitting on the floor of my living room, her back against the wall, legs outstretched.

'What the hell?' I exclaim. 'Have you been here all night?'

She doesn't look up. 'Obviously.'

She's staring with unnerving intensity at the untouched tumbler of whisky I poured for her last night, which she's placed on the floor between her feet. I have no idea what she's doing and I care even less.

'Why are you still here?'

'Because if I'd left, I'd have gone straight to the off-licence and bought myself a bottle of Jack Daniel's, and I'd be at the bottom of it right now.' She finally looks up. 'Trust me, once I know what happened to your daughter, I'll fall into that bottle and not climb out for a month. But I've been sober two hundred and three days and until I get this story, I'm off the sauce.'

She's not my responsibility. She's an adult, capable of making her own choices, and I didn't ask her to turn up at my house in the middle of the night. I didn't tell her to quit drinking or obsess over this story.

'Go home,' I say.

'Help me up.'

Awkwardly, I extend a hand and she stumbles to her feet. 'You need to take me to a meeting,' she says.

'What?'

'An AA meeting,' she says, impatiently. 'There's one in thirty minutes at the primary school down the road. I looked it up.'

'I'm not taking—'

'You owe me,' Quinn says.

'The fuck I do!'

'Then I'm sure you won't feel bad when I end up dead in a ditch.'

'Fine,' I say. 'If it'll get rid of you. Get in the car.'

'I could use a coffee first—'

'Don't fucking push it.'

She follows me out to my car. I don't offer to help when

274

she struggles with the seatbelt and I don't try to make conversation. I don't want anything I say now to be used against me later, when everything comes out.

'Where are you going?' Quinn asks as we turn onto Tooting Bec Road.

'I'm taking you to your bloody meeting.'

'And after?'

'None of your business.'

'Stay away from him,' she says.

I don't insult us both by pretending I don't know who she means.

'The fucker deserves to be hung by his balls with piano wire,' Quinn says. 'But he's your last, best hope to find Lottie. You need to be smart about this, Alex. Don't rush over there and blow it.'

The traffic snarls ahead of us, forcing me to a halt.

'I'm serious, Alex. You won't get another shot if you drive him underground.'

I don't want to hear this. Paul Harding knows where Lottie is. I want to beat down his door and shake it out of him.

'Let the cops do their job,' Quinn says. 'If she's still alive, they'll get her back.'

'What do you mean, *if*?'

Quinn shrugs, but doesn't answer my question.

'Do you think she's still alive?' I say.

'There's a chance he's got her stashed away somewhere,' Quinn says. 'A second home somewhere in Wales—'

'You don't really believe that, do you?'

'No,' she says, baldly. 'I think she's dead. I think she died within hours of being taken.'

The breath rushes from my lungs. 'But I *saw* her—'

'You asked me what I thought.'

The car ahead of us starts to move. Neither Quinn nor I

speak again until I pull up in front of the primary school and park.

'You're going to his house anyway, aren't you?' she says. 'Fuck. *Fuck.* Fine. I'm coming with you.'

'Get out, Quinn. This has nothing to do with you.'

Quinn twists in her seat. Her single blue eye conveys scorn and irritation in equal measure. 'Like hell it doesn't,' she snaps. 'I told you about Harding. This'll lead straight back to me. You think I'm going to let you go over there and make me an accessory to assault or murder?' She slams her head back against the headrest. 'Goddamn. I should never have told you about this till after he was arrested.'

'You told me because you wanted a good story,' I say. 'Well, here you go.'

'Fuck. You're enough to drive anyone to drink.'

'I didn't ask you to get involved. Go to your meeting, Quinn.'

Quinn stubbornly stays where she is. I shrug and plug Paul's address into my sat nav. If she thinks she's going to stop me with her impromptu sit-in, she's mistaken.

I've got more important things to worry about than Quinn Wilde.

My world has narrowed to a single, primal impulse: to get to Paul Harding and find my daughter.

I can't think beyond that.

I can't think at all.

chapter 52

alex

As soon as we turn onto Paul's street, I realise I'm too late.

The road is blocked by three police vehicles, all with their lights flashing. Clusters of neighbours gawk from the pavements. An officer stands in the middle of the street ahead of us, arm raised, palm outwards, halting traffic.

'Shit,' Quinn says. 'I didn't think they'd get here this quickly.'

Paul's glossy black front door abruptly opens. He's escorted down the steep flight of steps to the street by two police officers. He's not in handcuffs, but it's clear he's not with them voluntarily. One of the policemen even shields his head as he ducks into the police car waiting for them, as if this were a gritty televised drama.

Catherine appears at the top of the steps, still in her dressing gown. She watches, ashen-faced, as the police drive her husband away. I'm shocked to realise she's seven or eight months pregnant. I haven't seen her in a while and Paul never mentioned it.

'Find a place to park,' Quinn says.

'What's the point?' I smack my hand on the steering wheel. 'For fuck's sake, Quinn! You couldn't have waited before calling this in?'

'And leave the kids in those videos where they are for one more day?'

She's right. Lottie isn't the only child who matters, even if she's the only child who matters to *me*.

'I'm going home, Quinn,' I say, wearily. 'Obviously I can't talk to Paul now.'

'You can still talk to *her*. Come on, Alex. Get with the programme. We need to speak to her before she lawyers up.'

I reverse a few metres down the road and turn into a side street, driving slowly between the banks of parked cars until I spot a free space.

Quinn gets out as soon as the car stops moving, but I hesitate. The woman I saw with Lottie on the train was definitely not pregnant. It can't have been Catherine.

The certainty that brought me here suddenly ebbs. Maybe Catherine isn't involved, after all. She's *pregnant*. What sort of mother would knowingly have a child with a paedophile?

Quinn's already heading down the street towards Paul's house. 'Wait!' I call.

She turns. 'Don't get soft on me now.'

'I don't think Catherine has anything to do with—'

'Get real, Alex,' Quinn says, harshly. 'Even if Harding didn't take your daughter, Catherine *thought* he did. She invented the thin man, just in case. She *protected* him. And then she doubled down and took that video of Ian Dutton. She went to a lot of trouble to set him up and derail the investigation.' Her expression is scornful. 'Now you want to give her a pass just because she's knocked up?'

She takes off again. By the time I catch up with her, we're almost at Paul's house. Catherine has spotted me and is rushing down her front steps, her dressing gown flapping loose.

'Alex!' she exclaims. 'Thank God you're here! I can't believe what's happening, you have to . . .' She breaks off as Quinn takes advantage of the distraction to slip into the house. 'Who's that woman?' she says, uncertainly. 'Is she with you?'

'Unfortunately,' I say. 'Catherine, what did the police say? Why've they arrested Paul? Did they tell you?'

Catherine glances at the clusters of people still gawking in the street. I usher her inside, away from prying eyes and mobile phone cameras.

'It's ridiculous,' she says. 'It's obviously all a terrible misunderstanding. Paul's already called his solicitor to sort it out. You *know* Paul, how could anyone think—'

'Did they say anything about Lottie?' I ask bluntly.

'Lottie?' Catherine is suddenly wary. 'What does she have to do with this?'

'Please, Catherine. Where is she?'

'Mrs Harding, don't say another word.'

A woman in a charcoal trouser suit storms up the front steps and in through the front door, which no one has yet thought to shut. She pushes past me and steps in front of Catherine, as if ready to take a bullet for her.

'Mrs Harding, your husband called me,' she says. 'My name is Rebecca Miller. I'm a criminal lawyer.'

'I don't need—'

'Please, Mrs Harding. Let me do my job. I don't know who you people are,' she adds, as Quinn appears at the end of the hall behind us, 'but you need to leave.'

'Catherine, please,' I beg. 'If you know anything about Lottie—'

'*Now.*'

I'm about to protest, but the words die on my lips. I exit the house without another word.

Quinn has no choice but to leave with me. But as soon as we reach the street, she grabs my elbow, furiously spinning me towards her. 'You're going to give up, just like that?'

I shake her off. 'I told you before, this has nothing to do with you. You're not my friend, Quinn. You're a bloody jackal. Call yourself a fucking Uber and go home.'

I leave her standing in the street and go back to my car.

Quinn yells something after me, and then scowls and pulls out her phone. I wait till I'm sure she's not watching and then flip over the silver frame I just stole from Catherine's hall table.

Carefully, I prise off the velvet hardboard backing to extract the photo. There's a note scrawled in Biro on the back of the picture: *Ellie & me, South Weald Bay, summer 2019*.

It's the woman from the train.

In the wake of your friend's arrest, our hearts go out to you, but the truth is it's time to find some peace . . .

By Hannah Foster for the Sunday Post

Dear Alexa,

Can it really be two years since your little daughter Lottie disappeared? Since her three-year-old face first began to haunt us?

Who can forget her fierce expression blazing out at us from posters that went up everywhere, from airports to village shops.

Could she still be alive? Is she the prisoner of some twisted individual? I know that must be your deepest fear – indeed, it doesn't bear thinking about.

The fact that the evil sickness of paedophilia has now reached your inner circle must have shocked you to your core.

A man you trusted, who worked alongside you in the search for your daughter, turns out to be a monster.

How devastating that must be.

The scandal now engulfing the Lottie Foundation will pass, however soul-destroying it must seem now.

It's to your eternal credit that you've remained so resolutely optimistic, restating at every opportunity your unswerving belief that somehow, one day, Lottie will come back to you.

Over the years we've shared your hope and your nightmares. We've obsessed over the events of that fatal evening she went missing along with you. You must have relived those hours a million times and so have we.

So I hope it doesn't sound too callous to suggest that two years later, the world has moved on. Not because we have forgotten Lottie, but because time helps us heal and we forget, whether we want to or not.

No doubt that's what motivated you to give your impromptu press conference on the front steps of your house yesterday. To remind us. To shake us into caring again.

Clearly you are still tormented by not knowing what happened to your daughter and it's obvious that your agony is caused not just by loss, but by guilt, because you weren't there when she needed you most.

How else to explain what happened at Victoria station in London two weeks ago?

No one blames you for grasping at straws, but it's become painfully obvious to those who care about you that your pain has simply become too much to bear.

You saw what you wanted to see.

The terrible truth is, the chance that Lottie is still alive – never mind in London, 4000 miles from where she disappeared – is vanishingly small. Yet still you yearn to know what happened to her and who can blame you for that?

Perhaps if her body is found, you might finally achieve a glimmer of peace and be able to move on with your life. Maybe if you knew the truth, no matter how tragic that truth is, you might find it easier to bear.

You are not alone. Parents who lose children have told me how important it is to have something, even a body, to centre their grief on.

But two years on from Lottie's tragic disappearance, we have no more idea what became of her now than we did then.

The public's fascination with the story has been matched

only by the exorbitant amount of time and money spent on trying to solve the mystery.

First we had a nationwide US police investigation, which put the full resources of the most powerful country in the world at your disposal, to no avail.

Next came private detectives like Simon Green, who failed to locate Lottie despite trousering more than £500,000 in fees.

Then, at the behest of your local MP, the indefatigable Jack Murtaugh, Scotland Yard were called in.

An eye-watering £3 million of taxpayers' money has now been spent on the search, with no sign of a breakthrough.

Every witness statement and tip-off has been rechecked, every theory considered, no matter how unlikely. Each development raises fresh hopes and excites the media, but so far they have all come to nothing.

All of which goes to explain why the chief officer of the force, Ben Rich, has now suggested it might be time to pull the plug.

Mr Rich's remarks have inevitably sparked heated debate. #TeamLottie insists that the investigation must continue at any cost, but others have praised the officer for having the courage to voice the unsayable truth.

With a very heavy heart, I must say I agree with Mr Rich.

As the grandmother of three children who are roughly the same age as Lottie when she was taken and similarly cherubic, I dread to imagine how it must feel to be living in purgatory like you.

If, God forbid, I was in your shoes, I would want, demand and plead that everything humanly possible must be done to find my daughter, or, at the very least, to discover what became of her.

Like you, I would cling to the hope of a miracle, too.

No one is blaming you, Alexa.

On the contrary, the charity you set up, the Lottie Foundation, has done a huge amount to raise public awareness of missing children. You've become an unofficial global ambassador for the cause.

Despite everything that's happened, nothing can take away from that.

But after two years of false dawns and epic wild goose chases, I have come to the same conclusion as Ben Rich: enough is enough.

When I saw you on television this week, I was shocked by how vulnerable you seem and how unhappy. And no wonder.

Be assured, we have not forgotten Lottie or you. But grief, mourning and a carefully created memorial can bring healing.

And although we would not wish you to lose your commitment, we hope you find comfort in the knowledge that Lottie's name will live on in the foundation you set up.

Wishing you happiness as ever,

Hannah

two years and nineteen days missing

chapter 53

alex

I hold the photo up against my car window, comparing it to the landscape spread below me.

I'm in the right place; there's the same distinctive rock, shaped like a camel's hump, rising out of the sea a few hundred metres offshore. In the snap, which must have been taken on this same clifftop overlook, Catherine has her arm around the other woman – Ellie – and they're both smiling at the camera.

I toss the photo onto the passenger seat and pull back out onto the road.

South Weald village is a small place. I don't know Ellie's surname but, if she lives in the area, I'll find her. And it's a fair bet she does, given that Catherine grew up here.

A light November drizzle starts to fall as I follow the winding cliff-top road down to the village. I peer through the rain-smeared windscreen, looking for the turnoff to South Weald House. Even though the B&B has been sold into private hands, it's still as good a place to start as any. And I seem to remember it's only a few doors down from the village shop. Somebody there might recognise the photo.

But when I pull into the circular gravel driveway outside South Weald House, it's in total darkness. Clearly, no one is home. And then I remember it's Sunday afternoon: the village shop will be shut, too. I should've thought about that before I drove all the way down here from London.

Wearily, I park by the side of the road and get out to stretch my legs, which are stiff after five hours cramped behind the wheel. I tug the hood of my sweatshirt up over my head to protect myself from the rain, which is now coming down in earnest, and trudge down the road, wondering what to do next.

Jack was right: this is a wild goose chase. He told me last night not to come rushing down here. I should have listened to him. The police have Paul in custody; with all the evidence they have against him, surely it'll be in his interests to do a deal and tell them where Lottie is?

Assuming he knows, of course.

I finally face a truth I've been refusing to acknowledge: Paul probably passed my daughter on to one of the other bastards in his paedophile ring after he was finished with her. Who knows how many hands my baby has passed through since she was stolen from me? Paul may have no idea where she is now.

A delivery van swooshes through the puddles, drenching my jeans. It's not yet three in the afternoon, but it's already getting dark. I should just go back to my car and drive home, but I can't face leaving the village without getting some answers.

What if Paul *isn't* the one who took Lottie?

Given his proclivities, it's logical to assume he's guilty, but I can't shake my doubts. Ellie was the woman I saw with Lottie on the train, and Ellie is *Catherine's* friend. Maybe Catherine is the one who took her, though it seems hard to believe Paul wouldn't have known.

The questions swarm in my head like angry bees. *Who is Ellie to Catherine?*

Why would she have Lottie? How did Catherine and Paul get my daughter back to the UK undetected?

And always, *always*, the only question that really matters: *Where is she now?*

I round a bend in the road, shoulders hunched against the rain, and see the delivery van parked outside a stone pub on the left with a commanding view of the sea. It's the same pub my parents used to come every night when Harriet and I were secretly watching TV. I've never been inside, but my imagination conjures a cosy village inn with horse brasses and a roaring fire, an anachronistic blue fug of tobacco smoke swirling beneath its low ceilings. I could use some warmth and a bite to eat.

I push open the door. There is a fireplace, but it's not lit. The ancient beams have been painted white, and the stark decor owes more to chilly Scandi noir than *Midsomer Murders*.

It's not busy. I show the photo of Ellie to the few customers nursing pints at the bleached oak tables, but none of them recognise her. Perhaps my idea of the close-knit village community where everyone knows each other is as outdated as my assumptions about country pub decor.

'You could try the café,' the girl behind the bar offers. Her accent is strongly Eastern European and a snake tattoo writhes from her shoulder to her wrist. 'Louise knows everyone. She's there every day. Just follow the road along the cliff for a couple of miles, and you'll see it.'

I thank her and return to my car, not wanting to linger in the unwelcoming pub. It's stopped raining and, as I drive towards the café, the low winter sun casts a haunting monochromatic light across the landscape.

The beach below is almost deserted, other than a few hardy souls walking their dogs down by the water's edge. A biting wind crests the waves with white horses, bucking against the leaden sky.

It doesn't take long to find the café, which, judging from the lone car parked outside, is as deserted as the pub. South Weald is a summer village; its population increases tenfold in the months of July and August, during which time it makes enough money from holidaymakers to see it through the year. On a wet Sunday in November, the only patrons are locals.

I prefer it out of season, windswept and desolate. It matches my mood.

Unlike the pub, the café is warm and welcoming. Mismatched but inviting armchairs and sofas take up the bulk of the space with a small children's section in the corner filled with shelves of battered picture books and boxes of Lego. A small boy is kneeling on the floor beside two women sharing a squishy cinnamon sofa, writing his name in the condensation on the window with his finger.

Behind a counter, a young man with surfer hair is doing something complicated with a coffee steamer, all chrome pipes and frothing milk. He fills two thick-rimmed, chunky mugs with foaming liquid and takes them over to the two women.

There are no other customers and, when he returns to the counter, I order a thick wedge of homemade cheddar and asparagus quiche as much out of pity as hunger.

He doesn't recognise the photo of Ellie, and neither do the two women.

'You should ask Louise,' one of them says. 'She knows everyone. She's swimming now, but she'll be back soon to close up.'

I cast a glance at the pewter sea. The woman laughs. 'She swims in all weathers. Part seal, if you ask me.'

The quiche is surprisingly good and I wolf it down. By the time I finish, it's dark outside. I can't imagine swimming in this weather. I hope Louise turns up soon. I've got a long drive back to London.

The bell over the door rings as a woman comes in with her dog. The surfer kid crouches down beside the animal, a beautiful Irish setter, roughhousing with him for a few moments, to the dog's obvious delight.

The woman holds the door open, letting in an icy draft. She's clearly another customer, not the Amazonian swimmer Louise; her hair is dry and she's not alone.

'Come on, Flora!' she calls to the child behind her. 'Stop dawdling. We can get you another Squishmallow.'

'I want Henry! We have to find him!'

A little girl of about six erupts into the café. She's wearing an old-fashioned purple bobble hat, the kind a grandma might knit you for Christmas. I can't see her hair, but I don't need to.

She stops dead when she sees me.

'Mummy?' she says.

chapter 54

alex

The little girl backs towards the woman holding the café door open, taking refuge in the safety of her skirts.

'Mummy?' she says again, pulling the woman's hand. 'Can we go home now?'

I've frightened her. The intensity of my hunger must show in my face, but I can't look away. It takes every ounce of self-control not to run towards her and sweep her into my arms.

The world is full of girls who look like Lottie. A thousand girls, a million girls: girls the same age, the same height and weight. The mind plays tricks, I know this; the mind is not to be trusted; as everyone keeps telling me, you see what you want to see. You spot a girl turning the corner of the aisle at the supermarket, and you drop the glass jar of mayonnaise you were holding and don't even notice as it smashes on the ground. You shove shoppers out of the way as you run towards her, desperate to catch her before she disappears like a mirage. And then she turns round and you realise it isn't her. It hits you like a punch to the gut and you heave breath into your lungs as you back away, mumbling apologies. *It isn't her.*

She's just ten feet away. It's her. She's so tall and *thin*. She has cheekbones now, and her legs are long and rangy in jeans and a pair of navy wellington boots covered with tiny red printed hearts.

Her blue eyes meet mine and I know this is Lottie. Not a mirage, not a dream, not a girl-who-looks-like-her.

Lottie herself.

Real, flesh and blood.

I drink her in. I'm afraid to blink, in case this miracle vanishes. Lottie. My Lottie.

Not a dream of her. *Her.*

'Go and sit with Toof,' the woman says, giving the girl a little push. 'I'll get you some hot chocolate.'

'Can I have a biscuit?'

'*May* I. And I didn't hear you say please.'

'Please,' the girl says.

She's close enough for me to reach out and touch her as she goes over to the dog. She drops to her knees beside him and wreathes her arms around his russet body, laying her cheek against the top of his head.

There's something unfamiliar about her, something different that I don't remember and can't place; the tilt of her jaw, perhaps; the expression in her eyes. It's been two years, I remind myself. Of course she's changed.

I know she won't remember me. Memory is plastic, even in adults; explicit memories, the conscious recall associated with a time and a place, a *person*, don't start to form until a child is six or seven. Before that, memory is implicit, an unconscious, emotional recollection. Lottie was three when she was taken from me; she's spent a third of her life, the most recent, vivid third, without me. But I'm her *mother*. Deep down, surely she recognises that?

'Sit down properly, Flora,' the woman says. 'On a chair, please.'

The girl sighs and scrambles into a chair. She tugs off her

purple bobble hat and I see her hair has been cropped to her shoulders. It's darker than it used to be; darker, even, than I remember from the train.

The woman she called Mummy is not the same woman I saw on the Tube. She's at least thirty years older and has severe, salt-and-pepper hair. Biologically, she can't be this child's mother. She's too old. I have no idea who she is or what her relation to Ellie might be.

I slide my phone out of my pocket and pretend to be checking my emails as I surreptitiously take a photograph of the two of them. The police will have to believe me now. They'll be able to use facial recognition to identify the little girl as Lottie and that'll be enough for them to get a warrant for DNA to prove it. I text the picture to Jack, along with our location.

The surfer kid brings over their order – hot chocolate and a great wheel of shortbread for the girl, black coffee for the woman – and puts a bowl of water on the floor for the dog.

Lottie wraps both hands around her thick china mug, but the woman cautions her that it's hot and admonishes her to wait. Lottie puts the mug down again. *That's* what's different, I realise suddenly. The old Lottie would have ignored the instruction and burned her tongue.

Her gaze returns to me. Something about me is nagging at her, I can tell. Her brow creases, her nose crinkling. She knows me, but she doesn't know why.

The woman sees the girl staring and turns to look. It suddenly occurs to me that if she recognises me, if she realises who I am, all is lost. I could grab Lottie, here, now, but I can't physically escape with her. If I try, the woman and the surfer kid will stop me, and the police will be called, and, no matter what I say, there's a risk they'll return Lottie to this woman while they untangle the truth.

I have no credibility left after what happened in London.

By the time the police establish Lottie is mine, my daughter will be gone. The woman will run with her and I may never find her again.

But the woman doesn't recognise me. 'Finish your hot chocolate, Flora,' she says, turning back to the girl. 'We need to get home.'

I leave a couple of pound coins on the table beside my plate and go out to my car. I wait for them to come out, glad of the concealment afforded by the darkness and heavy rain. Jack still hasn't responded to my text, and I'm not letting Lottie out of my sight. I'll sleep outside their house if I have to.

Fifteen minutes later, the café door opens, spilling a wedge of golden light into the gravel car park. I assume they'll get into the only other vehicle parked in the lot, an old Volvo estate, but they walk past it, onto the main road, and I realise with a flicker of alarm they're walking home. I don't know why I assumed they'd driven here and parked before taking a walk along the beach. How can I follow them now?

After a few moments' hesitation, I get out of my car and head after them on foot. I don't want to get too close, but there are no streetlights along this section of the coast road and I can't risk losing them. I do my best to hug the shadows, terrified the sound of my breathing will give me away.

I'm soaked to the skin within minutes, my feet sloshing around in my thin plimsolls. I can hear Lottie up ahead, stamping and splashing in the puddles, clearly enjoying the inclement weather.

There's a dangerous moment when I nearly run into them as I round a corner, where they've stopped to wait for the dog to complete his business. I shrink back into the hedge, my heart thumping, but the rain and the sound of the waves crashing on the shore below covers any noise I make.

Less than fifty metres later, they stop in front of a small

stone cottage beside the road. The woman unlocks the front door and turns on the porch light. Lottie sits down on the thick stone step and starts to pull off her wellingtons. She stops, midway, and stares intently into the darkness, and for a second I think she's seen me.

The woman calls her name. She jumps and finishes taking off her boots, before running inside.

I edge closer to the cottage, watching from the other side of the road as a light goes on in the kitchen, and the woman puts on the kettle. I stay there even after she draws the curtains, blocking my view.

I can't believe I've found her. I can't trust the reality of this moment, because it's too incredible to be true. My daughter. In a café in Devon, four thousand miles from where I let her go. Lottie, splashing through puddles in her wellington boots. Lottie *alive*.

There's so much I want to know. Has she been here the whole time? Does she believe this woman is her mother?

Does she remember me?

I spot something pink lying in the dirt by the side of the road and pick it up between thumb and forefinger. It's a stuffed toy: the Squishmallow she lost.

My pulse racing, I cross the road and put the pink toy on the front step. It's wet, but clean; a few hours in a warm kitchen and it'll be good as new.

As I step back from the threshold, I see a movement out of the corner of my eye.

It's her. She's pulled back a corner of the curtain and is kneeling on a kitchen chair, looking directly at me.

Not daring to breathe, I lift my finger to my lips: *ssssh*.

For a long moment, she is motionless. Then, slowly, she presses her finger to her lips, too.

chapter 55

quinn

Quinn doesn't believe in giving people the benefit of the doubt. Nine times out of ten, in a case like Lottie Martini's – abductions, murders – the perp is someone close to the victim. She went hard at Alexa Martini in the beginning because she was trying to get at the truth. She's not going to feel bad about it now.

OK, maybe a bit bad.

But that has nothing to do with why she's committed to this story. *Obsessed*, according to Marnie. Which is fine with Quinn: she can live with obsessed. What she can't live with is failure.

She flips her six-month AA chip in the air and catches it again, slapping it on the back of her hand. Heads I win, tails you lose.

Christ, she wants a drink.

She makes herself a cafetière of strong Panamanian Hacienda La Esmeralda coffee (£90 a pound, but a girl has to have some vices) and settles into a large, comfortable armchair with her laptop. She's set aside the weekend to re-read all the original police interview transcripts from the wedding guests in the light of everything she knows now.

Everyone lies in a police investigation. About who they were with, what they were doing, how much they'd drunk. Rarely does it have any bearing on the case. But now and again, one small white lie has the power to change the course of an investigation. If Ian Dutton hadn't lied by omission, maybe the police wouldn't have been chasing their tails for the last two years.

She begins with the transcripts of the interviews with the members of the wedding party: the tabloids' 'twelve apostles'. She's got no idea what she's looking for, but she'll know it when she sees it.

Two hours later, the only thing she's learned is that Alexa Martini's a lousy judge of character. Apart from Dutton, Paul Harding and Catherine Lord clearly can't be trusted either, and Marc Chapman's not much better, in love with another woman on his wedding day. Alexa needs to pick better friends.

She grinds some more of her gold-plated Panamanian beans and brews another carafe of coffee. It's in here somewhere, she can feel it. The key to everything, buried in pages of banal details about wedding favours and who sat where.

Several wedding guests mention seeing Lottie talking to the bride's mother, the last verified sighting of the little girl, but when Quinn gets to the transcript of Penny Williams' interview, she's surprised to find the woman makes no mention of the conversation.

Mrs Williams recounts verbatim the discussion she had with her daughter's hair stylist and a last-minute panic over whether teal nail varnish on the bride's toenails counted as 'something blue'. And yet she doesn't even mention her conversation with a child who went missing less than an hour after she spoke to her.

Quinn's interrupted by the sound of her phone buzzing on the side table.

Fuck.

Much as she wants to ignore the call, when the editor of INN phones you from her personal mobile on a Sunday afternoon, you take it.

'*Dubai*?' Christie exclaims. 'What the fuck, Quinn?'

'Before you flip out, this is entirely on me,' Quinn says. 'Phil had no idea the trip wasn't sanctioned by the News Desk—'

'Never mind that you made an end-run around the News Desk to pursue your own personal agenda,' Christie interrupts. 'You're our senior UK correspondent, Quinn! You fucked off without a word to anyone, leaving a bloody intern to cover for you, and we got caught with our pants down. The Cambridge explosion led the bulletins on Friday, and we had a twenty-two-year-old kid stammering his way through a two-way on the early evening news. Fucking unprofessional.'

'I'm sorry about that, but if I'd told you what I was doing—'

'I know why you didn't tell me, Quinn. I took you off the story for a reason. Now I'm telling you, once and for all, as your employer and as your friend, to *back off.*'

Quinn knew there would be a price to pay for playing the lone wolf, but she didn't expect it to feel like this. Christie is right: it was beyond unprofessional to leave the UK bureau without proper cover. She should have come clean to her weeks ago, when it became clear her investigation was actually going somewhere. Christie would've taken her off-roster and let her see how far she could get with the story. Now, it's too late.

She's already had more final warnings than the rest of the reporters' desk combined. If she's fired, she won't be able to get a foot in the door of a local free paper, never mind an international news network. Her reputation precedes her and not necessarily to her advantage. She gets results and has the Emmy to prove it, but journalism is a small, incestuous world and she hasn't made friends on the way up.

There won't be many hands to catch her on the way down.

She hurls her phone against the wall in fury and frustration. It smacks to the floor, screen down, and bounces twice, before landing neatly at her feet.

Quinn shoves it in her pocket, grabs her denim jacket and heads for the door.

The kid behind the bar is new since she was last here. He looks about sixteen.

Quinn puts her AA chip down on the bar and pulls up a stool.

The kid looks at the chip, and then at her. 'Sure you should be here?' he says.

'Jack Daniel's,' Quinn says. 'Neat. No ice.'

He shrugs and pours her a single measure.

'Double,' Quinn says.

She finishes it before he's even racked the bottle.

'Again,' she says, rapping the bar with her AA chip.

In her pocket, her phone buzzes. Quinn switches it off without even glancing at the screen.

300

chapter 56

alex

It's impossible to keep watch on the cottage from the road. The house is on a bend, with uninterrupted views in both directions, and there's no cover: the road hugs the coast here and on the opposite side of the road from the cottage is a steep rock face, with no tree to hide behind, no hedges or stone walls. As soon as it gets light, anyone glancing out of the window will see me.

I weigh up the risk. Do I leave now and trust I can get the police to take action before this woman disappears with Lottie? I've no idea if this is a rented holiday cottage; they could be gone tomorrow.

Or do I stay and chance them recognising me and running again?

The front door opens suddenly and I shrink back into the shadows, heart pounding, thankful for the darkness cloaking me. The woman lets the dog out and he sniffs the air, and then immediately runs towards me, barking.

'Toof! Come here, boy.'

The woman comes out onto the porch, silhouetted against the light from the hall. The dog stops running and barks again. He's less than six feet away from me. I should've left when I had the chance. If she sees me now, she'll know I followed them from the café. She'll know I know—

'Stop it, Toof! It's just a rabbit!'

He gives a final bark and then reluctantly turns back. The woman lets him into a small garden to the side of the cottage, where he presumably does his business, and the two of them go back inside.

I don't realise I've been holding my breath until the door shuts behind them. I close my eyes and exhale as my heartbeat slowly returns to normal.

My car is still parked outside the café. I pull out my phone as I walk back to it and call Jack. I need him to get hold of the police and get things moving. If I call them, they won't take me seriously, not after the debacle in London. They'll say I'm *seeing what you want to see*. They'll delegate to the local plod, who may or may not get around to coming out here this week. Or maybe next. They'll sit down with my daughter's kidnappers over a cup of tea and shortbread and admire the view of the sea. *We have to check these things out, you understand. Well, I wouldn't mind another cup, if you're sure it's no trouble.*

Damn it, where *is* Jack? He still hasn't responded to my text, and now he's not answering his phone.

I can't just *leave*, not without my daughter. It's Monday tomorrow: for all I know, the woman may only be renting the cottage for the weekend. I'd feel slightly less frantic if I knew they lived here, but without the resources Jack has at his disposal, there's no way to find out. I don't know anyone else who can—

Quinn.

Like her or not, the woman has an uncanny ability to ferret out information. Maybe having a journalist involved will actually help me for once, putting pressure on the police to get their act together. Quinn Wilde has become part of my story as much as I've become part of hers. I have her number: my phone automatically stored it last time she called me.

But she doesn't answer her mobile either.

chapter 57

alex

The urge to beat down the cottage door and snatch my daughter back is almost as hard to resist as the drive to bear down during childbirth. I force myself to stay in the car, staring unseeingly into the darkness through the teeming rain as I think this through. I can't rush in, like a bull in a china shop. I only have one shot at this. I have to do it the right way, the legal way, or the woman will take Lottie and disappear again.

My phone buzzes and I snatch it up. But it's not Jack or Quinn.

'Alex, you need to come home,' Dad says, without preamble.

'Dad, I can't—'

'We're at the hospital,' Dad says. 'Your mum's not well. We're waiting for her to be seen. We're not sure what's wrong until we see a doctor, but she's in a lot of pain. It's like she's got appendicitis, but it's in the wrong place.'

My stomach goes into free fall. Mum's had cancer twice already; she's in remission, but we all know it could come back at any time.

'Is she going to be OK?'

'Darling, I'm sure she'll be fine, but I think she'd like to see you.'

He doesn't sound like he thinks she's going to be fine.

'I'm out of town right now,' I say, not wanting Dad to know I'm in Devon. He has enough to worry about without thinking I'm chasing phantoms again. 'I'll be back some time tomorrow. I'll come and see her as soon as I can. Can you let me know how she's doing in the morning?'

'There's no rush,' Dad says. 'It's quite busy here tonight. I think we could be in for a long wait.'

'Dad, you need to keep on at them,' I urge. 'Make sure they know she's had cancer. Don't let them just shove her to the back of the queue.'

'I've got this, Alex. Look, I have to go. I'll see you tomorrow.'

He hasn't got this.

My parents are decent, good people. They take their turn, play fair, pay their share, don't make a fuss. Dad will never go up to whoever is managing triage and demand my mother is seen. He'll sit patiently waiting for her name to be called, while a mouthy girl with a stubbed toe creates such havoc she gets whisked to the front of the line just so they can be rid of her. He'd never dream of making a nuisance of himself.

I have no such compunction.

But I can't just leave Lottie. What if the woman disappears with her again? I have to wait here until Jack mobilises the police. I can't let her out of my sight.

I check the live wait times at the Mid-Surrey Hospital. Six hours. Mum can't be left on a trolley for six hours! Dad'll never get her bumped up the queue. And in her immune-compromised state, a wait like that could kill her.

No one should have to choose between their mother and their child. I slam the palm of my hand against the wheel in fury and jump as the horn blares. A light goes on in the café and I freeze in place till it goes off again. I don't want to draw attention to myself.

I have to make a decision. Do I stay or go?

Lottie isn't in imminent danger; she's clearly well-cared-for. My mother is sick and getting sicker. Mum would tell me to stay with my daughter, but if I don't get to the hospital and fight for her, she could die on a hospital trolley waiting to be seen.

I don't think I've ever felt this alone. I'm so *tired*. Tired of having to be strong, of never allowing myself to doubt, of supporting everyone else no matter how defeated and beaten down I feel. My parents have done their best to look out for me and I wouldn't have survived the last two years without the support of everyone at the Foundation, but, at the end of the day, when everyone else has gone back home to their lives and families, I'm alone with my grief. Luca was a lousy husband in many ways, but he was a wonderful father. We didn't agree on much, but we were united in our love for Lottie. No matter our differences, if he'd been here, at least I'd have had someone with whom to share the pain of the last two years, someone who'd understand.

Someone to make me feel just a little less lonely.

My phone buzzes with an incoming text and, as I read it, I realise the decision has been taken out of my hands.

chapter 58

We have to move again soon. We've already been in one place longer than I'd like. But the child seems happier here and I'm tired of fighting her.

She's used to me now and she's accepted her new name – she even calls me Mummy. I trust her enough to let her play on the beach below our new cottage without me and sometimes I take her to a café in the village. She makes friends with the owner's dog, and now and then the man lets us take him down to the beach with us to frolic in the surf. It's the only time I see the child smile.

But then one day a woman stares at us a little too hard when we're in the café, and I'm sure I see her watching us again later, when we're walking back home. Maybe I'm being paranoid, but I haven't stayed one step ahead of the police all this time by taking chances.

I've got too comfortable here. It's time to move on.

The girl won't be pleased when I tell her. Our truce is fragile and she'll blame me for dragging her somewhere new, just when she's got settled. But I'm only trying to protect her. She belongs with me. I can't let them take her away.

I'd rather die.

In the afternoon, while she's playing on the beach, I start packing. We travel light: a few changes of clothes, some toys, my iPad. It doesn't take long to fit everything into a holdall. We can be ready to leave first thing tomorrow.

I check the leaflet I got at the café for local bus times to the nearest train station. By nightfall tomorrow, we'll be hundreds of miles away. It won't matter then if the woman recognised us.

We'll be long gone.

306

chapter 59

alex

Dad said in his text Mum was being rushed into emergency surgery, but he didn't say why. When I arrive at the Mid-Surrey Hospital a little after midnight, the receptionist informs me Mum's still in intensive care, but she can't, or won't, tell me what's happened.

My fear intensifies as I follow the woman's directions up to the ICU on the third floor. I thought I'd come to terms with Mum's mortality after her cancer diagnoses, but I feel blindsided by the suddenness of this. She's had surgery and chemo and radiation, she's lost her hair, and aged ten years in less than two, but never, for one moment, have I believed I might actually lose her until now.

Dad's text left me no choice but to come. Mum might die; of course I had to be here. I just pray to God Jack gets my messages and mobilises the police before the woman leaves the cottage. I can't find the house on any property rental websites like Airbnb, so perhaps she and Lottie live there after all. And I'll go back first thing tomorrow, when Mum's out of the woods.

If.

Dad's by her bedside when I'm buzzed into the ICU. His eyes are frightened above his mask. Mum is unconscious on the bed and more pale than I've ever seen her, more pale than I've ever seen anyone still living. I tell myself the wires and tubes and monitors around her bed make things seem more alarming than they are.

I apply another liberal pump of hand sanitiser and take Mum's hand. 'I'm here,' I say softly. 'It's Alex. I'm here, Mum.'

She doesn't open her eyes. Tenderly, I stroke her hair back from her forehead.

Her skin feels cool, almost clammy, to the touch. She's not spiking a fever, at least. That has to be good, doesn't it?

'What happened, Dad?' I ask. 'What's wrong with her?'

'Let's go and find some coffee,' Dad says. 'You must be tired after your drive. They've got some fairly decent biscuits in the waiting room.'

I don't want to leave Mum's side, but I recognise Dad needs a break. I follow him to a small waiting area just outside the ICU. We're the only ones here; this late at night, any visiting relatives are sitting with their loved ones, keeping vigil.

Dad inserts a coffee pod in the machine and pours me a cup, then makes a second for himself.

'She started complaining of pain in her stomach yesterday morning,' he says. 'It got worse all day, but you know your mother, she doesn't like to make a fuss. Then this afternoon she started vomiting, like nothing I've ever seen. She didn't want me to bring her in but I had to. She was in so much pain she couldn't even speak.'

I voice the fear that haunts us both. 'Is her cancer back?'

'The doctor said the CT scan showed a perforated bowel. It can be quite serious, so they whipped her straight into surgery. Mr Terpsichore said it went well, but she's obviously going to be a bit under the weather for a while.'

'But what caused it? The chemo?'

308

'They don't know. The important thing is, they caught it in time.'

He's part of a generation that always believes the men in white coats and doesn't like to challenge their authority by asking questions. I don't blame the doctors for trying to project optimism, but I want to know the truth, however hard it may be to hear.

'I'd like to speak to her surgeon,' I say. 'Find out exactly what's going on. Is Harriet on her way here?'

'Oh,' Dad says.

I feel a brief pang of compassion for my sister. 'Don't worry. I'll phone her.'

'Thanks, love. I'm going to get back to your mum,' Dad says. 'I don't want her waking up and me not being there.'

'Why don't you go home and get some sleep? I'll stay with—'

'It's all right, love. I wouldn't sleep anyway.'

As we return to the ICU, we're met by a doctor. She looks tired and anxious. Her hair is very dark and cut into an asymmetric bob. She's wearing a neat pair of gold earrings, shaped like horseshoes.

'Mr Johnson, I was just on my way to find you.'

'Is Mary awake?'

'Are you family?' the doctor asks me.

'I'm her daughter,' I say. 'Alexa Martini.'

'Naomi Todd. I'm sorry to meet you under such circumstances.' She sighs. 'I'm afraid your wife's taken a bit of a turn for the worse, Mr Johnson. Her heart rate's up and her temperature's started to climb. We don't want to concern you, but we'd like to pop her back into theatre.'

'More surgery?' I say. 'Are you sure that's necessary?'

'The doctors know best, love,' Dad says.

'Your mum is worrying us a bit, Alexa,' Todd says. 'Her bowel must have perforated quite some time before she arrived at A&E. There was considerable faecal matter in the abdomen, enabling all sorts of nasties to get into her bloodstream. We'd like to stay ahead of this thing, if we can.'

'Can I see her first?' Dad asks.

'Just for a couple of minutes.'

'I'll be right there, Dad,' I say.

I wait until the doors to the ICU have swooshed shut behind him.

'What's the prognosis?' I ask bluntly.

'It's still very early days—'

'Dr Todd, I'd appreciate whatever facts you're able to give me.'

Her grey eyes appraise me. 'Your mother is very sick,' she says, after a moment. 'The biggest danger is sepsis. Mr Terpsichore is going to try to stabilise her condition with an abdominal washout, and he'll also put in a drain. He may need to remove more of her large bowel. I'm afraid, after that, it's very much a waiting game.'

The ground shifts beneath my feet. I have gone from *they caught it in time* to *very much a waiting game* in just a few minutes.

'Is she going to die?'

'We're going to do everything we can.'

'My sister lives in the Shetlands,' I say.

A beat passes.

Naomi Todd's voice softens. 'In an otherwise healthy patient, the overall mortality rate, in a case such as this, is roughly thirty percent,' she says. 'Your mother has metastatic cancer, and the infection was already well-established before we were able to operate. If there are members of the family who might like to say goodbye, now would be the time to call them.'

two years and twenty-one days missing

two years and twenty-one days missing

chapter 60

alex

Harriet doesn't come.

She doesn't come when I tell her Mum is in a medically induced coma, fighting for her life. She doesn't come when Mum's organs start to fail, one by one: her kidneys, her liver, her heart. She doesn't come when the doctors try a Hail Mary pass, obtaining an emergency licence from the General Medical Council to try a new drug that still hasn't completed its clinical trials, but is showing promise.

She doesn't even come when that fails, and Naomi Todd tells us there's nothing more they can do.

Mum's sister, Julie, has travelled twenty-six hours nonstop from New Zealand to be by her side. Her oldest friend, Sharon, whom she's known since primary school, makes the long journey down from Newcastle. But for Harriet, it's *too upsetting*.

'I couldn't bear to see her like that,' she says, when I phone again to tell her if she doesn't come *now*, it'll be too late. 'It'd break my heart, Alex. I'm not strong the way you are. I love Mum so much, watching her fade away would kill me.'

I ignore the implication that I must therefore love Mum *less*.

'Dad wants us all to be together,' I plead. 'He's needs you. He's falling apart, Harry. He still refuses to accept this is really happening.'

313

'I wouldn't be any use,' Harriet says. 'It's you Dad needs, not me. You know he relies on you.'

'What about me?' I say. 'What if *I* need you?'

'You don't need anyone, Alex. You never have.'

The hospital has given us our own family suite now, the one they reserve for relatives when there's no hope left. It has a bed made up with fresh sheets, a kitchenette, even a tiny shower. In the adjacent sitting room, there's a sofa and a couple of armchairs, and a vase of fresh flowers on the coffee table: *From the Friends of Mid-Surrey*, a small card reads beside them. Despite all the thoughtful touches, grief and loss seep like moisture from the bland, beige walls.

Only two people are permitted in the ICU with Mum at any one time, so we take it in turns. We only leave her when the doctors come in to carry out more of their tests.

Dad is sitting on the sofa with Aunt Julie and Sharon, while I pace the room restlessly. I haven't smoked since I was in college, but I itch for a cigarette now.

'We're going to have to get some sort of rota going,' he says suddenly. 'Once Mary comes out of hospital, she's going to need to convalesce. I'm happy to do the lion's share, but I don't want her to get bored. We'll need to keep her spirits up with visitors, once she's up to having people over.'

My aunt and I exchange a look. My courage deserts me; I can't be the one to tell my father that Mum's not coming home.

'Tony,' my aunt says, gently. 'I think you need to be prepared for the worst.'

'I realise that,' Dad says. 'I know Mary could be in this coma quite a while. And Dr Todd's told me she could have significant deficits when she wakes up. She'll need rehab, and even then she might never get back to where she was. I know all that. But we'll get her through it.'

He nods several times, as if to convince himself.

I sit down next to him. 'Dad, she may not wake up,' I say.

'Of course she will. We just have to give it time,' Dad says.

When Naomi Todd returns and tells us Mum's near the end, Dad still refuses to accept it. Aunt Julie is the one who asks the parish priest at my parents' local Catholic church, Father Jonathan, to come and give Mum the last rites.

It's been less than forty-eight hours since Mum arrived in casualty.

Dad isn't the only one who can't get his head around what's happening. I'm in the grip of emotional whip-lash: I've finally found my daughter, only to lose my mother.

I'm desperate to get back to Lottie, but I don't even know if she's still at the cottage. And I have no way of finding out: Jack's on a fact-finding mission about climate change in Alaska, and won't be home for another two days, and I haven't even heard back from Quinn. I can't call the police, who'll either dismiss me as crazy, or blunder in to talk to the woman and send her running again the moment they leave. I don't think I've ever felt this powerless.

The doctors have lifted the limit on who can be with Mum now, so we all gather at her bedside. Outside, it's dark. The nurses have turned the lights down low and drawn the curtains around her bed.

Father Jonathan opens a small vessel of oil and anoints Mum's forehead and hands with the sign of the cross.

'Through this holy anointing, may the Lord in his love and mercy help you with the grace of the Holy Spirit,' he murmurs. 'May the Lord who frees you from sin save you and raise you up.'

I'm not religious. While Mum sought comfort and aid from a higher being on her knees in church, for me, Lottie's disappearance was the final proof that if a god existed, it was a bitter, vengeful one, undeserving of our attention.

But there's something soothing about the soft cadences of Father Jonathan's prayers, the tangible faith of more than two millennia that he represents. It's hard not to find a kind of solace in the belief of others, even if I can't join them. I felt its power when I married Luca in his maternal family's ancient chapel in Sicily, walking down an aisle worn smooth by the passage of thousands of feet. I felt it again two years later, when I stood in front of the same altar a few feet from his coffin as the priest eddied clouds of incense from the gold thurible around us. A strange calm, as though I'd put myself in the hands of something larger and unknowable. Not faith, exactly. But a sort of surrendering.

Dad and I stand at the head of Mum's bed, on either side, holding her hands.

The nurses have turned off the monitors, so there's no beeping, no alarms. Father Jonathan and Aunt Julie flank her feet, with Sharon between them. Mum is encircled by love.

I don't know if she's aware of us, but Naomi Todd has told us hearing is the last sense to go. 'It's OK,' I whisper, bending next to her pillow. 'I've found Lottie. I'll bring her home, I promise. You can go now. I'll look after Dad.'

A small tear appears at the corner of her eye. I wipe it away and tuck the precious tissue in my pocket.

Her breathing is so shallow I can barely make out the rise and fall of her chest. I can't believe my mother is leaving me. She's only fifty-nine. She'll never get to see Lottie come home. Never celebrate another Christmas with us.

I try to remember the last conversation we had, and fail. It would have been about Lottie. It was always about Lottie. I don't think I've seen, not really *seen*, my mother since the day my child was taken. I need to apologise to her for that—

Naomi Todd gently touches my shoulder. 'She's gone, Alex.'

Mum looks as if she's sleeping. And yet I can tell instantly she isn't here any more. The essence of her, who she is, who she loved, has gone.

Dad presses Mum's hand to his cheek and lays his head on the pillow next to her. He looks utterly broken.

'Come on, love,' Aunt Julie says. 'Let your dad have some time alone with her.'

'Someone should tell Harriet,' I say.

'In a minute,' Aunt Julie says.

In the waiting room, Sharon presses a hot mug of tea into my hand. I don't know why I'm so felled by this. I feel stupefied. I'm thirty-one years old. I haven't needed my mother for a long time. I'm not sure I can even remember how to breathe.

Aunt Julie sits next to me and rubs my back. 'You're all right, love. You're all right.'

'Someone should tell Harriet,' I repeat.

'Do you want me to call her for you?'

I should be the one to tell my sister, but I don't trust myself. 'Let me give you her number,' I say.

'I've got it, love. She gave it to me when I saw her at the airport.'

My mind is fogged. I can't seem to make sense of anything.

My aunt steps out into the corridor to make the call. I grip the cooling mug of tea with both hands, as if it's all that's tethering me to the ground.

'Harriet's leaving Shetland tomorrow morning,' Aunt Julie says, when she returns. 'She'll let us know her flight details as soon as she has them.'

'When?' I ask.

'When what, love?'

'When did you see her at the airport?'

'The day Lottie disappeared,' she says, patiently. 'I ran into her at Heathrow. Now, stop worrying, love. We'll get things sorted.'

I finish my tea, even though it's cold now. I've got so many things to do, but my thoughts are disjointed and out of order. It's as if each of them has been written on pieces of paper that've been tossed willy-nilly into the air.

A man who looks like my father joins us in the family suite. He's wearing Dad's clothes and Dad's glasses, but this man is hollowed out, empty, a husk of a man. He sits on the sofa, his hands hanging uselessly between his knees, and I can't bear the pain of seeing him shrunken and diminished like this.

I can't let my father collapse in on himself. If I don't do something, he'll sink without trace. I'm the only one who can restore the heart of this family.

And I made a promise to my mother.

two years and twenty-five days missing

two years and twenty-five days missing

chapter 61

quinn

Quinn's bender lasts six days. A record, even for her.

She gets thrown out of the pub when she's so drunk she literally can't stand up. The kid behind the bar manhandles her into the street, shoves her AA chip in her face and tells her to sort out her shit. So she stops by the off-licence on her way home and buys a case of Jack Daniel's.

Shit sorted.

She only sobers up when she's burned her way through all six bottles of whiskey, and there's no alcohol left in the house. She's even drunk the shitty peppermint schnapps she found in the cupboard under the sink when she moved into her flat two years ago, after her stint in Washington ended.

From the minty stains on her shirt, she's guessing she threw up on herself at some point. She's been wearing the same clothes for almost a week; even she can smell the stink coming off her. She needs to clean herself up or they won't let her back in the off-licence.

She strips off and gets into the shower, steadying herself against the tiles with her good hand as the cold water sluices off her back. Her stomach is practically concave, because she hasn't eaten in nearly a week. Food absorbs alcohol, which makes it an inefficient way to get drunk.

When she's drunk, she gets maudlin. When she's maudlin, she rings Marnie, who pities her enough to take the calls, even though it's been two years since they broke up. Quinn figures she'll have some damage limitation to do while she's sober enough to be coherent so, after she's pulled on a fresh shirt and a pair of clean jeans, she searches her apartment for her phone.

The battery's dead, of course. She plugs in her charger and gives it a minute for her recent calls and texts to load, then scrolls through them, squinting to read through the cracked screen. No drunk-and-dial calls to Marnie, thank fuck. Her battery must've died before she had the chance.

But there's a voicemail from Alexa Martini, left six days ago.

She should delete it. That woman's brought her nothing but trouble. If she opens the door again, she'll fall back down the rabbit hole. She'll lose her job.

She's not going to delete it. Of course she's not going to delete it.

She plays the message. *I've found her. I know where she is. I'm looking at her house right now. If you want your damn story, Quinn, call me back.*

Jesus fuck.

It's been six days. If Lottie Martini has been found and *she's missed it*, she'll slit her fucking wrists.

Quinn grabs her computer and fires it up, her hangover dissipating as adrenaline completes the job the cold shower started. But a search for Lottie's name reveals no fresh developments in the Martini story since Alexa yanked the emergency brake on the Tube three weeks ago. There's nothing new on AP or Reuters, nothing anywhere.

Her heart rate returns to normal. Alexa Martini is either crazy or trying to fuck with her head. She should never have let herself sober up. She needs a drink.

But she clicks on the INN website, just to be sure.

Christ on the fucking cross.

She can't believe what she's reading. Just when she thought the Lottie Martini case couldn't get any more twisted.

Quinn hits speed dial on her phone.

chapter 62

We don't leave the next morning as I'd planned. The child is sick and running a temperature. What kind of mother would I be if I took her out now, in the cold and rain, and dragged her halfway across the country on a bus? The woman who was staring at us in the café hasn't returned. The child needs rest and sleep and plenty of liquids. We can leave in a day or two, when she's feeling better.

But she doesn't get better. She gets worse.

She's always been a voracious eater, but now she has no appetite. She's listless, curled up on the sofa, staring blankly out of the window at the grey, rain-sheeted beach below. She doesn't want me to read to her; she doesn't even want to watch TV. This difficult, wilful child is suddenly biddable and compliant, and it terrifies me.

I make her favourite tomato soup but she eats a spoonful and then pushes the bowl away. Her eyes are sunken into her skull and her skin is pale and clammy. I can't believe the transformation in her in just a couple of days. She looks almost consumptive. Maybe it's flu. She's been sick before, but not like this, never like this. I don't even have any Calpol to give her to bring down her temperature and I can't leave her to go into the village to get some. All I can do is try to keep her comfortable.

On the morning of the fourth day since she got sick, I have difficulty waking her.

She cries out when I open the curtains, flinching from the light.

My stomach plunges.

I lift the top of her pink pyjamas and note the telltale rash across her chest. My heart in my mouth, I pick up the empty glass beside her bed and press it against the rash. The spots do not disappear.

Meningitis.

'My head hurts,' she whimpers.

Can I risk taking her to hospital? Even if I give a false name, there'll be so many questions. There won't be any record of her in their computers. They'll want to admit her and, with every moment she spends in the hospital, the chance someone recognises her will increase.

I could leave her there. I could take her to A&E and just leave her there.

But if I do that, I won't be able to go back. I'll lose her forever.

We'll ride it out. I have some penicillin I bought online. It's past its expiry date, but those don't mean anything. I'll keep up her fluid intake and crush a couple of paracetamol into a spoonful of jam to help with the headache. If I can get some food into her, that'll help, but fluids are the important thing. And we need to get that temperature down.

I run her a tepid bath – not cold, that would be too much of a shock to the body, that's the mistake everyone makes – and gently help her out of her pyjamas. She lets me sponge her down without complaint, and then I lift her out of the bath again and wrap her in a soft, fluffy white towel.

She leans her hot head against my shoulder. 'I love you, Mummy,' she says.

It's the first time she's ever said that to me.

chapter 63

alex

From my hidden vantage point, I watch Lottie run down the beach, her blonde hair streaming like a bleached flag behind her. She's pretending to be a plane, or a bird perhaps: her arms are stretched wide as she swoops and dives across the sand.

No one is with her. No one is watching her.

Except me.

Lottie stops suddenly, plopping down on her fat bottom in the sand like a much younger child. She tugs off her sandals and flings them into the cold, grey sea, laughing with delight as the tide quickly whips them away. Watching her, it's hard not to smile. Even at nearly six, she's still young enough to be unfettered by *should* and *ought*. She's impulsive, living in the moment, just as I remember. She skips joyfully along the chilly beach in her bare feet, her skirts flapping wetly around her calves, and I wonder briefly at what age we stop skipping and surrender to the pedestrian discipline of walking and running.

I'm glad she's having so much fun now, because I know she'll be frightened when I take her. I can't help that, but I'll make sure the scary bit is all over as quickly as I can.

Lottie veers closer to the shoreline, oblivious to my presence as I emerge from the rocks behind her, and I quell my instinct to pull her back from the water's edge and tell her to be careful, that the tide is stronger than it looks. Life is dangerous. If she doesn't know that by now, she soon will.

And the biggest threat to her doesn't come from the sea.

It comes from someone like me: a stranger to her, lurking in the shadows.

My pulse quickens as I step out from behind the rocks. I'm about to cross a line and set in motion a train of events from which there'll be no going back.

The first year I was at Muysken Ritter, one of the partners represented a French woman whose baby son had been snatched from his pram when he was ten months old. Four years later, he was found in Johannesburg, being raised by a couple who'd innocently adopted him after he'd been trafficked to South Africa. The High Court in Pretoria decided it was in the boy's best interests to stay with the only parents he'd ever known. The biological mother was permitted to see her son once a month and even those visits were supervised, in case she tried to snatch him back.

Four days ago, I promised my dying mother I'd bring Lottie home. I'm not waiting for the police to act, for the courts to grind their way towards a decision that might give my baby to another woman. I've got nothing left to lose, now.

I'm done playing by the rules.

It's a crisp, sunny morning and unseasonably warm, one of those rare November days that feels more like early autumn. The beach is dotted with dog-walkers and local families taking advantage of the watery sunshine. I deliberately waited till Saturday to do this in the hope there'd be people around, so Lottie and I would be able to blend in more easily, but I've been luckier than I dared dream. I choose to take it as a good omen. A last gift from my mother.

Lottie looks up from her playing and sees me. She hesitates a second, and then raises a finger to her lips: *ssssh*.

327

My heart turns over. She remembers me.

She has no idea who I really am, of course. To her, I'm just the lady from the café, the lady who returned her toy. But when I beckon, she comes to me, her eyes bright with curiosity.

My daughter, just three feet away.

She should know better than to go so willingly to a stranger, but she's always been one of those children who likes breaking the rules. I fight the urge to pull her close. More than anything, I want to touch her, to know she's really here, but I hold myself in check.

'No Squishmallow today?' I say.

'Not at the beach. I don't want him to get wet again.'

'Of course. Silly me.'

She laughs.

'I have a little girl your age,' I say. 'You won't believe how many Squishmallows she has. And something even better.'

'Even better?'

'Even better.'

'Like what?'

I shrug. 'Oh, you'd have to see it.'

'Can you show me?'

'I could. It's not very far away,' I say. 'But I don't think you're allowed.'

She frowns, considering. And then she raises her fingers to her lips again, *ssssh*, her eyes dancing with mischief.

I smile and turn as if to leave, knowing curiosity will be her undoing. She catches up to me and takes my hand, because she trusts me.

My daughter's hand in mine.

We walk together in plain sight along the beach, past dozens of people. No one even tries to stop us.

I can't believe it's this simple. This is the moment of greatest risk, the only period of time when, for all the planning of the last few days, events are largely beyond my control. If someone sees her with me and challenges us, I have my excuse ready. But no one even notices. We're made invisible by our very ordinariness, Lottie and me.

I walk a little faster. The clock's already ticking. Lottie may be missed at any moment. Time is of the essence.

I turn onto a stony path leading away from the shore. Lottie's barefoot, though she doesn't complain. But she's slowing us both down as she hops gingerly from foot to foot, so I pick her up and she doesn't protest.

My daughter in my arms.

She frowns for the first time when I open the door to the back seat of my rental car. I didn't want to risk using my own vehicle, in case there's a CCTV camera I missed, though I think I've managed to avoid them. The ID I gave the car hire company is obviously false; you'd be shocked how quickly you can obtain a fake driving licence and passport online. Thanks to Simon Green and Berkeley International, I know my way around the dark web all too well.

'Where's my car seat?' she says.

'Aren't you too old for that?' I ask, although of course she isn't.

'Yes,' she says, pleased.

She doesn't ask questions as we drive to a cheap hotel just forty minutes from South Weald village, other than a request to use the bathroom, which I deny, since by then we're nearly there. I deliberately chose somewhere nearby, so as not to panic her with a long drive, but she doesn't seem at all concerned. I keep stealing looks at her in my rear-view mirror, unable to believe she's really here. She's here, with me. We're making our escape. This isn't a fairy tale, this isn't my imagination: this is real. Lottie is real.

I force myself to concentrate on the road. I've been careful to pick a route with few traffic cameras and no road tolls. I don't think the woman who stole my baby will be stupid enough to raise a hue and cry but, just in case, I've taken steps to ensure we won't be found, until I'm certain she's slunk back into the same dark hole from which she emerged. I don't care about revenge, about punishing her. I have my daughter back.

In a few days, I'll be able to take her back home to London. It won't matter how I found her. It's not a crime to rescue your own child.

The nightmare is almost over.

chapter 64

quinn

No one else makes the connection, but Quinn does.

A logo on a sweatshirt.

A child missing in Devon.

I've found her. I know where she is. I'm looking at her house right now.

'What the fuck have you done, Alex?' Quinn mutters, as the woman's phone goes straight to voicemail yet again.

She leaves another message and shoves her phone into her jeans pocket. She'd love nothing more than to climb back into a bottle of Jack, but that's not going to help her find Alexa and Lottie Martini. That's not going to give her resolution on this motherfucking, screwed-up, bastard of a story. She's got to see it through to the end and fuck the consequences.

Quinn might as well admit it: it's not just about the story. She's got a raging crush on Alexa Martini. The woman is difficult and damaged and fucking fixated on getting to the truth, and that's enough to hook Quinn right there. Alexa's been subjected to the kind of character assassination no man in her place would ever have had to endure and she just keeps right on going, unbroken and undaunted, sticking up two fingers to the world: *You are the trailer park. I am the tornado.*

Quinn throws the empty whiskey bottles into the recycling

bin and cleans up the puddles of vomit on the sofa and beside her bed. She grimaces as she scrubs at the stains. Jesus, she really knocked it out of the park this time.

When she's done, she makes herself a bowl of porridge – the only food in her flat – and grinds the last of her Panamanian beans. She sits back down at her computer, awkwardly cupping her good hand around her coffee as she thinks it through.

She has no idea if Alexa Martini has actually found her long-lost daughter or if she's out-of-her-head crazy and has grabbed an innocent kid off the street. The photo of the missing child is similar enough to Lottie that it *could* be her, but it's hard to be sure: the most recent pictures of Lottie are two years out of date now, and kids this young change so quickly. But right now, it doesn't really matter. Clearly *Alexa* believes she's found Lottie. She's a smart woman. She must have a plan. She knows she can't hide out forever, so what's her endgame?

Quinn kicks herself for the umpteenth time for not answering the phone six days ago when Alexa called. She might have been able to talk her out of this. Or at least been part of the story, instead of playing catch-up. Alexa could be anywhere by now, though Quinn bets she's probably still in the country.

Where would you go if you were on the run with a young child?

Quinn puts her coffee down. She's looking at this from the wrong angle. Trying to find the particular hotel or B&B where Alexa has holed up is akin to looking for a needle in a haystack of needles. She's learned from experience that tracking someone down is like playing tennis: you aim not for where the ball *is*, but where it *will be*.

If Quinn were in Alexa's shoes, she'd want incontrovertible, DNA proof from a trusted testing centre if she was going to pull a stunt like this.

Find the lab and she'll find Alexa.

There are only a dozen reputable, government-accredited DNA test centres in the UK. It's a slow, tedious trawl, but this is the kind of tradecraft Quinn specialises in. It takes her three days and costs her £500 in backhanders to underpaid record clerks, but eventually she hits the jackpot.

Like everything else about this story, it comes with a twist that's even more fucked-up than she could've imagined.

chapter 65

alex

At first, Lottie thinks it's an adventure. She's excited when I tell her we're going to play a game and hide from everybody until my special surprise for her is ready. I say we need to cut her beautiful, distinctive blonde hair and, instead of objecting, she asks me if she can do it herself. I hand her the scissors and she hacks off a huge hunk and flings it on the floor, laughing.

'When are we going to see the surprise?' she asks.

'Soon,' I tell her.

My plan was to stay at the hotel for a few days and then explain to Lottie who I really am, and take her home with me.

But to my shock, the woman who calls herself Lottie's mother *does* go to the police. Her name is Helen Birch, and she says she adopted Lottie – she calls her Flora – from Poland two years ago, when the little girl was four.

I don't know if she's lying or if somehow my daughter was traded to an intermediary and Helen Birch is a victim, just as I am.

This changes everything. Even though I knew it might happen in theory, I never really thought it'd come to this.

The enormity of what I've done hits home for the first time. As far as the world's concerned, I've kidnapped an innocent child from her mother. I've become the monster of my own nightmares. I can't take Lottie home now until I can prove, beyond doubt, that she's my daughter.

I go online and select a DNA testing centre accredited by the Ministry of Justice, which follows strict procedures to maintain chain of custody, meaning its results are court-approved and accepted by family law courts.

I bag up the toothbrush I bought Lottie, along with my own, and post them to the centre, using Jack's office as the return address. Because of a backlog, it'll take two weeks to get the results, but I want them in the public domain. It's the only way I can show I'm telling the truth.

I follow every development in the story obsessively, waiting till Lottie's asleep before going online and trawling through news sites and social media. The police parade Helen Birch on television, and she doesn't come across well. It doesn't take long for the press to turn on her, just as they did me.

A part of me feels sorry for her. I know what it's like to blame yourself. I know what it's like to tell yourself you only took your eyes off your child for a second, that it could've happened to anyone, even though you know it isn't true. It didn't happen to anyone, it happened to you, because *you* looked away.

But it's not all plain sailing my end, either. As the novelty of our adventure wears off, Lottie starts to chafe against my rules, even though I explain they're for her own good. I don't risk taking her out in public, except when I'm forced to get food. She's more of a handful than I expected and I find it harder to bond with her than I'd hoped. Stressed and confused, I lose my patience with her quite quickly.

'Where's my mummy?' she demands, with increasing frequency.

My heart cracks open. I know it's too early, that she's not yet ready for me to tell her the truth, but in the end I can't help myself.

'I'm your mummy,' I say.

She flies into a rage, kicking and biting. My legs are soon covered with bruises and I give her my iPad to placate her. She plugs herself into YouTube and watches Minecraft videos for hours on end. She never used to like watching TV; she always had too much energy to sit still for anything.

It makes me realise anew how much I've missed, how much has been stolen from me. The child I knew has gone. This girl is like a stranger to me.

None of this is going the way I thought it would. I expected Lottie to be upset at first, but surely she realises by now I'm doing this for her? I know it's foolish to expect her to remember me, but it hurts she can't see how much I love her.

Her precious 'mummy' wasn't any kind of real mother to her. I watched them together for several days before I finally made my move. Helen Birch didn't pay any attention to Lottie, letting her play on the beach alone for hours at a time. I doubt she even misses her now she's gone.

Whereas I've proven my devotion. I've risked everything for her.

But Lottie doesn't make it easy. She's sulky and rude, and throws a tantrum whenever she doesn't get her own way. She behaves like the three-year-old toddler she was when she was taken from me, rather than like a child of nearly six, and I wonder if, by taking her, I've caused her to regress. She seems well-cared-for, but I've no idea what she's been through in the last two years. And we're both suffering from cabin fever, trapped within the same four walls day after day.

So I try to make allowances, but when I give an inch, she demands a mile. I feel as if I'm failing her all over again. I've never been a hands-on mother before; Luca was the one who looked after Lottie. I'm building the plane as it flies.

I realise now I've constructed a rose-tinted view of my

daughter, which is running up against hard reality. I tell myself this is *good*. This is what mothering is all about and I'm not going to run away from it this time.

Jack and Quinn keep calling, but I let my phone go to voicemail. They're both smart enough to have made the connection between me and a missing child from South Weald. I'm gambling on their loyalty – to me, to the story – to stop them from going to the police until I've had a chance to explain myself. I need to keep them at bay for a while yet.

But I'm staying in constant touch with Dad. He wants me home, but I've told him I need some time on my own to process Mum's death. Harriet's with him; it's about time she pulled her weight. He's insisted on an autopsy, because he still refuses to accept there was nothing that could be done to save Mum, and while this breaks my heart, it buys me time, because a funeral can't be held until it's done. Lottie and I will be back home before then, once the fuss dies down and I have the DNA results.

But the fuss doesn't die down.

Flora Birch's name is on everyone's lips. I see her photograph everywhere. I move us to a B&B in a rundown part of Barnstaple and pay cash in hand. Our room smells damp and musty, and Lottie complains the sheets feel slimy. She's fractious and complaining, and constantly, *constantly* hungry.

I realise I've made a mistake: we stand out like sore thumbs in this sketchy part of town, with our clean hair and white faces. We need to blend in with people who look like us.

We drive north to Manchester and I check into a smart hotel in Didsbury. No one gives us a second glance but Lottie is restless and bored, cooped up inside all the time. I take her on a few day trips around the city, risking the crowds and anonymity of the train, but it's not enough. If we're going to make this work, she needs to be outside every day, somewhere she can run around and play. She's starting to look peaky.

So I take her to Anglesey and rent a cottage near Traeth Mawr, on the coast in the middle of nowhere, paying three months upfront in cash. The skinny kid at the lettings agent doesn't even ask for ID. He's too busy counting bank notes.

Lottie seems a little happier here, but it's been too long since she had playmates. She requires constant attention, constant entertainment. I worry she's been irrevocably damaged by everything that's happened to her.

I worry I've made everything worse.

After ten days together, she's finally grown used to me – she even calls me Mummy. But there's a fear in her eyes, a wariness, no child should have. Something's wrong between us and, despite my best efforts, it grows with every passing day. I want to show her I trust her so I let her play on the beach below our cottage without me, and sometimes I take her to a café in the village where she makes friends with the owner's dog.

But then one day a woman stares at us a little too hard in the café, and I'm sure I see her watching us again later, when we're walking back home.

I decide we'll drive to Scotland in the morning. I know Edinburgh well; it'll be easy to lose ourselves there. It's only another week or so until the DNA results come back. Then Quinn can run the story and it'll be safe for me to bring Lottie home. No one will take my child from me again.

But the next morning, Lottie's running a temperature. She's tired and listless, clearly too sick to travel. She needs rest and sleep and plenty of liquids. We can leave in a day or two, when she's feeling better.

Except she doesn't get better. She gets worse.

two years and thirty-five days missing

Two years and thirty-five days missing

chapter 66

alex

When Lottie tells me she loves me, it's like a bucket of iced water has been flung over me, sobering me in an instant.

What does it matter if I'm arrested? I'd rather the court returns Lottie to Helen Birch and lose her forever than have anything happen to her. It doesn't matter if they fling me in jail. Saving my daughter is all that matters.

We're less than forty minutes from the hospital at Bangor, but it's the longest forty minutes of my life.

I can't believe how quickly Lottie deteriorates. She's been listless and running a temperature for several days, but in just the last hour her fever has rocketed to 41°C. As I buckle her into the car, she vomits a dark, seaweed-green bile that fills me with terror. Her pallid skin has an unhealthy sheen to it, giving her an eerie luminescence, and her cropped blonde hair is plastered to her skull with sweat. She can't bear the brightness of daylight, so I cocoon her in a blanket and drive as fast as I dare.

What was I *thinking*, feeding her out-of-date penicillin and crushed paracetamol? She needs expert care – specialised antibiotics, intravenous fluids, oxygen, steroids – not tepid baths! I should never have left it this long to seek help. I *know* about meningitis; a child at Lottie's playgroup nearly died from it.

One of the teachers recognised the signs and called an ambulance; her quick thinking saved the little boy's life, but sepsis ravaged his small body and cost him both his feet. If my delay robs Lottie of her limbs, if anything happens to her, God forbid, I'll never be able to forgive myself.

I'm just minutes away from the hospital when I check on Lottie in the rear-view mirror and see her suddenly go rigid, her body stiffening like a marionette. Then she starts to convulse, thrashing against the confines of the car. I realise she's having a seizure.

Every second counts now.

I pull out into the oncoming lane, my hand on the horn, my foot to the floor. My urgency must convey itself: cars pull onto the hard shoulder in both directions, letting me through. I drive straight up to the ambulance bay outside A&E, ignoring the yellow cross-hatching telling me not to park there, and leap out, yanking open the door to the back seat.

'My daughter's having a seizure!' I shout, as a paramedic climbs out of a stationary ambulance parked nearby and runs towards me.

I unbuckle Lottie and lift her out. I'm shocked by how light she suddenly seems.

'I think it's meningitis,' I say, panic making me breathless. 'Her temperature's forty-one degrees and she's got this strange purple rash all over her chest.'

The paramedic pulls up the sleeve of her sweatshirt. 'It's spread to her arms,' he says. Even as we look, more dots appear on the insides of her wrists, the rash spreading literally before our eyes.

'She's burning up,' the paramedic says, scooping her out of my arms. 'You did the right thing bringing her in so quickly.'

He's already striding into A&E and I jog to keep pace alongside him. Lottie's limp in his arms, her eyes rolling to the back

342

of her head. There's a sudden storm of activity as medical personnel in scrubs converge on us from all directions. The paramedic transfers Lottie to a trolley and a doctor is already tapping the inside of her forearm to insert an IV line as she's whisked away along a corridor and through a pair of sliding doors.

I try to go after her, but the paramedic puts a detaining hand on my shoulder.

'Can't go back there, love,' he says. 'Try not to worry. She's in good hands. The best there is. Someone will take you through to her as soon as she's stable.'

As he returns to the ambulance bay, the doors swoosh open again and a nurse in primrose-yellow scrubs appears, holding a computer tablet. 'Are you Mum?'

'Yes. Is she going to be OK?'

'She's in excellent hands.' The nurse pecks at her screen. 'I just need to take some details. What's your daughter's name?'

I hesitate only briefly. 'Charlotte. Lottie.'

'Last name?'

There's a sudden commotion behind us: shouts for help, crying, running feet.

The sound of glass breaking, of chairs being overturned.

A fight has broken out in the waiting room. Two men in their early twenties are aggressively squaring off, both already bleeding from split lips and broken noses. Each is backed by a cluster of two or three friends, some nursing injuries of their own, all yelling abuse and encouragement. A couple of young women wearing identikit gold hoop earrings, high heels and toothpick jeans are ineffectually trying to calm them down.

A deafening alarm suddenly blares, cutting off all conversation. Two burly security guards wade into the fracas, forcibly separating the lads from each other.

'Sorry about that,' the nurse shouts, over the din. 'Security alarm. Happens all the time. Can you tell me your daughter's last name again?'

I could lie. Use the name and birth date on her false ID, fabricate a home address. In this chaos, maybe it'd go unnoticed. For now. But sooner or later, the hospital will discover the child with the fictional name I've given them has no medical records, and that there's no National Insurance number attached to her date of birth. I'm tired of running. Lottie's *my* daughter. The DNA test will prove that. Why should I have to hide it?

The alarm stops abruptly.

'Martini,' I say, my voice loud in the sudden silence.

The nurse doesn't even look up. If Lottie's name means anything to her, she gives no sign. 'Any allergies?' she asks. 'Penicillin, anything like that?'

'No,' I say. 'No allergies.'

She asks for details of Lottie's vaccinations, how long she's been sick, when she last ate. Has she visited a farm in the last two weeks? Been exposed to any chemicals? Travelled to sub-Saharan Africa?

I answer every question, trying to conceal my mounting frustration.

'When can I see my daughter?' I say, finally.

'The doctor will come through and update you soon.'

Order has finally been restored in the waiting room and the two young men are now sitting on opposite sides of it, glowering at each other. I take a seat as the nurse suggests, but I'm soon back on my feet again, pacing the corridor. My little girl is fighting for her life in there and I've no idea what's going on.

My mobile rings.

'No phones in here,' the receptionist says, from across the room.

344

I pull out my mobile to silence it. Quinn's name is on the screen. A text message.

Only a few words are visible: **Call me ASAP! Flora** . . .

But before I can tap through to the full message, I hear someone call my name.

Two uniformed policemen are coming towards me. Leading the way is the nurse in yellow scrubs who took down Lottie's details.

So, she *did* recognise the name, then.

'Mrs Martini?' one of the policemen says again. 'We'd like a word.'

And then I read Quinn's text.

two years and thirty-nine days missing

two years and thirty-nine days missing

JESS: I think – and it goes without saying, our hearts go out
           to both women and it's really sad, I feel for them both
           – but at the same time, we have laws, there are proce-
           dures in place for a reason.

ZEALY: It's really sad, yes.

JESS: As Alexa Martini's best friend, you must be devastated
           for her.

ZEALY: Yes, we all are.

JESS: You were one of the twelve so-called 'apostles', weren't
           you? You were actually at the last supper the night
           before Lottie disappeared.

ZEALY: I wish people wouldn't call us that.

JESS: For the sake of our viewers, the other apostles at that
           dinner were your half-brother, Marc Chapman, and his
           bride, Sian, her parents, Penny and David Williams, and
           Marc's dad, Eric Chapman, plus the parents of one of
           the little bridesmaids, Felicity and Jonathan Everett. Ian
           Dutton was there too – well, we all know about him.
           And the last two people at the dinner were Catherine
           Lord, Sian's maid of honour, and Paul Harding, whom
           Catherine later married, is that right?

ZEALY: Yes.

JESS: Who's since been charged with child sex abuse.

ZEALY: Yes.

JESS: There's been a lot of talk about you and the other apostles over the years, hasn't there? A lot of speculation. Can you tell me, Zealy, what it's like to have the finger of suspicion pointed at you?

ZEALY: It's nothing compared to what Alex has gone through.

JESS: Zealy, you've avoided the spotlight till now – I believe this is the first interview you've given to the media, is that correct?

ZEALY: Yes.

JESS: Can you tell me, why are you speaking out now?

ZEALY: Because someone needs to set the record straight. It's easy to judge Alex, but what she's been through, she's been incredibly – it's a mother's worst nightmare, none of us know what we'd do in her shoes.

JESS: But it's a nightmare *she* inflicted on another mother, didn't she?

[long pause]

JESS: Helen Birch.

ZEALY: I'm sorry for Mrs Birch, too.

JESS: Flora's abduction has been all over the news for weeks, hasn't it? Even the prime minister mentioned her in an interview the other day. As a person of colour, does that make you angry?

ZEALY: What?

350

JESS:	To see another white child given all this attention, all these resources.
ZEALY:	No, of course I'm not—
JESS:	Do you think if Flora Birch had been Black, the prime minister would've been appealing for her safe return?
ZEALY:	What I think is you don't care either way. You're playing up the race thing to get ratings.
JESS:	What Alexa Martini did was inexcusable, wasn't it?
ZEALY:	The police weren't doing anything—
JESS:	Are you saying you support Alexa's decision to turn vigilante?
ZEALY:	She's not a vigilante!
JESS:	If she really thought Flora Birch was her daughter, she could've gone to the police.
ZEALY:	She went to the police after she saw Lottie on the Tube and they didn't do anything.
JESS:	But it was *Flora* she saw on the train, with her au pair, not Lottie.
ZEALY:	Yes, but Alex didn't know that.
JESS:	So, you think she wasn't wicked, but deluded?
ZEALY:	[pause] She thought the little girl was Lottie. They look so similar—
JESS:	But DNA tests proved the child *wasn't* hers. If Alexa Martini had just allowed the police to do their job, she'd have spared Helen Birch ten days of hell, wouldn't she?

351

ZEALY: Alex's mother had just died. She was desperate, she
            wasn't thinking straight—

JESS: So you're saying she's mentally unstable?

ZEALY: No, I didn't say that.

JESS: Flora nearly *died*.

ZEALY: And as soon as she realised how sick Lottie – Flora –
            was, Alex took her to hospital. She'd never have put
            her in danger.

JESS: Would you say Alexa Martini is a good mother?

ZEALY: Of course!

JESS: Do you think a good mother leaves her child unattended
            in a hot car?

ZEALY: She made a mistake. She was working crazy hours,
            she—

JESS: Do you think a good mother has sex with a stranger
            instead of looking after her child?

ZEALY: You're twisting everything. Even if Alex was a terrible
            mother, she didn't deserve to have her baby stolen! She
            didn't do anything wrong!

JESS: She kidnapped a *child*.

ZEALY: That's not what I meant—

JESS: A lot of people think Alexa shouldn't have been allowed
            out on bail, after what she's done. Do you think she's
            been given special treatment, because of who she is?

ZEALY: How would putting her in prison help anyone?

352

JESS: That's a matter for a jury to decide.

ZEALY: After all she's been through, surely she deserves some compassion? Helen Birch got her daughter back, but Alex's daughter is still missing. Can you imagine what she's feeling right now?

JESS: Do you believe Lottie Martini is still alive?

ZEALY: I think Alex will never stop looking for her.

JESS: Isn't it time, as her friend, you took her aside and told her to stop?

[silence]

JESS: Do you think she should stop looking, Zealy?

[long pause]

ZEALY: If it was your daughter, would you?

chapter 67

alex

My hands are shaking with nerves. I tuck them beneath my thighs and take a slow, steadying breath. I can't believe she's agreed to see me. I'd never be as forgiving in her place.

We're meeting in my lawyer Jeremy's office, at his insistence. The police have made it clear they intend to pass my file to the Crown Prosecution Service, with a recommendation to press charges. *As per the Child Abduction Act 1984, it is an offence for a person to take or detain a child under the age of sixteen so as to remove him from the lawful control of any person having lawful control of him, or, so as to keep him out of the lawful control of any person entitled to lawful control of him without lawful authority or reasonable excuse.*

I've no idea whether the CPS will decide to prosecute, but Jeremy seems to think it's a fair bet they will. There's a lot of public pressure to throw the book at me, as a deterrent to other would-be vigilantes tempted to take the law into their own hands, should they think they've stumbled across their kidnapped child. Because there are so many of us out there.

There's a soft knock at the door. 'Are you ready?' Jeremy asks.

I stand, wiping my palms on my skirt.

Helen Birch is younger than I remembered. When I saw her

354

in the café, I put her in her early fifties, but now I can see she's probably a decade younger than that. She has a thick middle and short legs, a droopy bosom. Her best asset is undoubtedly her startling leaf-green eyes, fringed by long, dark lashes. I'd have noticed them before, but I was only really paying attention to Lottie.

To *Flora*.

Helen extends a hand and then withdraws it. 'Sorry,' she says.

I don't know whether she's talking about her gesture or the awkward situation in which we find ourselves.

'Please, would you like to sit down?' Jeremy says, indicating the two armchairs on the opposite side of his desk. 'Can I get you two ladies some tea?'

Jeremy is no more than thirty-five, but from his manner and conversation you'd think he's seventy.

'Thank you,' Helen says.

He steps out of his office to see to the tea, briefly leaving the two of us alone. Helen still doesn't sit down.

'How is she?' I ask, unable to help myself.

'Flora's doing much better, thank you,' Helen says. 'The doctors say she can come home tomorrow.'

The emphasis on her daughter's name is subtle, but unmistakable.

'Thank you for agreeing to see me,' I say. 'I wouldn't have blamed you if you—'

'Why am I here?'

Her tone is not particularly hostile, but those green eyes are cool.

I've no idea what to say to her. This meeting was Jeremy's suggestion: he says the CPS is less likely to pursue prosecution aggressively if Helen isn't demanding retributive justice from the rooftops. She has no reason to be sympathetic to my cause,

355

and for my sake I don't much care whether I go to prison or not.

But if I'm behind bars, no one will be looking for Lottie.

The Met has made it clear that when the current tranche of government funds runs out, they won't apply for more. As far as they're concerned, this is now a cold case. And the Lottie Foundation is fatally compromised: the twin blows of Paul Harding's arrest, and now mine, has sent our donors running for the hills. Even Jack has been forced to distance himself from us in public, though his support in private is the only reason I'm even out on bail.

'I need to apologise to you in person,' I tell Helen, finally. 'I know that can't begin to make up for what I put you through. But I just needed to look you in the eye and tell you how sorry I am.'

Helen says nothing. But when Jeremy returns with the tea, carrying a tray of old-fashioned floral porcelain teacups and saucers, she sits down.

'I was so *sure*,' I say. 'I can see now she's not Lottie; her eyes aren't even the right colour. But at the time, I looked at her and I really *saw* my daughter.'

It wasn't just that she resembled a little girl who could be my daughter. I saw *Lottie*. I was as certain of that as I am of gravity, of the ground beneath my feet. And yet I lied to myself. I'm the unreliable narrator of my own story.

And if I've lied about this, then nothing I say can be trusted.

'I was so sure,' I say again, 'and then Mum died and I'd promised I'd bring Lottie home. I'm not asking for sympathy,' I add. 'I just wanted to explain. I never meant to hurt you, or Flora. I thought I was *rescuing* her.'

There's a long silence. I look down at my hands. I've done exactly what I said I wouldn't do: I've asked for her sympathy.

'I don't need to tell you what you did to me,' Helen says,

keeping her emotion in check with a visible effort. 'When I went down to the beach and she wasn't there. The terror. The panic. I felt like I was drowning. The pressure in my chest . . .' She hesitates, collects herself. 'I don't need to tell you.'

'I'm so sorry—'

'All those nights when I couldn't sleep,' Helen says. 'When I was imagining what'd happened to Flora, who might've snatched her. The *men*.' She stops again, remembering to whom she is speaking. 'I prayed it was someone like you who'd taken her. A woman who'd lost her own child and needed mine. Someone who'd look after her; love her, even. I prayed, and I promised God, if Flora was returned to me, safe and well, I wouldn't ask for anything else. *Just bring her back to me.* That was the bargain I made.'

My throat closes. I've made the same pleas, the same promises.

Helen's knuckles turn white as her hands twist together in her lap and I know how much this is costing her. 'I promised I'd take the gift of my daughter and let everything else go,' she says. 'I promised I wouldn't seek vengeance or punishment. No matter who'd taken her, if I got her back safe, I'd forgive them. And then a miracle happened.' Her voice is suddenly filled with wonder. 'Flora came back.'

We both know she's right: it *is* a miracle. The police will have maintained a facade of optimism while they searched for Flora, but Helen must have googled the truth, as I did, and learned that, after the first three days, only one in twenty children who go missing are found alive. Murderers and paedophiles usually kill their victims long before that. And of those children who are recovered, nearly all are runaways or have been abducted by family members in custody disputes. After ten days, the chances that a child taken by a stranger will be returned safe and well are slim indeed.

After two years?

'You were my miracle,' Helen says. 'You were my nightmare, and then you were my miracle.'

My daughter has been missing for seven hundred and seventy days. There's been no verifiable sighting of her, no trace, in all that time. Now I know I didn't see Lottie on the Tube after all, the tiny flame of hope I've cherished for the last five weeks has no oxygen to feed it. We're back to square one.

In my heart, I know my child must be dead. But if Lottie is still alive, *if*, my prayer is that she's been taken by a woman like me. A deluded, broken woman who believes my child is hers and is keeping her safe. I pray Lottie has forgotten me and thinks of this woman as her mummy. I pray she's loved and warm and happy.

Helen stands. 'I hope you find your daughter,' she says. 'I pray to God she comes back to you, as Flora did to me. And if she does, you have to pay it forward, Alexa, like I'm doing. You have to let the hatred and anger go. You have to *forgive*. That's the deal you've done with the universe.'

And because I would do anything, agree to everything, to have Lottie home, I say yes.

two years and forty-one days missing

two years and forty-one days missing

chapter 68

alex

It's not the funeral my mother deserves. I stole the last two years of her life when I lost her granddaughter and now I'm robbing her of the dignified, public farewell she should've had.

It's impossible to hold the service at my parents' parish church, as Mum wanted, because of the media feeding frenzy surrounding me after my arrest six days ago. So we're forced to say goodbye to her in a small, private chapel set within the grounds of a nearby Benedictine monastery, whose high walls and rolling fields keep the press at bay. We have to limit the ceremony to just a few family and close friends, which is all the tiny church can admit.

For the second time in three years, I stare down at the cold, still face of my dead, pillowed on satin and oak. If there is a god, he's no god of mine.

Dad turns to me, as always, for support. I take his arm and help him to a pew at the front of the chapel; I put my arm around his shoulder when he sobs, broken and bereft, as Father Jonathan urges us to celebrate my mother's life; my voice is clear when I give the reading Aunt Julie chose: *In my house there are many mansions: if it were not so, I would have told you.*

But I can't cry. I can't feel. My heart is flint. The flickering ember of hope for Lottie that sustained me is no more than grey ash in my soul.

When the brief service is over, we spill outside into the chill November afternoon. The pallbearers load Mum's coffin into the hearse for the short journey to the cemetery a few miles away. It's only two-thirty, but the pale sun already hangs low in the grey sky.

I'm surprised to find Jack waiting for me on the gravel pathway behind the chapel, standing beneath an ancient cedar to shelter from the drizzle. He's wearing a smart, thick black wool coat, but his jaw is stubbled and he looks like a man who hasn't seen his own bed in two days.

My frozen heart lifts at the sight of him, in all his shambolic dishevelment.

There's something comforting about his worn-down, worn-in, worn-out cragginess, and I have to resist the temptation to turn down his crooked collar, straighten his tie.

'It was a beautiful service,' Jack says. 'She'd have been very proud of you.'

'I didn't realise you were here.'

'I stayed at the back. Didn't want to intrude.'

'It was kind of you to come.'

Beneath the platitudes, a deeper exchange is taking place. Jack exhales, his breath a puff of white carried on the cold air. It brushes my skin, warm, like a kiss. He smiles and I feel the heat spread to my bones.

Harriet calls out to me from across the car park. 'We should go,' she says. 'Dad and Aunt Julie are waiting in the car.'

'One minute,' I say.

'You should go be with your family,' Jack says. 'I just wanted to let you know, the CPS won't be taking your case any further. It's not official yet; we need to wait for public interest to die down. But if you agree to see a counsellor for a few months, they won't press charges.'

For a moment, I find it hard to speak. Jack must have called in a dozen favours to make this happen.

'Thank you,' I say.

'Don't thank me. Flora's mother lobbied very hard on your behalf.' He hesitates. 'Alex, I'm sorry I wasn't there when you needed me. If I'd picked up your messages when you first saw Flora—'

'It wouldn't have made any difference.'

'You know that's not true.'

'It doesn't matter, Jack. None of this is on you.'

'I was looking for Amira,' Jack says, abruptly. 'My wife.'

I remember who she is.

'It took me a few days to track her down,' he adds. 'I haven't seen her in more than six years. And I didn't want the press getting wind of it, so I took myself off-grid for a bit.'

'You don't have to explain—'

'I asked her for a divorce, Alex. She's got citizenship, now. She doesn't need me.'

His breath mingles with mine in the chill air.

'You don't have to rescue me, Jack.'

'Maybe I'm the one needs rescuing.' He brushes a fallen leaf from my shoulder. 'I'll see you when you get back to London,' he says.

It's a promise. A fragile thread to the future.

Harriet cranes around me as I climb into the car, and the cortege starts to move. 'Who's that?' she asks, watching Jack as he shambles away.

'No one you know,' I say.

My sister exchanges a look with Aunt Julie. There's an air of complicity between them, and I know they've been talking about me.

I shiver, as if someone's walked over my grave.

363

chapter 69

alex

We bury Mum in the cold earth of an ancient cemetery, beneath a juniper tree. Later, at my parents' house, where the wake is being held, I pour myself a thick measure of gin in her memory, savouring the bitter taste.

No one stays long. Aunt Julie passes around platters of curling sandwiches and mini quiches, while Dad sits inert in his armchair, gazing at nothing. He's lost ten pounds in as many days and his skin is thin and loose over his bones. It's as if he's joining Mum in her decay beneath the ground, collapsing in on himself, his blood and muscles and bones turning to putrefaction and rot.

I could tell him: grief is the price we pay for love.

Aunt Julie confers with Harriet in the kitchen, their eyes on Dad as they whisper together. I hadn't really noticed the resemblance between them before, but they could be mother and daughter. They both have the same thick, dark hair, though Aunt Julie's is greying now and caught up in a neat bun, while Harriet's reaches halfway down her back. If Harriet was my cousin rather than my sister, maybe she'd be happier.

After the last of the mourners has gone, I help Harriet wash up. Mum's handbag is still on top of the microwave, next to a pile of unopened bills. Her apron still hangs on the back of the kitchen door.

'Did Aunt Julie say how long she's going to stay here?' I ask.

Harriet hands me a platter to dry. 'A few more days, I think.'

'What about you?'

'I'm leaving tomorrow.'

'Harry—'

'I've already been here three weeks,' she says. 'I've been commissioned to paint a mural at a school in Brae. I can't afford to take any more time off.'

My sister doesn't need to say it: *it's your fault we had to wait to hold Mum's funeral.* Her rigid back does all the talking for her.

We finish washing-up in silence. Aunt Julie is sorting through photographs in the dining room and Dad has gone upstairs to lie down. Grief is wearying; of all its unimaginable aspects, the intensity of the physical symptoms is what takes you by surprise. After Lottie disappeared, I was exhausted all the time.

'Do you think you can come home for Christmas?' I ask Harriet, as we put Mum's best china back in the sideboard. 'I know Dad would like us both here.'

'Maybe,' she says. 'It depends on Mungo. He's got a family, too.'

I feel a wave of sadness. The distance between us has never felt as unbridgeable as it does now. I know she blames the stress of the last two years for driving Mum into an early grave. Blames *me*. But I don't want the next time we see each other to be years from now, at Dad's funeral. I want us to be sisters again.

Harriet's barely spoken to me since she came down from the Shetlands. When I enter a room, she leaves, as if she can't bear to be anywhere near me. I don't think she's looked me in the eye once since she got here. I could understand if this was about Flora Birch, but she's been acting like this towards me for months.

Ever since Lottie went missing, in fact.

I know she blames me for losing Lottie. But if anyone has the right to be upset, it's me. When Lottie was taken, Harriet didn't come to Florida to help look for her. She's my *sister*. How could she not be there for me?

'Aunt Julie said she bumped into you at Heathrow,' I say, suddenly remembering. 'The day Lottie disappeared.'

Harriet has her back to me and I'm not sure she's even listening. She shifts the coffee table an inch to the left and then steps back to consider it, as if its precise positioning is the most absorbing thing she has ever done.

'Where were you going?' I ask, curiously.

'When?'

I suppress a sigh of irritation. 'When Aunt Julie saw you at Heathrow.'

'Mmmm? Oh, yes, we did run into each other. But that was years ago, when Mungo and I were going off on honeymoon. She must've got it muddled.' She nudges the coffee table another inch. 'Does that look like it's in the middle to you?'

Aunt Julie was quite clear. *I ran into her at Heathrow, the day Lottie disappeared.*

In our family, the day my little girl vanished is like 9/11, the death of Princess Diana, the 7/7 bombings on the Tube. We all know what we were doing, where we were, who we were with.

It's not the kind of thing you get confused about.

In the last two years, I've relived the final hours I spent with my daughter a thousand times, a hundred thousand times, slowing and stopping time to examine every detail, hoping this continual, slow-motion reconstruction will help me find the clue that'll lead me to her.

Lottie shoving pieces of paper beneath the bathroom door.

Lottie splashing in the pool.

Lottie holding my hand as we walk along the powdered sand to face the ocean.

Lottie treating Sian with the contempt she deserved.

I've always fast-forwarded through my brief phone call with Harriet, concentrating instead on the moment I turn round and see Lottie talking to a strange man who has his hand on her shoulder.

But now I remember.

I remember the sound of a flight announcement in the background of the call. I remember asking my sister: *Are you at the airport?*

And her answer: *It's just the TV.*

chapter 70

alex

It's not possible.

Harriet would *never*.

My sister may not approve of me or the way I was raising Lottie, but she'd never take my baby away. She'd never put me through this. She'd never put *Mum* through this.

Aunt Julie comes into the sitting room, an album in her hand. 'Some of these photos,' she says, fondly. 'Our *hair*. Look at your mum, in those flares. I can't believe we went out like that.'

'Do you remember when you bumped into Harriet at Heathrow?' I say.

'What, love?'

'You said you ran into her at the airport.'

'When did I say that?'

'After Mum died.'

Aunt Julie glances at Harriet, and then back at me. She closes the album and holds it against her chest. 'I don't think so, love.'

'You said you saw her at the airport the day Lottie disappeared,' I repeat.

'Which airport?'

'Heathrow,' I say, impatiently.

'What would I have been doing in England, love?'

'I don't know! But you said—'

'Alex, I was at home in New Zealand, with your Uncle Bern, when Lottie was taken,' she says. 'I didn't fly out to Florida to help you look for her till days later. I think you've got confused, sweetheart.'

Harriet sighs. 'I told you, Alex. It was when Mungo and I were on honeymoon.'

Suddenly, I feel dizzy, as if I have vertigo. I know I didn't imagine it. I remember: *I ran into her at Heathrow, the day Lottie disappeared.*

But my memory can't be trusted, can it? The debacle with Flora Birch proved that: my need to find my child is so overwhelming, I conjured a mirage so real I couldn't tell the difference between truth and fiction.

Perhaps Harriet and my aunt are right. Maybe I'm remembering fragments of a conversation and splicing them together in my imagination. Harriet has no conceivable reason to lie to me.

Does she?

'Your mum had just died,' Aunt Julie says, touching my arm. 'You were probably in shock, love, and got your wires crossed. Best not to dwell. Now, why don't I make us all a cup of tea, and we can look at some of these photos of your mum together?'

Harriet's voice is surprisingly kind. 'You can't keep on like this, Alex,' she says. 'You need a break. Somewhere you can get away from the press for a bit.'

'I'm on bail,' I say. 'They've taken my passport. I'm not going anywhere.'

That night, as so often, I can't sleep. I tell myself I'm being paranoid, but I can't shake the sensation Harriet and my aunt are hiding something from me.

Harriet knows Aunt Julie much better than I do. She took a gap year while I was at university and spent six months in New Zealand. Neither of them have children; Uncle Bern

369

already had three by his first wife when he met my aunt and didn't want any more. Maybe the two of them—

The two of them *what*? Stole their niece and great-niece and smuggled her to New Zealand or the Shetland Isles? Hid her in an outbuilding somewhere?

I feel as if I'm going mad. I need a break: Harriet was right about that.

The clock on my bedside table says 4.54 a.m. Flinging back my bedcovers, I grab a thick cardigan and fumble my way downstairs in the dark, careful not to tread on the creaky step fourth from the bottom. I let myself out into the back garden and tiptoe through the frost-rimed grass in my bare feet, almost running because of the cold. My breath comes out in white puffs and hangs heavily on the chill night air.

I perch on the mossy stone bench beneath the beech tree, hugging my knees to my chest and curling my feet beneath me for warmth. This is where Mum and I used to sit and chat. She'd be on the deckchair, there, and I'd unburden myself of whatever was troubling me: boys, exams, work.

Lottie.

I close my eyes, listening for her voice, and hear only mocking silence.

The sun hasn't yet risen, but the dense blackness of night is softening into the strange, grey half-light that precedes dawn. I feel as if I've been trapped in this moment of non-being, caught between two worlds, ever since Lottie disappeared. For those who grieve, time is not a linear experience. My purgatory is both endless and rawly fresh.

My eyes sting with sudden tears. I can't keep careening from one crazy conspiracy theory to another, the way I have been ever since I thought I saw Lottie on the Tube. My feet need to touch bottom.

Somehow, I have to find a way to climb back out of the

abyss. For two years, I've clung to the hope of being reunited with my daughter. It's time I figured out how to let her go.

First, I need to heal the breach with Harriet. Whatever's happened between us in the past, we're sisters. Mum would be heartbroken if she could see how wide the rift between us has become. Perhaps I should go back to the Shetlands with Harriet for a while and really get to know who she is. We might surprise ourselves and actually like each other.

With a sudden sense of purpose, I uncurl and head back towards the house. The kitchen is still in darkness as I let myself in. Before I make peace with Harriet, I need to make peace with myself. I can lay my doubts to rest with a single phone call. I unplug my mobile from its charger on the kitchen counter and shut myself in Dad's study at the front of the house, where I won't be overheard.

Mungo answers on the second ring. I'm aware it's still not yet six, but he works shifts on the rigs and I have no idea when a good time would be.

'Mungo, it's Alex,' I say. 'I'm sorry to call so early. Do you have a moment to talk?'

'Two minutes,' he says.

My brother-in-law has always been a man of few words but, even so, I'm surprised by the gruffness of his tone.

'It's about Lottie,' I say. 'The day she disappeared. You were at home that week, weren't you? On the islands, in Brae?'

'Yes.'

'I know this might sound ridiculous, but was Harriet with you?' I wait for him to say, *Yes, of course, where else would she be?*

The silence swirling between us is thick and dense, like fog rolling in from the North Sea.

'What's this about, Alex?' Mungo says.

'I'm just trying to get things clear in my head,' I say.

'You should talk to your sister.'

371

My mouth is dry. 'I'm asking you, Mungo.'

The clock in Dad's study ticks loudly. I can hear the radiator pipes in the walls as the house breathes.

'I've no idea where Harriet was,' he says, finally. 'I have no idea where she *is*. She left me. I came home from the rig one day and she was gone.'

The ground beneath my feet falls away.

'When?' I stammer. 'When did she leave you?'

'That summer. Before your girl was taken.'

That summer.

Two and a half *years* ago.

Why didn't Harriet tell me she'd left Mungo? Why didn't she tell *any* of us? Mum bought her and Mungo an anniversary card only a few weeks before she died. Why keep it a secret?

'Look,' Mungo says. 'I'm sorry. I heard about your mum. She was a nice lady.'

'Thank you.'

'It's been a shit few years,' he says.

'Yeah,' I say. 'Shit.'

'Anyway. The lads are waiting for me, so—'

'Mungo, just one more question. When Lottie disappeared, was Harriet still on Brae?'

'No. She left the island after we split up. She hasn't been back since. I don't know where she's living now. Alex, I'm sorry, but I really have to go.'

I put down my phone and stare at the photograph of Harriet and me on Dad's desk. It was taken seven years ago, at my wedding to Luca. My sister and I have our arms around each other's waists, our heads tilted towards each other, almost touching.

Our smiles are wide and open.

She lied to me.

She wasn't on the Shetland Islands, at home, in Brae.

So where was she?

chapter 71

quinn

Quinn chucks her phone onto the sofa with an exclamation of disgust. The most basic of errors, right at the very start of the police investigation. Christ on the cross.

Those so-called detectives should be strung up.

It's not Penny Williams.

The last official sighting of Lottie Martini, talking to the quote-unquote bride's mother on the beach at the end of the wedding ceremony? *She wasn't talking to Penny.*

Quinn knew there was something off when she read the woman's interview transcript. Mrs Williams remembered verbatim her banal discussion with the hair stylist the morning of the wedding, and every word of the debate with her daughter about the teal nail varnish. But she'd forgotten her entire encounter with a child who's been at the centre of a global manhunt for the last two years?

Nope. Quinn wasn't buying it. So she went back and re-read the interviews with the four wedding guests who'd said they'd seen the little girl talking to Mrs Williams.

They'd all described an older woman with dark hair, wearing a pale blue dress, whom they'd taken to be the bride's mother. But when Quinn tracked them down and spoke to them herself, she discovered not one of them actually *knew* Penny Williams.

All had made an assumption based on the woman's age and the colour of her outfit. And the Florida police had never questioned that assumption by showing any of the witnesses a photo of Mrs Williams, to be sure they were talking about the right woman. Every line of inquiry since the very beginning has been based on the same faulty information. And despite millions of pounds spent by the Met, no one had ever thought to go back and actually *check*.

So Quinn emailed the four witnesses a photo of Penny Williams in her wedding outfit. She's just got off the phone with the last of them.

And now she knows for sure.

Penny Williams doesn't remember her conversation with Lottie because *she wasn't the woman the little girl was talking to*.

The dark-haired woman they saw chatting to Lottie was about the same age as Penny Williams, and her dress was a similar colour. But now the witnesses have seen a photo of the bride's mother, they realise the woman they saw was much more tanned, and thinner. They feel terrible, they just *assumed* . . .

Quinn makes herself some more of her fabled Panamanian coffee and goes back to her computer. She's got a sense she's running out of time. Not to rescue Lottie, but to save Alex.

It's clear the woman's on the edge of a nervous breakdown. And Quinn *owes* her. If she'd answered her phone when Alex called instead of going on a six-day bender, she might've been able to talk her off the ledge. At the very least, she'd have persuaded Alex to get hold of a DNA sample from the girl she was so sure was her daughter and wait for the results *before* taking the law into her own hands. Like it or not, she feels responsible for what happened. The two of them are in this together.

Quinn has skin in this game.

She spends the evening poring over every photo and video clip submitted by wedding guests and tourists to the Florida police department when they made their first appeal for help. She didn't exactly come by them legally, exploiting a source within the police investigation, but in her view the ends justify the means.

She's no idea if the mystery woman Lottie was seen talking to has been captured in any of the photos, but she won't know till she's been through every frame to check. The woman isn't one of the wedding guests; she's already established that. But the beach was open to the public during the wedding ceremony and there are any number of tourists and other hotel guests hovering in the background of photos, enjoying the spectacle from the water's edge. Perhaps she'll get lucky.

Perhaps not.

By 3 a.m., she's been at it for sixteen hours. Her head aches and her back is sore.

She's been through thousands of photos and found nothing.

She goes into the kitchen and grinds yet more beans, wondering if she's reached the end of the line. She'll loop the Met investigation team in tomorrow and let them know what she's learned but, without a photo of the woman, she's not sure what good it'll do.

The trail is over two years old and this is likely to be another red herring, anyway. The woman's probably got nothing to do with the inquiry. Just a sweet old grandma who stopped to tell a bridesmaid how pretty she was and moved on.

Quinn takes her coffee back to her computer and keeps looking.

two years and forty-two days missing

two years and forty-two days missing

chapter 72

alex

'I *am* telling you the truth,' Harriet says.

My sister is sitting opposite me in Mum's deckchair, across from the old stone bench. The sag of the chair is filled with wet leaves, and the bench is cold, but neither of us care. This isn't a conversation we can have in the house, where Dad might overhear us.

'Why should I believe you?' I say.

'Because it's true. I don't know what else to say.' She spreads her hands. 'I've told you everything, now. Why would I lie?'

'Why did you lie *before*?' I say. 'Not telling any of us you'd left Mungo is one thing. I think it's crap, but OK. Maybe you really didn't want to upset Mum. But all the rest of it?' My voice rises. 'You're full of shit, Harriet.'

'Sssh,' Harriet says. 'We don't want Dad to come out.'

My anger suddenly leaches away. I stand up, wrapping my cardigan more tightly around myself, staring out at the small copse of trees behind my parents' house. Harriet and I used to play for hours on end in the woods, building dens and tree-houses, swinging on the tyre Dad had hung from an old oak tree, stuffing our faces with blackberries in the autumn until we made ourselves sick.

Back then, she was my best friend.

'Every single morning,' I say, 'I wake up and there's a moment, a split second, when I think it's all been a terrible dream. A part of me wants to stay in that moment forever, and I'm finding it harder and harder to let go of the fantasy and come back to the real world.' I turn back to face her. 'I just abducted a child I thought was Lottie. I *kidnapped* her. I'm on the edge, Harry! And you made me believe I'd imagined an entire conversation. You had me thinking I was going mad.'

She looks uncomfortable. 'I never meant it to go this far.'

'You *gaslighted* me. How could you, Harriet?'

An odd expression passes across her face. '*I* gaslighted *you*? I've spent my entire life being gaslighted by you!'

'What does that—'

'It means I grew up thinking I was stupid and dull, when the only thing wrong with me was that I wasn't *you!* Don't pretend you didn't know,' Harriet adds, fiercely. 'You loved being the centre of Mum and Dad's world. You sucked up all the attention and they'd got nothing left for me. I had to move to the bloody Shetlands to get out from under your shadow. The last two years of Mum's life have been entirely about you: you and your drama, you and your tragedy. It's all we *ever* talked about. Mum never once called to ask how *I* was doing.'

'Jesus, Harriet! My daughter was *abducted*!'

'You think I *like* being this person?' she cries, leaping to her feet. 'Most of the time, I can't bear to look myself in the mirror!'

I'm taken aback. I know she's always felt left out, but I had no idea she was this jealous. This *angry*.

'I didn't tell Mum and Dad I'd left Mungo because I didn't want them to be any more disappointed in me than they already are,' she says. '*Poor old Harry, can't have kids, useless job, broken marriage.* There's no sinister explanation why I didn't tell anyone about it, Alex! I just wanted a chance to lick my wounds for a bit before I had to face everyone, that's all. I was waiting for

380

the right time to tell you, but then Lottie disappeared, and the right time never came. It wasn't about *you*,' she adds, bitterly. 'It's not always about you.'

'But why lie about where you were that day?' I say. 'Why pretend you were at home with Mungo? Where *were* you?'

'I don't have to tell you everything!'

'You do when it concerns my daughter!'

'What kind of monster d'you think I am?' Harriet demands. 'Do you really think I had *anything* to do with what happened to Lottie? I love that little girl more than anyone!'

'Maybe that's the problem!'

We face each other, our breath coming in short, sharp pants that linger like smoke in the crisp air.

When Harriet speaks again, her tone is conciliatory. 'Alex, I know you're hurting, but this is crazy. Even if I wanted to, I wouldn't know how to begin to pull something like this off. Come on. This isn't you—'

'Did Aunt Julie help you? Is that how you did it?'

'You're sick, Alex. You need help.'

'Don't walk away from me!' I shout, grabbing her arm as she turns back to the house. 'You didn't answer my question. Where were you when Lottie disappeared? Did you get Aunt Julie to lie for you? Is she in on it, too?'

'You know why you're so frantic to get her back?' Harriet cries, shaking me off. 'It's not because you love her so much, Alex! It's because you didn't love her *enough*! You feel guilty because you never really wanted her! *That's* what all this is about!'

I reel, as if I've been sucker-punched.

It's because you didn't love her enough.

Seven words that damn me to hell.

She's right.

Only a sister knows exactly how to pierce your defences

and strike right at your soft underbelly. *I'm* the reason Lottie was taken. I'm the reason my little girl is rotting in the earth somewhere or trapped in a living death in a cellar. From the moment she was born, I handed her off to Luca, to nursery, to anyone who'd take her for five minutes.

I deserved to lose her, because I didn't want her enough.

'I didn't mean it,' Harriet says, looking stricken. 'I take it back. I didn't mean it.'

'Yes, you did.'

'Alex, please. I didn't mean it. I know you love Lottie, of course I do.'

I turn towards the house, sickened to my stomach. The words can't be unsaid. She can't retract them, because they're true. Guilt has underpinned every waking moment since the day my daughter was stolen from me: Harriet just gave it a voice. She calls to me across the lawn. 'I was having an affair,' she says.

I stop.

'The day Lottie disappeared. I left Mungo because I'd met someone else,' Harriet adds. 'I was flying out to Cyprus to be with him.'

It totally takes me by surprise. It's ridiculous, of course: Harriet's as human as anyone else. And yet I never saw this coming. She may be an artist, but she's always been such a rule-follower, so proper and conventional.

'Why didn't you just tell me?' I say. 'Why make such a secret of it?'

'Because he's married,' she says, a flush stealing across her cheeks. 'And after Luca . . . I know how you feel about that sort of thing. It's over now,' she adds quickly. 'He went back to his wife after four months. Serves me right, I know. I moved back to the Shetlands a few months ago, but I haven't told Mungo. I didn't want to make it any worse for him.'

'Oh, Harry.'

382

'I should never have lied. I'm so sorry, Alex. I didn't take Lottie, I swear—'

'I know you didn't. I'm sorry I ever—'

She pulls me into a hug, the first I can remember sharing with her since we were kids at South Weald House. After a moment, I wrap my arms around her and hug her back.

Only much later, on the drive back to London, does it occur to me to wonder why my aunt lied about being at the airport, too.

two years and forty-three days missing

chapter 73

quinn

Quinn finds the mystery woman.

Of course she does: she's Quinn Wilde.

It takes her forty-two hours and so many Panamanian coffee beans she'll never sleep again, but there she is: the dark-haired woman in the lilac dress, right at the edge of a photo taken by one of the wedding guests.

From the timestamp, it was evidently snapped at the end of the ceremony; the bride and groom are facing their guests, preparing to walk back down the sandy aisle together as man and wife. Whoever took it must've been sitting towards the rear of the rows of chairs because much of the foreground comprises a blur of the back of people's heads.

But the woman in lilac is in perfect focus.

She's standing by the shore with several other tourists who've stopped to watch the ceremony. Quinn almost didn't spot her, because most of her distinctive lilac outfit is obscured by the photographer's fat finger. But there she is, staring at the wedding party under the canopy.

At Lottie.

Quinn crops everyone else out of the photo and runs it through some enhancing software, enlarging and sharpening the image of the woman until her features are recognisable.

She's in her mid to late sixties, at a guess. Her skin has the deep caramel tan of someone who's spent a lot of time in the sun over many years, not just a few weeks on their summer holidays, suggesting she's either a native Floridian or lives somewhere warm, like Australia. Her dark hair is heavily greying and pulled back from her face in a ballerina bun at the nape of her neck. There's nothing remarkable about her; had Quinn not been looking for her, she'd have been just another face, lost in the crowd.

She can see why the four witnesses confused the woman with Penny Williams. They resemble each other quite closely and they're wearing similar dresses. If this woman's the kidnapper, she certainly had luck on her side.

Those spidey senses of Quinn's tingle. The woman could just be a local who was taking a sunset walk along the beach and stopped to enjoy the romantic spectacle. Complimented Lottie on her dress, perhaps, or told her not to go too near the water.

But Lottie's abduction was on every news channel and in every newspaper for weeks afterwards. There were posters of her in supermarkets and bars all over St Pete Beach; the president even made an appeal for her safe return. Unless this woman lived under a rock, she must've known there was an international manhunt underway for the little flower girl she'd stopped and chatted to.

So why didn't she come forward?

Quinn copies the enhanced image into a text message to Alex, and then hesitates. She doesn't want to send the poor woman down a conspiracy rabbit hole again, especially since she's got no actual proof the woman in lilac has any bearing on the case. She knows the chance Alex will recognise her is remote at best.

But if this woman *is* the one who took Lottie, then clearly the little girl felt comfortable enough to go with her without making a fuss. Which means Alex *met* her.

In a nail bar, maybe. Handing out towels by the pool.

It's got to be worth a shot.

Quinn hits send.

chapter 74

alex

I recognise her instantly.

Of course I do. She's *family*.

Lottie would've gone with her without protest. She'd have believed any story she was told.

I want to throw up. Lottie was probably on her way to Tampa airport before I even knew she was missing. She'd have been on the other side of the world by daybreak.

We never had any hope of finding her.

With a howl of fury that comes from the depths of my soul, I sweep everything from my desk, blind with rage. I hurl books from my shelves, rip pictures from the wall, throw anything and everything I can get my hands on, as two years of pent-up fear and grief and guilt course through me like molten lava.

I've spent seven hundred and seventy-four days in a circle of hell even Dante couldn't have imagined. I've tormented myself with images of what my little girl might be enduring at the hands of sick, evil men, and pictured her last moments, the terror my baby must have felt, on a nauseating, inescapable loop in my head for more than two years. I've heard her voice in the middle of the night, calling out for her mummy. I've known the excruciating torture of praying my child is dead, rather than suffering.

And the woman who did this to me, who put me through this indescribable nightmare, is someone I once thought of as family.

My berserker frenzy eventually abates and I lean on my empty desk, panting. Now the red mist has lifted, all that's left is a cold, unyielding hatred. I finally know where my daughter is. As soon as I knew the *who*, the *where* was obvious. I'm going to find Lottie and I'm going to lay waste to this woman's life.

We won't both walk away from this. Which means I need someone to make sure my girl gets home safely, no matter what happens to me.

Someone who isn't afraid to break rules.

I find my phone amid the debris on the floor and pull up Quinn Wilde's number.

two years and forty-four days missing

chapter 75

alex

I scan my boarding pass through the reader and hand over my passport. My heart pounds as the woman on security swipes it through her scanner. I used the same false ID to make the hotel and car hire reservations when I snatched Flora Birch and I cross my fingers some bright detective hasn't thought to put out an all-ports alert on my alias as well as my real name.

But the security guard barely gives *Alicia Emma Douglas* a second glance as she waves me towards the body scanner.

It's Quinn who triggers the alarm, with her metal spinal rods and plates and screws. It takes twenty minutes for a female officer to be found to pat her down, my agitation growing with every second.

'You need to chill,' Quinn says, as she's finally cleared and we head towards our gate. 'Take a bloody Valium if you're nervous. You're going to attract attention.'

'What if someone recognises me?'

'In that get-up?'

I've tucked my hair beneath a grey beanie, and I'm wearing combat trousers and an oversized plaid shirt, a far cry from my usual crisp, tailored suit and brogues. But I won't fool facial recognition software or a sharp-eyed reader of the *Mail*.

I haven't slept in more than thirty hours but I'm so wired

I find it hard to keep still. My body vibrates with adrenaline as we take our seats on the plane. *Lottie is alive.* I know it in my soul, in the very marrow of my bones. She's alive and she's just one plane ride away from me.

'Remember what you promised,' I tell Quinn. 'Lottie's all that matters. If something goes wrong, you don't wait for me. You take Lottie and you leave.'

Quinn nods brusquely.

I lean back in my seat and close my eyes, trying to steady my jangling nerves. I made the right decision when I asked Quinn along. Jack would try to rescue me if I was in danger. I need someone who can walk away.

The woman must think she's safe now; that she's got away with it. After all, in more than two years, I've never even come close to guessing the truth, even though it was right under my nose. In her own warped, distorted way, I know she loves Lottie. She thinks she's keeping her safe. But I've got no idea what she'll do when she's cornered.

Which is what makes her so dangerous.

Quinn and I don't talk much on the drive from the airport. The air-conditioning in our rental car isn't working, so I power down the windows, since it's surprisingly warm given the time of year.

I'm not used to driving a manual vehicle and repeatedly crash the gears as I negotiate the mountain's sharp hairpin bends.

'Jesus,' Quinn says, after the third or fourth time. 'Want me to drive?'

'Very funny,' I mutter, struggling to get into third.

The landscape is barren and arid, one long undulating mass of sun-scorched fields littered with abandoned houses and farmsteads. Pockets of eucalyptus suddenly give way to stretches of scrubby grassland. Isolated mountaintop towns glower down on modern roads that have passed them by. It's a beautiful, uncompromising land; a timeless vista of silent, sunburnt peaks, grey stone villages and forgotten valleys.

'There,' I say suddenly.

I point. It takes Quinn a moment to locate the villa, squatting on top of a small crag. Its ancient stone walls blend perfectly into the parched landscape.

'Fuck. You weren't kidding,' she says.

There's no way to approach the property unseen. The villa is effectively a small fortress, perched on its lonely mount with a clear view in every direction. It was built to defend itself against medieval marauders and I have no time to lay siege. I want my child back.

So I'm going to march up to the front door and ask for her.

The road forks a few metres ahead of us. I turn right, onto a narrow, unpaved track that corkscrews up the peak towards the villa, jolting in first gear over rocks and deep, sun-baked ruts.

The track stops in front of a low stone wall encircling the building two-thirds of the way up the mountain. We'll have to make the rest of the way on foot.

Quinn struggles to keep her balance on the uneven ground, but I'm too keyed up to wait for her. I'm almost running up the steep slope now, sending stones skittering down the hillside behind me.

I stop when I reach the entrance, a latticed iron door which opens onto a large, tranquil courtyard. Colonnaded archways lead off to cool, open-sided rooms on three sides of the courtyard, while a small fountain surrounded by stone benches burbles quietly in the centre.

The villa seems deserted, but I know our approach must have been heard. As Quinn finally reaches the top of the hill, panting with exertion, I open a small wooden panel in the wall to the right of the door and reach for the bell pull within.

We wait, the sun beating down on us, as the bell echoes distantly within the villa. The final reverberations die away, leaving behind a silence broken only by the sound of water splashing in the fountain and the rasp of cicadas.

I'm about to reach for the bell pull again when a door slams deep inside the villa. We hear footsteps coming towards us.

My stomach fizzes with nerves. My chest tightens and it's suddenly hard to breathe.

A woman approaches the latticed door.

The woman from the photograph: the woman who stole my child.

chapter 76

alex

Luca's mother raises the edge of her hand to her eyes, blocking out the sun. We're backlit against it, our faces in shadow, and it takes her a moment to recognise me.

Her reaction is absolutely the last thing I expect.

'*La mia bellissima figlia!*' she exclaims. '*Vieni qui! Vieni qui!*'

She beckons us forward, her face wreathed in smiles as she unlocks the latticed iron gate.

'Roberto!' she shouts over her shoulder. '*Vieni qui presto, sono Alexa!*'

'What the fuck?' Quinn mutters.

Elena Martini presses her palms on either side of my face, squeezing my cheeks, and then clasps her hands joyfully to her heart, shaking her head in wonder.

'*Mio cara! Questo è un miracolo!* Roberto!' she shouts again.

She looks much older than I remember. It's only three years since I last saw her at Luca's funeral, but her hair is almost entirely white now and her weathered skin has an unhealthy yellowish cast to it. There's a vacant look in her eyes, too, that makes me wonder how advanced her dementia is. She's always been a petite woman, but now she looks fragile and insubstantial, as if a puff of wind might blow her across the courtyard.

Roberto doesn't appear. Elena ushers us through an archway

and into a cool sitting room on the far side of the courtyard. A flight of stone steps in the corner of the room leads down to a second, lower courtyard filled with bougainvillea, the purple blossoms a vivid splash of colour against the mellow gold stone. A window set high in one wall reveals sweeping views of the valley below.

I remember being shown into this same room when Luca brought me back to meet his parents. Then, as now, I was struck by its strong Arab influence: the kilim rug in muted shades of blue and red, the engraved Moroccan silver coffee table, the blown glass hookah beside the fireplace. Sicily is as much Arabian as it is Italian, a legacy of the island's conquest by Saracens in the ninth century, and more than two hundred years of subsequent Muslim rule.

When I first came here, I'd been to Italy several times before with my parents, and I'd even spent one summer waitressing along the Amalfi coast. But the tourist Italy I'd known hadn't been *this* Italy. Sitting in that Moorish room seven years ago, I'd been struck by a truth whose significance I only realised after we married: Luca and I might both be cosmopolitan Europeans on the surface, but we came from very different cultures and backgrounds.

Elena waves us towards a semicircle of white linen sofas scattered with mirrored cushions. '*Caffè? Acqua? Tè alla menta? Solo un momento, per favor.*'

She returns to the courtyard and we hear her call out to an unseen maid. My sense of dislocation grows. I feel as if I've slipped into a parallel universe, in which my child is not missing and my mother-in-law and I are in the habit of spending the afternoon drinking mint tea.

'My Italian's pretty basic,' Quinn murmurs, 'but I think your mother-in-law just went off to kill the fatted calf.'

'I told you, she's crazy,' I say, going over to the window.

'She saw us coming up the hill. Roberto must be hiding with Lottie while she tries to get rid of us.'

There's only one road down the mountain: the same way we came up. It's impossible to approach the villa unseen, but equally impossible to leave without being spotted. If Roberto, or anyone else, tries to spirit Lottie away while Elena distracts me, I'll see them from here.

'You *are* sure it's her in the photo, right?' Quinn asks.

'Of course I'm sure!'

She looks sceptical. I don't blame her: despite my confident assertion, suddenly I'm not sure at all.

Could a senile old woman really kidnap a child and smuggle her thousands of miles across international borders? Quinn had to enhance that blurry photograph with some high-tech software to make the woman's face recognisable. Maybe the process made a passing resemblance appear much stronger than it was. Maybe I *wanted* to see Elena's face, because that would mean my daughter was still alive. Would she really have welcomed me with such open arms if Lottie was hidden somewhere in the villa?

I was wrong about Flora Birch. Am I wrong about this, too?

My former mother-in-law returns and sits down, patting the sofa for me to join her. I pretend not to notice, keeping my vigil at the window.

'*Quindi, chi è questo?*' Elena asks, indicating Quinn.

'She's a friend of mine,' I say.

'*Alexa, cara*, why you are here? You have news *della mia bella ragazza?*'

Her beautiful girl?

I'm suddenly filled with anger. After Luca's funeral, Elena cut me off as if I'd never existed. She never once got in touch with me to see how I was or asked to see her granddaughter. I didn't pursue it, because of her dementia; when Lottie disappeared, it was Roberto, not Elena, who sent me a brief letter of condolence, offering to send money and promising to pray for Lottie.

I'm not her *bellissima* daughter and I never have been. This sweet old lady routine is all an act.

I pull up the photograph on my phone and thrust it in front of her. Elena peers at the screen. '*Chi è questo?*' she asks.

'You know who it is,' I say.

She glances from the phone to me and back again, confused.

'It's you,' I say, impatiently.

She bursts out laughing. '*Sono io?*' she exclaims. 'No!'

'It's you, on the beach in Florida,' I say, struggling to control my temper. 'The day Lottie disappeared.'

'*No, non sono io. Questa donna è molto più grassa* – more fat than me!' She wags her finger in a mock admonishment, still laughing. 'I am not such fat woman, Alexa. Not such old.'

We're talking about the kidnap of my daughter – her own granddaughter. As crazy as she is, I can't see how she can find anything about this conversation amusing.

'If it's not you, Elena, do you know who it is?' Quinn asks.

The old woman shrugs helplessly. '*Non sono io,*' she says again.

She seems genuinely perplexed by our questions. Is this all part of her dementia? Does she even remember what she's done?

'This isn't getting us anywhere,' I say, frustrated.

'Can we look around the villa?' Quinn asks, gesturing to make herself understood.

Elena beams. '*È bello, sì?*'

'Very beautiful,' Quinn says. 'Please, I'd love you to show it to me.'

I want to rip the villa apart stone by stone, not shuffle around after this demented old woman admiring tapestries.

'Trust me,' Quinn murmurs, as she offers the old woman her arm.

She's effusive in her praise as Elena gives us a tour and the old woman visibly blooms as she shows us around. She proudly shows us hidden passageways and concealed rooms we'd never have found without her. There's no sign of either Roberto or the maid.

And there's no sign a child lives here, either.

No toys, no scribbled pictures, no unmade bed, no children's books, no small shoes tumbled near the door.

Lottie isn't here.

We search the villa from top to bottom. My daughter isn't here and clearly never has been. I was wrong about the photo. It wasn't Elena on the beach, after all. This is yet another false trail, one more dead end born of wishful thinking and the same dysmorphic longing that caused me to see Lottie in another girl's face.

Elena isn't a crazy kidnapper. She's just a lonely, half-senile old woman who's lost both her son and her granddaughter. She welcomed me into her home when I turned up unannounced on her doorstep and I hope she never knows why I was really here.

I'm suddenly as desperate to escape the villa as I was to reach it.

'I need to get out of here,' I tell Quinn as we return to the courtyard.

'Just because Lottie's not here now, Alex, it doesn't mean—'

'I was wrong, Quinn. It's not her.'

'Are you sure?'

'Look at her,' I say, as Elena sinks onto a stone bench by the fountain. Her mouth is slightly open and her eyes are dull. 'She couldn't shoplift a lipstick, never mind kidnap a child.'

'Your call,' Quinn says.

I can't do this any more. I always said I'd never stop looking for Lottie, but I can't keep riding these tsunamis of alternating hope and despair. I'm jumping at shadows, suspicious of everything, trusting no one. In the last two days, I've accused my sister and my former mother-in-law, with little evidence for either. It has to stop.

'Mind if I use the bathroom?' Quinn asks Elena.

She points to a door near the iron gate. '*Questo è il più vicino.*'

As Quinn tries to open the door to the lavatory, it jams. Something is evidently caught beneath it, and she struggles to free it with just her good hand.

I go over to help her and then stop. My blood turns to ice.

The reason the door won't open is because, crammed beneath it by little fingers, are a dozen small pieces of paper.

chapter 77

alex

Lottie, here.

My daughter, here, in this villa, pushing small scraps of paper beneath the bathroom door.

She's been here all the time.

The next second, I have Elena by the shoulders. 'Where is she?' I shout, shaking the woman so hard her head whips back and forth. 'What have you done with her? *Where is she*?'

Quinn tries to pull me off, but my rage is so visceral, so primitive, so filled with all the fear and pain and grief of the last two years that I'm beyond reach. I'm consumed by a fury that will engulf us all.

'Jesus! You're going to kill her!' Quinn cries. 'Alex, for God's sake! She can't tell you anything like this! Let her go!'

She finally penetrates the red mist. With a feral howl, I shove the old woman away from me. Quinn catches her before she falls. 'Alex, what the hell?'

'Lottie was *here*,' I say. Disgust thickens my voice like mucus. 'The bitch has been lying to us from the beginning. Those pieces of paper under the door. It's something Lottie used to do when she was anxious. She was *here*.'

Quinn withdraws her comforting arm from Elena's shoulders. This time she doesn't need to ask me if I'm sure.

'She isn't here now,' Quinn says. 'We've searched this place top to bottom.'

'Perhaps they don't keep her here. Maybe Roberto has taken her somewhere else. Perhaps they keep her in a fucking dungeon!'

Elena starts to sob, rocking back and forth on the bench, her hands covering her face. I watch her with something close to hatred. I don't care how old she is, how senile, how lonely. She stole my child from me. There's no punishment I could mete out that would be fittingly cruel.

I crouch down in front of her and grab her hands, roughly forcing them from her face. '*Dov'è* Lottie?' I demand. 'Where have you taken her? Where is she?'

'*Non capisco, non capisco—*'

'You understand,' I say, grimly. 'Where is she, Elena?'

'*Non lo so,*' the woman whimpers.

I brandish my phone in front of her, forcing her to look at the photograph. 'This is *you*! You were *there* the day Lottie disappeared! Where is she?'

'*Non lo so. Non lo so!*'

I don't know. I don't know.

'Goddamn it,' I say, rocking back on my heels.

'She's fucking terrified, Alex.'

'She should be,' I snarl.

I suppress the urge to put my hands around the woman's throat and squeeze the truth out of her. Lottie loved her nonna; before Luca died, he often took her to see his ailing parents in Genoa, knowing how much it cheered them. Lottie would have gone with her grandmother willingly. How could Elena do this to me? Did she just wake up one day and decide that because she'd lost her child, she'd take mine? Or is she simply mad?

Without pity, I seize Elena's wrist and haul her to her feet. She's so light, she can't weigh more than a child herself.

'I don't care if we have to tear this place apart,' I tell her. 'If Lottie is here, we'll find her. Do you understand, Elena? *Capisci?*'

'Wait,' Quinn says suddenly.

Footsteps echo from within the villa. Roberto: the tread is too heavy to be the maid. There's no attempt to approach quietly; either he doesn't know or doesn't care that we're here.

Quinn edges out of sight, behind an archway, her phone in her hand.

'Roberto!' Elena cries.

She twists free of my grip with surprising strength, breaking towards him. He opens one arm, pulling her into a casual embrace and dropping a kiss onto the top of her white head. His black eyes don't leave mine for one second.

My mouth is so dry my tongue cleaves to the roof. There's a burning sensation behind my eyes, a jangling in my ears. I try to speak, but the muscles in my cheeks are numb with shock.

'Hello, Alex,' Luca says.

chapter 78

alex

Everything seems to stop and spin. I don't know if the sound in my head is the wind whipping through the courtyard or the blood rushing to my ears. My stomach swoops, as if I'm falling into an abyss. My gut churns and my lungs constrict and it's suddenly hard to breathe.

It's not possible.

Luca is dead. I was there when he was buried.

I *saw* him go into the ground.

I watch my dead husband saunter across the courtyard, solicitously seating his mother back on the stone bench by the fountain. A pungent, sweet smell is suddenly strong in my nostrils: the woody, spicy scent of incense, eddying around the courtyard. I hear the clink of the chain as the priest raises his gold thurible, the muffled sound of stifled sobs, the shuffle of feet on the flagstones, the ancient pews creaking as mourners take their seats.

My brain struggles to process conflicting images, superimposing them on each other like a photographic double negative:

Luca in his coffin, beautiful and pale and still.

Luca in front of me, tanned and vital and alive.

'I'm impressed,' he says to me. 'You actually found us. I wondered if you might. Mamma here was certain you'd give

408

up, but I told her, you don't know Alex.' He smiles fondly at Elena. 'She doesn't remember much, these days. She hasn't been the same since Papà died last year. She doesn't know what day it is, most of the time. She thinks I'm my father, and I don't have the heart to correct her.'

Shock is the mind's way of protecting you, a shutdown mechanism designed to buy you time to repair your shattered defences. The external world fades from view; sound and sight are put on hold as the brain eliminates distraction, while it reconciles your lived experience with the impossible. Only when your mind has caught up does the real world come roaring back, vivid and unstoppable.

My first thought:

'Where is she?' I say.

'Lottie's safe,' Luca says. 'Whatever you're thinking of doing right now, Alex, stop. If you want to see her again, that is.'

I clench my hands against my thighs, my nails digging into my palms, to stop myself from flying at him and gouging out those come-to-bed eyes, ripping the flesh from his beautiful bones.

He faked his own death.

I can't imagine how confused Lottie must be. He's not just the narcissist I always suspected him to be; he's a psychopath. His very existence is living proof: there's nothing this man won't do.

But even as I try to wrap my head around this, I'm aware the ice I'm standing on is perilously thin.

I've seen him, now. His cover is blown.

He can't let me leave.

Quinn is still hidden in the shadows of the loggia and I realise Luca hasn't seen her. For the briefest of moments, I catch her eye, and she nods.

Lottie's all that matters. If something goes wrong, you don't wait for me. You take Lottie and you leave.

409

'I buried you, Luca!' I cry, making sure his attention stays on me. 'You were dead. I *saw* you!'

'You saw what you were meant to see.'

'How? How is it even possible?'

Luca rubs a pale scar on his forehead. 'I *was* in the Genoa bridge collapse. That wasn't a lie. I was in a coma for more than six weeks. In a state like that your body shuts down, and your breathing slows way, way down. Your circulation slows, too: you're pale as death, and it's hard for someone to find a pulse. You'd think I *was* dead, to look at me. Unless you touched me and realised I was still warm, you'd never know I was alive.'

'You staged your own funeral,' I say, incredulously.

'Actually, my mother did that,' Luca says.

I glance at Elena, sitting silent and slack-jawed on the stone bench, gazing blankly into the distance. She was very careful no one got too near his coffin, I remember suddenly. Flowers were heaped all around the catafalque, making it hard to get near: I was at least six feet away from Luca, perhaps more. And the only people at the funeral were Luca's Sicilian family, who'd have closed ranks around Elena. But she still must have had nerves of steel to pull this off.

Looking at her now, it's hard to imagine her capable of it. But dementia isn't linear, of course. Elena had just been diagnosed with the disease when Luca went to visit her nearly three-and-a-half years ago, but he said she was still fully coherent and functional: unless you spent time with her at close quarters, you'd never have guessed she was beginning to lose her mind. Her behaviour at the funeral seemed perfectly rational to me, especially in the context of a mother's grief. There was no sign of the moonstruck, senile old woman she is now.

Luca's father must have been part of the lie too, I realise.

410

Elena couldn't have managed deceit on this scale without his cooperation. She was always the dominant one in their relationship: he'd have done whatever she asked.

Luca frowns. 'I still get headaches. It's hard, sometimes, to concentrate.'

There's a shadow in his eyes, a darkness, a confusion, as if he himself can't quite remember how he got here any more. 'Mamma thought she was doing it for the best,' he says. 'A gift from God, she called it. *Un dono di Dio.*'

'Luca, you're not making any sense.'

He rubs his hand over his face. He's lost weight, I realise, more than is healthy; beneath the tan, his beautiful face is drawn. You could cut diamonds on his cheekbones.

'I was in trouble, Alex, after we divorced. There was a woman.' He sighs. 'I know. Always a woman, right? She was Genovese; I met her when I was visiting my parents. It turns out she was married.'

His eyes dart nervously around the courtyard.

'Her husband's a bad guy, Alex,' he says. 'I got in over my head. *Way* over my head. He's got connections everywhere. I couldn't go to the police, because half of them were working for him. I didn't know what to do. I was scared to come home, to London, in case I led him to you and Lottie, scared to go back to my parents. And then the bridge in Genoa collapsed and, the next day, they found my car, crushed to nothing. Everyone thought I was dead.'

I have no idea how much of this is true and how much just paranoia. But Luca evidently believes it.

'I didn't have any ID on me and I was admitted to hospital as a Mario Rossi – what would you say? John Doe? Or is that just in America?' He shrugs. 'When my father finally found me, after three days, he had me transferred to a hospital here, in Sicily, using my mother's name. Luca Bonfiglio.'

411

'Why didn't you tell *me*?' I say. 'How could you let *us* think you were dead?'

'It wasn't my choice,' Luca says. 'I swear to you, Alex. I was in a coma for weeks and afterwards I had to learn how to do everything again. How to walk, how to eat. It was months before I learned what my parents had—'

'But it was your choice to keep the charade going!'

His expression darkens. He is Luca, but not Luca, I realise suddenly. He's changed. The accident has left invisible scars deeper than the one above his eye. He seems brittle, volatile, as if he doesn't know himself which way he's going to break.

'We were divorced, Alex,' he says, coolly. 'Why should you care if I'm alive or dead?'

'Of course I care! And what about Lottie?'

'I came back for her,' Luca says.

'You *stole* her! You didn't even let me know she was alive!'

'You didn't want her. *I* was the one who looked after her. It's better she's with me. I'm not the only one who thinks so.'

There's something in his smile that gives me pause. A spite I've never seen before.

'What does that mean?' I say.

'How d'you think my mother knew to be on the beach at that time, on that day?' he says. 'Work it out, Alex.'

Someone told him about the wedding.

Someone close to me, someone I trusted.

'Who?' I say.

He laughs. 'Ask your boyfriend,' he says.

412

chapter 79

alex

It feels as if I've been punched in the throat. Suddenly it's hard to breathe.

Marc set me up.

He's the reason Elena Martini was on the beach that day.

He's known where Lottie was all along.

Marc was never my boyfriend, of course, but that's what Luca always called him: *Your boyfriend's on the phone. Off to have dinner with your boyfriend?*

'Marc knows you are alive?'

'No, he doesn't know. It was a lucky coincidence. I'd resigned myself to never seeing Lottie again, but then he contacted my mother a few months after I "died" and they arranged it between them. He thought he was sending Lottie to her grandmother.'

Somehow Marc's treachery is the worst of all. Luca is Lottie's father; however deluded he is, he does at least have some claim to her. He didn't play the role of devoted friend, campaigning and fundraising to find a child whose whereabouts he already knew. He didn't hold my hand and comfort me as I sobbed my heartbreak to him, knowing he could alleviate my grief and misery in a moment.

'*Why?*' I say.

413

'Why d'you think?'

I suddenly remember the last time I saw Marc: *After all I've done for you*.

He didn't mean what he'd done to *help* me.

He meant what he'd done to *win* me.

I want to vomit. Did he think with Lottie out of the way I'd have time for him? Or perhaps it's even darker: he wanted me to suffer, believing, *in extremis*, I'd turn to him.

And for a while, at least, he was right.

Marc's the one who broke into my house, I realise. He wanted to see how close we were getting. How near to the truth.

He must've stolen that photo of my sister and me eating ice-creams on the lawn at South Weald House to distract me – unless there's a more sinister reason he wanted a picture of me as a child. My stomach curdles when I think that I let him tuck Lottie into bed.

'I'm tired. I need to sit down,' Luca says, abruptly.

He crosses the courtyard towards the shade of the loggia, his movements those of a much older man. His left foot drags slightly and, when he sits down, he does so carefully, positioning a cushion in the small of his back.

I feel an unexpected pang of loss. Luca might not have died three years ago in Genoa, but the young, handsome, vibrant man I knew did vanish that day. I don't recognise the thin, haunted stranger who's taken his place.

'Where is she?' I demand. 'Is she here?'

'She's with her family.'

'I'm her *mother*!'

His beautiful eyes suddenly blaze with anger. 'You have no right to call yourself that! You were fucking a stranger when you should've been looking after her! If my mother hadn't rescued her, who knows what could have happened!'

I want to slam his head against the stone wall behind him. For two years, I've been tormented by visions of *what could have happened*: my daughter chained in a cellar, passed around among depraved men, rotting in a makeshift grave.

Luca could have spared me that agony with a single text.

It takes a huge effort to swallow my rage. But the only thing that matters now is giving Quinn enough time to get my daughter safely away from this man and his insane mother.

I crouch down before him. 'Luca, I know I wasn't the perfect mother,' I say, my tone conciliatory. 'But I've loved the very bones of our girl, since the moment she was born.' My voice cracks. 'When she was taken from me, it was like my heart had been ripped out while it was still beating. I may not have been a natural mother or even a good one. But I *am* her mother, Luca. And she needs me.'

For a moment, I think I've reached him.

'You were never there,' he says. 'How many times did you actually give Lottie a bath? Feed her or change her? The only thing you ever cared about was *work*.'

'My job never mattered more to me than Lottie! Do you have any idea what the last two years have been like for me, Luca? Can you even imagine?'

'I follow the news,' he says, shortly.

'Then you know I've flown all over the world looking for her! Every time there was a sighting, I was on another plane! Morocco, Algeria, Thailand – you broke my heart a thousand times!' I can no longer control my anger. 'How could you do that to me, Luca? How could you put me through that? You destroyed my life!'

'I missed her, too!' Luca says. 'I thought I'd never see her again, and then Marc called my mother and offered a solution. What was I supposed to do?'

I'm exhausted by the futility of it all: our missteps, our

415

mistakes. All the damage we've caused the child at the centre of our conflict.

'Luca, this has to stop,' I say wearily. '*We* have to stop. We have to do what's best for Lottie now. She needs a normal life.'

'She *has* a normal life.'

'Does she have friends? Go to school?'

'Of course! I don't keep her in a cage, Alex. She goes to the school in the village. We use my mother's name. She's Carlotta Bonfiglio now. Carli.' His voice fills with pride. 'She's the tallest in her class. The smartest, too. She's happy, Alex. She has everything she needs.'

'Except her mother!'

'She has her nonna,' Luca says.

I glance over to the stone bench where Elena was sitting, but the old woman has gone inside. 'Your mother isn't well,' I say. 'She shouldn't be looking after a child.'

'Alex, I know you've missed her, but she's settled here now. She's safe, and she's happy. If you want what's best for her, leave her where she is.'

'Living a *lie*?'

'Living a normal life,' Luca says. 'She doesn't know anything else, Alex. She doesn't remember her life in London with you. This is her home now. And you know what'll happen if you take her back. The media won't leave her alone. She'll spend the rest of her life in a goldfish bowl. Is that really what you want for her?'

For the first time, I feel a twinge of doubt. Luca's right: Lottie Martini is public property. She'll never be left in peace. But Carli Bonfiglio is just an ordinary child, albeit with an extraordinary story.

'I can't leave her,' I say. 'I can't lose her again, Luca.'

'So stay with us.'

'*Stay*?'

416

'What d'you have to go back to?' He gestures around him at the beautiful villa, the fountain, the vast, rocky expanse surrounding us. 'Think about it. You could stay here and be Signora Bonfiglio, a normal wife and mother. You could escape your media prison and live here, with us.'

For a brief moment, I'm tempted.

A normal wife and mother.

'We could be a family again,' Luca says. 'Isn't that what you want?'

'We haven't been a family in a long time, Luca.'

He puts his hands on my shoulders, so I've got nowhere to look but at him. 'I never wanted to leave you,' he says. 'I didn't want the divorce; not then, not now. You've no idea how many times I've wanted to call you. We can turn back the clock, Alex. It can be like it used to be, before your work got in the way. Remember how good we used to be together?'

My body remembers.

Luca presses his advantage. His thumb traces the line of my jaw and I feel an electric tug at my nipples.

'Stay with me,' he says softly. 'We can give Lottie her family back. You'll be free of the media circus. It'll be you and me again, *cara*. Just the three of us. Even better than before.'

417

chapter 80

alex

He makes it sound so easy. And he's right: I could stay here. No one knows where I am, apart from Quinn, and I can trust her. I flew here on a false passport. Luca and I could live here quietly, under the radar, an ordinary family again.

Or I could wait till Quinn comes back with the cavalry and take Lottie back to England. Try to rebuild our lives and continue to juggle work with raising Lottie. Maybe one day even fashion a future with a man I can trust, a man like Jack. But at what cost to Lottie? Luca did a wicked thing when he snatched her from me, but tearing her life apart a second time won't fix that. And it'll all play out in the fierce glare of the press.

Lottie's age won't save her from the media storm.

Staying here is a lovely fantasy. But that's all it is: a fantasy.

I can't trust Luca. I'm not even sure he *is* Luca, not really.

A head injury that leaves you in a coma for six weeks could cause permanent brain damage. Judging by his scar, the blow was to the front of his head, which houses the part of the brain that controls personality and impulse control. I can't believe the man I knew would've kidnapped our daughter.

But even if by some miracle Luca and I managed to revive our relationship, I can't stay home and make pasta from scratch for the rest of my life, and I'm not qualified to work in Italian law. What would I do, once the novelty of being a stay-at-home mamma wears off? Have more babies? Sit at home looking after Luca's crazy mother while he chases anything in a skirt?

I hear the sound of a car in the distance. There's a crunch of gears and I realise Quinn must've reached our vehicle. I need to distract Luca.

I press my body a little closer to his.

'What would we tell Lottie?' I ask, as if I'm weakening.

'The truth,' he says. 'She thinks she came to live with me because her mamma had to go to work and help people. And now you've come back.'

'But you said she won't remember me.'

'I said she doesn't remember her life in London. Of course she remembers *you*. I'm not a monster, Alex.' His lips brush my neck. 'I talk about you all the time. We need you. We both need you.'

'I have to think about it, Luca. You need to give me some time—'

But I don't have time.

Something hits me, hard, in the lower back. I stumble against Luca, caught off-guard. I'd fall if he weren't there to catch me.

'It's OK,' I say. 'I'm fine.'

I try to find my balance again, but my legs won't work properly. My chest feels oddly tight; I can't seem to suck in enough air.

'I need to sit down,' I say, dizzy.

Black spots dance before my eyes. Luca staggers under my dead weight, unable to hold me up, and the two of us slide to the ground. I lean against the courtyard wall. The pain in my back is getting worse.

Everything starts to take on an unreal quality, as if in a dream. Luca is holding me and shouting at his mother in Italian – *Mamma, cosa hai fatto?* – and Elena is laughing.

She has a knife in her hand.

Luca says something about calling for help. *I'll be back in a minute, Alex, just stay with me.* I slide down the wall, until my left cheek rests on the flagstones. I can smell the bougainvillea in the planter just a few feet away.

I think I always knew it would end like this. But it's OK. Lottie will be safe. Quinn will take her to Harriet and my sister will look after her. Luca and I have failed spectacularly as Lottie's parents, but Harriet will do better.

He's on the phone now, demanding an ambulance, but I know it'll get here too late. Everything is swimming in and out of focus. The ground rocks gently beneath me, as if I'm being cradled in a warm bath.

The darkness is closing in. My vision narrows, like an old-fashioned camera, the shadows creeping in from the outside. And then suddenly Lottie is standing in front of me. Her hair is longer now and lighter than I remember; her skin is tanned and her brown legs are long and skinny. The baby fat has gone. Lottie, but not Lottie.

In my dream, I tell her to run. *Run!*

Don't look back.

When I blink, she's gone. Luca's holding me in his arms, trying to stop the bleeding. I think I tell him not to cry, but I'm not sure if the words are just in my head. I don't hate him any more. I'm not even angry.

You have to pay it forward, Alexa, like I'm doing. You have to forgive. That's the deal you've done with the universe.

I have no regrets. I knew coming here was a risk, but I made my choice a long time ago.

I chose Lottie.

HIDDEN HEARTBREAK OF LOST GRANDPARENTS

COMMENTARY by Emma Donovan

THE love between a grandchild and their grandparent is often the sweetest and most precious bond a child can know, untainted by the arguments and stresses of everyday family life.

But it can also be a hidden source of agony.

As we rightly celebrate the miraculous safe return of Lottie Martini, 6, snatched from a wedding in Florida more than two years ago by her estranged Italian grandmother, we should spare a moment to consider the grief of a woman driven to take such extreme measures.

Of course, no one condones 77-year-old Elena Martini's actions for a moment. It's impossible to imagine the suffering that Lottie's mother, Alexa, 31, endured, not knowing if her cherished only daughter was alive or dead.

But if this tragic story teaches us anything, it's that the importance of the bond between grandparent and child cannot be understated.

Every child should have the right to access to their wider family, especially their grandparents, unless there is good reason to keep them apart to protect the child.

Across Britain, thousands of grannies and granddads are denied access to their grandchildren, creating a hidden well of heartbreak.

Many are the collateral damage of divorce – especially if they're the father's parents. For many isolated older people, particularly if they've been bereaved, grandchildren are literally a lifeline.

When they lose touch with those children, they feel they've lost everything.

Exclusion

Even in the happiest of families, the delicate mother-in-law/daughter-in-law relationship can be complex and sometimes competitive.

If it comes to a fight, the younger woman will always win, armed with the ultimate weapon – exclusion.

The sad fact is, in the event of a family breakdown, grandparents have no legal rights. Even if they can afford to hire a solicitor to take their case to Family Court, it's a long and costly process.

Little wonder many become so desperate they consider ending their lives. Some describe the estrangement from their grandchildren as a 'living bereavement'.

Elena Martini's son, Luca, became Lottie's primary carer following his divorce from her mother, in February 2018.

He took his daughter to see her grandparents in Italy at least once a month, until his tragic death in the Genoa bridge collapse in August that year.

No doubt struggling with her own grief, Alexa Martini then broke off all contact with Luca's parents, driving Mrs Martini to take matters into her own hands.

For the Martinis, it's too late to call a truce, but for so many other families, surely it is not beyond hope that peace could be declared?

After all, in these cruel family conflicts the victims, as they are in so many wars, are the children.

six months later

chapter 81

quinn

Quinn hates memorial services. She's not a big fan of funerals or hospitals either, but at least you can be miserable at a fucking funeral. No one expects you to quote-unquote *celebrate a life well-lived* or, even worse, *find closure*.

She avoids the journalists and photographers clustered near the church steps.

She's not here in a professional capacity today. She's here as Alex's friend.

Alex's sister, Harriet, hands her an order of service as she enters the nave. 'It was good of you to come,' she says automatically.

Quinn glances at the smiling photograph on the pamphlet. It looks nothing like Alex.

'How's Lottie doing?' she asks.

'I know people say kids are resilient, but it's amazing how quickly she's bounced back,' Harriet says. 'And she seems to like the Shetlands – oh, Mrs Harris. It was good of you to come.'

The service is moving but unsentimental and mercifully brief. A touching eulogy from Alex's father, some uplifting readings; the usual Henry Scott Holland poem, *death is nothing at all*, and then 'Jerusalem'. Quinn's an atheist, but the faith of those gathered in the packed church is oddly touching and for a moment she wishes she shared it. And then she remembers what happened in Sicily and she's glad she doesn't believe in God.

Afterwards, everyone adjourns to a nearby pub. Quinn hadn't planned to go – she's sober again, and her new six-month chip is burning a hole in her pocket – but she overhears Harriet say Lottie's going to be there and Quinn wants to see the kid for herself. She needs to know the little girl is flourishing, despite everything that happened. She needs to know she did the right thing.

Lottie's all that matters. If something goes wrong, you don't wait for me. You take Lottie and you leave.

What kind of fucking psycho fakes his own death, for God's sake? Quinn's spidey senses had been telling her all along there was more to this story than met the eye, but she'd never have picked a zombie husband back from the dead.

She hadn't wanted to leave Alex alone in that courtyard with him, but she'd promised she'd take care of Lottie and she wasn't going to let her down. *You take Lottie and you leave.*

It was just dumb luck she'd spotted Lottie running away from the villa. The little girl must've been hiding somewhere: under a bed, maybe, or behind one of the massive bougainvillea planters in the courtyard. Quinn had caught sight of her from the car, a tiny figure scrambling down the rocky slope to the road.

The poor kid had been terrified when Quinn finally caught up to her, clearly convinced she was about to be murdered. Quinn knows her eye patch can freak people out; the little girl thought Quinn was some sort of homicidal maniac who'd killed her mother. She'd never have got her in the car if the child hadn't been so exhausted. The poor kid hadn't even got any shoes on. She'd cut her bare feet to bloody ribbons.

If Quinn had headed straight to the airport there and then, things would've ended very differently. She should have taken the little girl home, as Alex had told her to do. It's why she'd called Quinn for help and not Jack Murtaugh.

But she'd broken her promise.

She'd gone back.

Lottie had been semi-comatose in the back of the car. Quinn had pillowed the little girl's head on her jacket and double-locked the doors, cracking the windows so the child had some fresh air.

Then she'd slipped back into the villa the same way she'd left. She could hear shouting again, but this time it was in hectic Italian: Luca and his mother. She hadn't heard Alex's voice.

And then she'd realised why.

Even from across the courtyard, Quinn had been able to see the red bloom blossoming on Alex's back.

Luca hadn't noticed Quinn's approach because he was grappling with his lunatic mother, who'd somehow climbed onto the battlements. Something was flashing in her hand as she ranted at her son and it'd taken Quinn a few moments to realise it was the sun reflecting off a blade.

Even as she'd watched, the crazy old woman had backed further along the low, wide wall, and Luca had climbed up after her. *Stai attento, Mamma!*

Be careful!

The villa was a mountaintop fortress, designed to keep the owners safe from invading Saracen hordes. Perched atop a crag, three sides of the villa held commanding views of the countryside. The fourth rose seamlessly from a sheer cliff that dropped hundreds of feet to the rocks below.

Luca had suddenly seen Quinn. 'She's going to fall!' he'd shouted. 'Help me!'

He'd lunged towards his mother, knocking the knife from her hand. It'd clattered onto the flagstones and skittered across the courtyard, coming to rest at Quinn's feet.

Red with Alex's blood.

Luca had managed to get one arm around Elena, but she was fighting him, spittle flecking her lips.

He'd held out his free hand to Quinn. 'Please! Help me get her down!'

So Quinn had run towards them.

And pushed.

chapter 82

alex

I'm in the pub garden with Lottie, savouring the first really warm day of summer, when Quinn comes outside looking for us. I invited her to Mum's memorial service weeks ago, but I didn't think she'd actually show up.

I wave her over. I haven't seen her since I came out of hospital, nearly six months ago, and I'm surprised how much healthier she looks. Clearly giving up the booze and getting back into the field to be shot at and bombed has done her good. She's still got the rakish eye patch, of course, but she no longer resembles a heroin addict searching for her next fix.

'You've just made Lottie's day,' I say, making room on the wooden bench.

'Other way round,' Quinn says.

Lottie clambers onto Quinn's knee, unselfconsciously moving the reporter's withered arm out of the way to make room. Anyone else watching them might be surprised by my daughter's uncharacteristic affection, given they haven't seen each other in six months, but they struck up an unlikely bond in Sicily: the hard-bitten, childless war correspondent and my difficult, awkward, immeasurably brave daughter.

Or perhaps not that unlikely, after all.

'So,' I say. 'How was Nagorno-Karabakh?'

'Lively. The ceasefire's broken down again, so I'll probably be on my way back in a day or two. How are the Shetlands?'

'Unbelievably dull. Thank God.'

'When are you coming back to London?' Quinn asks.

I glance across the pub garden to where Jack is in deep conversation with my father. The two of them hit it off the first time they met, while I was convalescing at Harriet's cottage. My sister has been my staunchest supporter over the last few months. I couldn't have managed without her. I'm really going to miss her when we leave.

'At the end of the summer,' I say. 'Lottie's going back to school in London in September. She seems ready.'

'I'm sure he'll appreciate the shorter commute,' Quinn says, dryly.

My relationship with Jack is still under wraps, for now, but I know our secret's safe with Quinn. I'd never have thought I'd say this, given the way we started, but I can literally trust this woman with my life.

She was the one who saved it, after all.

I don't know exactly what happened that day at Elena Martini's villa. I've got no memories of anything after she stabbed me. I nearly died: according to my medical records, my heart stopped twice on the helicopter to the hospital in the Sicilian capital, Palermo. So I don't suppose I'll ever know how Luca and his mother came to be lying at the bottom of the cliff. But I can guess.

A tragic accident, the Sicilian police decided. It appears Signor Bonfiglio – a distant cousin of the old lady, apparently, although no one is quite sure of the relationship – was trying to save his elderly relative, who suffered from dementia, and the two fell to their deaths. No one else was home at the time.

When I regained consciousness, six days later, I was in a private room at St George's Hospital in London, the victim of an apparent mugging near my home. Jack must have called in quite a few favours to pull that off.

We debated long and hard whether to tell the world Lottie had been found. After Quinn had spirited my daughter out of Sicily, she'd taken her to Harriet in the Shetlands, and when I was discharged ten days later I flew up to join them. Perhaps I could've passed Lottie off as a relative of my late husband, using the alias Luca had given our daughter, but I'd had enough of lies and deception. I didn't want to spend the rest of my life looking over my shoulder, waiting for the truth to come out. I wanted Lottie to know who she was.

A simple press release was never going to work. There'd been too much interest in the story for too long to get away with that. So I finally gave Quinn her exclusive, and sat down for a ninety-minute TV interview.

We stuck to the truth as much as we could. Quinn told the moving story of a bereaved grandmother, driven by the death of her beloved son to commit an unforgivable act. A woman who, when she was diagnosed with Alzheimer's, returned Lottie to her mother and then took her life at her mountain home in Sicily a few days later. There was no mention of the unfortunate Signor Bonfiglio.

Quinn knew how to sell the story. INN promoted the interview across its domestic and international channels, and followed it up with a series of scoops: the first pictures of Lottie, playing in the garden; access to the villa where she'd been kept; interviews with my dad and Harriet. INN sucked the life out of the story, and although the other networks and newspapers covered it, they'd lost the initiative and they knew it. In journalism, there's no such thing as second place. Besides, the story had suddenly become a lot less interesting: instead of the dramatic, stranger-danger abduction that fed into every mother's worst nightmare, the Lottie Martini kidnapping had

431

turned out to be nothing more than a convoluted custody battle. A few commentators wrote opinion pieces about the rights of grandparents and then the news cycle moved on.

Lottie spies a puppy playing with a family at a table a few feet away and abruptly wriggles off Quinn's lap. '*Posso andare a giocare con il cucciolo?*' she asks me, folding her hands in mock-prayer.

'In English, Lottie.'

She scowls. 'Can I go and play with the puppy, Mummy?'

I nod and she runs off.

'Must be hard to let her go,' Quinn says.

'It was harder when she was too scared to leave my side,' I say.

When Quinn arrived in Brae with Lottie, my poor girl was so terrified and confused she wouldn't speak. It was only when I finally came home to her she really believed I wasn't dead, and for months she refused to let me out of her sight.

It was the same for me. At night, I'd lie on the covers of her bed next to her, watching her as she slept. I couldn't stop looking at her, the miracle of her. Stroking that white-blonde hair, still not able to quite take it in. Restored to me. My girl.

It's taking time for us to find our way back to each other. She's changed in so many ways and I don't know how much of that is part of the natural process of growing up, and how much is because of what she's been through. And yet, despite her long absence, she seems so much like herself, the same stubborn girl who refused to let anyone help her tie her shoelaces, who ripped off her nappy when she was two and demanded to use the toilet. Lottie's come through this, not unscathed, no; but intact, herself.

And she remembers me. When I find myself filled with rage against Luca, I remind myself of that. He didn't try to erase me. He told Lottie I'd gone away, but he kept my memory alive. Did he know, deep down, I'd find them one day? Was this his way of atoning for the terrible wrong he did me?

I've forgiven him. I often remind myself of Helen Birch, the extraordinary compassion she showed me. *You have to let the hatred and anger go. That's the deal you've done with the universe.*

I don't mourn Luca's death, because for me he died years ago, but I do grieve the loss of the man he used to be; the man I married. That's the father I want Lottie to remember. I'll keep him alive for her, as he did for me.

For Marc, there's no such absolution. He's in prison now, caught up in the Paul Harding paedophile sting. Jack saw to that. Marc may be innocent of the charges that landed him in jail, but I don't feel guilty. He deserves to be there.

Lottie comes running back to me now and grabs a swig of her lemonade, spilling a little on the table as she thumps the glass down, before racing off again. She looks like any happy, carefree six-year-old playing in the June sunshine.

I knew we'd turned a corner two months ago, the first time she let me leave Harriet's cottage in Brae without her. Until then, she'd always insisted on coming with me wherever I went, even if I was only popping out for a pint of milk.

I'd got my shopping list together and gone into my sister's art studio, where Lottie had been lying on her tummy, colouring a picture of three baby owls sitting on a branch.

'Are you coming, darling?' I asked.

'Can I stay here with Auntie Harriet?' Lottie had asked, without looking up. 'I want to finish my picture.'

Harriet's paintbrush had frozen in mid-air.

'Are you sure?' I asked. 'You don't mind if I go out without you?'

'I'm sure,' she'd said, reaching for a different-coloured pencil. She'd glanced at the baby owls, an illustration from her favourite story book, and then looked back up at me, and smiled.

'Mummies always come back,' she said.

Acknowledgements

I am exceptionally lucky to have an inspired and committed team behind me at Avon and HarperCollins, which has worked tirelessly to champion my books in the most challenging of times. I could not wish for better publishers, and I thank all those who've laboured behind the scenes to make this novel a success.

Special thanks to my editor, Rachel Faulkner-Willcocks, who has been a cheerleader for my writing from the first, and has made this book so much better in every way. It's a joy to work with you.

Thanks also to Rebecca Ritchie, for her thoughtful insights and passionate support, and for listening to my midnight terrors with endless patience.

And thanks to my marvellous copy editor, Rhian McKay, for picking up all those loose threads I left hanging. I don't know how you do what you do, but you saved me much embarrassment!

I'm grateful to Juliette Wills and Two Magpies Media for designing and creating www.tessstimson.com, distilling my vague vision into a brilliantly simple website.

Thanks to my wonderful stepmother, Barbi, for reading the manuscript at lightning speed and providing encouraging feedback.

And thank you to my dear friends Linnie and Bamby (who kindly lent her name to one of my characters!). You provided a lifeline of sanity this tumultuous year.

Thanks always to the NetGalley readers and bloggers and book lovers who take the time to review my novels. It is appreciated more than you know.

And across the globe, thanks to all the readers and listeners, to all the buyers and sellers and lenders and givers of books who ensure that our stories find a home.

Last, though never least, thanks to my husband Erik, my sons Henry and Matt, and my daughter Lily, who endured lockdown with her crazy mother with grace and good humour. Thank you all for ensuring that the life of a writer is never dull.

Don't miss Tess Stimson's other addictive
suspense novels . . .

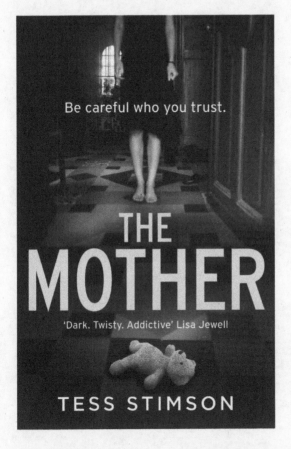

Be careful who you trust.

THE
MOTHER

'Dark. Twisty. Addictive' Lisa Jewell

TESS STIMSON

'More chilling than *Gone Girl* and twistier than
The Girl on the Train' Jane Green

Out now